'Fresh and utte̶r̶ a fantastical fight for ̶f̶r̶e̶e̶d̶ all costs.' — Heidi Heilig, at ̶ ̶ ̶ere

'This intensely readable, satisfying fantasy asks questions about identity, choice, power and obligation, against a vivid, richly imagined backdrop of west African-inspired magic.' – *Guardian*

'A fresh, phenomenal fantasy that begs readers to revel in its brilliant world.' – *Kirkus*, starred review

'Ifueko's mesmerising debut stuns as it weaves a tale of loyalty, fate, destiny, family and revenge. Moreover, it places a dark-skinned heroine front and centre, who is beautiful and powerful, deadly and compassionate, and vulnerable and tough, giving YA literature more of the diverse representation teens need.' – *Booklist*, starred review

'By crafting a world plagued by imperialism, poverty and institutionalised misogyny, and a mythology that literalises the power of love, purpose and sacrifice, Ifueko illustrates the need for social change and inspires readers to fight for it.' – *Publishers Weekly*, starred review

'Ifueko's debut is full of lush world building and detailed, Nigerian-inspired mythology, giving life to a myth of epic proportions and a tale that is bound to stick with readers long after they finish it. – *Bulletin of the Center for Children's Books*, starred review

REDEMPTOR

REDEMPTOR

JORDAN IFUEKO

HOT
KEY
BOOKS

First published in Great Britain in 2021 by
HOT KEY BOOKS
4th Floor, Victoria House
Bloomsbury Square
London WC1B 4DA
Owned by Bonnier Books
Sveavägen 56, Stockholm, Sweden
www.hotkeybooks.com

A CIP catalogue record for this book is available from the British Library.

Paperback ISBN: 978-1-4714-1013-0
Hardback ISBN: 978-1-4714-1107-6
Also available as an ebook and in audio

1

Printed and bound by Clays Ltd, Elcograf S.p.A.

Hot Key Books is an imprint of Bonnier Books UK
www.bonnierbooks.co.uk

For young revolutionaries,
who have chosen the loneliest job in the world.

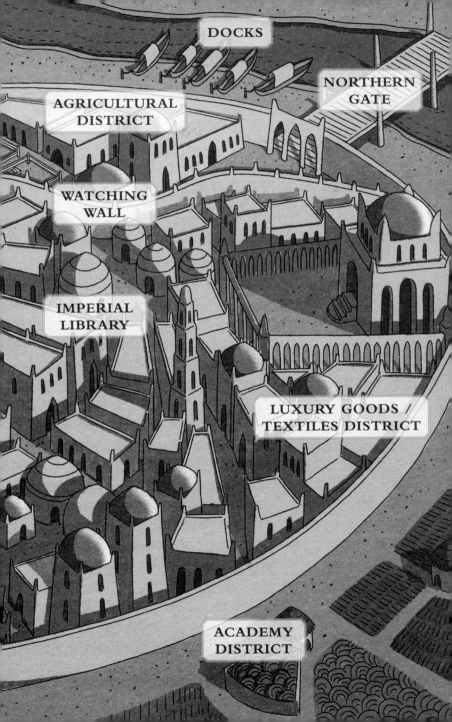

PART 1

PART I

CHAPTER 1

MY NAME WAS TARISAI KUNLEO, AND NO ONE I loved would ever die again.

I stole down the palace hallway, my sandals slapping the words into music—*never again, never again.* I would play this song until my soles wore thin. Griots, the sacred story-tellers of our empire, shaped the histories we believed with their music.

I, too, would sing this story until the world believed it.

Tar? The base of my scalp hummed as Kirah connected our Ray bond, speaking directly into my mind. *Are you all right?*

Kirah, my council sister, and Mbali, the former High Priestess of Aritsar, stood ahead of me in the broad palace hallway. I caught up to them, smiling manically before remembering that they couldn't see my face.

We wore ceremonial veils: colorful beads and shells that dangled to our chests, concealing our faces. Tall leather hairpieces, stained crimson and shaped into flames, circled our heads. Our costumes honored Warlord Fire, creator of death, and disguised us as *birinsinku*: grim women of the gallows, on our way to perform holy death rites on imperial prisoners.

I'm fine, I Ray-spoke to Kirah, gritting my teeth. Then I willed my voice to be light and chipper, speaking aloud for Mbali's sake. "Just—you know. Excited for Thaddace."

Servants and courtiers danced out of our way as we swept through An-Ileyoba Palace. Rumor warned that birinsinku spread foul luck wherever they went, and so as we passed, onlookers warded off evil with the sign of the Holy Pelican. No one guessed that I, Mbali, and Kirah hid beneath those glittering veils, plotting to free the most hated man in Aritsar from prison.

Dayo had named me Empress of Aritsar exactly two weeks ago. Until then, the world had believed that only one Raybearer—always male—existed per generation. The Ray was a blood gift, passed down from Aritsar's first emperor, Enoba the Perfect. Its power granted emperors near immortality, and allowed them to form a council of bonded minds, uniting the sprawling mega-continent of Aritsar.

But Enoba had lied about the gift in his veins. He had never been meant to rule alone, for two Rays existed per generation—one for a boy and one for a girl. That Ray now swelled in my veins, upsetting five hundred years of Arit tradition. My sex alone had made me plenty of enemies, but if that hadn't been enough . . . with one impulsive vow, I had placed the entire empire in grave danger.

For eras, demons called *abiku* had plagued our continent, causing drought and disease, and stealing souls down to the Underworld. Enoba achieved peace through a treaty, sating the abiku by sending children into the sulfurous Oruku Breach—three hundred living Redemptors, or sacrifices, per year. I had voided that treaty, offering myself instead as a final Redemptor. The abiku had accepted on one mysterious condition: Before I descended to the Underworld, I had to anoint the rulers of all twelve Arit realms, forming a council of my own.

They had given me two years. If in that time I failed to anoint a council and cast myself into the Oruku Breach . . . the abiku would raze the continent. No one would be safe then, not even the priests in their lofty temples, or the bluebloods in their gilded fortresses.

Enraged, the nobles had plied me with tests. If my Ray was fraudulent, my promise to the abiku could be voided, and the old treaty reinstated. But before hundreds of gaping courtiers, I had walked across hot coals, chugged goblets of pelican oil, and submerged my face in gourds of holy water—all tasks, legend had it, highly lethal to any but a Raybearer.

The strongest proof of my legitimacy, however, shimmered in lurid patterns on both my forearms: a living map of the Underworld, marking me as a Redemptor. The abiku would not have accepted my treaty, relinquishing an eternity of child sacrifices, for anything less valuable than a Raybearer. To win my soul, the abiku had made a promise—and a deal made by immortals, once sealed in blood, could not be broken.

Dayo had begged me not to provoke the nobles further. "Just for a while," he had pleaded. "I want them to love you, Tar. To see you as I do." Out of guilt for making him worry, I had promised to keep my head down. And I would. Really.

Right after I broke an imperial traitor out of prison.

The late morning sun glowed through An-Ileyoba's unglazed windows, casting arch-shaped halos on the rainbow floor tiles as I swept through the palace with Kirah and Mbali. A song wafted from the courtyards outside. Courtier children chanted with morbid glee, watching as Imperial Guard warriors erected an executioner's platform.

When you meet Egungun, will you have your eyes-o?
Tell me, will you hear him, if you have no ears-o?
Dead man, dead man, fell like a coconut
Round head rolling
on the red hard ground.

Brats, Kirah Ray-spoke soothingly, sensing my anger through our blood bond.

I hunched my shoulders. Arits believed that upon death, all souls followed after Egungun: the first human being, born of Queen Earth and Am the Storyteller. Egungun roamed the Underworld beating a drum, leading souls in a parade to the paradise of Core. Those children were mocking Thaddace, who faced beheading in a matter of hours.

The former High Judge of Aritsar had done the unspeakable, an act that until two weeks ago, many had believed to be impossible: For the first time in five hundred years, an Anointed One had murdered his own Raybearer.

But Thaddace had only acted as my mother's puppet, killing Olugbade in order to save Mbali's life. I had revealed Thaddace and Mbali's relationship to The Lady, giving her leverage to force his hand, and so ultimately . . . this was all my fault. Besides, Thaddace was *mine*. Like my council siblings, and High Priestess Mbali, and Melu the *alagbato*. Even Woo In and Kathleen, my mother's Anointed Ones, held cherished places in my story.

I had pined my whole life for a family. Now that I had cobbled one together, dysfunctional and cursed as it may be . . . nothing would snatch it from me. Not even an imperial execution.

I forced my brow to relax. If my plan with Mbali and Kirah succeeded . . . Thaddace would not dance for Egungun anytime soon. Laugh at those children, I told myself. Float, confident that you will win in the end.

But an intrusive thought shook my resolve: *Isn't that what your mother would do?*

My jaw hardened. For too long, Aritsar believed girls could only be two things: virtuous servants of the empire, or devious villains, like The Lady. But it was time I silenced those voices.

My lioness mask lay hidden against my chest, a bump protruding from beneath my wrapper. My fingertips warmed as my Hallow summoned hazy memories of Aiyetoro, the only other *obabirin*, or empress. She had lived too long ago for my Hallow to retrieve her thoughts. But the remains of her haughty confidence put a spring in my walk. Of course I could rescue Thaddace. Who could stop a divinely blessed Raybearer? Who could keep the sun from rising?

You are Tarisai Kunleo. And no one you love will ever die again.

Thaddace waited in the open-air prison of Heaven, a platform atop the tallest tower of An-Ileyoba. Kirah, Mbali, and I had made good time crossing the palace. The corridors were still sparse but for a few sleepy courtiers. Funeral shrouds bundled on our backs concealed supplies to aid Thaddace's escape. Birinsinku tools completed our disguises—tiny vials of burial herbs and holy water, jingling on our birinsinku belts as we ran.

"We're going to make it," I said, laughing in spite of my nerves.

"He won't accept help," Mbali warned when we arrived at the steep staircase to Thaddace's prison.

I shoved down the nugget of doubt in my throat and smiled at her. "Of course he will." I tried to forget that only yesterday, a servant had slipped me a calfskin letter. The writing had been burnt directly into the hide—a marker of Thaddace's Hallow.

I have heard of a plot to secure my escape. If these rumors are true, then you are a fool.

I killed an emperor, for Am's sake.

I was not forced. I was of sound mind, and despite any loyalty you have for me, I am only reaping what I have sown. Your position is precarious enough. Do not join me in my ruin and make Aritsar lose faith in your legitimacy.

I once told you that there is no justice, only order. But I was wrong. Sometimes justice and order are one and the same.

Leave me to my fate, protégé. I join Egungun's Parade.

Thaddace had not signed the letter. His seal ring had been confiscated, and he had known, besides, that a signature was unnecessary. Every time I touched the calfskin, my Hallow caused the memory of my former mentor's hands, the sting of his pain and resolve, to chafe my skin. He had likely heightened his feelings on purpose, knowing that they would seep from the paper and coerce me.

"You can convince him to escape," I told Mbali. "I know he's worried about ruining my reputation, but we won't get caught. All we have to do is—"

"He won't come," repeated Mbali. "This isn't about you, Tarisai. He's only pretending it is."

We stared up at the landing. Kirah reached for my hand and squeezed. The last time we had stood here, eleven arrows had been aimed at my mother's heart. The Lady had survived the botched execution, only to be accidentally poisoned by Woo In, her own council member. Beneath her veil, I was sure Mbali looked haunted as well.

"Thaddace was supposed to protect Olugbade at all costs," Mbali said. "That is the point of being an Anointed One, and why I was ready for The Lady to drop me from this very tower. But Thaddace . . ." She sighed. "He couldn't let me go. He broke the most sacred vow he'd ever made, and now he feels the universe is owed a debt."

Cold crept down my arms. "He *wants* to die?"

Mbali nodded, the beaded strands of her veil clinking together.

"That's . . ." I sputtered. "That's insane."

"No," Mbali deadpanned. "That's just Thaddace."

Kirah crossed her arms. "The High Lord Judge does love one thing more than order, High Priestess. And that's you. I've seen it."

"You shouldn't call me that anymore," Mbali scolded her quietly. "You became *High Priestess* Kirah the moment Olugbade died. Likewise, Thaddace is not the High Lord Judge. Not anymore." She turned sharply to me. "The sooner you both embrace your roles, the better."

I sensed Kirah's determination surge through the Ray. "Well, I still think you can convince him, High . . . Anointed Honor. When you walk into a room, he changes. You're his Core." She used a stubborn tone that I suspected she got from her mother. "And you know it." Then she held out four gobs of wax.

Mbali looked doubtful, but sighed, shrugged, and plugged her ears. I plugged mine as well, and Kirah cleared her throat and sang into the rafters. The sound was muted, but I recognized the same lullaby Kirah had sung when we first met, waiting for our turn to be tested in the Children's Palace.

Even with my hands clapped over my plugged ears, the jangling timbre of Kirah's voice seeped into my limbs, reminding them of how tired they were. Of how sweet it was to rest. How surely a nap, even here on the cold tiled floor, was precisely what I needed . . .

I shook my head and hummed a counter tune, clearing the fog from my mind. The guards at the top of the stairs were not so lucky. When their shadows appeared on the steps, the four warriors were hunched with exhaustion, yawning as they squinted down at us. Three made it a few steps before slumping in the stairwell, their spears dropping with a clatter as they began to snore. The last guard seemed to realize what was happening, but before she could cry for help I bounded up the stairs, clapped her head, and stole the last few moments of her memories. Guilt pricked me as she stared at my veiled face, her own washed of emotion.

I gritted my teeth and pressed her temple again, erasing the entire morning, as well as the day before. Years of trying to coax away Sanjeet's nightmares had taught me that minds were dangerously resilient. With enough context, people could reconstruct their stolen memories, like filling in the missing tiles of a mosaic. If Thaddace was to escape, I couldn't let guards remember who had helped him.

The guard succumbed to Kirah's song at last, slumping

against me. I laid her gently on the landing, then wiped the memories of the three other guards, taking no chances.

How many days of stolen memories, I wondered, did it take to erase who someone was? Suppose I erased a crucial moment or epiphany—was that akin to murder?

I swallowed hard, trying not to think about it. For the few memories I stole from the guards, Thaddace would survive to make thousands more. That made it all right—didn't it? Sacrifice of the few for the many . . . I shivered, hating the cursed arithmetic of empresses.

One of the guards wore a necklace of keys; I lifted it over his head and lurched up the stairs. There, behind the iron-barred door that led out to Heaven, stood Thaddace, hands clapped firmly over his ears.

I beamed with relief. If Thaddace hadn't recognized Kirah's Hallow in time, we would have had to drag his sleeping body from the tower.

"Anointed Honor," I said, parting the birinsinku veil, "it's me. We've come to get you out." My smile faded at Thaddace's empty stare. A sharp ammonia smell rose from buckets at his feet, and a threadbare tunic, pulled up like a hood over his head, served as his only protection from weeks of beating sun and wind. Livid burns speckled his pale skin. His hair and beard had been recently shorn—more mercy than humiliation, where prison lice were considered. I wondered who had snuck him the razor, and why—though the thought sent me shivers—he had not used it to end his misery.

He uncovered his ears. "I told you," rasped the former High Lord Judge, "not to come."

"I've never been good at following directions," I reminded him, and fumbled with the ring of keys, racing through the guards' stolen memories. An image of the correct key surfaced in my mind. I held it to the lock . . . then yelped and dropped the key ring, sucking my blistered finger.

"Really?" I accused Thaddace, gaping in shock. "Using your heating Hallow on the iron? That's low, Anointed Honor."

He said nothing, green eyes dull and sullen.

"You could have melted the whole lock," I said then, realization dawning. "All this time, you could have freed yourself!"

"I have not spent my life," said Thaddace in his thick Mewish brogue, "enforcing the laws of this empire to flout them now. In a few hours, I will lay my head on that chopping block. And so help me gods, I will settle my debts at last . . ." He trailed off as his gaze fell behind me, where Mbali and Kirah stood.

The former High Priestess removed her veil. "And what about the debt you owe to me?"

The resolution in Thaddace's jaw crumbled, like a pillar of salt in water.

"What of your siblings, who have suffered enough?" Mbali asked, reaching through the bars to stroke his weather-scarred face.

They tried to speak without words, eyes filled with mute longing. But no energy crackled through the air—no sparks crossed the space between them.

They don't even have a mental bond anymore. Kirah Ray-spoke, her horror sharp in our mental bond. *I guess their Ray abilities disappeared when the old Emperor died. Tar . . . that just doesn't seem fair.*

No, it didn't. I was still reeling at how quickly the old Anointed Ones had been stripped of their power. After Emperor Olugbade's death, Arit law required his council to be permanently exiled from An-Ileyoba so that the our council's new power would go unchallenged. Olugbade's Eleven now resided at a cloistered temple just outside Oluwan City. After a complicated series of disguises and bribes, Kirah and I had just managed to smuggle Mbali back into the palace, knowing she was our only hope of coaxing Thaddace from prison.

Thaddace and Mbali can still be together, I pointed out to Kirah, trying to comfort myself as well. *They don't need the Ray to survive.*

But I wasn't sure if I meant it. I thought of my nights with Sanjeet since returning to An-Ileyoba: our bodies pressed into the shape of each other, sugary nonsense drifting between our minds until one of us dropped asleep. I would love him without the Ray, of course. But when I imagined the mental link vanishing, erecting a wall of adamant between our minds forever . . . I shuddered.

Thaddace wept into Mbali's palm. "I have to stay,"

he whispered. "We lived to build an empire. To shape order from chaos, a world where rules matter. If you think I've gone insane—"

"I think," Mbali said bitterly, "that you're the same fool I fell in love with. The one who thought the right set of laws could save humanity."

They held each other through the bars, and I realized with frustration that their features were resigned. They *were* giving up. They were saying goodbye.

"Laws aren't everything," I blurted, stamping my foot like a child. "Even if they keep empires running. Order is not enough."

Thaddace turned to me in surprise, raising an eyebrow. "Unwise words from Aritsar's new High Lady Judge," he said dryly. "You're still in charge of court cases, you know—even as Empress Redemptor."

I barely heard him. The tritoned voice from the shrine at Sagimsan rang in my ears, warming every limb. I had never told anyone what had happened that day—when a spirit spoke to mine on the hillside, propelling me on Hyung's back toward what I thought was certain death. I barely understood it myself. Even now, a fearful thrill shot through my veins as I stammered those words—the ones that had carried me across lodestones.

"'*Do not ask how many people you will save,*'" I said. "'*Ask, To what world will you save them?*' What makes a world worth surviving in?" I nodded at Thaddace's and Mbali's hands. "Well . . . what if it's this, Anointed Honors? What if?"

Thaddace scanned Mbali's face, drinking her in. Cracks grew in his suicidal resolve.

"Thaddace of Mewe," I said. "I order you to escape this tower."

He blinked at me in surprise, but I only smiled. "Obey your empress, Anointed Honor." I cocked my head. "You wouldn't want to break the law, would you?"

CHAPTER 2

THADDACE OF MEWE LAUGHED: A DESPERATE, rasping sound that dissolved into coughs.

"Stand back," he managed at last, and the iron lock on the grate began to smolder, melting in on itself until the door creaked open. Thaddace gathered Mbali to his chest, gasping beneath her torrent of kisses.

"I'm sorry," he mumbled against her neck. "I've been a fool."

"My fool," Mbali agreed. Kirah and I looked awkwardly at our sandals, and after several moments, the former Anointed Ones seemed to remember they weren't alone. Thaddace glanced at me over Mbali's head. "Well, incorrigible one? What next?"

"Change into these," I ordered, pulling an Imperial Guard uniform and dust mask from the bundle on my back. "Then we'll have to split up. Groups of two are less conspicuous."

As he changed, I listened at the landing. My pulse hammered when I heard the squeak of a cart, a muffled *thump* at the bottom of the stairs, and the pattering away of anxious footsteps.

"That was the drop I ordered. Sanjeet said he'd leave a decoy body. Kirah, Anointed Honor Mbali—can you handle dragging the corpse up to the landing?" They nodded. "Good. Once you've brought it up, dress it in Thaddace's clothes. Use the torches to set it on fire, so it looks like a dishonor killing. Then get out of here as fast as you can. By then, Thaddace and I should have reached the palace gates."

Kirah winced. "What if you get stopped?"

"We're leaving the palace, not entering. They won't have reason to search us thoroughly."

"Still"—Kirah gestured at the sinister charms and holy water vials dangling from my belt—"make sure the guards see those. And the marks on your sleeves. It's bad luck to touch a birinsinku who has just delivered last rites. Or at least, that's what people believe." She smiled thinly. "Let's hope those guards are superstitious."

Thaddace planted a last, lingering kiss on Mbali's full lips, beaming as she murmured against him: "A world worth surviving in."

His green gaze darted across her face. "Almost there," he said. Then my old mentor took my ringed hand in his sunburned one, and we disappeared down the landing stairs.

An-Ileyoba was waking up, and the halls had grown dangerously crowded. Courtiers shot curious looks at the masked Imperial Guard and veiled birinsinku woman

16

hurrying through the passageways.

"We'll head through the residential wing and cut around to the back gates," I told Thaddace, keeping my head down. "Fewer witnesses."

I guessed correctly: The palace bedrooms were sparsely populated, and we were able to run without drawing attention. Just a few more corridors and we'd be outside. Then Thaddace would be through the gates, and I would have one less horror, one less death, on my conscience.

"It's almost over," I breathed, and then we rounded a corner. A single child stood in the center of the hallway . . . and I gasped in pain.

The Redemptor glyphs on my arms burned, glowing bright blue.

"Greetings, Anointed Honors," the boy monotoned.

At first glance, I would have said the child was a ghost. But he was flesh, not spirit, feet planted firmly on the ground. Ten, perhaps eleven years old, with matted straight hair and pale skin like Thaddace's. The strength of the boy's Mewish accent surprised me. The cold, green kingdom of Mewe was thousands of miles north of Oluwan, but most realms weakened their regional dialects in favor of the imperial tongue, for fear of sounding like country bumpkins. This boy sounded like he had never seen an imperial city in his life. Most confusingly . . . Redemptor birthmarks covered his body. Unlike mine, his glistened purple—the mark of Redemptors who had satisfied their debt to the Underworld.

"Y-you are mistaken," I stammered. "We are not Anointed Ones. I'm a birinsinku." The veil hung thickly over my head and shoulders. This boy couldn't know who we were. Well . . . the marks glowing through my robe might give me away. But Thaddace's mask was still in place. Either way, we needed to keep moving. I advanced briskly, intending to pass him, but the boy fell to his knees in front of Thaddace, staring up at him with translucent eyes.

"Bless me," he whispered. "Please."

"You're being silly," I snapped at the child, beginning to panic as the boy clutched Thaddace's tunic. "Let him go."

"Please—"

"Shh!" Thaddace hissed, glancing around the empty hall. When no one came to investigate, Thaddace tried to shake the boy off, but the child began to wail: a high, keening sound.

"I don't like this," I whispered.

"Can't be helped." Thaddace shrugged and sighed. "Transitions of power are always hard on peasants. I'll just give him what he wants."

Hair rose on the back of my neck. The child . . . smelled. Not like an unwashed body, but like earth and decay, or the rotting musk of burial mounds, steaming in wet season.

Something was very, very wrong.

Thaddace bent down, holding out his hand to touch the child's head. "By the power of the Ray, formerly vested in me, I bless—"

I heard the knife before I saw it. The scrape of metal against leather as the boy slipped it from his boot, and the soft, wet hiss as a line of crimson bloomed across Thaddace's throat.

My vision dimmed as blood soaked Thaddace's collar, and he sputtered and gasped.

"Run," he told me, but my feet had lost all feeling.

"Long live the Empress Redemptor," Thaddace gurgled, hand locked around the boy's wrist. With a stagger, Thaddace turned the knife back toward the child. The boy did not resist, eerily calm as his own blade impaled him.

Then Thaddace collapsed on the tiles, dead before he hit the ground.

I backed away, shivering from head to toe. No. Thaddace could not be dead. Thaddace was mine, and I was Tarisai Kunleo, and no one I loved would ever . . .

The thought faded to white noise as the boy stood over Thaddace's body, removing the knife in his own chest. He did not bleed.

"You're not human," I whispered. "What are you?" He didn't look like an abiku. No all-pupil eyes, no pointed teeth or ash-gray skin. Besides, the abiku did not kill humans unless the Treaty was breached, and I still had two years to make my sacrifice. So if not an abiku, then . . . what?

The creature cocked his head. "I am your servant."

"You killed Thaddace." The world was spinning. "Why? For Am's sake, why?"

"Thaddace of Mewe murdered the late Emperor

Olugbade," the creature replied. "The Empress Redemptor was aiding a crown traitor."

"But it wasn't his fault," I sobbed. "My mother made him. Thaddace wasn't going to die; I was going to save him—"

"The empress must not engage in actions that damage her reputation," the boy continued. "For our purposes, your image must remain unsullied. You must retain the trust of the Arit populace."

"Whose purposes?" I shrilled. "Who do you work for?"

His childish features wrinkled, as though I had asked a question for which he had not been fed the answer. "I am your servant," he repeated. "The empress must not . . ." He took a step forward. I fumbled for a weapon, but my hand found only the trinkets on my belt. With a cry, I unstoppered a vial of holy water and hurled its contents at the boy.

The water would have dissolved an evil abiku, turning it to ash. But the boy merely flinched, staring emptily at his splattered clothes.

"What are you?" I demanded again, seizing his shoulder and attempting to take his memories.

For seconds, all I saw was a long, yawning void. I blinked—this had never happened before. Even babies had *some* memories, though fuzzy and disorganized. But after a moment, my Hallow managed to salvage the dimmest echo of a memory, lifting it to the surface.

The boy stumbled back from my grasp, his gaze growing suddenly childlike. Unfocused . . . as though recalling a distant dream. "I'm," he mumbled, "I'm called Fergus. I was born in Faye's Crossing. Far north, in Mewe."

"Who do you work for? Who are your people?"

The boy shook his head slowly. "My parents . . . went away. No. They died in battle. At Gaelinagh."

"Gaelinagh?" I echoed the foreign word, and battle records raced through my memories. "But that's impossible. The Battle of Gaelinagh was a Mewish civil war, and they haven't had one of those in centuries. Not since—"

Disbelief stole the words in my throat.

Peace had been established in Mewe five hundred years ago—during the reign of Emperor Enoba. Back when Redemptors were born all over the continent, and not just in Songland.

The Mewish child was sinking before my eyes. The ground was—was *swallowing* him. My fingers grasped at his clammy pale skin, but my Hallow found nothing—only cold emptiness.

What kind of creature had practically no memories at all?

"Your map's still blue," he said. The monotone had returned, and he nodded absently at the symbols on my forearms. "It'll go purple once you join us." Then the ground closed over him. He vanished, leaving me alone with Thaddace's body as a gaggle of courtiers rounded the corridor.

CHAPTER 3

"YOU CAN'T HIDE FOREVER, YOU KNOW," said Kirah.

"I'm not hiding," I lied, humming with manic cheer as I swept through the gilded Imperial Suite hallways, balancing a sloshing tureen on one hip and a bundle of scrolls on the other. "I'm busy. You haven't had your coneflower tea yet, have you?"

"Tar."

"Can't forget your tea. Temple duty tomorrow. The crowds will expect you to sing, and you'll never heal all those people without drinking your—"

"We're going to be late," Kirah said, in the same dire tone she used on stubborn camels.

Several flights of stairs away, a festive commotion rumbled from the Imperial Hall. I pretended not to hear, inhaling the chatter of our council siblings instead. Their voices skittered, specter-like across the jewel-toned wall tiles. Griot voices undulated in the dark courtyards far below, and moonlight glowed through the halls of our council's new home: the private Imperial Suite of An-Ileyoba.

Five floors comprised our private wing of the palace. A labyrinth of gilded sandstone, the Imperial Suite was a castle in its own right, with a treasury, bathhouse, kitchens, salons, and sleeping chambers, crowned by a sprawling rooftop garden. Lurid green vines crept over the balustrades, hanging down to the open-air windows of our central apartments below. The vines flowered daily, coaxed to life by my council sister Thérèse's Hallowed green thumb, and covering the suite with their hallucinatory perfume.

Healers traditionally used *kuso-kuso,* the blossoms draping the suite walls, as a dreaming aid. But Thérèse altered the plant to heighten our senses. The scent extended the power of our Ray bond, allowing my siblings to move through the suite in a haze of constant intimacy, even when rooms apart. Unfortunately, kuso-kuso also strengthened my Hallow . . . and every stool, vase, and gilded divan hummed with the memories of previous Anointed Ones, including the ones who had wanted me dead. For days, I had wielded my Hallow like a scouring brush, cleansing the suite furniture of memories until my temples burned.

Gauzy mosquito netting wafted over corridor windows, lifting in the warm night breeze, and grazing my cheek as I passed.

Usurper, whispered a disembodied memory. *Where is she. Where is she, whereisshe . . .*

I shuddered, hurrying past. Dayo's father used to pace

the suite hallways, ranting about my mother. I'd have to cleanse the netting later.

"Tar." Kirah trotted to keep up with me. "I know you're still upset about Thaddace. But you've barely left the suite in a week."

My council siblings knew what had happened to Thaddace, and we had opted to keep the undead phantom boy a secret. With the court still unsettled by my promise to the abiku, rumors of Underworld creatures haunting An-Ileyoba Palace were the last thing my reputation needed.

Sanjeet and his best warriors had scoured the grounds day and night. I had rifled through the memories of every potential witness, searching for clues. But the search proved fruitless: The mysterious Mewish boy seemed to have worked entirely alone.

"We're doing all we can to find Thaddace's killer," Kirah went on. "But the more you hide, the worse people will gossip. Besides . . . what will all the vassal rulers think if you're late to your own banquet?"

"Silly me," I chattered, as if she hadn't spoken. "Of course you haven't had your tea. The garden's out of coneflowers, and Thérèse needs more seeds from Swana. I promised her I'd send for them . . ."

Kirah planted herself in front of me, tendrils of hair escaping from her prayer scarf. "That banquet," she puffed, "is happening whether you're there or not. How will Dayo convince those royal strangers to be *your* council siblings, all on his own?"

"Ai Ling's going," I reminded Kirah, swooping around her. "She's the new High Lady Ambassador. Handling the vassal rulers of each realm is her job."

"And your job," she observed, "is to be empress of Aritsar."

Goat's milk spilled from the tureen on my hip onto the floor. I groaned, mumbling, "I'll mop that up."

"You've never mopped a single thing in your life." Kirah pinched her nose with a delirious laugh. "You know what you *have* done before? Defied an immortal emperor to his face. You can do this, Tar. So send a servant for this mess, and get dressed for your party."

"Servants don't like it in here," I said evasively.

Kirah's cheeks flushed with frustration, but I was telling the truth. The crackling energy of Dayo's Ray, heightened by kuso-kuso, sent our voices like ghostly whispers through the halls, setting palace staff on edge. As a result, few servants worked in the suite. But we Anointed Ones liked it that way, craving only one another for company. Still, the more ambitious attendants stuck around: courtiers, beauticians, hair braiders, and clothiers whiled away the hours in the suite's anterooms, breathlessly waiting for Anointed Ones to make use of them. Whenever I left or entered the suite, servants started in eager attention.

But I hadn't left the suite's inner sanctum in days. No doubt the attendants had noticed, fueling the gossip already ringing from every rafter in the palace.

The Empress Redemptor is a murderer.

"Your hair's not even done." Kirah trailed me with difficulty, restricted by her formal High Priestess garments. She wore a jade tunic and matching headscarf, trimmed in the silver coins of her home realm, Blessid Valley. In contrast, I wore only a linen undershift and sandals, my cloud of coils wrapped haphazardly in a black silk sleeping scarf.

"Dayo's dressed already," Kirah continued. "He'll—"

She broke off as I turned into one of the suite's spacious bedrooms.

A cacophony of thoughts had seeped into the hallway, crackling through the Ray before I even parted the door flap. But I still gasped, scrambling for a grip on the milk as six bodies, chests rising and falling in Ray-synced unison, shone from behind an embroidered mosquito canopy. Kameron, Theo, Mayazatyl, Umansa, Zathulu, and Emeronya lay crammed together on a downy bed pallet. Each person rested on someone else's stomach or cradled another's face. The dappled tones of their skin glowed in the flickering sconce light.

I nearly dropped the pile of scrolls. "Ah." I cleared my throat, voice unnaturally high. "Sorry to interrupt."

My council brother Kameron laughed, sliding his pale freckled body from beneath Theo's. "Don't apologize," he said in his thick Mewish brogue. "It was rude of us to have our mental shields down. I'm guessing our thoughts were pretty loud?"

"Welcome to join in," crooned my Quetzalan council

26

sister, Mayazatyl, flopping so she grinned at me upside down. Her silky twin braids dangled over the bedside. "You too, Kirah."

I rolled my eyes, and Kirah's face flushed red.

When we first moved into the suite, the private bedchambers had shocked me. In the past, my siblings and I had slept shoulder to shoulder in the Children's Palace's Hall of Dreams, or in a pile on the Yorua Keep floor. All the better to ward off council sickness: the fever and slow madness that plagued Anointed Ones when we separated for more than an hour. It also made us less likely to sneak off for romantic trysts, knowing we'd have to risk waking the others.

But the Imperial Suite of An-Ileyoba boasted twelve pristine—and separate—bedchambers. They were arranged in a circle, with a hallway on the outer perimeter and an airy salon in the center. Past Anointed Ones, it seemed, had strengthened their Ray bond with age, rendering group slumber unnecessary. But thanks to Olugbade's untimely death . . . our Ray bond was less than five years old. We were the youngest Anointed Ones to rule in Arit history.

Thérèse had solved the problem with kuso-kuso vines, heightening our connection and keeping council sickness at bay. Still, out of habit, we often crowded three or more to a bed . . . and some of my siblings were enjoying the benefits of our newfound privacy more than others.

"It's not what it looks like," blurted Emeronya, my Biraslovian council sister, and the youngest at fourteen.

She primly adjusted the lopsided veil she wore over her short dark hair, shooting a guilty look at Kirah. Both Blessids and Biraslovians belonged to People of the Wing, the most prudish religious sect in Aritsar. "We were only telling stories. Seeing if we could give one another dreams, like Tar used to do. Back before she got busy with all her treaties and banquets."

"Banquets to which *we* aren't invited," added my council brother Zathulu of Djbanti, tilting his shaved head.

Kirah crossed her arms. "You know why tonight's banquet is special. Tar couldn't invite everyone. And if you're only telling stories . . . why are you all half naked?"

"The Ray works better skin to skin," said my Spartian council brother, Theo, draping a sculpted arm around Kameron's torso.

"Is the great Tarisai Idajo going to condemn us with a ruling?" deadpanned my Nyamban council brother, Umansa. He flashed a smile, bright against his dark skin, which glittered with constellation tattoos. Sensing my location through the Ray, he turned his sightless white eyes on me, holding out his wrists to be cuffed.

I cringed at the honorific, hugging the bundle of scrolls to my chest. Idajo—*the Just*. As High Lady Judge, enforcing imperial law was technically my job.

"She would have to arrest herself," Emeronya pointed out, in her usual prim monotone. "When Tar forgets to raise her mental shields at night, her dreams about Sanjeet do not usually involve clothes."

My cheeks grew hot. The law forbids Anointed Ones from any behavior remotely romantic or sexual—except, of course, with our Raybearer, whom we had sworn to serve in any way he wished.

In private, however, the law was seldom enforced. I hadn't even cared about it until Thaddace and Mbali's tryst had led to Olugbade's death. After all, if they had never fallen in love . . . Thaddace could not have been blackmailed. He would never have killed the emperor, or been imprisoned, or had his throat slit by that boy in the—

I blocked out the thought. "No one's getting arrested," I said. "It was just a story game. None of you were breaking the law."

"Yet," Theo coughed.

"Just be careful next time," I said, more sternly than I intended. "All of you."

Emeronya wrinkled her elfin features, managing as usual to resemble a child and a grumpy old woman at the same time. "Tar, you don't look so good."

"Don't be paranoid," I said breezily. "I'm— I'm just—"

I was just terrified of everyone I loved dropping like flies. Like Thaddace bleeding in the hallway. Like The Lady pierced with poison. Like Dayo beneath Enitawa's Quiver, my knife in his side.

I was terrified of everything but the thick, perfume-drugged halls of the Imperial Suite, where I could search the memories of brick and tile, and ensure that no ghostly assassins lay in wait behind them.

"I'm not too busy to give you dreams," I said brightly, sidestepping the question. "I can make up any memories you want—so long as they're not too naughty." I dropped the scrolls: sources I'd collected for Mayazatyl's latest weapon designs. Then I set the tureen of goat's milk on the floor: supper for Kameron's latest adoptees. Immediately, two silky black panther cubs dashed from a pallet in the corner, rubbing their coats on my bare legs before lapping up the milk.

"Don't encourage them," Theo groaned. "Ever since Kameron became High Lord of Husbandry, the palace has become a zoo. Those monsters gnawed on my best harp."

Kameron's teal eyes sparkled wickedly. "Maybe if you'd write more love songs about me instead of flirting with servant boys," he said, trapping a blushing Theo in a burly headlock, "my bairns would chew your harp less often."

My siblings laughed and rolled their eyes as Theo made a show of trying to escape from Kameron's embrace, though we all knew both men would rather stay just as they were.

"The puppies *could* have been baby war buffalo," Mayazatyl told Theo, rolling off the bed pallet and riffling through the yellowed scrolls. "So count your blessings. We've been studying how the empire can breed buffalo with tougher skin. If I can design armor big enough, the buffalo can replace our old-fashioned war machines."

I frowned. "War machines? What for?"

"In case you don't appease the abiku," Mayazatyl replied, never one for sparing feelings. "And the continent goes to war. Also, some rabble-rouser's been interfering with the palace supply lines. Calls himself the Turtle, or Crocodile, something like that. Anyway, if war machines don't scare him away from your iron quarries, a war buffalo certainly will."

"Right," I said dazedly. "Dayo and I . . . own things now."

"They're a lot more than *things*," Umansa, the newly crowned High Lord Treasurer, said with a laugh. "The Kunleo family claimed nearly every massive natural resource on the continent after establishing the empire. Quarries, river mills, lumber farms. Why do you think the Imperial Treasury never runs dry? The Kunleos generate so much wealth from raw resources, they barely even touch their revenue from taxes."

"Oh." My head spun. "But don't all those places have workers? Villages that depend on them? How are Dayo and I supposed to keep track of them all?"

"You don't," Mayazatyl said cheerily. "Nobles manage the mills and quarries for you. Taking a cut for their trouble, of course. The crown only interferes when nobles need reinforcements."

"Reinforcements?"

"Muscle." She grinned. "Like war buffalo."

"Right." I nodded uneasily. "Well, you don't have to read all those scrolls—I've read half of them already. I'll give you my memories of what they say."

"Or," said Mayazatyl, "you could leave imperial defense to me, since it's my job, and address the twelve realm monarchs waiting for you downstairs?"

I bristled, glancing busily around the chamber. "Umansa, did you ever find your lost weaving shuttle? You can't chart your prophecies without it . . ."

"My shuttle is where it's supposed to be," Umansa said dryly. "You, my sister, are not."

"Why," I muttered, "is everyone so obsessed with this stupid banquet?" I set my jaw and wheeled to leave the room in disgust.

I barreled straight into a wall-like chest. Someone had filled the doorway. When the intoxicating wave of leather and polish hit me, I grimaced, knowing the jig was up.

"Tar?" Sanjeet held my shoulders to steady me. The gold and steel of his High General regalia glinted in the sconce light. Grim, tea-colored eyes ran perplexed patterns over my clothes. "Sunshine girl . . . why aren't you dressed?"

Behind him stood my council sister Ai Ling, resplendent in formal state wear. She watched me worriedly, and the room seemed to freeze. The hair on my neck prickled as my siblings began to use the Ray, pulsing words and feelings through the air. I knew they were discussing me, though when I tried to listen, they blocked me out with mental shields. Irritation surged through me. I pressed into the Ray again, and fractured phrases slipped through their barrier.

. . . have to stop her. She hasn't been the same since—

. . . handle being empress. She's stronger than Dayo. But maybe I was wrong. We shouldn't have encouraged her—

. . . protect her, even from herself. Even if it means—

I hardened my own mental shields to adamant, plunging the voices into silence.

"Need air," I breathed, and pushed past Sanjeet and Ai Ling.

"Best leave her," I heard Kirah say behind me. "I've been trying all evening." But Sanjeet and Ai Ling followed anyway, hard on my heels. I regressed to an old instinct, one I had used as a child whenever the gilded walls of An-Ileyoba threatened to suffocate:

Escape to the roof.

CHAPTER 4

WHEN I STUMBLED UP A NARROW STAIRCASE to the suite's elevated garden, night air enveloped me in a citrus-scented balm. Herb beds, dwarf palms, and potted fruit trees lined the flat sandstone roof, nestled prettily between the golden palace domes. My council sister Thérèse of Nontes stood swaying among the fragrant vines of kuso-kuso. Moonlight bleached her frizzy yellow hair as her Hallow forced waxy kuso-kuso leaves to sprout, flower, wilt, and sprout again, over and over until they achieved her prim standard of perfection. When I burst onto the roof, Sanjeet and Ai Ling close behind, Thérèse barely flinched.

"The others are right, you know," she said without turning around, her Nontish accent pinched and breathy. "Tarisai, *ma cherie* . . . you cannot hide forever. You have been *very* helpful lately, though. Did you ever find my coneflower seeds?"

"You heard my argument with the others?" I asked with dread. "From two floors away?"

"Only the parts they Ray-spoke." Thérèse gestured

34

at the vines. "My kuso-kuso is especially strong tonight. I could probably hear you Ray-speak from the peaks of Nontes."

"Talk to us, Tar," Sanjeet coaxed. Through the Ray, he sent a gentle beam of warmth up my spine, making me shiver. "You're not well. What can we do?"

I bit my lip, staring at the dark indigo sky, dotted with stars and pulsing lavender sprites. "I can't do it," I said at last. "I can't face those people."

"Those stuffy vassal rulers?" Ai Ling laughed, clearly trying to lighten the mood. "That courtier chicken coop? Trust me—they're no match for our Empress of Aritsar."

She sounded sincere, but then again . . . Ai Ling always did, when she needed to.

That was unfair of me. Ai Ling never used her persuasion Hallow on her council siblings. She rarely used her coercion powers at all, though that was hard for the public to believe. After two weeks as Imperial Ambassador, Ai Ling had already calmed two rowdy crowds who had arrived at the palace to protest my rule, swaying them with her speeches. She'd brokered a trade deal between Songland and Aritsar, despite Songland's reasonable distrust of Aritsar. But Ai Ling's melodious voice—her quick wit, and sharp negotiation savvy . . . those were no Hallow. They were just *her*: my sister, the unflappable Ai Ling of Moreyao.

"Sorry I'm being so much trouble," I mumbled, and grimaced at her stunning formal wear. Her outfit had sprouted wrinkles after she chased me up to the garden.

Torchlight glimmered on her peach silk *hanfu*—the flowing robes of her home realm—and pearl ornaments dangling in her hair.

Ai Ling had arranged tonight's Peace Banquet single-handedly. She had convinced all the continent rulers to remain at An-Ileyoba, instead of leaving after I had sabotaged the Treaty Renewal. Floors below in the Imperial Hall, twelve rulers waited for me to seduce them into loyalty. Into bonding their minds with me for life. But—

"They think I murdered Thaddace," I protested. "They all do—the court, the rulers. Everyone. How can they love an empress who kills in cold blood?"

Dimples appeared beneath Ai Ling's keen dark eyes. "At court," she said, "being known as a killer isn't always a bad thing."

I made a face. "I . . . almost don't want you to explain that."

"The only difference between a murderer and a hero is who tells the story." Ai Ling cleared her throat, then lifted her hands as if addressing a throne room, her voice cool and imperious. "Thaddace's death," she said, "removes any remaining suspicion that our Empress Redemptor was in league with The Lady. On the contrary: Empress Tarisai is our empire's savior. She prevented a dangerous convict, an imperial traitor, from escaping the palace. She is so dedicated to justice, so loyal to Olugbade's memory . . . she would kill her own mentor in cold blood. Such courage." Ai Ling let a delicate sob shake her voice. "Such majesty!"

I lurched away and vomited into a nearby potted palm tree.

Ai Ling swore, bustling over to rub my back. "Am's Story, Tari darling. I should have thought. I didn't mean to . . ." She winced, the confidence draining from her voice. "You'd think a speaking Hallow would prevent me from being an ass."

"You're not an ass," I mewled. "You're right. You're always right, and I'm already failing at being empress."

Thérèse unhooked a vial from her belt and tipped its contents down my throat. Astringent peppermint stung my nostrils, but the nausea abated. My skin prickled as Sanjeet scanned me anxiously with his Hallow, searching my body for illness. He would find nothing but cowardice, thrumming through every vein.

"The only thing you've failed to do," he said quietly, "is let us help you. We're your family, sunshine girl. Tell us what you need."

"Come with me," I squeaked. "To the banquet. All of you."

Ai Ling tensed. "You know that isn't a good idea," she said gently. "Fewer companions are better optics. It sends the message that you're there to make new friends, not hide behind old ones. But Dayo's going, so you won't be alone. So will Kirah and I, since we're handling peace negotiations with Songland."

The phrase *making friends* sounded much too casual for tonight's endeavors. The abiku had accepted my sacrifice on one condition: that I become a full-fledged Raybearer, anointing the vassal rulers of every Arit realm to create my own council of eleven. If I failed at anointing the rulers, then the abiku would deem my body too cheap a sacrifice. Aritsar would never know peace again.

I asked, "How can those rulers love me if they think I just murdered someone?"

"Oh, Tar. Love is delightfully complicated." Ai Ling placed my hand on her brow, offering me her memories. The sour faces of several foreign monarchs flashed through my mind. "Ever since the Treaty ceremony, the vassal rulers have been staying at guest villas, here in Oluwan. So I thought I'd pay them a visit," she explained. "Sniff out how they felt about you. Turns out, you made a good impression on the empire when you repealed that Unity Edict. But you also branded yourself as impulsive. Overearnest. A little naïve. In other words, none of the vassal rulers took you seriously. You were a mere child to them, until . . ."

"Until they thought I killed my own mentor. And now they hate me."

"They're scared of you," Ai Ling corrected. "Which is way more useful. People can't love someone they don't respect. And, well—fear's a step in the right direction."

"Ai Ling," Sanjeet muttered, his Hallow no doubt sensing the anxiety spike in my bloodstream. "Thérèse . . . can I speak to Tar alone, please?"

My council sisters glanced between me and Sanjeet,

exchanged a coy look of wiggled eyebrows, and disappeared downstairs without a word.

Once alone, I drank him in, lingering on the curve of his ears, the slant of his eyebrows. I'd never scold my council siblings for illegal romances again—I was the biggest lawbreaker of them all. He smiled at me, tea-colored eyes resigned with exhaustion, and opened his arms. I pressed my ear to his armored chest, sending Dayo's Ray in tendrils over his earth-scented skin.

"I'd rather not Ray-speak," he said, consonants plosive with that deep, Dhyrmish accent that reminded me of a talking drum. He gave a rumbling chuckle. "Not now, anyway. The others mean well, but we both know they aren't above eavesdropping."

"You're going to lecture me." I turned up my head, resting my chin between the pectorals of his leather breastplate. The cold, gilded spikes proclaiming his new High General status pricked me, but I didn't mind. Already the panic was leaching out of me, drawn by the poultice of his steady heartbeat. "I wouldn't, if I were you. Kirah tried all day, and she didn't get far."

"No lecture," he promised, murmuring into the silk of my hair scarf. "Tar, if you don't want to go to the banquet, then . . . don't."

I would have stumbled back in shock if his solid arms hadn't held me there. "You can't be serious." I blinked up at him. "Of course I have to go. It's my banquet."

If my contradictory moods surprised Sanjeet, he didn't

show it. "You are empress," he said simply. He traced the raised oval where my obabirin mask lay hidden beneath my shift. "Do whatever the hell you want."

I shook my head, speaking slowly as if he no longer spoke Arit. "The fate of the entire continent depends on what I say at this party. You know that. Are you—" I squinted suspiciously. "Are you trying to guilt me into going down there?"

"By saying the opposite?" His bushy eyebrows knit. "That sounds . . . complicated."

I breathed a laugh. "Sorry," I said, standing on tiptoe to kiss his cheek. "You've never had the mind of a courtier. You're too straightforward for that. But I don't get it—Jeet, what side are you on?"

"The hardest side to be on: the one that keeps you alive." He smiled, though the bitterness in his tone bled through. "Between challenging Underworld demons and planning prison heists, you seem . . . determined to heighten security risks."

"I was *born* a security risk."

His smile faded. "You know I don't mean your mother's curse. Tar . . . Aritsar hasn't seen someone like you in centuries."

I heard what he would not say outright: Unlike Dayo, I was a ruler who could still be assassinated.

And with a twisting sensation in my stomach, I knew he was right. Until I anointed a council, I was only immune to fire. Still—

"You encouraged me to be empress," I reminded him. "Back when Melu first told me I was a Raybearer, and I was still in denial. So you shouldn't want me to hide. The others are right—I can't cower in the Imperial Suite forever."

Sanjeet's chiseled features went blank, and a shiver chased up my arms. I hated it when this happened. Whenever Sanjeet couldn't trust himself to speak—to do anything with complete control—a wall rose around him, like the impenetrable enchanted barrier around Bhekina House. The wall had appeared more often when we were younger—when Sanjeet was still a candidate in the Children's Palace, haunted by the danger of his own Hallow. If he wanted, Sanjeet could sense the physical weakness in anyone, and to avoid the temptation of control, he had taken to cloistering himself whenever he felt angry, helpless, or both.

I'd spent years tearing that wall down. But ever since I'd offered myself to the abiku as a sacrifice, acting as Aritsar's final Redemptor . . . the distance between us had returned with rising force. Sometimes I felt the wall even when we slept, nuzzling into the shape of each other at night.

He sighed at last, shoulders sagging as, for now, the barrier crumbled. He ran his fingers through his loose dark curls. "The truth is," he said in a strange, rough voice, "you're not safe anywhere in An-Ileyoba. Even here in the suite. I've doubled defenses at every palace entrance. Posted Imperial Guard warriors in every major thoroughfare. But I still haven't figured out how that creature who killed Thaddace breached the palace walls. And now the Imperial Guard has new concerns with the Crocodile and his riots . . ."

My brow furrowed, remembering what Mayazatyl had said about a new vigilante. "Crocodile?"

He blinked, as if regretting he'd brought it up. "Some new troublemaker." He waved a hand. "Stirring up unrest around the realms. Don't worry—I'll handle it. Am knows you've got enough on your plate."

I frowned at the dismissal, but then stringed griot music surged from the courtyards far below, and my stomach flipped. "Do you really think I have a chance at winning over those monarchs?" I asked, swallowing hard as I stared out into the night. "I doubt they're eager to be wooed after what happened to Thaddace. No matter what Ai Ling says, the timing wasn't exactly ideal."

"You had to try and save him," Sanjeet monotoned. "It's who you are."

"You think I was foolish," I accused. "You think I should have left Thaddace alone. Let him die for my mistakes."

A thought formed on Sanjeet's brow, only for him to suppress it, his clay-toned features carefully neutral.

"Say it," I told him.

He avoided my gaze. "Say what?"

I sighed and reached to lace my fingers behind his neck, smiling up at him. "Whatever you're thinking, Sanjeet of Dhyrma, that you don't know how to sugarcoat."

He scanned me with those deeply steeped brown eyes. Goose bumps sprouted wherever his gaze landed, from my exposed collarbone to the lurid blue marks on my forearms. Then his lips lowered to mine, rousing an army of dragonflies in my stomach. The kiss was slow, thoughtful. A meditation.

"Nice distraction," I gasped, knowing his Hallow could sense my heart hammering. "But you still have to say it."

Sanjeet laughed softly, resting his chin atop my hair again. "I was thinking," he said, "that you should get used to people dying for you."

I stiffened in his embrace. "Because I'm a cursed Raybearer? Who brings death wherever she goes?"

"No." He fed me a memory then: the day of my First Ruling, only through his eyes instead of mine. He had watched the crowds packing the tiered seating of the Imperial Hall, his heart teeming with fear and wonder as they all had chanted my name. *Idajo. Idajo. Tarisai Idajo.* "You should accept it, because people die for what they believe in. You're used to everyone hating you. But Tar . . . someday, you'll have to carry a burden much, much harder." He gestured down to the courtyards glimmering with festive torchlight, where a hundred souls waited to be seduced to my cause. "You'll have to prepare for everyone loving you too."

CHAPTER 5

WITHIN AN HOUR, I STOOD IN A VAST, GAILY lit corridor with Ai Ling, Kirah, and Dayo, waiting before the two-story-high Imperial Hall doors.

"At your signal, Your Imperial Majesties," boomed an Imperial Guard warrior.

I swallowed hard, willing my elaborately painted palms not to sweat. "Just a moment, please," I croaked.

The guard waited patiently, ready to order that the massive doors be hauled open: a feat made possible by a dozen burly servants and a pulley system of thick rope looped through rings in the noses of carved lions, which shone from the polished wood. Ever since the Treaty Renewal, the doors made me shiver every time I saw them. I hadn't told anyone why.

Somehow—after I had ridden across the empire and Melu rejuvenated me, bringing me back from the edge of death—I had managed to open those doors myself.

I had burst through what was likely several tons of solid wood and iron, desperate to stop Dayo from completing the Treaty Renewal. In my feverish determined haze, the massive doors had seemed to spring open at my touch, creaking forth with a deafening roar. Since that day, they had not opened on their own again.

Wooden doors were rare anywhere in Oluwan, as they were impractical in the heat, and far more expensive than linen door flaps. Legend dictated that an Oluwani alagbato—a fairy guardian like my father, Melu of Swana—had crafted the Imperial Hall doors centuries ago, sacrificing sacred trees of golden-white mahogany. The alagbato commanded that the trunks hew themselves into smooth planks, and then she had pulled iron from her own heart, fashioning it into nails. As a finishing touch, she had carved intricate glyphs and patterns into the door, symbolizing an ancient pact between alagbatos and the Kunleo dynasty, who had been the first humans to raise cities on Oluwan's fertile plains. But what that pact had promised . . . no one seemed to remember. Apparently, the alagbato had now been dormant for generations, as often happened to nature spirits after industry thrived and land was heavily developed. Occasionally I had touched the doors out of curiosity, but only human memories seeped through: the clamor of sumptuous court celebrations and the volleying voices of nobility and Anointed Ones, holding centuries of Imperial court.

In that hall, the rulers of every realm on the continent awaited my entrance. What thoughts and whispers were those ancient doors soaking up right now?

You're going to be fine, a warm tenor Ray-spoke in my head. *Take your time, Tar.* The sound blossomed as it always did—right behind my eyes, as if we shared a soul. *You're worth the wait.*

Emperor Ekundayo Kunleo, *oba* of Aritsar, reached for my hand, the sun-and-stars of his solid gold seal ring pressing into my fingers. These days, I found it hard to look at him. Circles pooled beneath his eyes—exhaustion that I blamed myself for.

Dayo had always been gangly. But the past weeks had reduced his tall dark frame to bone, aging him and accentuating the latticed burn scar that stretched from his jaw to his collarbone. The fatigue showed only in his face. He shimmered in Olugbade's old banquet *agbada*, a sweeping purple kaftan with swaths of fabric furling over each shoulder. It tripled Dayo's size and swayed around him with every step, metallic threads catching the light. He didn't look like a sleep-deprived boy grieving his father. He looked like someone's emperor.

"Don't worry about me," I told him aloud, touching his cheek. "You need rest more than anyone."

"It's funny." A *V* formed on Dayo's smooth dark brow. "I should feel worse than I do about Father."

"Worse?"

"Sadder." Dayo chewed his bottom lip, staring up at the massive doors shimmering with his family's legacy. "But the truth is . . . Father barely let me know him. Didn't let anyone, really. I always assumed when I was older, I'd understand, but . . ." He trailed off.

46

"Grief isn't simple, Dayo," Ai Ling said. She watched him with pity and another emotion I couldn't quite name. The air crackled as I felt her reach for Dayo with the Ray— then she stopped, throwing up her mental shields abruptly, as though afraid of what her thoughts might reveal.

"I feel numb about Thaddace too," said Dayo, not seeming to notice Ai Ling's secrecy. "It doesn't make sense. He helped raise me, and I loved him, I really did. But whenever I try to mourn Uncle Thad, I just feel . . . empty."

"He killed your father," Kirah observed.

"But it wasn't that simple," he protested. "Uncle Thad had to make an impossible choice."

"I know." The silver coins on Kirah's tunic jingled as she patted his arm. "But Dayo . . . it's still okay to be mad at him."

He opened his mouth, shut it, and then wilted. I reached out to cup his cheek, running my thumb over his jaw. I had only just begun to see the resemblance between our features—the same rounded nostrils and subtle chin, gifts from our shared grandfather.

"Woo In of Songland didn't mean to kill my mother either," I said quietly. "But I still have to forgive him every day. And . . ." I shifted my jewel-studded sandals. "I get it if you keep having to forgive me too."

Dayo's large black eyes widened in horror. "I don't blame you, Tarisai."

"I know. But you should." The words stuck in my throat.

"If I hadn't told The Lady about Mbali and Thaddace, she never would have had the leverage. Your father would still be alive. So would Thaddace. And—"

I looked away in embarrassment as tears pooled in my eyes, making streaks in my intricate face paint and highlighted cheekbones.

"Your beauticians are going to throw a fit," Ai Ling tutted, coming to dab at my face with her flowing peach hanfu sleeves. Then she stood back as I sniffled, cocking her head. "You know, less makeup might actually be the look we want. Vulnerability could prove useful. After all"—she winked at me—"tonight's about falling in love."

"And convincing them I'm not a cold-blooded murderer."

She only shrugged. "It's like I said before, darling—fear is a tool."

People had been afraid of me my whole life. I had never tried to make it an asset before.

Ai Ling straightened the cowrie shell necklaces festooning my shoulders and adjusted the ivory adornments in my hair. Elaborate braided knots crowned my hairline, while the rest of my coils floated in a black halo. "You know," she mused, "there are limits to my Hallow, but I could—well—*encourage* the continent rulers to join your council. I can't exactly make them love you. But I can make them want to try. They'll resist me at first, but they can't keep their mental guards up forever. And once they get to know you—"

"No." I shook my head. "If I'm going to have my own council, I want it to be like ours. A life we chose." I exchanged a look with Dayo. "A family."

"Families aren't usually chosen," Ai Ling pointed out. "We just got lucky." She shot an inscrutably affectionate glance at Dayo, and her words rang ominously as drumbeats vibrated the ground.

I glanced at my multiple reflections in the mirrored hall ceiling. Arit courtiers wore garments that honored their home kingdoms, and my attendants and beauticians had dressed me in a diplomatic balance between Oluwan and Swana. The clothing was purposely outdated, a tribute to the traditional garb of each realm. I wore nothing on top but a wide, tiered necklace of gold-encrusted cowrie shells, secured with cords at my neck and back. Even this was a modern concession—ancient Oluwani women hadn't covered their breasts at all. A skirt of *ashoke*, the luxury textile of Oluwan, hugged my curves in a woven sheath, dusky indigo shot with threads of gold and white. The fabric stopped at my knees, and on each leg I wore tassels of dried grass, hanging in a layered fringe to my ankles: a tribute to the fashions of Swana.

Beyond the Imperial Hall doors, the banquet opening ceremonies were building to a frenzy.

"Funny," I observed absently. "In two years, I'll throw myself into the Oruku Breach to enter the Underworld. But this feels like the scary part." I smirked. "After this party, dying will be easy."

I knew it was a mistake the moment I said it. All three of my council siblings froze.

"But you aren't going to die," Dayo said, and the sharpness in his tone surprised me. "You're coming back from the Underworld. Like you promised."

"Right." I nodded quickly, pulse hammering. "I misspoke. I'm sorry."

"Like you promised," Dayo repeated, and my heart twinged. I wasn't lying—I truly didn't plan to die in the Underworld. But nothing was certain . . . and Dayo had never done well with uncertainty. I feared another loss would break him. In the space of a year, he had witnessed the massacre at Ebujo Temple, recovered from me stabbing him, and grieved his father's murder.

"Yes." I tried to smile. "I promise, Dayo."

"Good." He nodded once, looking petulant. "Because . . . because I won't get coronated. Not until you return."

I started in shock. "That's impossible," I said slowly. "I'm not going to the Underworld for two years. You can't hold off a coronation for that long."

"Says who?" he asked, signature cheer returning to his voice. "We're already emperor and empress, as far as the Ray is concerned. The coronation's just a symbol. Besides, if we wait until *after* you save the Redemptors, you'll be crowned as a hero. Aritsar will have to accept you then!"

I doubted that very much, but knew not to challenge him any further. His desperate expression betrayed his true intention for delaying our coronation: If Dayo could convince the empire that I would return from the Underworld, he might just start believing it himself.

We nodded at the warrior, and the doors groaned open.

A solid wall of music and light accosted us, briefly blinding me.

Oh. Dayo's flabbergasted voice echoed in our minds. *Ai Ling, I knew you said the party would be grand, but this is . . . incredible.*

Sconces, sprite-lamps, and free-standing torches blazed on every surface, reflecting off the marble tier seating lining the walls, which could hold thousands at full capacity. The vast chamber appeared suspended in time, high noon in the dead of night. Lighting a room this large would have cost an emperor's ransom in palm oil. A daytime banquet would have cost much less, but considering the favor I was about to ask of our royal guests . . . well. Maybe the luxury would put them in a good mood.

It's all about signaling, Ai Ling gushed through the Ray, her mind brimming with excitement. *Show those vassal rulers that to negotiate peace, the Emperor and Empress Redemptor will spare no expense.*

Secretly, I wasn't sure *peace* was the message echoing from the hall's glowing rafters. All of it—from the black-and-gold tapestries of wax-dyed cloth, to the multistory-high statues supporting the hall on giant obsidian shoulders—spoke the same words in a resounding voice:

Kneel, or be cut down.

An elaborately costumed choir sprung to attention when we entered, playing hand drums and chanting the ancient call-and-response:

Of what use—Tell us!
Of what use is an empty throne?
We have found someone worthy—Have you found someone?
Aheh, Kunleo is worthy to fill it—Yes, Kunleo is worthy to fill it.

Our banquet guests—all one hundred of them—joined in, and my bladder threatened to send warm rivulets down my thighs.

I am not allowed to be terrified, I reminded myself. I was a Kunleo, and this was our court. Our palace.

If this was a den of snakes, then Dayo and I were the cobras who ruled it.

I had heard the ancient call-and-response before—*Kunleo is worthy to fill it.* But it still made my face burn. Whenever Dayo and I left the palace, children sang to us in the streets, tossing petals and handmade effigies onto the roof of our palanquin. The adoration of strangers had always unnerved me. But as I scanned the faces of my banquet guests, wincing at their hostility . . . I supposed being feared by strangers wasn't much better.

The new Kunleo seal blazed on the distant domed ceiling: two overlapping suns, representing the joint reign of two Raybearers, circled by a wreath of interlinked hands. Long, low feast tables lined the hall, golden in the festive lamplight. Ai Ling, Kirah, and Dayo took their places near the head of the tables, sinking onto tasseled velvet cushions. I remained standing.

Now, Ai Ling Ray-spoke.

Just as we had rehearsed, I lifted my hands toward the multistory windows, sweeping my arms in a flourish. The banquet guests gasped as hundreds of lavender *tutsu* sprites poured through the arches, congregating above us in the ombre of the domed ceiling.

Sprites never left the land they were born in, unless poached to be sold as lamps and baubles. So no one had been prepared when, three weeks ago, a cloud of Swanian tutsu had congregated outside my window at An-Ileyoba Palace.

I told everyone the truth, naively thinking it would help: My father was Melu the alagbato, a guardian spirit from Swana. After liberating myself from my father's curse, my scent now seemed to attract sprites from leagues away. The announcement dazzled Arit commoners and terrified palace courtiers, with few opinions in between.

To all of Aritsar, I was either a god or a demon.

The sprites arranged themselves in twinkling constellations, recreating the Oluwan night sky. My stomach flipped with relief. Tutsu sprites strongly disliked being indoors, and it had taken days of practice before the creatures entered when I summoned them.

The crowd applauded, some with delight, others with wariness. Many recognized that a flex of power, however beautiful, could just as easily be a threat. Where some saw a blanket of stars, others saw a glittering army over their heads.

Ai Ling's words echoed—*Fear is a tool*. So I only smiled, attempting to look aloof and serene. Let them be a little afraid.

Feasting began when I lifted a bowl of kola nuts above my head, intoned a greeting, and then passed the bowl around—an ancient gesture of welcome. Queen Hye Sun of Songland, her heir Crown Princess Min Ja, and the eleven vassal rulers of Aritsar sat in silence at my table. Nerves frazzled my concentration, and the multicomplexioned faces blended together as I tried to take them in. The oldest monarch could easily be my grandfather, and the youngest, to my surprise, looked barely thirteen. Each ruler touched the bowl and nodded, signaling their acceptance.

Dayo and I did not touch the platters of seared goat, savory jollof rice, roasted pear skewers, and fried plantains, nor did we touch chalices of palm wine and herb water. We had taken tinctures before the banquet to suppress our appetites, as it was considered a display of weakness for Raybearers to eat or drink in public, or to leave a function to relieve ourselves. Every court custom served to reinforce that ancient fiction: that Raybearers were near deities, handpicked by the Storyteller to rule over Aritsar.

I hadn't needed the tincture—the anxious knots in my stomach were more than enough to spoil my appetite. But once the dining bustle died down, I donned an imperious mask, washed my hands in the ceremonial water bowl at my elbow, and stood.

"Welcome, everyone," I began, jumping at the amplification of my voice. Ai Ling had placed an enchanted echostone behind my seat cushion. Throughout the hall, the scrape of earthen dinnerware stopped, and the ambient drums and plucked zither music melted into the quiet. A sea of eyes surged to rest on me.

"I am especially grateful for the presence of Aritsar's vassal rulers, as well as our guests from Songland. Thank you for prolonging your stay. I know you were eager to return to your home realms, after I . . . transformed our treaty with the abiku." I smiled tightly, choosing to ignore scornful whispers. "What you choose tonight decides the fate of the empire. I want to be the last Redemptor ever sent into the Oruku Breach. To ensure that no child—Arit or Songlander—is ever sacrificed again."

"Hear, hear," Dayo interrupted with eager applause. The guests awkwardly followed suit.

"But the abiku won't accept me," I went on. "Not unless I anoint a council of the twelve rulers of Aritsar. I know it's . . . a lot. What I'm asking. A pact for life, binding our minds, our blood. But I've been in your shoes. I'm an Anointed One too, after all, so I know how daunting that feels. But if we don't try . . ." I inhaled—then bit down on the kernel of dried kuso-kuso I'd been hiding under my tongue. The fragrant herb went sharply to my head, and a green haze crept at the edges of my vision. The Hallow flowing in my veins—the gift from my father the alagbato, who drew stories from the earth—boiled beneath my skin, begging to leach memories from every surface I touched. Instead, I used my temporarily heightened power to conjure a memory, and send it as a mass hallucination into the brows of every guest at my table: the massacre at Ebujo, with visions of bodies littering the temple floor, ripped apart by vengeful creatures from the Underworld.

CHAPTER 6

MY BANQUET TABLE FELL INTO CHAOS. SOME of the rulers stood, upsetting their chalices and clutching their temples as if to claw the vision out. I winced. It had been a risk, invading their minds like that. It was unlikely they would forgive me for it soon—but forcing the memory of Ebujo had been the quickest way to get my point across.

"This could be the fate of the entire continent," I said over their indignant cries. "I had to make you see. Please sit down. I—"

They clamored over me, some dignitaries threatening to leave the banquet then and there. No. My palms sweated. They couldn't leave; this was my only chance to save Aritsar. To prevent thousands of child sacrifices. Millions. Desperation sped my heartbeat, and heat rose in my chest. When I spoke again, my voice sounded lower, and the echo-stone brought my altered voice to a bellow.

"Please," I thundered. *"Sit. Down."*

Beneath my necklace of cowrie shells, the obabirin mask

seared like a coal. For a moment, I could have sworn the mask glowed.

Then as if in a trance, every Arit ruler lowered to their seat cushions, features startled and mouths slack. When the heat receded from me and my pulse returned to normal, they still sat, stunned as though they had just awoken from a strange, powerful dream.

I was as surprised as they were. Only the dignitaries from Songland continued to stand, seemingly unfazed by whatever had subdued the other monarchs.

"Please," I said again, dropping the bass from my voice. The Songlander royals scowled . . . but after exchanging a wary glance, voluntarily sat back down with the others.

"Thank you," I said shakily, feeling as dazed as my guests looked. "I was . . . just trying to convey the danger. If monsters pour from the Oruku Breach, not only will they kill us, they'll also turn our realms against each other, just like at Ebujo. The empire could splinter overnight, leaving us just as weak as we were five hundred years ago. I think—if we don't form a council to appease the abiku—all of Aritsar could be at risk."

Though calm now, the Arit rulers had clearly not recovered from my mental invasion. Some squinted into their chalices, as though they might have been drugged. A few shot pleading glances at Kirah, making the sign of the Pelican.

"You have nothing to fear from the empress," Kirah assured them, using her lofty High Priestess voice. She gestured a blessing over the table. "The empress's warning was a gift."

"Of course it was," Dayo announced. "We have only two years to avoid the fate of Ebujo. And so," he said, standing and taking my hand in solidarity, "the Empress Redemptor and I would like to extend an invitation: Stay in Oluwan City. All of you."

"Not indefinitely," I added quickly. "But we can't risk too much lodestone travel. You need only stay until—"

Until you love me and bind your minds to me for life.

"Until you've tried to join my council," I finished lamely. "And the fate of the empire is secured. We would house you all in the utmost comfort, compliments of the crown. High Lord General Sanjeet has seen personally to each villa's safety." I steeled my shoulders. "We open the floor for questions."

Cacophony from wall to wall. The rulers and their retinues roared over one another, shaking their heads and gesturing in protests that upset platters and toppled chalices.

Calmly, Ai Ling joined me on the echo-stone and said, "It would be better, perhaps, if questions were posed one at a time."

The Hallowed suggestion fell on the room like a thick mudcloth blanket. A few stubborn-minded people still muttered at their seats, but most hushed at Ai Ling's request, looking vaguely ashamed of themselves.

First to speak was King Helius of Sparti, a graying man with sea-whipped skin. Curling chest hair bristled around a gold-edged chiton. "With all due respect, Your Imperial Majesties," he sputtered, "whether or not we are willing to *try* to love the empress is immaterial. Suppose you succeed. What then? We live in Oluwan forever, stuck to her side, neglecting our own countries? Sacred Oceans—my absence in this past month alone has stalled the launch of several ships! Sparti's trade will grind to a halt, and our fisheries won't be far behind."

The other rulers grunted in agreement, and the rumble threatened to return.

"We have a plan for that," Ai Ling piped up, digging in her pocket and placing a sachet of dried leaves on the table. The smell hit me instantly, sharp and heady.

"The kuso-kuso herb?" asked Queen Danai of Swana. Silvery white locs shone in intricate patterns on her head, and she appraised Ai Ling with keen eyes. "But that is a dreaming aid. How will that help us?"

Ai Ling smiled mysteriously. "It's true—in some regions of Aritsar, entire villages inhale kuso-kuso smoke together, allowing for communal dreaming. But our council has been experimenting with ways to send messages across long distances, improving communication between realms." She paused for effect. "Turns out, you don't have to inhale kuso-kuso in the same room to dream together. If two or more strongly bonded individuals dream at the same time . . . their minds unite. Wherever they are. The dreams are as potent as speaking in person, alleviating council sickness through the Ray."

Dayo beamed at Ai Ling, and she colored. "It's brilliant," he said. "Once each monarch is anointed, they won't even have to stay in Oluwan. So Tarisai's new council can commune anytime, anywhere."

Impressed voices rippled down the table. Then Crown Princess Min Ja of Songland's alto cut through the others, smooth and piercing. "What I don't understand," she said, "is what any of this has to do with Songland."

I tried not to quail beneath her stare. Min Ja seemed to glow in her traditional Songlander attire—a full skirt and matching jacket of crisp pastel silks, blues and whites icy against her golden skin. She had the satiny black hair and fine bone structure of her younger brother, Woo In, and shared the same glint in her jaded dark eyes. The last time I had seen that expression—bristling grief masked by anger—Woo In had been holding a knife to my mother's cheek, unaware of the poison seeping into her bloodstream.

Tread lightly, Kirah Ray-spoke to me.

I tensed at the warning. *You've been getting to know the queen and the princess, right? What should I know?*

Kirah bit her lip. *Queen Hye Sun hasn't been the same since her son Woo In disappeared. She's a little better, now that she knows he's alive—but they say she's still a husk of her former glory. And Min Ja is—* Kirah sucked in a breath. . . . *a puzzle. She's barely ten years older than us. Yet she's the sole heir to the Songlander throne. Even over Woo In.*

That's weird, commented Dayo, cocking his head. *Don't Songlander dynasties usually pass from father to son? They don't*

61

even include daughters in their genealogies. Hye Sun only ruled as a widow regent. Why would the throne go to Min Ja instead of Woo In?

Woo In's a Redemptor, I pointed out. *Perhaps that made Hye Sun nervous.*

Ai Ling said: *Woo In wasn't Hye Sun's first male child.*

An ominous chill pricked at my neck. *He wasn't?*

There were seven total, Ai Ling continued to Ray-speak, after an unsettled pause. *Seven healthy sons, all older than Min Ja and Woo In. But something happened. None of my spies in Songland can be sure, but . . . it's widely spoken that when she was younger, Min Ja murdered her own brothers.*

The crown princess of Songland appeared to be relishing the silence. She drew a gold-tipped nail around the rim of her chalice, causing a low, resonant whistle. At last she smiled tightly and said, "Your empire admitted to massacring thousands of Songlander children. Your council has hurried to facilitate reparations," she acknowledged, nodding at Ai Ling and Kirah. "A process that I intend to be painful, especially to Aritsar's bottomless treasury. But as far as I'm concerned, our business ends there. The abiku asked you to form a council of *Arit* rulers. Songland is not part of the Arit empire, nor shall it ever be. So why," she asked with that cold, coy contempt, "are we here?"

"You are here," I replied, "because your people have gone centuries without a voice on the continent. I won't pressure you to join the empire. I won't try to rule you. But it's time Songland had a seat at the table."

Min Ja examined me for several moments, her expression inscrutable. "How noble," she monotoned. "Unfortunately, I don't believe in heroines. Not even pretty ones, who go on suicidal joyrides across Aritsar on giant magical leopards. How do I know this isn't just another Kunleo ruse? A trick to gain control of my people again."

"I'll have no power over Her Majesty." I nodded shyly at the old Queen Hye Sun, who blinked back at me with rheumy, absent eyes. "And she can make sure of that. If the queen joins my council, after all, we'll be bonded in mind and body. She'll have access to my thoughts. My dreams. I couldn't keep secrets from her—not easily, anyway."

Min Ja appraised me severely, until the beautiful young woman beside her whispered in her ear. She looked Min Ja's age, with the fat figure coveted by Oluwani court ladies. Brown eyes twinkled over floral lace, which masked the bottom half of her full, flushed face. As the woman spoke, Min Ja looked chastened, eyeing her companion with annoyed vulnerability. When the woman gestured, I blinked in surprise. Pink sleeves fell back to reveal amputated arms, severed and scarred over just below the elbow.

That's Da Seo, Ai Ling Ray-spoke. *The princess's consort. Lady Da Seo lost her arms intercepting an attempt on Min Ja's life several years ago. Afterward, Min Ja named Da Seo her equal. The Songlander court has tried to pressure Min Ja into producing an heir with a man. But she refuses. Where the princess goes, Da Seo goes.*

Presently, Min Ja addressed me again. "Your mother," she said slowly, "once controlled my baby brother. That

witch made him forsake his own sister. His own family."
Her upper lip wrinkled, as though my mother's memory
tasted bitter. "But my consort's heart is softer than mine. Da
Seo reminds me that for some reason, Woo In trusted you
enough to return to Songland. My brother has never been
a good judge of character. Still—" She gave a begrudging
sniff. "Because of you, my baby brother came home. And
for that reason alone . . . Songland will consider your
offer. But it won't be my mother inside your head, Little
Empress." Min Ja flashed a mirthless smile. "It will be me."

As the hall looked on in confusion, Min Ja gently patted
her mother's arm. The elderly queen blinked back at her
sleepily.

Min Ja said, "We were going to wait to announce it. But
we should tell them, Ommah."

Hye Sun expelled a phlegmy sigh from deep in her lungs,
nodded once, and reached for the thick gold pin piercing
her elaborate silver top knot. She handed it to Min Ja, and
with a gasp from the entire hall, the princess threaded it
through her own shining dark bun.

"As Regent, I thought I could be what Songland
needs," Hye Sun croaked, seeming to summon strength
for the short speech. "But these past few weeks has made
one thing painfully clear—Songland does not need a doting
grandmother. It needs a warrior queen. And so," she
rasped, "before this hall of witnesses, I abdicate my crown
and bestow it on my daughter, Min Ja, my late husband's
chosen heir of Songland."

Surprised murmurs filled the hall. I gaped like a fish.

I don't like this. Ai Ling's wary voice sprang into my mind. *Tar, you weren't planning to anoint Min Ja. It's not too late. There's still time to back out.*

Min Ja's gaze fixed haughtily on mine. For a moment I quailed—but then I saw another face. A young Redemptor girl, Ye Eun, scowling with agonized determination before plunging into the Oruku Breach.

The abiku may not care if I anoint Songland, I told Ai Ling. *But I do.*

I raised the chalice at my side to Min Ja. "To the new queen of Songland," I said quietly. "Whom I hope to call my sister."

Min Ja lifted her cup, expressionless as the baffled court applauded. Then she asked in her blunt, clipped voice, "If I join your council, will you require me to wed you?"

If I had been allowed to drink my palm wine, I would have choked on it.

"Wed—me?" I gasped. "I . . . of course not!"

"There is no *of course* about it," another realm ruler spoke up. It was Maharani Sadhika of Dhyrma, an amber-skinned queen covered in bangles. She flared a jewel-studded nostril, tossing a glossy braid. "Anointed Ones swear fealty to their Raybearer, no? In mind *and* in body. But some of us already have spouses. Concubines." She gestured to the retinue of pretty young men who sat around her. "Do you expect us to forsake them for you?"

"No. I mean . . ." I sputtered. "Celibacy is custom, yes.

But I won't require it. It's certainly not necessary to accept the Ray."

A strident tenor remarked, "How disappointing."

My face burned in surprise. Scandalized whispers tittered throughout the hall. Heart pounding with irritation, I met the speaker's eye.

Zuri, King of Djbanti, stared straight back.

He looked my age, with waist-length locs tied back in a sweeping ponytail. His form, though athletic, sprawled drunkenly across his seat cushion. A gold ring winked in his ear over a smooth jawline. His lips curved generously, a permanent kiss.

"I, for one," he slurred, "was looking forward to meeting our empress's private needs. After all, the law requires Raybearers to produce heirs with their Anointed Ones. We must obey the law, Lady Empress."

Ignore him, Ai Ling Ray-spoke, rolling her eyes. *Zuri's beauty is the only interesting thing about him. He was crowned barely a year ago, and he spends all his time hunting and gambling on games of mancala. Djbanti's true rulers are merchants. Zuri's nothing more than a puppet. At least . . . that's what my spies report. I didn't get much out of him directly.* Ai Ling paused. *My persuasion Hallow didn't . . . work on Zuri, exactly. He avoided direct answers to my questions, and so I don't know what he thinks of you. He came to the banquet anyway, obviously. But I'm still trying to figure out why I couldn't influence him.*

You have to have a brain to be persuaded, I retorted, and Ai Ling's laughter vibrated through the bond.

Then I told Zuri of Djbanti, "Traditions are made to be broken."

His dark features shifted in surprise, then he erupted in laughter. The low, musical sound infected the hall, easing the tension and causing others to join in. I smiled instinctively, though something about Zuri's laugh made my brows knit. He didn't sound insincere, exactly. Just . . . precise. As though his voice were a song practiced to perfection—an instrument carefully tuned.

"I meant no offense, Your Imperial Majesty," said Zuri, flashing a pearly smile that left me—just a little—breathless. "I look forward to falling in love with *all* of you." He scooped up his chalice, sloshing the wine. I was dimly aware that while other guests had drained cup after cup, Zuri's had stayed full. Still, he loafed on his cushion, slurring as he tasted. "To peace," he declared, with a flourish.

"To peace," the hall echoed, and the mood lightened from Zuri's antics.

Ji Huan, the boy king of Moreyao, blurted out, "But we don't have powers." He looked no older than thirteen, and drowned in a red silk robe embroidered with blossoms. "Anointed Ones are Hallowed, aren't they?"

"I won't require Hallows of my Anointed Ones," I told him with a wink. "This council . . . I want it to be different. It won't exist to protect me, but to save the empire. To build bonds of trust that can withstand attacks from the abiku." I still wore the sunstone from the Nu'ina Eve festival at the base of my throat, and it warmed as the words poured out of me. "This is bigger than me—than any of us. If we create a new council, we won't only save thousands of children. We'll have created a future for Aritsar beyond the Redemptor Treaty. No one remembers how weak our isolated kingdoms were before the empire, but if the history scrolls are true, then we're safer—and stronger—together. Please . . . help me keep it that way."

The faces around the table grew still, stunned and thoughtful. My heart surged with hope—and then a cold, breathy voice asked:

"What if we can't love you?"

Blue eyes framed in crow's-feet peered at me from beneath a fringe of straw-colored curls. Queen Beatrix of Nontes fluttered two lace fans, an affectation of distress. "I mean no offense," she mewled. "But in order to accept the Ray, we have to love you, yes? The trouble is—I find it much easier to have respect for men. I do not get along with girls. Women together, we are . . . " Queen Beatrix gestured airily around the table, though her fan stopped on me. "Irrational. Emotional. I can't imagine ruling an empire with a woman. Let alone having one in my thoughts."

I took several deep breaths, blinking at her. "I . . . don't understand, Your Majesty. You are a queen. And I've had girls in my head for years. Frankly, I couldn't imagine ruling *without* them."

Beatrix looked doubtful. Ai Ling and Kirah made faces when the queen wasn't looking, wiggling their eyebrows at me from across the table. *I forgot to tell you,* Ai Ling Ray-spoke gayly. *Beatrix is one of* those *ladies. You know—the ones who think it's sexy to have an inferiority complex.* I stifled a snort, and my sisters' laughter rang in my mind.

I wished suddenly that Mayazatyl, Emeronya, and Thérèse could be here too. No—I wished that we were back at Yorua Keep, giggling on a sun-soaked beach, with no worries but our scrolls and riddle games, as we fed one another figs and cornrowed each other's hair. I had the best sisters I could ever ask for.

So how could I ever anoint someone like *Beatrix*?

I sighed, praying to the Storyteller for patience, and forced a smile. "Love is complicated," I told the Nontish queen. "All I ask, Your Majesty, is that you're willing to try."

"But what if it's impossible?" Beatrix pressed. "Impossible to love you?"

My jaw ticked. But before I could say something I'd regret, Dayo made an announcement.

"I have a theory," he said grandly, while Ray-speaking privately: *I have a surprise.*

My arm hair stood immediately on edge. Dayo had notoriously poor instincts for surprises. For my seventeenth birthday just last week, he had presented me with a pearl-pink albino baby elephant—an attempt to make up for all the years he had tried to make me forget about Swana.

"It's to remind you of the grasslands," he had said eagerly. "Elephants have amazing memories, and you have your Hallow. You two are going to be best friends."

The calf had proceeded to escape its pen near the

Imperial Suite, get high grazing on kuso-kuso, and break into the bathhouses, where it splashed muddily into a pool of screaming noblewomen. Last I'd heard, my new best friend had been penned in the northern palace orchards, giving the poor imperial orange-pickers gray hairs.

But before I could interrogate Dayo further, he was addressing the entire Imperial Hall. "I've given a lot of thought to why Anointed Ones are so faithful," he said. "So intimate with each other. It doesn't make sense, when you think about it, right? Anointed Ones are strangers as children. They swear fealty to the Raybearer, not to each other. Yet in five hundred years of councils, Anointed Ones have never betrayed each other. Why?"

After a pause, King Nadrej of Biraslov ventured in his guttural accent, "Fear of council sickness, of course." The mustachioed king wrapped his fur-lined garments closer about him, which he had insisted on wearing even in the Oluwan heat.

King Uxmal of Quetzala agreed, stroking jade crystal gages that hung low in each of his ears. Embedded crystals of turquoise and pyrite flashed in his teeth. "Any rivals would endure each other's company, if the alternative was going mad."

"I don't think that's the answer," Kirah said. "Forced companionship makes people hate each other as often as not."

"Then it's because Anointed Ones share a common goal: to protect the Raybearer," suggested Chief Uriyah, ruler of the Blessid Valley clans. "Just as we Blessids are many tribes, but we unite to preserve our way of life."

"But the Blessid nomads have more in common than just one goal," Dayo replied. "You have customs. Religion, histories. Anointed Ones hail from different realms, often with conflicting cultures and values. So why do they love each other?"

Silence spread across the table, and Dayo bounced on his heels with excitement.

"It's the Ray bond," he announced. "Ray-speaking. Having someone else's thoughts and desires feel like your own. If one person understands another completely—from their deepest pain to their most passing thought—I think they can't help but love each other. I think . . ." Dayo gave me a small smile and shrugged, crinkling his burn scar. "When you take someone's story as your own, it's no different than loving yourself. Tarisai can't Ray-speak with you yet. But she can share her memories. All of them."

Every bone in my body turned to ice.

"It shouldn't take more than a few weeks per person, I think," Dayo went on brightly. "Her memories work like dreams, hours compressed down into seconds, and"—

Are you out, I screeched at him through the Ray, *of your yam-loving mind?*

—"though it might feel strange, once you get to know Tar . . ." He grinned. "You can't help but love her."

71

Dayo, you're going to get me killed. How can I show these people my memories? They hate me enough already!

He blinked, confused at my distress. *But it's the only way. They can't bond with you if you don't open up a little.*

Open up? I was hyperventilating. Open up? *Dayo, this won't be like sharing a few secrets after a night of honeywine. This is my life. My whole life. I tried to murder you, for Am's sake.*

They'll know why you did it, though, Dayo protested. *They'll feel your love for your mother. Your love for me. Tar . . . your memories tell your story better than you ever could.*

My throat closed with fear. *I won't survive this,* I thought numbly, and Ai Ling took my hand.

Dayo, she Ray-spoke, *you should have asked Tar first. Announcing it like this wasn't fair. If she does this, there's no going back.*

Dayo deflated with guilt, fumbling with the mask on his chest. *You're right. I'm sorry, Tar. I was just trying to help.* He paused. *But they don't have to like you to love you, you know. They only have to understand.*

As I processed this, Ai Ling said aloud, "A good time to go around the table, I think."

She signaled to the attendants, who passed kola nuts to every ruler, and then held up the empty vessel. "If you accept the invitation of the emperor and empress to stay at An-Ileyoba and secure the future of Aritsar," Ai Ling said, "then place your token in this bowl. Or, if you would rather risk a future of eternal child sacrifice, permanently interrupted trade, and another War of Twelve Armies against the Underworld . . . keep the token to yourself."

The air in the room chilled. But as I watched with both relief and terror, one by one, kola nuts dropped into the bowl.

"Accept—accept—accept."

Reluctant words of assent from Min Ja, Uriyah, Helius, Sadhika, Ji Huan, Nadrej, Edwynn of Mewe, Danai, Kwasi of Nyamba, and Uxmal. Zuri threw in his kola nut with a flourish and a wink. Even Beatrix tossed hers in, with a haughty shrug.

My banquet had been a success. But still my hands sweated, numb with fear. I may have promised to enter the Underworld . . . but nothing scared me more than the promise to which Dayo had bound me: exposing my ugliest memories to twelve complete strangers.

CHAPTER 7

WERE IT UP TO ME, THE NIGHT WOULD HAVE
ended then, letting me escape this den of strangers to be
with my council siblings, who would ply me with sweets
and kisses, stories and honeywine. Instead, Ai Ling rose and
dismissed the tables, gesturing for the court musicians to
play . . . and the reveling portion of my Peace Banquet
to begin.

You realize those are dance accessories, right? Dayo Ray-
spoke, nodding at my grass leg tassels with a mischievous
smile. *They'll expect us to lead the first set.*

I will dance in front of these people, I replied testily, *when it
snows in the Blessid Desert.*

Everyone at court knew that I didn't dance. Most girls
from the center realms—Oluwan, Djbanti, Nyamba, and
Swana—had been raised on festival drums and rhythm
games, learning to bounce and wind while still babes tied
to their mothers' backs. But my world had been Bhekina
House: dusty scrolls, plaster walls, and windows boarded up
so tightly, no music bled through.

Come on, Tar, Kirah chided, already on the arm of a Songlander dignitary. *You made history tonight. Loosen up a little.*

Ai Ling sidled to my rescue, taking my place at Dayo's side. "The Empress is recovering from an injury," she announced to the court, tinting the words with a hint of her Hallow's persuasive power. "She will not be joining the dancing tonight, and conveys her regrets."

I bowed serenely to the guests, tossed a grateful smile at Ai Ling, and retreated to watch the banquet from my throne, which stood on a dais overlooking the Imperial Hall.

Traditional Oluwani dances were performed by groups or individuals—never in pairs, as was custom in the distant northern realms. As the empire had grown, however, Oluwan courtiers had adopted the *ijo agbaye*, a dance with elements from all over the empire, including individual partners.

I winced as revelers took the floor. To this day, my council siblings teased me about the ijo agbaye. It was, famously, the only test I had ever failed as a Children's Palace candidate.

"Just give me a logic puzzle," I had sputtered at age twelve in the Hall of Dreams, hot with humiliation after colliding with my partner for the fifth time. "I'll behead sparring dummies. I'll memorize every law in the Imperial Library. Just don't—make me dance—again."

Still, as I watched revelers gyrate and twist from my

throne on the Imperial Hall dais, longing pricked at my feet.

Ai Ling and Dayo darted like revolving fireflies as they led the ijo agbaye, first dancing without touching, in the Oluwan style of outstretched arms and rolling hips. Then they danced together, Ai Ling's hands on Dayo's shoulders as he lifted her from the waist and spun. She threw back her head and laughed, hanfu sleeves streaming in pale peach ribbons as Dayo's purple agbada swept the floor. Her hair hung loose to her waist. The front looped in a bun, glinting with pearl flowers and bead ornaments that jingled as she twirled in Dayo's arms.

My hips twitched absently, infected by the beat. For just a moment, I considered recovering miraculously from my illness and joining the dancers below, melting into the din of color and sound.

But how can you celebrate?

I jumped, pulse racing as my eyes searched the dais. The glyphs on my arms stung like acid. The lisping treble voice spoke at my ear . . . but no one was there. Then I saw it—barely visible in the bright light of the hall, a child stood. A Redemptor, like the one who had killed Thaddace—though this one hovered, an apparition whose features were so decayed, I could not guess its sex.

"Are you all right, Your Imperial Majesty?" asked a fidgeting cupbearer, pausing on the steps to my dais. The servant had clearly approached out of concern, offering me a chalice of wine, though she knew decorum forbade me from drinking it. I rose from my seat and snatched it anyway, tense as a cornered hare.

"Don't you see it?" I hissed.

The cupbearer opened her mouth, then closed it. "I . . ." She followed my gaze to the apparition, then said, her tone warily neutral, "What would you like me to see, Lady Empress?"

The revelries continued around us. And with slow, cold dread, I realized that no one could see the child except me.

I sat back down.

You are not real, I thought at the child, trying not to hyperventilate. *The boy who killed Thaddace was real, but you aren't. I'm sick. After the banquet, I'll have Kirah sing to me, and I'll be healed, and you will go away.*

The apparition cocked its head as if I'd spoken aloud.

It is true that I am not here, it said in a patient monotone. *I am with the others. But I am real. You did not answer my question. How can you celebrate?*

Stop it, I thought, shaking my head over and over. *Stop it. You're not real.*

How can you celebrate? the creature repeated, hovering closer. *How can you smile and throw parties, when so many of us have died? The child Redemptors that your empire murdered will never dance or sing again. Don't you care?*

All of a sudden, the joyous banquet display, the whirlwind of light and color dimmed in my eyes. A wave of guilt crashed into me, overwhelming.

"I'm sorry," I breathed. "I—I know Aritsar has done wrong. I'm trying to fix it. That's why I'm anointing Min Ja. That's what this banquet is for."

The creature stilled, and for a moment, its icy aura crossed the dais, goose bumps traveled up my arms and neck. Then its voice roared in my ears.

DO MORE, it said. *Do more.*

And once again I was alone, as though the child had never been. I lifted the chalice to my lips, hands trembling as I gulped down its contents.

"Er—more wine, Lady Empress?" the cupbearer squeaked, and I jumped.

I had forgotten she was there. The color had drained from her face, and I realized with chagrin that she'd seen me talking to myself. I sighed, pinching the bridge of my nose. Well, half the court already thought me a witch. I supposed it was no different if they thought me a loon as well.

"No," I said at last. "I . . . think I'd better pace myself tonight."

I vowed to see Kirah the moment the banquet was over. She would sing the madness out of me, and everything would go back to normal.

Until then, I just had to survive the night.

In between sets of the ijo agbaye, the realm rulers and their retinues performed regional dances in my honor, with some instruments and costumes that I had never seen before. Nadrej and his Biraslovian attendants spun in colorful dervishes; Ji Huan's courtiers pantomimed with Moreyaoese masks and ribbon streamers—even stuffy Beatrix performed, stepping with her ladies in a Nontish procession of poses called a *pavane*. With every display of silk, gold, and precious jewel adornments, I thought of what Mayazatyl had told me before the banquet. How many of those treasures came from mines and mills that Dayo and I owned?

Exactly how rich was I?

The moon sank in the hall's arched windows. Sweat shone on the brows of winded dignitaries as they collapsed on cushions, fanning flushed cheeks and nursing chalices of mango water. But before the night drew to a close, King Zuri of Djbanti stepped onto the dance floor.

At his back stood a throng of Djbanti warriors, bare chests painted intricately in red, yellow, and white. Each wore a leg rattle of seed pods, and they pounded rhythms into the ground with colorful staves. The warriors chanted in harmony as Zuri mounted the steps to my throne. He bowed, locs falling over his chiseled dark shoulders, and grazing the folds of his draping red tunic.

"My empress," he announced, "this dance requires a partner."

"I'm sorry to hear that." I gave a crisp smile. "Because your empress doesn't dance."

Zuri blinked in innocent confusion. "But your part won't require dancing, Imperial Majesty. Warrior's honor. All I ask for," he said in that measured tenor, "is your full attention."

Then he held out his hand. A gold cuff glinted on his upper arm, pressing ever so slightly into his skin. It was a popular accessory for wealthy young men, and so I didn't know why it made me shudder. Why I thought suddenly of Melu in his grassland, bound by a will not his own.

Still, beneath the weight of a hundred curious eyes . . . I reached out and took Zuri's hand.

As his fingers closed around mine, I felt the gentle scrape of calluses. Strange, for a man who spent all his time gambling on mancala.

"Think of this as a game," he told me as we descended to the dance floor. The warriors continued to pound their staves, the beat rising in tempo. "Keep your eyes on me, and you win. Lose track for more than seven beats, and you lose. Your prize is to ask me a question. Anything you like." He backed away from me, and I realized too late that the warriors were forming a circle around us. Before he disappeared outside the circle, enclosing me inside, he winked. "My prize, of course, is the same."

I retorted, "But what if I don't want to answer your—"

The warriors drowned out my question. They had begun to sing in brassy voices, grinning at me facetiously.

Can you see him, girl?
(Is she clever?)
Can you hear him, girl?
(Is she pretty?)
The bird that will lead you to honey?

If you find him-o
(Are her lips full?)
If you catch him-o
(Are her hips wide?)
Pretty maiden, you had better come hungry!

Giggling whispers peppered the Imperial Hall. My face heated.

A courting game. Zuri—this cheeky, empty-headed fop of a king—had dragged me into a *courting game*.

I narrowed my eyes at him, determined now to win the game, if only to demand what made him so presumptuous. I could just make out the top of his locs as he danced, a lithe shadow behind the circle of warriors. The warriors stepped in the opposite direction, as though to confuse me further. Zuri danced back and forth, shifting directions sharply, causing me to do the same. I realized then he had timed the shifts, forcing me to move in time to the song. My scant top of cowrie shells chafed against my skin. I swabbed my damp brow, cracking a smile.

"Well played," I panted. He had tricked me into dancing after all.

The song increased in tempo until I grew dizzy, and lost sight of Zuri's hair. I whirled in desperation, but the beats sped by—five, six, seven—and the game was over. Zuri broke the circle, sinewy chest glistening with sweat, and grinning as the warriors chanted and closed around us.

I scowled, crossing my arms . . . but before I could register what was happening, Zuri had lifted me by the waist, just as Dayo had lifted Ai Ling in the ijo agbaye. I gasped, hands flying to his shoulders. He whirled me in an elegant spin, set me on my feet, and leaned down to my ear.

My breath grew shallow.

He smelled sharp and sweet, like spear polish masked with agave. His lips brushed my cheek. And in a moment of temporary insanity, I almost—almost—wished he had found my mouth instead.

Then he asked, in a voice as cold as silk, "Who killed Thaddace of Mewe?"

I recoiled like he had slapped me.

He looked immediately regretful. "Forgive me, Tarisai. I meant no—"

I wrenched out of his arms. The hall was tilting around me. The towering obsidian statues blurred and fell together in great pillars of black, and then I was back in that abandoned hallway, Thaddace's blood streaming across the tiles. The boy was wailing at me, convulsing with words I didn't understand. Then he was crumbling to dust, and Thaddace was dead, and it was all my fault, and . . . and—

The Imperial Hall rose to meet me. Zuri lurched forward, breaking my fall.

"I'm an idiot," he breathed as he braced me up. The satin had vanished from his voice. "That was a tasteless joke; curiosity got the best of me. I'm sorry, Tarisai."

"That's *Her Imperial Majesty* to you," Ai Ling said, slapping Zuri's hands from my waist. She, Dayo, and a flock of Imperial Guards had crowded onto the dance floor. "Or Lady Empress. In that order. You would do well, King Zuri, to remember protocol."

"Is it poison?" Dayo asked, his face crumpled with worry. "Tar, are you all right?"

"Check the king of Djbanti for weapons," Ai Ling demanded.

I tried to object, but the vision of Thaddace was too fresh. Words stuck inside me like knives.

The Djbanti warriors clucked in protest, unsheathing concealed weapons, but Zuri barked at them to stand down.

"I did not mean to hurt her." The young king held up his hands in surrender. But after shooting me a guilty glance, his face went blank . . . and his signature expression of vapid cheer returned. "My humor shocks our delicate sovereign," he announced in a wine-soaked drawl. "Allow me to make amends. I relinquish my prize. Most excellent Imperial Majesty"—he bowed with a flourish—"ask me anything you like."

My shoulders rose to my ears, where Ai Ling's words echoed: *None of the vassal rulers took you seriously. You were just a little girl to them. People can't love someone they don't respect.*

I balled my hands into fists. When I spoke again, the lioness mask warmed at the base of my throat. I imagined a beast crouching in tall grass, and willed my words to be just as calm. Just as deadly.

"I have no questions for King Zuri of Djbanti." I did not look at him as I spoke, but turned to mount the echo-stone on my dais, and addressed the entire hall. "The Peace Banquet is over. Your empress bids you good night."

I turned on my heel, preparing to sweep from the room. Blood drained from a hundred faces as sprites descended from the ceiling, swarming behind me in a burning train of light. But before I could go, Dayo seized my hand.

It shouldn't end this way, he Ray-spoke. *Tonight was supposed to be about peace. Please, Tar—let me fix this.*

Then to my surprise, Dayo faced our guests again, voice ricocheting from the echo-stone with uncharacteristic gravity.

"I am Emperor of Aritsar," he began, "as Tarisai is your empress. However, I am also King of Oluwan, a title the empress could not share with me, as she represents Swana on my council. This means that Tarisai, while ruler of all Aritsar, is ruler of no single realm."

I raised an eyebrow at him. *Where are you going with this?*

He only winked. "Tarisai promised the abiku she would form a council of twelve Arit rulers—one for each realm. This includes Oluwan. As a result, I proudly claim the first place on the Empress Redemptor's council."

Ignoring gasps and whispers, Dayo lifted a golden chain from his neck, dangling a vial of pelican oil—the same one he'd used to anoint me so long ago, in the Children's Palace. He unlatched the vial and held it out to me. "I love the empress already," he announced, grinning boyishly, "and so I require no more deliberation. Tarisai of Swana, will you accept me on your council?"

Murmurs across the hall. I took the vial with reluctant hands, staring at him in confusion.

I just realized something, I Ray-spoke. *If I anoint you and Min Ja, I'll have a council of thirteen. How is that even possible? Raybearers gain an immunity for every anointing. There are only twelve deaths—besides old age—and no one can be immune to that.*

Dayo grinned. *Maybe you'll become immortal.*

Don't joke like that, I said, giddy with terror. *If there's any job I don't want forever, it's this one.*

In response, he leaned in and kissed my cheek, sending a pulse of courage down the bond. *I guess we're about to find out.*

My heart hammered in my chest. But when he began to kneel, I stopped him. *Stay standing,* I Ray-spoke.

Why?

I bit my lip. One reason was that every noble in this room already suspected me to be a usurping witch, controlling Dayo like a puppet master. But the other reason—the one I told him—was more important.

Because the time for kneeling is over, I told him. *The original Raybearers were always meant to be equals, Dayo. It's time we stand shoulder to shoulder.*

He nodded, features shining.

Now I hesitated. What in Am's name was I supposed to say? The traditional proposal of Raybearers was *Shall you be moon to the morning star*—but that didn't seem right. Not anymore. I waited, summoning that warm, mysterious spirit from the cave in Sagimsan Mountain, letting the right words fall quietly, lastingly, into place. My eyes shut, and I seemed to float above my body, watching the scene from above, and then I was everywhere at once, enveloped with a formless Someone I had met only once before.

When I spoke, my voice was not my own, though I felt more myself than ever. A force had borrowed my lungs, filling the hall with tritoned harmonies that rang from the dais echo-stones.

"More stars fill the sky than any soul could count," said the interloper. "Each brighter and hotter than the last. Yet there is somehow room for all of them. So, Ekundayo of Oluwan: Will you shine beside Tarisai of Swana? Do you accept her hand in councilhood?"

If Dayo feared the spirit possessing me, he did not show it. Instead, his broad, guileless features creased in a peaceful smile, and tears filled his pure dark eyes. "I will," he said, "and I do."

Then the foreign spirit glowed, washing us both in a wave of ancient joy—and it was gone. I stood on the dais, myself again, human and trembling.

Half the hall had fallen, prostrate on their faces. The rest were on their knees, brushing their chins in the sign of the Storyteller.

Thank you, I thought to no one.

In response, a low rumble shook the dais, like a grunt of laughter . . . or the throaty call of a pelican.

"Well," Dayo asked, "aren't you going to offer me your Ray?"

I straightened my stance to focus. I used Dayo's Ray all the time, slipping into the minds of my council siblings. It was easy, like gliding into a coursing river, letting its strong current move me along. But this time, *I* would be the river, trying to join Dayo's stream to mine.

I concentrated on the heat in my chest, letting it congregate at the sunstone around my throat pendant. *Focus.* It rose, a pleasant, sweltering haze at the base of my neck, sending invisible tendrils across my scalp.

"Ekundayo of Oluwan," I whispered, "receive your anointing."

Then I joined the tendrils into a single beam, aiming it at Dayo. He inhaled sharply, as if pierced . . . then relaxed.

Well, he laughed in my head. *That was easy.*

I jumped. His voice vibrated through every bone in my body, louder than it had ever been. It sounded . . . doubled. As though he spoke with two sets of vocal cords, the second one strangely feminine.

You're speaking with my voice, I told him, wide-eyed.

Then he was his turn to look rattled. *And you're speaking with mine,* he said. *I guess this is what happens when two Rays coexist in a body. Does it . . . bother you?*

No, I said after a moment. *I think it feels . . . nice.* I shivered with pleasure at my new, multitoned voice. *Very nice.*

Me too.

Then I flinched, watching in fascinated horror as lacy patterns grew up my arms and splayed across my chest, azure glyphs glistening against my dark skin. My Redemptor map had grown. Once I anointed a full council, I suspected, no inch of me would be left uncovered.

The crown of banquet guests gasped, then lapsed into fearful awe. Ai Ling took control of the room's mood, clapping her hands. "All hail Ekundayo," she declared, raising a chalice and grinning at us both. "Anointed One of the Empress Redemptor, first of many! To peace in Aritsar!"

The hall surged into applause, first stunned, then manic with enthusiasm, and many raising chalices in toast. The musicians struck up a triumphant phrase, and my sprites pulsed to the rhythm. With a signal from Ai Ling, servants in the lofty rafters rained down petals and bits of shining cloth—the finale of our banquet's spectacle.

Dayo lifted me off my feet, spinning me in a hug until laughter bubbled from my lungs, and the joy I felt then could have given me wings. Then he set me down—

And the hall vanished.

Or rather, all the people in it. And I was standing in a cavernous, silent room, every coronation guest replaced with a small, unsmiling child. The smell of death rose from two thousand dirt-covered bodies, blank eyes fixed on mine.

My heart slammed in my chest. "What are you?" I rasped, clawing at my skin, on which glyphs now burned in patterns like streams of fire ants. "Where did you all come from? *What do you want?*"

The children regarded me, expressionless, for a long moment. Then they spoke in a monotone, words overlapping in a treble din.

Justice—no one cared—should have saved us—gone, all of us gone—why don't you care?—do more—do more—pay for all our lives—justice—have to pay . . .

I covered my ears, but it made no difference. The glyphs on my arms gleamed, threatening to melt my skin to the bone. "What do you want?" I asked again, growing shrill. "For Am's sake, *just tell me what you want!*"

They fell silent at once. Then a sea of filthy fingers lifted to point at my chest, and the children spoke together as one:

Redemptor. Redemptor. Empress Redemptor.

Then I was back in the Imperial Hall, still in Dayo's arms, ears ringing with the banquet's cheerful music as cold sweat prickled my skin.

"Tar?" Dayo was scanning my face, his smile cracked with worry. "You left us for a moment there. Everything all right?" I returned his stare, numb with shock. He hadn't seen them.

No one had seen those children but me.

"Of course," I said, throat bone dry, and forced a wavering smile.

Dayo lifted our joined hands in triumph, egging on the chant of the crowd as petals flurried down from the ceiling, a cascade of crimson and bone-dust white.

Long live the emperor.

Long live the Empress Redemptor.

PART 2

PART 2

CHAPTER 8

WHEN DAYO, AI LING, KIRAH, AND I RETURNED to the Imperial Suite, the usual Ray-speak whispering through the halls had gone dormant. We found our council siblings fast asleep, strewn across one another in the suite's common salon. They snored and mumbled, clutching drained cups of honeywine and half-eaten bowls of *fufu*. It seemed they had tried to wait up for us. My heart twinged fondly at the sight of the sleep-softened faces of my motley family, drooped across tufted divans and rugs, their chests rising and falling in Ray-synced unison. I brushed my fingers over each of their brows, sending dreams into each one. Though I'd missed them all night, I was relieved that they slept.

If they had been awake, I would have had to tell them I was going insane.

The palace rumor mill would let them know soon enough. A cupbearer had seen me speak to thin air, and the entire court had watched a divine spirit possess me. The more religious of An-Ileyoba might revere me for the incident, but sanity and intimacy with gods were not known to go hand in hand. I needed Aritsar to take me seriously as empress, not cloister me like an oracle in a gilded temple.

But that was tomorrow's struggle. I bid good night to Dayo, Ai Ling, and Kirah, but not before noticing that one body was missing from the common room huddle.

Jeet? I asked the air, sending the Ray-like fingers through the suite halls. *Where are you?*

The answer was a mind jolted awake, and then a surge of apologetic warmth, flooding my veins.

Here. Sorry, I meant to wait up.

I followed the voice and found Sanjeet in my bedchamber, sitting on the raised dais platform of my bed pallet. My chamber, swiftly added to the Imperial Suite after my rise to the crown, still felt foreign to me: muraled walls and a high, domed ceiling, with slanted skylights that let me spy on my sprites among the stars. Sanjeet's copper features were hazy in the low lamplight, and when I entered, he rose to offer a bowl-ridden tray: stew and fried plantain, gone cold but still fragrant with spices.

"Saved it from dinner," he mumbled, voice rough with sleep. "I know they don't let you eat at those parties."

"I could kiss you," I moaned, and sank onto a pelt-covered sofa, inhaling the feast with unrefined gratitude.

Sanjeet chuckled and sat beside me, his molten eyes contemplative as he took in my ensemble—especially my scant top of cowrie shells. "So," he observed in a carefully neutral voice, "I'm guessing the continent rulers swore fealty on sight?"

I snorted and wiped plantain grease from my hands, not feeling at all captivating. My intricate face paint and gold-powdered shoulders had faded with the revelries, and my necklace and wrapper skewed in disarray . . . but still, Sanjeet's steeply slanted eyebrows rose with appreciation.

"Hardly," I told him. "But at least they're planning to stay for a while. Dayo basically offered them my head on a platter." He recoiled, so I hurried to explain. "I have to give them all my memories. Even the bad parts. Don't ask—it's supposed to make them love me, or something." I stared at my ring-covered fingers. "I don't really want to talk about it."

I banished any further thoughts about my sanity. It seemed easier, while apparitions of undead children lurked in the corners.

Sanjeet wisely asked no more questions. Instead, he reached his foot across the floor to nudge my ankle, where tiny bells jangled on a golden chain. The cowrie shell from his mother's anklet gleamed against my skin, where I wore it always. "You know," he said, tea-colored gaze glinting with mischief. "Amah would be disappointed if you never danced in that."

My face heated, and I raced to banish a smug, hateful Djbanti face from my mind. "I doubt it. My rhythm would insult your amah's memory."

He shook his head. "She would have loved you."

Imperial Guard drums thundered from the outer palace walls, announcing the late hour. He stood and rubbed the back of his neck, glancing at the door. "I guess we should get to bed."

"I guess." I played with a coil of my hair. "Where is that, tonight? The others are in the common room." Amidst all the moving and upheaval, we hadn't spent a night alone together since I returned from Sagimsan. Sanjeet had a private bedchamber like I did, of course, but we were too often bombarded by our affectionate wolf pack of siblings to find each other there.

"I hadn't decided yet," Sanjeet replied, darting a shy glance at me. "Do you want to be alone?"

I thought of dead-eyed children scaling walls in the shadows and suppressed a shudder, smirking instead. "No," I croaked, giving a shaky little laugh. "I'd rather you stay."

He nodded without a word, and I rose to undress. My room was a maze of chests, cushions, and gilded side tables, covered with cosmetics whose functions I had yet to memorize. The sparkling theater of An-Ileyoba life was a sharp contrast to the barefoot simplicity of Yorua Keep, and the military order of the Children's Palace. I dug through several ornate chests, sneezing at perfumed sachets of myrrh and amber before finding a linen night shift, embroidered at the collar with a chain of sunbursts. Sanjeet, already in the low-necked tunic and trousers he wore to bed, stared studiously at his sandals.

For the first time, I registered how little I was wearing . . . and how difficult it would prove to remove my cowrie necklace.

The sparkling shells hung to just above my stomach, secured in two places, with a clasp at my neck and with an unreachable knot at the center of my back.

"Um," I said. "Could I have a hand?"

I didn't look up, only heard him cross the room. His calloused fingers brushed the small of my back as he loosened the necklace. A thrill crept up my spine as his breath warmed my neck, pinning me in place.

He released the second clasp. The necklace fell noisily into my hands, and for a moment neither of us moved, the heat of our skin burning between us.

Then I moved away, unwinding the wrapper from my waist and slipping the shift over my head. The hem fell to my ankles, covering me at last—though the soft chafe of linen against my hips somehow made me feel more naked.

Shakily, I swabbed my face with rosewater from my nightstand. While I wrapped my hair in its satin scarf, Sanjeet freshened up at my washbasin. Water beaded on his curls as he raked them with his fingers.

The oil lamps smoldered low, making wisps of fragrant smoke in the air. An open arch led out to my balcony, where the hum of cicadas drifted in from the night.

"Well," I said. "We should get some sleep."

"We should," he echoed.

"Busy schedule tomorrow. Sparring practice. Court sessions."

"Full day," he agreed.

And then my arms locked around him. His lips found

my neck, collarbone, earlobe—every inch of me that could sing and shiver. When my hands peeled off his shirt, a crackle of energy danced across my skin. He was using his Hallow. Tracking the pleasure as it strummed through my body—targeting areas he knew would be weakest.

"That's not fair," I mumbled.

His voice was thick. "Neither was that necklace."

He lifted me from the ground. I could feel his pulse against mine, pounding and erratic as he climbed the short steps to my sleeping dais and we fell toward the silk-covered pallet. As my council siblings tended to migrate between bedrooms, I had barely slept on the dais twice before . . . and I wasn't about to now.

Sanjeet suspended himself above me on a clublike arm. His eyes burned shades of murky amber. My fingers found the peaks and caverns of his chest, savoring my favorite parts. Rosewater glistened on his burnished copper skin. His free hand caressed my lower legs, and my shift moved slowly up my thigh . . . until he stopped.

"Tar." He was still. "Do you want this?"

I fought to gain control of my lungs. "I love you," I squeaked, and he gave me that rare, butter-melting smile.

"I know, sunshine girl. But we haven't done this before." He dropped a kiss on my shoulder, and his fingers drew intoxicating circles on my leg. Still, he watched my face. "I want you to be sure."

The back of my throat burned. I felt his Hallow scan my body with the precision of Aritsar's High Lord General, mapping territories, campaigns to set my skin alight.

The answer to his question was *yes*. I wanted everything about him. But . . .

A vision flashed in my mind. A bundle with soft hair and tea-colored eyes; the Ray glowing in a new, tiny body.

I stiffened, and Sanjeet's hand dropped immediately from my leg.

Heart racing with indecision, I reached for his chiseled face. He turned to catch my fingertips in his mouth, and I swallowed, fighting to retain my focus.

"There are risks," I said at last.

"Mm." He nodded thoughtfully. "There are herbs for that, you know. Droughts. Potions."

"Yes. But we don't have those right now. And I don't feel like sending a servant to get them." There were enough empress-related rumors circling the servants' quarters tonight. "So . . ." I withdrew my hand. "Not tonight, Jeet. I'm sorry. For not knowing how I felt until—"

"Don't apologize. Not for that." He kissed the top of my head and fell beside me, chuckling ruefully. "Though in the future, if you're planning to wear that necklace . . . we might need a backup plan."

I snorted, leaned to kiss his cheek, and then buried my face in his shoulder. "Is it . . . strange, do you think? That I'm not sure about having babies? After all, I was supposed to have Dayo's. You'd think I'd get used to the idea by now." I scowled into the darkness. "Why am I always so different?"

Sanjeet was still for a long time, staring at the lavender

sprites twinkling through skylights. "For what it's worth, sunshine girl," he said at last, "you have always been my kind of different."

I sighed, shutting my eyes. "That's only because you're as strange as I am."

His chest rumbled with laughter. I settled against his cavernous heartbeat, savoring my time as a love-drunk girl before dawn transformed me, once again, into the mad Empress Redemptor of Aritsar.

CHAPTER 9

I HAD WORRIED ABOUT COURT GOSSIP FOR nothing: My antics at the Peace Banquet was old news by morning.

"A volcano did *what*?" I demanded, after Dayo shook me and Sanjeet awake.

"Destroyed one-third of Oluwan City," gasped Dayo, thrusting travel clothes into my hands. "Well. Not yet, exactly. But soon."

Dawn had barely flooded the suite as Sanjeet and I stumbled into the hallway behind Dayo, joining the rest of our council in the main salon.

"What's going on?" Sanjeet demanded.

Our siblings were darting in circles, stuffing packs with clothing, weapons, and healing droughts.

"Umansa's tapestries," Dayo breathed. "He just deciphered the prophecies. He didn't spot the pattern until he finished the last one, just an hour ago."

Umansa's prophetic tapestries lined the salon walls. A tall loom rested in one corner, shadowed in the weak morning light, where Umansa had spent every evening weaving in a fugue. His Hallowed tapestries—which featured the only images his milky white eyes could see—told stories in fractured pieces, each blazing in a chaos of glyphs and constellations, empires rising and falling with the capricious turn of planets.

"Nothing's been destroyed yet," cut in Umansa, turning his ear toward Dayo and me. "The volcano may not even have erupted. My visions aren't clear on timelines."

"But we have to stop it," Dayo said, wringing his hands as I pulled off my satin sleep scarf, still groggy from dreaming. "It could happen at any moment."

"Can't we at least wait until after breakfast?" mewled Emeronya. Amidst the packing chaos, she was sitting cross-legged on the floor, peering into her glass scrying orb. "I've searched the city borders. No sign of fires, lava, anything. If Umansa's vision is so urgent, why didn't he say something earlier?"

"I did," Umansa retorted, crossing his tattooed arms. "Or at least, my hangings did. But they weren't clear until now." He gestured at the sandstone salon walls, where his last few weeks of tapestries glittered in black, ochre, and crimson. The latest tapestry still hung from the beams of the loom. It appeared to depict a mountain with teeth, flashing claws, and unsettlingly human eyes. The rocky beast reared on its haunches, spewing lava from its mouth. Glyphs and planets bordered the tapestry—coordinates of the monster's location.

Zathulu, my bookish council brother and Archdean of the Imperial Academy, scribbled furiously on a slate, glancing up at the tapestry and squinting over reference scrolls. "That can't be right. Umansa's tapestry puts the volcano in the same place as Olojari Temple."

I frowned. "The Ember mountain forge?"

The Ember religious sect revered Warlord Fire, one of Aritsar's principal deities. His devotees built mines and holy forges all over Aritsar, hoping the elemental god would bless their efforts with rich veins of gold, iron, and coal.

"The forge belongs to the Ember," Umansa said. "But the quarry beneath it is imperial property."

"Oh." Yet another place that Dayo and I owned. I supposed the nobles ran the quarry for us too.

"I've been tracking its shipments to the treasury," Umansa went on. "Recently, some rebel group has been interfering with supply lines. I thought my prophecies pointed to some kind of bandit uprising—but I guess I was wrong. Looks like the real danger is that mountain exploding."

"But Olojari is seventy miles from here," Kirah said. "Something that far away couldn't destroy Oluwan City."

"Not something," Sanjeet murmured. "Someone." He had already found and tightened his weapon halter. Wordlessly, he crossed the room to Umansa's new tapestry, grimacing as he traced the mountain's livid features. "I've seen a face like that before," he said, sending an image down the Ray bond.

My siblings stiffened as Sanjeet's vision flooded our

103

thoughts: a tall, pole-like being with wings of cobalt fire and blazing yellow eyes that slanted all the way to his temples.

"I don't understand," said Ai Ling. "Why would Swana's fairy guardian set off a volcano in Oluwan?"

"That isn't Melu," I protested, swallowing hard as I examined the tapestry. "It *is* an alagbato, I think. But that creature isn't my father."

"If not Melu, then who?" Zathulu objected. "Oluwan doesn't have nature fairies, at least, none that I've heard of. Most alagbatos died when we razed the land to build cities."

"It's Malaki," said Kirah.

We all turned to stare at her in surprise. She worried the edge of her prayer scarf, blinking with shocked realization.

"Malaki the Mad, Malaki of the Mountain . . . there are songs about her. I'd forgotten until now. No one's sure, but . . . High Priestess Mbali believes Malaki's the alagbato who made the doors to the Imperial Hall." With a jolt, I remembered the legend—an alagbato had fashioned the Imperial Hall doors with iron from her own heart. Kirah brushed her chin to ward off bad luck. "No one talks about her. Some elders think it's bad luck to say Malaki's name within the palace walls. Anyway, no one's seen her for a century, though she's guarded that mountain range for millennia. Mbali wasn't even sure she was still alive."

"I don't see why you're all so worried," said Kameron. He grinned, making his freckles pop as he slung a burly arm around my shoulder. "We've got an alagbato of our own. Tar'll talk down Mad Malaki—won't you, Tar?"

"I'm not a fairy," I sputtered, wriggling out of my brother's embrace. "I'm not even immortal, except for what I get from the Ray. What do you expect me to do?"

I absently fingered my lioness mask. To my surprise, anointing Dayo hadn't given me a new immunity. Instead, the lone red stripe on my mask, representing my birth immunity to burning, had grown more vibrant, framing itself in gold. The Ray, it seemed, would allow me to have an extra council member. But just like every other Raybearer, I would be immune to only twelve deaths. It comforted me to know I would die an old woman . . . assuming I survived the next two years.

Kameron shrugged. "Dunno. But Melu seemed to like you well enough. If I've learned anything training magical beings, it's that species smell their own—no matter what they look like on the outside."

"One problem," Umansa announced quietly. "Olojari isn't the only disaster."

He gestured at the tapestries lining the salon. Slowly, I noticed that every loom depicted a different creature with glowing eyes—some causing floods in lakes and rivers, others rising from quaking grassland, and some charging through blizzards of snow, or bellowing amidst blazing jungles and forests.

"It's everywhere," Umansa confirmed. "Alagbatos are awakening all across Aritsar, threatening crucial raw materials."

A dazed pause chilled the room.

"We have to go back to our home realms," Mayazatyl realized slowly. "All of us."

"We have to stop them," Theo agreed. "Or at least figure out what they want. It'll be harder once we split up, but—"

"Split up?" I interjected, head spinning. "What about council sickness?"

"There's no other way to reach all the realms in time," said Sanjeet, scanning a map on the salon war table. "So we'll just have to endure. Travel quickly. Treat our symptoms another way."

"That's impossible," I protested.

"Not with kuso-kuso," said Thérèse, tremblingly lifting a vial of smelling herbs to her nostrils. "It won't be easy. But if we all take my new strain at the same time—the Ray can unite our minds across space. Not forever—the herbs aren't that strong. But if you take them every day, we'll stay connected for a while. Five months. Maybe six."

"Good." Sanjeet nodded curtly. "If we're lucky, Aritsar will never know it was in danger. Prevent the disasters before they happen."

My pulse began to race. Five or six months? My council siblings had never separated for that long. Not ever. What if something happened to us?

Mayazatyl dusted off her hands with satisfaction, patting a leather bundle that bristled with weapons. "Look, I'll miss you all and everything, but . . . Am's Story, I can't *wait* to leave court. I've been streamlining my inventions ever since the abiku attacked Ebujo. My new cannons can shoot twice as much holy water as the old ones, and I'm dying to test them out."

"The abiku at Ebujo were demons," Kirah reminded her. "Holy water won't work on alagbatos. Besides, alagbatos aren't evil, or at least they aren't born that way. We should try to appease them first."

"I'll bring my lyre," offered Theo. My council brother from Sparti slipped the instrument from a sling on his back and patted the strings. "If my songs can put Kameron's pet beasts to sleep, I'm sure they can handle a fairy."

"Dayo and Tarisai will stay in Oluwan, of course," Ai Ling said, pacing. "They can handle the alagbato in Olojari, but we can't risk them going much farther from the capital. Not after convincing all the continent rulers to stay. I'll stick around a little longer, to help Tarisai manage the monarchs. But after that, I should go to Moreyao."

"I'll delay leaving for Dhyrma," muttered Sanjeet, staring grimly out at the Oluwan City skyline. "At least for now. There's too much to do here. If Malaki doesn't listen to Tarisai, then I'll have to mobilize the Imperial Guard. Order evacuations. Build barricades, trenches. Camps for refugees."

Everyone began to talk at once, faces brightening as they planned their departure, and traded strategies to wrangle alagbatos. They . . . were excited to leave. All of them. My family wanted to flee the safety of our home. They were eager to face danger, eager to leave me. My jaw tightened as

I remembered the apparitions of undead children filling the Imperial Hall. Ghostly, lisping shadows crept at the edges of my vision.

"Stop it," I bellowed, and my siblings froze, turning to stare at me. "Sorry. I . . . I just—" I stammered, picking anxiously at my hair, until my coils lay in mats. "You're moving too fast, all of you. It isn't safe. Scattering across the continent. Abandoning the capital, abandoning each other? This isn't how our family is supposed to work. This isn't right. It's foolhardy. It's—" My fear blazed into anger. "Selfish."

After a beat of shocked silence, Mayazatyl emitted a sharp laugh. "Well *that*'s rich. Coming from you."

I blinked at her. "What in Am's name is that supposed to mean?"

"What do you think?" She avoided my gaze, twisting her silky twin braids angrily in one hand. "Tar, if abandoning our family on a whim is selfish, then . . . then you're more selfish than any of us."

I scoffed, then gaped, waiting for the others to leap to my defense. But instead, my family fidgeted where they stood, avoiding my eyes—even Kirah.

"You all agree with her," I breathed. "You've been talking about me behind my back. And you think Mayazatyl's right."

"No. It's not like that," Kirah said, coming to put a placating hand on my arm. Then she traded a glance with the others. "Well—not exactly. It's just—"

"It's just you offered yourself to the abiku," Emeronya

blurted. She glared at her orb, trying to conceal a trembling lower lip. "You came back from Sagimsan, and called off the Treaty, and swore you'd go to *hell*. All without asking what any of us thought. Without thinking how we would feel if you d–died—" She broke off, not trusting her voice to continue. I saw her grief mirrored in the rest of my siblings' faces . . . even in Sanjeet's. Even Dayo's.

"For the last time," I said. "I'm not going to stay in the Underworld."

"You can't promise that," Theo said, plucking despondently at his lyre. "And Tar . . . ever since you came back from Sagimsan, you've been different. Distant. Angry."

My confusion drained away, replaced by a throbbing sadness. "You're my only friends," I said. "You're all I care about."

"We used to be," Zathulu said. "But you've changed, Tar. I'm not saying it's a bad thing. We're just . . . still getting used to the new Tarisai. The one who upsets laws, and plans prison heists, and runs off to Songland to unearth old injustices—"

"Old injustices?" I cut in, slowly repeating after him. "Like the two hundred children who were sacrificed last year, and the thousands of children before that?"

My siblings paused uncomfortably.

"No one's saying the empire's perfect," Mayazatyl said then, crossing her arms. "But you disappeared for months. And now that you're back, all you care about is *changing* things. New treaties! New councils! We support you as empress, Tar, but did you stop and think that some of us—well—love Aritsar just the way it is?"

Kirah's grip on my arm tightened. "Don't misunderstand, Tar," she said gently. "We know you had to change the Treaty. More than anything, we just want you ba—" She bit her lip. "Want you to be happy."

But I had caught what she almost said.

We just want you back.

I tried to unhear it. Tried to tell myself I was misunderstanding, that I was being unfair. I could fix this. I could give my best friends what they wanted. But when I scanned their guilty faces, realization seared me, like the sun on a parched savannah, the truth a lethal ember among rushes.

My family missed the love-starved girl from Swana. The one who worshipped her friends, and whose anger could be cooled with a kiss. They missed the tree in its gilded pot. The girl so afraid of herself, and so grateful for a family, the world could burn to ash, and she would smile and call it paradise.

And though I loved my friends—though I would still die and live for them—I would never be that Tarisai again.

"There's something I need to tell you all," I whispered then, staring emptily at the eye-filled tapestries. "I've been getting visions. Apparitions of children like the one who killed Thaddace. I saw one last night at the banquet—and another, after anointing Dayo. I can't tell if they want to help me or hurt me."

"Really?" Emeronya, who studied the supernatural as High Lady Magus, perked up in alarm. "When do the creatures usually appear? When you're doing something? Thinking, feeling something specific?"

I considered, chewing the inside of my cheek. The first child had appeared when I was full of hope, thinking I'd succeeded at rescuing Thaddace. And when the second vision appeared, I had been watching the hall full of dancers, basking in the triumph of my Peace Banquet. Finally, moments before I had hallucinated the hall as a mass mausoleum . . . I had just celebrated Dayo's anointing.

Why should you celebrate? the ghosts had hissed. *Why should you live happy when we are dead? Do more—do more—pay for our lives.*

"I'm not sure," I said at last. "Not exactly. All I know is, before the visons appear . . . I almost feel like I'm enough. Like I'm doing the best I can, and I deserve to be Raybearer. Deserve to be empress. Then the voices make me feel . . . useless. Like there's so much evil, so much injustice, and I have to fix it."

"This is strange," Emeronya said, peering again into her scrying glass. "I have heard of Underworld apparitions before, but—"

"Do you think they're shades?" I asked hopefully. At least if the apparitions were real spirits, it would mean I was not going mad.

"Not exactly," she said slowly. "Shades are souls that died recently. They visit our world only when summoned, and sometimes not even then. Afterward, they join Egungun's Parade, traveling to their final resting place at Core. Some shades never make it to paradise, though. They just . . . linger in the Underworld. Unable to find rest. And sometimes—" She paused. "It's said that abiku consume lost souls. Defile, reshape them until what's left are creatures between death and resurrection. Beings that can appear as both spirit and flesh, known for mixing lies with the truth. Tar . . . you're being haunted by *ojiji*."

"It can't be ojiji," Kirah objected, as shivers chased up my glyph-covered arms. "Those are bully spirits—they coerce people into doing evil. To destroy themselves and others. They don't coax people to solve injustice."

"Maybe they're taunting me," I whispered. "Maybe they know that no matter how much I care, no matter how hard I try . . . it'll never be enough."

My voice broke. As hot tears sprang to my eyes, invisible caresses warmed my skin. Immediately, all eleven of my council siblings had bathed me with the Ray, expressing a depth of love that words never could. I closed my eyes, caressing them back—each member of my forever family, each branch of my external heartbeat.

Ours, they sang in wordless harmony. *Tar is ours, and Tar is enough.* And right when my shoulders began to relax . . .

It happened again.

A translucent Redemptor child shimmered into being, gliding across the salon floor and passing through the bodies of my siblings. The glyphs on my arms smoldered. The creature smiled emptily, holding a grimy finger to its lips.

The ojiji's mouth did not move. Still, it said: *Don't tell them.*

"It's happening now, isn't it?" demanded Kirah. She felt my forehead, her hazel eyes sharp and grave. "Tell me, and I'll sing for you."

Your friends do not see what you see, the apparition sighed. *They are spoiled by privilege. Numb to the true cost of change.*

I recoiled at the words, which rang true. I had just been thinking the same thing earlier, when Mayazatyl had whined about my desire to improve the empire. But Emeronya had said these creatures meant me harm. That they told both truth and lies.

They are blind, great Empress Redemptor. They are blind, and you are alone.

What was truth, and what was a lie?

My eyes slid to Kirah. I knew then, with grim intuition, that I did not have an illness my friends could cure. Kirah could sing down the moon and stars, and my siblings could cover me in hugs and spells and promises . . . and that undead child would still be there, lisping its cold, pure truth.

You are alone.

Woodenly, I pressed Kirah's hand. From a distance, I heard my voice say, "Go on, all of you. I was overreacting. Do the jobs you've been training for. You're right—I've been different. But now, I'll be fine." A smile stretched on my face as my stomach sank, sour with the certainty that this lie would be the first of many. "I'll be just fine."

CHAPTER 10

EIGHT OF MY ELEVEN COUNCIL SIBLINGS vanished toward the corners of the continent, and within hours, I stood with Dayo before the craggy Olojari Mountains, clutching my stomach from the lodestone journey.

"I wonder why that never gets easier," Dayo mused as we left the guarded port.

I laughed shortly and stuck a finger in my ear, which still rang with enchanted vibrations. Thankfully, the ojiji appeared not to have followed me through the lodestone. Still, I wondered if they lay in wait, always just beyond human sight. Sweat beaded on my brow, and not just from fear. In contrast to Oluwan City with its cool coastal breezes, the Oluwani province of Olojari was several miles inland, with hot, dry air that tasted of soot.

"Getting dissolved, transported seventy miles, and slapped back together isn't a skill you can practice," I pointed out.

"Well, you'd be the expert," Dayo said cheerily. "After

twenty-six lodestones in a row. Maybe you'll get immune."

"I nearly died," I reminded him. "I think I *did* die, for a minute. That part's still a bit hazy. What I do remember involved a lot of puke."

"Don't say 'puke,'" Dayo begged, then rifled through his gold-trimmed trousers to produce a vial of amber liquid. After tossing some back, he offered it to me. "New from Thérèse."

The potion tasted strongly of ginger and burned as it went down, but did wonders to settle my stomach. I looked guiltily at the empty bottle, wishing I'd thought to share with our Imperial Guard escort. Sanjeet had stayed back to secure the capital and had sent a cohort of trusted warriors in his place. They followed a respectful distance behind as we neared the holy forge, trying their best not to look queasy.

The Holy Olojari Forge and iron quarry rested in the heart of a scruff-covered mountain, hollowed out over centuries for the purpose. As the temple prospered, a chain of villages had sprouted up at the mountain's feet, servicing the forge with generations of miners, blacksmiths, and inns for the year-round influx of Ember-sect tourists.

At first, we passed through a patchwork of sumptuous noble villa estates, roofs dotted with iron statues of bluebloods—the same nobles, I imagined, who had managed the quarry on my ancestors' behalf for generations. Every now and then, an orange fleck buzzed near my ear, and something sharp and piercingly hot accosted me in the face. Once, I slapped my neck and brought my hand away to reveal the squashed carcass of a tiny winged creature.

"*Ina* sprites," Dayo observed. "Fire spirits. With so many, the forge must be thriving."

But the closer we got to the temple, the more I sensed something terribly, terribly wrong. The villages, while numerous, were little more than tenements and mudhouses crowded together, with the occasional tourists' inn surrounded by beggars. As far as I knew, the forge had employed Olojari commoners for hundreds of years. So why did so many live in squalor?

The narrow streets and markets lay spookily bare.

"Where is everyone?" I asked Dayo, careful to keep my voice low. "Do you think word got out about Umansa's prophecy?"

"I don't know," Dayo replied. "But *that's* not a good sign, is it?"

He pointed to a plume of smoke slowly filling the horizon. The mountain appeared to be steaming—unearthly tendrils of red, gold, and black rising from craggy rock.

We soon discovered where most of the villagers had gone. A crowd of thin, soot-covered commoners blocked access to the forge. Armed priests guarded the forge entrance: a tall, wide arch carved into the face of the mountain. Twin statues of Warlord Fire, depicted as a barrel-chested giant with billowing hair and wicked amethyst eyes, framed the arch. A phrase in large script, mottled with ash and soot, had been carved into the entryway:

IN THE EYE OF KUNLEO,
OLOJARI WILL PROSPER.

Some in the crowd bore picks and iron mallets, others simply lifted bruised and calloused hands, as if in prayer. But all of them swayed, voices lifted in rasping song and jaundiced eyes alight with hunger. From the sidelines, well-dressed bluebloods looked on with nervous scorn. As for the Ember priests of the forge, who stood out in costumes of red and gold, their sympathies appeared to be split. Some acolytes stood with the poor and rioting, joining in their music, and blessing them in red clouds of incense. Other acolytes stood with the wealthy, sneering at the rabble, and making signs of the Pelican to ward off evil.

Alarmed at the unrest, our Imperial Guard escort fell in place around us. But barely anyone had noticed our arrival. Instead, the crowd fixated on a wiry man standing above the arch, teetering on a ledge in the mountain. His hair was tied up in a bulky bun, and his face was concealed by a green, scaly mask made of leather trimmed by jagged rows of animal teeth. Wide bands of green leather decorated his chiseled arms.

From the hubbub below, I caught an excitedly whispered name: the *Crocodile*.

He was beating a talking drum, leading the crowd in song:

My sister's bones, they have no ears,
Ah-ah—but is my sister deaf?
Bones will turn to dust,
But Malaki lives forever.

My mother's skin is mottled clay,
Ah-ah—but is my mother dead?
Skin may turn to ash,
But Malaki lives forever.

Energy crackled from the ground, rising through my sandals and making the hair on my calves tingle. Perhaps this man was a sorcerer of the Pale Arts: His song was an incantation.

My gaze traveled slowly to the lurid steam rising from the mountain.

Skin may turn to ash,
But Malaki lives forever.

No, I realized with cold dread. Not an incantation: The song was a summoning.

Dayo sensed it the same moment I did. "Stop," he cried, hailing the man in the mask by waving his arms. "You don't know what you're doing!"

The stranger continued to direct his rabble choir, though he cocked his head toward us and seemed to start with surprise. Then his shoulders shook—he was laughing. A chill crept up my spine. I couldn't shake the feeling that, though Dayo and I had hidden our imperial seal rings, and a long-sleeved linen tunic hid my Redemptor marks . . . this stranger knew exactly who we were.

"He's doing this on purpose," I growled.

A crimson glow emanated from the forge's mouth . . . and then a smoldering hand the size of a boulder punched through the top of the mountain.

She burst forth in a mushrooming cloud of ash and fire sprites: a giant of smooth, obsidian rock. The force blew back my hair, and bluebloods scrambled for cover while all around me, the rabble ululated in rapture. The creature rose until her legs straddled the mountain's ruined peak, thighs gleaming like marble pillars. Plumes of smoke burst from her scalp, and wings like black sails filled the sky, plunging the day into hazy night. With an agonized roar, the alagbato beheld the forge with bright white coals for eyes.

In that moment, a thought occurred to me and my mouth ran dry:

I may never have seen my father in his truest form.

If he wished to—if my mother had not enslaved him—could Melu of Swana have grown to the size of a mountain? What power had my mother harnessed when she slapped a cuff on that guardian's arm?

Over the arch, the masked man called the Crocodile crowed with triumph. "She has heard your cries," he bellowed at the jubilant crowd below. "See what your suffering has wrought! If you cannot profit from the fruits of your labor, no one should! We give their wealth to Malaki!"

"He wants Malaki to destroy the mine," Dayo said slowly. "But why?"

"I don't know," I said through gritted teeth. "But he's an idiot! If Malaki sets off an explosion, the Crocodile will have a lot more than the mine to answer for. Doesn't he know volcanoes can explode for miles?"

"Feed their stolen wealth to the flames," the Crocodile cried, pumping a fist before leaping down into the crowd. "And now we must go. Take your children; go, take cover! Watch from afar as justice takes its course!" But to the man's apparent chagrin, many of the villagers ignored him. Instead, they turned worshipful eyes to the mountain, numb to the Crocodile's pleas for their safety.

With a tremor that shook the ground, Malaki spoke:

"*IRON. IRON. ALWAYS—THEY DEVOUR. MY HEART—MY HEART—*"

She bellowed in a dialect I barely made out—some form of Arit that had died centuries ago. Ash poured from her lips, making the back of my throat smart. Malaki let out a hoarse, thundering cry, as if speaking hurt her.

"*SO—MANY—STORIES,*" she rasped. "*END THEM—END THEM ALL—*"

And from the yawning caverns of her eyes, lava flowed in rivulets.

"Run!" I hollered. "She's going to blow. She's—" I seized Dayo's arm and tried to tow him up the path. But he wrenched away.

"Tar." His dark eyes fixed on Malaki with pity and

wonder. "I think . . . I think she's crying." And then Dayo—my large-hearted, brave, and utterly stupid better half—threw himself up the side of the mountain.

As I watched in disbelief, he scrambled up the rock face, calling out over the hubbub. "Malaki, what do you want?" His burn scar prickled with sweat. "Tell us. Let us know how to help you!"

"That thing doesn't need help!" I shrilled, clawing at his tunic to bring him back down. "We do!" But it was too late. The moment Dayo said Malaki's name, the alagbato paused, turning to stare in wild confusion.

Then a massive hand descended from the sky, blotting out my vision, and snatched up me and Dayo in a swift, bone-crushing fist.

My head snapped back, then forward.

Thérèse's nausea potion threatened to immediately resurface. I screamed, clinging to Dayo, and in turn he clung to the alagbato's fingers, trembling . . . but still he met Malaki's gaze.

"Please," he said, gagging on smoke as Malaki brought us to her ancient, smoldering face. "We . . . we just want to help."

Lava continued to stream down Malaki's cheeks. *"ALWAYS—MORE,"* she said, in a hot, strangled rasp. *"FALLING—HERE. FILL—MOUNTAIN. PAIN—MORE—STORIES."*

For the first time, Malaki's eyes locked on mine. We both stilled, girl and alagbato, trapped in mutual horror and confusion. I held my breath, preparing for an early journey to the Underworld . . . but just as Kameron predicted . . . a spark of familiarity lit Malaki's face.

Species smell their own.

"*STORIES,*" she rasped, though this time her tone sounded focused. Determined. "*YOU . . . TAKE THEM.*"

Then she raised her other hand, and pressed a massive, rocky finger to my forehead.

Grief, as wide and troubled as the Obasi Ocean, filled every crease of my brain. I cried out, eyes streaming with the tears of peasants. Paupers who descended into the mine before sunrise and emerged with the moon, raking a pittance wage to fill the bellies of infants they rarely saw. I knew the agony of child workers, trapped beneath the collapsed walls of shafts, clumsily erected for the rising profit demands of bluebloods. I groaned through the discontent of scar-handed blacksmiths, fleeced into buying iron of paltry quality, while nobles whisked the best specimens far away to the Imperial Armory.

But the sharpest, most lasting pain was that of the mountain itself. Olojari teemed with generations of tragic memories, stories that had seeped down, down, into the rock, weakening the spirit who lived there. Malaki remembered a time long ago, before Raybearers, before emperors or kings of any kind, when the people ruled themselves, and took little more than what they needed. A time when the stories that trickled down into Malaki's bones were made of music—the laughter of souls well fed, the beat of picks on stone, bodies lean from strength, not hunger.

Then Malaki lifted her finger. I gasped with relief as the memories subsided, then coughed as Malaki's smoke filled my lungs. She held me, quiet for now, with an expression on her face like understanding and mild contempt.

"What does she want?" Dayo asked me in a whisper, still gripping the alagbato's fingers for dear life.

I almost replied that I didn't know—and then I realized that wasn't true. The day's events came together, piece by piece, in my mind, which had always excelled at puzzles. The tapestries surrounding the suite common room. The elegant noble villas and the ramshackle village. The peasants swaying before the mountain, filthy hands lifted in prayer.

"She wants me to fix it," I said slowly. "And so I will." I pressed my hand into Malaki's giant fingers, sending visions of a hopeful future—of a mountain filled with music. "You won't have to feel those stories anymore," I told her. "I promise, Malaki. But if you destroy the mountain now, it will only cause more pain. More—bad stories. So give me time." I sent her visions of many sunsets, and of moons charting their course across the sky. "More—time."

Malaki eyed me warily, her grip tightening around me ever so slightly. But right when I thought she would crush us to dust—she heaved a great, ashy sigh.

"*LAST CHANCE,*" she bellowed, and plunged forward, tossing us back at the foot of the mountain. Dayo and I tumbled to the ground, wheezing and scraping our limbs on the gravel before scrambling to our feet. Then, in a burst of lurid, searing sparks . . . the ancient creature vanished. Malaki disappeared back into the mountain, taking every drop of lava with her.

For now.

Our Guard warrior escort immediately surrounded us, clucking and inspecting us for wounds. They formed a barrier between us and the awestruck peasants, trying to herd us away from the mountain. But I broke their ranks, returning instead to the tall arched entrance of the Holy Olojari Forge. Malaki's grief had shaken the temple, sending bits of rock, iron, and coal skittering across the clearing. I considered the entrance arch, then snatched a broken lump of coal from the ground.

Dayo looked on in confusion. *Tar?* His concerned voice blossomed in my head. *We should go. In case Malaki changes her mind.*

She won't, I replied. *Not if we fix it.*

I was wrong to put you in danger like that, Dayo added. *I'm sorry. It's a miracle you calmed her down. I'm still not sure what you did.*

We both stopped her, I objected. *If you weren't so annoyingly kind all the time, I'd never have figured out what she wanted.* I turned to smile at him. *Guess we make a pretty good team, Oba of Aritsar.*

He dimpled, highlighting a smudge of soot on his cheek. *Guess so, Obabirin Redemptor.*

Speaking of which . . . mind if I borrow those long legs of yours?

I sent a vision of my intention into Dayo's mind. His eyebrows rose when he saw . . . but he nodded, as usual trusting me without question. He crouched low so I could roost on his shoulders, and held my legs so I wouldn't topple. The crowd—villagers, priests, nobility, and the man in the crocodile mask—watched as I directed Dayo to the arch.

Then I set my jaw, gripped the hunk of coal, and slashed at the ancient inscription.

When my vandalism was done, the blessing that had once invoked the power of blood dynasty, the moneyed name of my ancestors, was now reduced to three words.

OLOJARI WILL PROSPER.

I drew back my sleeves, revealing the bright blue marks on my forearms. Then I called my mask by its name, and light burst from beneath my tunic, drawing scandalized gasps from the crowd. The majority of the priests and villagers sank to genuflect in the dirt. But others, especially the gentry, just stared, frozen in shock.

"By the power vested in me as Empress Redemptor," I announced, "with consent from His Imperial Majesty the Emperor . . . I officially forfeit the mine beneath the Holy Olojari Forge. From this day, the quarry and all its resources belong to the miners of the province, who may select delegates among themselves to facilitate trade with the capital. The nobility of Olojari," I went on, nodding at the apoplectic huddle of well-dressed lords and ladies, "who have until now, so *deftly* managed the mine on the crown's behalf, are hereby relieved of this service. Let the record be sealed—my word is passed."

A wave of gasps and guttural cries rose across the temple clearing, and it took several moments before I recognized the sound for what it was: celebration. Dayo laughed, squeezing my legs where he held me for balance. My heart pumped with fear, hope, and elation . . .

And right on cue, a specter child floated above the crowd, gazing down at the happy display with sunken, bottomless eyes. Then in a chilling gush of wind, the ojiji's treble voice hissed at my ear.

You helped them, but you did not help us. It's too late—too late. Do more.

Pay for our lives.

Guilt overwhelmed me. The child was right. How dare I stop and celebrate when there was still so much work to be done? The mine was only the beginning.

When the apparition vanished, I climbed down from Dayo's bony shoulders with unmajestic awkwardness, then pointed, panting, into the crowd.

"You." I indicated at the masked man called the Crocodile, who watched me from a distance with what seemed to be wary fascination. "I've heard of you. You've been inciting insurrection across the continent. And this was only the beginning, wasn't it? You want to wake all the alagbatos. Start disasters everywhere."

The man stiffened in surprise. I clearly wasn't supposed to know about the other alagbatos—and wouldn't have, if it weren't for Umansa's prophecies. The Imperial Guard warriors lurched for the Crocodile, who moved a hand to his weapon hilt. My accusation had been more than enough to have him seized and imprisoned. But I held up a hand to detain the warriors. If this man had agents throughout the empire, waiting to summon the other alagbatos . . . perhaps only he could call them off? Besides, after his seemingly accurate tirade about stolen wealth, I felt strange about imprisoning him. Still . . .

"You're either a fanatic or an idiot," I told him bluntly. "You almost got these townspeople killed. And when the quarry was destroyed, what then? These people are miners. How were they supposed to live?"

From an ever-so-slight hunch of the Crocodile's shoulders, I could tell my reprimand had hit home. Still, with a low, mask-muffled bravado, he replied, "They were to live free from the yoke of exploitation. As long as that quarry continued to line the coffers of your gentry sycophants, the people of Olojari would never be liberated." He paused, again seeming off balance, then conceded coolly, "But Your Imperial Majesty, it appears, has improved on my plan. Well done, Empress Idajo."

"Call off the other attacks," I snapped, "and I'll continue my improvements."

The man considered me. Then, in a single elegant movement, he genuflected, touching his head and heart in the imperial salute. "Let the will of Idajo be done," he said. He began to mutter a rapid series under his breath. The onlookers gasped, backing away as his limbs convulsed, and the tendons in his muscles glowed gold. He yelped in pain and grasped his leather-banded arm, where his veins bulged grotesquely—then he vanished.

"Track him," I ordered the guards, disbelieving my eyes. He must have darted behind a building. Created an illusion. But after an hour of searching the town, the imperial warriors returned empty-handed.

The Crocodile was gone.

CHAPTER 11

"WE DON'T HAVE TO DO THIS," DAYO SAID A week later, as we crossed the palace courtyard to stop at the An-Ileyoba gates. "We can postpone the Emperor's Walk. You're still recovering from Olojari."

"I'm fine," I said, rolling my eyes. "I may not be immune to death, but I'm not made of glass. Besides, we owe this to the city folk. They deserve a holiday."

News of our cancelled coronation ceremony, which Dayo still insisted on postponing until I returned from the Underworld, had shocked the volatile social world of Oluwan City. Combined with news of my forfeiting the mine—and depriving, without warning, the nobles of its profits—the atmosphere at An-Ileyoba court had been coldly sullen for days.

My gaze traveled to the skyline below, where whitewashed high-rises glowed against the velvet night sky. All around Palace Hill, the citizens of Oluwan City had pretended to fall asleep.

The Emperor's Walk was a five-hundred-year-old

tradition. The night before a coronation, the Imperial Guard imposed an early curfew, and the million residents of Oluwan City took to their homes in quiet revelry—feasting, storytelling, burning lamps all night . . . and peeking if they dared from their windows, hoping for a glance of their future emperor as he walked the streets in the dark. Tonight, they would look for two figures instead of one.

"I wish our family was home," I said, staring back wistfully at the moonlit An-Ileyoba turrets. "Emero, Maya, Kam—all of us. It would make the palace seem less . . . ominous."

"We can't be sure what the Crocodile will do," Dayo reminded me. "I miss the others too, but it's best they keep watch for alagbato attacks in their realms."

I nodded glumly, picking at the sachet of dried kuso-kuso I kept folded in my wrapper. I placed a leaf under my tongue whenever I needed to feel my council siblings, to sync my heartbeat with theirs, scattered thousands of miles away. Occasionally, I caught snippets of words:

Love—

Tar—

Miss—

Flashes of their faces and voices that I savored each night, like drops of cool, clean water in dry season. Missing Kirah was the worst. And I'd received word that she might not return for several months, continuing from Blessid Valley to start her campaign in Songland, facilitating reparations for the Redemptors.

Dayo nudged my ribs. "The Emperor's Walk can wait," he said again. "Am knows you need the rest. Don't you have your first . . . ah . . . intimate meeting with the vassal rulers tomorrow?"

I stiffened, battling the unsettling memory of King Zuri's arms around me at the Peace Banquet, and the inviting smell of agave wafting over me as he leaned toward my ear. Of all the vassal rulers I had to convince to love me, Zuri unnerved me the most.

"I'm trying not to think about it," I told Dayo. "And it's not an Emperor's Walk anymore. It's our walk."

I closed my hand around his. Imperial Guard Captain Bunmi, along with four of her cohort, stood in the gate's shadow, waiting to escort us to the city. She saluted me and Dayo as we passed through. "Evening, Your Imperial Majesties. We've secured your route through the city."

The warriors were dressed in plainclothes, pupils dilated with childish excitement. I winked at them, and Bunmi suppressed a smile.

"Evening, fellow commoners," I said, dipping my head.

"Just out for a stroll," Dayo added, in the worst working-class Oluwani accent I'd ever heard, making all of us burst into laughter.

Festive body paint covered our arms and faces, and our skin smelled sharply of lemon and peppermint, a balm to keep mosquitoes at bay. In theory, we were supposed to blend into a crowd of commoners. But tradition required Dayo and me to wear clothing from the reign of Enoba the

Perfect. The outdated costumes did little to conceal our identities. They were also unnecessary, thanks to the city-wide curfew . . . but the old customs still held.

"Ready to meet the ancestors?" Dayo whispered, linking his arm through mine. The beat of drums and shakers pulsed from the city below, muffled from celebrations confined indoors. Overhead, my sprites sparkled against the cloudless night sky. I had tried to convince the creatures to stay at the palace, but they would have none of it. Now they followed me and Dayo in a chirping, glowing parade, announcing our approximate location to the entire city.

The Watching Wall, several stories tall and glistening with muraled plaster, began at the base of Palace Hill, and cut for miles through the city. We would walk its full length, stopping to honor past Raybearers and their councils.

Enoba the Perfect's shrine began our pilgrimage. Dayo and I knelt on cushions before the image of our eight-times-great-grandfather. I had to crane my neck to glimpse the late emperor's face, and even standing, we barely reached Enoba's ankle.

"We pay homage," Dayo murmured. The warriors passed him a chalice, from which he sipped palm wine and poured a libation.

I did the same and echoed him. "Homage." But as I stared at Enoba's serene broad features, his ringed hand lifted in blessing, all I could think was: *How many?*

How many Raybearing daughters did you send away? Would you have wanted me standing here at all?

We knelt the longest at Olugbade's mural, emptying the chalice at the late emperor's feet. I sent tendrils of comfort down the Ray bond, watching Dayo for signs of anxiety. But his eyes remained dry.

"Strange," he said, touching the cold stone of his father's likeness. He smiled weakly. "This was how it felt when he was alive too."

I grimaced and nodded. The Lady had parented me from the opposite wing of an isolated manor. And Olugbade had loved Dayo the only way he knew how—from a distance.

We continued down the wall, kneeling and paying tribute every half mile. Moonlight glowed across the broad gravel avenues, and lamps twinkled festively in every window. Faint music wafted into the streets from closed shops and high-rises. Children's voices lifted in praise of Dayo, placing his name in the ancient hymn of Aritsar: *Eleven moons watch the sun dance: Black and gold, Ekundayo!*

But every so often, a new song spilled into the streets. I'd heard the melody before, mocked by nobles in the palace . . . but these commoners sang it in full voice, sending a thrill of joy and terror down my arms.

> *There is no night in Oluwan, nse, nse*
> *The sky is bright in Swana—awaken, bata-bata.*
> *They lie awake in Moreyao; nse, nse*
> *They sing in Nontes and Biraslov; snow melting, gun-godo.*
> *Djbanti and Nyamba rise, tada-ka, tada-ka*
> *Look, their children never sleep! Eyes open, bata-bata!*

Why, you ask? Why?
The Pelican has spoken!

A sun for the morning, a sun for the evening,
And moons for years to come.

Dhyrma, Blessid Valley, nse, nse
Sparti's tears have all dried up; tada-ka, tada-ka.
Quetzala grins and shields its eyes; nse, nse
Mewe will shed its heavy skins; gun-godo, gun-godo.

Why, you ask? Why?
The Pelican has spoken!

Tarisai for the morning!
Ekundayo for the evening!
And peace for moons to come.

"Do you think they mean it?" I whispered. "That they've accepted me already?"

Dayo grinned up at the high-rise buildings. They twinkled like beacons over the empty, mist-filled streets, and the vibrations of drums and voices shook the earth beneath us. "Sure sounds like it," he said.

When I didn't look reassured, he checked to make sure the guards were out of earshot, then turned me to face him.

"You're meant to be here, Tar," he whispered, pouring

his kind black eyes into mine. "I'm more certain of that than I've ever been of anything."

My heart raced. Then it slowed, as if the Ray had crept between us unbidden, matching my pulse to his. His dark features eased into a smile: the same one I had seen my first day in the Children's Palace, square and radiant. The smile that had convinced me to stay.

Dayo's lean chest rose and fell. His breath synced with mine, and an urge blossomed inside me, seizing control. I slid my hands to Dayo's shoulders and pressed my lips to his cheek. The kiss was shy. Nothing like the deep, core-shaking ones I gave Sanjeet.

But I still winced when I stepped back, dry-mouthed and mortified.

"I'm sorry," I whispered. "I should have asked. I . . . I know you don't like . . ."

"Kisses are fine," he said slowly. His features wrinkled with confusion. "Tar—is there something you're trying to tell me?"

"Yes. No. I'm sorry, it's just—" I shook my head, trying to make sense of the fog. "Dayo . . . ever since I was little, there's always been this dread. This haunting thought that I'm doing something wrong. That I *am* wrong, that I'll always be alone, that everyone will always leave me. I never even realized the voice was there . . . not until I met you, and it was gone. I don't feel that way with anyone else. Not with Kirah. Not even with Jeet. Just you." I bit my lip, hiding my face in my hands. "I'm sorry. I'm not making sense."

"Of course you are."

I peeked up at him. "I am?"

He gave a lopsided smile, using his thumb to wipe my cheek. I must have smudged my body paint when I'd kissed him.

"If there's anything I've learned from having eleven partners bonded to me for life," he said gently, "it's that there are all kinds of love, Tar. You talk about things with Kirah that you never share with Jeet. And you have—things— with Jeet . . . that you'll never have with me. And that's fine. We're the only Raybearers on earth. What we have is . . ." He trailed off, words failing, and flooded my mind instead.

Warmth coursed from the roots of my scalp to the soles of my feet. All of a sudden, everything was Dayo—his thoughts, his earthy smell, his steady heartbeat—and yet I was more myself than ever. On both our chests, the oba and obabirin masks glowed, and for a moment, they almost seemed to float, drawn to each other like two halves of a perfect whole. Then Dayo withdrew and the masks faded.

The guards were glancing back at us. Sheepishly we fell in step again, and Dayo linked my arm through his.

"You're doing it again," I mumbled, resting my head on his shoulder. "Making me feel like I belong."

Faintly, the glyphs on my arms began to sting. I shuddered, fighting off the surge of ghostly whispers.

Not enough. Not enough. He is blind. Do more.

Dayo paused, considering. Then he dipped to drop a kiss, experimentally, on my cheek. "That's fun," he concluded.

"I can do without the rest, I think. But we should kiss more often."

I laughed, shoving him as he aimed another peck at my nose. "I'm not sure how Jeet would feel about that."

"He stole your heart," Dayo pointed out. "He can spare your nose every now and then." He dimpled, then grew suddenly distant. "This world is going to be so much brighter for future Raybearers. Can you imagine, Tar? Just think. Now that we know there are two, they'll have soulmates . . . instead of growing up lonely. Like we did." He draped an arm around me. "I mean, it, Tar. When you and Jeet finally have children, it'll be the best thing that ever—"

I stopped dead in my tracks, dropping my arm from his.

Dayo blinked. "What's wrong?"

"When Jeet and I *what*?"

Dayo smiled, shifting his feet. "You know. I just assumed. Since you and Jeet are always finding excuses to slip away, be alone together . . . I figured it was . . . bound to happen. Eventually."

"We haven't been together like that," I said, my voice shrill. "Not yet. And even if we had been . . ." I thought of my panic that night with Sanjeet, how I froze in his arms. A realization formed in my stomach, hardening into conviction. "Dayo, I don't think I want to be a mother. Ever."

"Oh." He looked stunned. "Well, not now, maybe. But later . . ."

"Later I'll change my mind?" I crossed my arms. "What makes you think that?"

His shoulders sagged. "I'm sorry. I just . . ." He sighed. "We have to make more Raybearers somehow. And what it takes is—you know. Not in the stars for me." He leaned against the Watching Wall, looking queasy.

My anger drained away. I slipped my hand in his, and he squeezed it tiredly.

"I asked Ai Ling," he said after a pause. "If something was wrong with me."

My eyebrows rose. "Why Ai Ling?"

"I don't know." Dayo squirmed, considering. "She's just so easy to talk to. Have you noticed that? And she listens better than anyone, even when she pretends not to care. I wonder why she . . ." Dayo trailed off, looking sheepish, and picked at the grain of his wrapper. "Anyway. She's pretty sure there are others like me. Some who can't stand sex, some who like it but don't feel drawn to anyone, and others who just . . . feel nothing." He shrugged. "I'm the first kind. And I don't know how to change."

"Then don't," I said. "Why change for some dusty legacy? We didn't ask to be Raybearers."

"But we are, all the same." He smiled ruefully. "You know what's funny? I think I'd be good at raising children. Watching a brand-new person grow—what could be better than that? I'd never send them away. Not like Fath—" He inhaled and broke off again, hunching his shoulders.

I slunk against the wall beside him, letting the stones chill my back. "Dayo, if I birth an heir for the empire . . . I'll be doing exactly what The Lady did. Having a child, just to fulfill some imperial purpose—one they didn't even ask for. And that scares me. A lot. What if . . . what if I'm just like her?"

My palms broke into a cold sweat. I imagined cradling a small, sleeping creature with my coiling dark hair and Sanjeet's tea-colored eyes. I imagined all the knowledge I would crave to give it. All the power and protection. I would want to polish every detail of its tiny life to a rosy gleam, and love would surge inside me, hot and domineering, curling in my breast until a song dripped from my lips, sharp as crystallized honey:

Me, mine. You're me and you are mine.

No. *No.* I would hide myself away before it came to that. Make sure I'd never hurt it . . .

Just like The Lady had hid herself on the other side of Bhekina House.

Bile rose in my throat. "I can't do it," I told Dayo. "I won't. I'm sorry."

"Don't be sorry, Tar. It's fine." He nodded as if trying to console himself as much as me. "We'll just . . . figure something out. I know we will."

"Keep moving, Imperial Majesties," said Captain Bunmi, scanning the area. "It's safer not to linger." As we walked, Bunmi and her cohort traded signals with other Imperial Guard warriors, stationed at corners and on every rooftop.

I suppressed the thought of heirs and baby-making as we neared the center of the city. Here, the murals faded into a long, blank wall: space for future Raybearers and their councils.

"Have you seen it before?" Dayo asked with a nudge.

"Of course not. I was waiting for tonight. Have you?"

Dayo bit back a smile and shrugged.

"You have!"

"I peeked," he admitted, laughing and dodging my blows to his arm. "A few days ago. I'm sorry! I couldn't wait. But it's better this way—I get to watch you see it instead."

The wall curved, so we rounded a corner . . . and there it was.

"Well?" Dayo breathed. "What do you think?" But tears drowned any sound I could make.

I noticed the anklet first. *How strange*, my mind thought, retreating immediately to denial. *The cowrie shell anklet on that enormous painted foot looks just like mine.*

". . . incredible attention to detail," Dayo was saying, his voice faint in my ears. "The artisans outdid themselves. I could barely believe my . . ."

My eyes traveled up the wall, up the shapely brown legs, tall as tree trunks, up the towering torso and rainbow-colored wrapper, and stopping, at last, at the distant face. Dark eyes surveyed the city with proud serenity, framed by a billowing black mass of hair.

"Well?" Dayo repeated.

"Eep," I replied.

He beamed and pulled me close. "That's what I said too."

Dayo's likeness stood shoulder to shoulder with mine,

majestic and clear-eyed, the long, latticed burn scar giving him an air of heroic solemnity. Close around him stood our council siblings, faces wise and unsmiling. The murals were so lifelike, I expected the massive Sanjeet to sigh and run fingers through his curls, and the giant Kirah to wink and fray the ends of her prayer scarf.

The space behind me was conspicuously empty. The artists had left space for my soon-to-be council—the vassal rulers of Aritsar. I gulped and looked away, concentrating on my siblings.

Our unlined faces struck me the most. Every other likeness on the wall was hardened and wrinkled with dignity, but ours were smooth and vivid, the youngest rulers ever to grace the Watching Wall. I wondered if, deep down, that bothered Dayo. Our glory had come at the cost of his father's life.

"Don't be too long, Imperial Majesties," Captain Bunmi said, squinting up at the high-rises. "I'd like to secure the perimeter."

"It's secured," said one of her warriors, flagging a shadow on one of the rooftops, which slowly gestured back. "Whoever's posted up there returned the signal."

"I know. I just . . ." Bunmi bit her lip, frowning. "Something doesn't feel right."

"How should we end the pilgrimage?" I asked Dayo, giggling with nerves at our giant doppelgangers. "Should we bow to ourselves?"

Dayo genuflected with a clumsy flourish. I copied him,

both of us slightly tipsy from the wine chalice.

"We pay homage, oh Dayo the Gullible and Tarisai the Maleficent," he caterwauled, and I shushed him, doubled over with laughter. My sprites danced overhead, as if in on the joke. Dayo grinned at me. "We pay homage, oh shiniest—"

Then an arrow lodged with a *thwack* in the Watching Wall, inches from my head.

Dayo threw himself in front of me, right as another arrow sailed through the air . . . and lodged, firmly, in his back.

"Cohort, to me!" Bunmi screeched. "Get down. *Get down!*"

CHAPTER 12

THE STREET ECHOED WITH POUNDING FEET and the hiss of unsheathing weapons. Bunmi's cohort surrounded us, lifting their long oval shields above their heads to form a covering. But before they could finish, a second arrow whizzed through a gap in their formation and lodged in Dayo's shoulder.

Someone was keening, screeching unintelligible curses. I didn't realize the person was me until Dayo, still shielding me against the wall, cupped my face with both hands.

"Tar. Look at me. I'm fine."

"You have to get away," I wailed, hyperventilating. "I won't let you die; this cannot happen again—"

"Tar, *look*." And as chaos ensued around us, Dayo grimaced, reached around to his back, and pulled out each arrow.

The bleeding holes in his back clotted before my eyes. His oba mask glowed as new skin crept across each wound, darkening into scars.

"These arrows aren't for me. I can't die," he whispered,

143

features taut with fear. He nodded at the lioness mask on my chest, its single stripe announcing my vulnerabilities to the world. "They're for you."

Blood from my grazed ear trickled down my neck. Shafts continued to thud, one by one, against the warriors' shields. A single assassin, then—stationed on top of a nearby high-rise.

"We've been set up," Bunmi growled, signaling warriors to enter the building. They broke down the door, and the confused cries of high-rise residents spilled onto the street as the warriors scrambled to reach the roof.

Still the arrows streamed, unnerving in their accuracy. The assassin began to target the legs and feet of the guards surrounding me, their lower halves unprotected by shields. One by one the warriors cried out, breaking the barrier around me and Dayo.

Bunmi locked eyes with us. "Run," she rasped.

Heart in my throat, I seized an abandoned shield and fled the wall. The sound of revelry still floated in the streets, a ghostly anthem.

Why, you ask? Why?
The Pelican has spoken!

Adrenaline burned in my ears. The assassin had picked their hunting ground well—I ran in an open square, flooded with lamplight, with no shelter or alleyways in sight. An arrow grazed my shin. I hollered in pain, my flight reduced to a limp. My sprites spun in the sky, seeming to dim and quail as my own pulse weakened. Had I been thinking clearly, I would have willed them to help me—to dive in a glittering army, swarming my would-be killer. But my mind was a panicked fog, and tutsu sprites—curse them all—did not act without being commanded.

Dayo caught up with me and slung my arm around his shoulder, helping me hobble across the square. But we weren't moving fast enough.

A sun for the morning, a sun for the evening.
And moons for years to come.

Another arrow struck the shield, nearly knocking it from my hand. Faintly, I could see the silhouette of a burly figure atop the roof, pausing to replenish its quiver.

And then the children came.

I thought they were animals at first. Small, dirt-covered bodies rose from the ground, scaling the walls of the high-rise like beetles. First there were two, then four, then seven human creatures, limbs blurring as they clambered up the walls with chilling precision. Beneath the building, Imperial Guard warriors froze in terror, making the sign of the Pelican to ward off evil.

By the time the assassin noticed, it was too late. A scream pierced the air as the shadow children set upon the figure, clawing, biting, tearing at the assassin's limbs like jackals. Barely visible beneath the swarm of small bodies, the figure staggered, teetered . . . then pitched, children and all, over the edge of the eight-story high-rise.

They landed with a sickening crack. Dayo and I clung to each other, watching the mound of bodies in the pale-lit square. The children were still at first, covering the assassin's corpse. Then, in slow, disjointed movements, they rose from the ground.

"Can you see them?" I whispered to Dayo, and he nodded slowly, heart thudding against mine.

Layers of earth and grime muddled their faces, but closer up, their features varied greatly. Some dark with coiled locs, some pale with matted tresses, others tan and golden. Children from different ends of the continent, and all of them covered in purple Redemptor birthmarks.

"How?" I croaked. It didn't make sense. After the reign of Enoba, every Redemptor had been born in Songland, but these children came from all over the empire. If they were truly Redemptors, they must have been born in the original wave, which made each child five hundred years old.

Then I remembered Emeronya's warning: *They can appear as both spirit and flesh.*

These too were ojiji. My stomach twisted with both horror and pity. These children had once been alive. I had assumed that when Redemptors failed to return from the Underworld, they simply died and passed on to Core. These children had not been so lucky. The abiku had

146

enslaved their souls—perhaps forever. Exactly how many Redemptors had been turned to ojiji?

"Why are you protecting me?" I asked softly. "What do you want?"

As one, the pack of children turned their dull, translucent eyes on me—just like the boy who had killed Thaddace. Their voices, a quiet hiss that raised every hair on my neck, echoed across the square.

"Justice," they said, and crumbled into dust.

When Dayo and I returned to the palace, the Guard warriors sequestered us in the Imperial Suite, where Ai Ling and Sanjeet—along with an army of healers, attendants, and courtiers—flocked to greet us in the anteroom. I had barely crossed the threshold before a muscular pair of arms enveloped me, burying my face in a broad, solid chest.

"I'm all right," I mumbled into Sanjeet's bicep. But he barely seemed to hear me. He rasped curses in Dhyrmish, scanning me over and over with his Hallow as he buried his face in my hair.

"We heard the news," gushed an advisor, gawking at the blood staining my neck and ankle. "How *horrible*, Lady Empress. Let us attend you—"

Then everyone was talking at once. The air grew thin. My chest began to palpitate, and before I knew it, I had stepped out of Sanjeet's grasp and gestured sharply at the carved anteroom doors.

"Out," I rasped. "Everyone, except for the emperor, Anointed Ones, and Captain Bunmi."

"You should at least keep the healers," Dayo objected. "Your ear. And your leg—"

"Out," I barked again, and an exodus of servants and courtiers stampeded for the door. Once they were gone, I exhaled . . . and the room swayed beneath my feet.

Sanjeet picked me up in one efficient movement and stalked wordlessly to the suite common room. Bunmi and my siblings followed close behind. Sanjeet set me down on a low salon chair, rummaged through the cabinets above his war table, and produced salve and linen strips. He attended grimly to my wounds as I stared at Umansa's dire prophetic tapestries, watching the colorful glyphs and patterns pitch and swirl.

Bunmi genuflected at my side, offering up her spear with open palms.

"Your life was endangered on my watch, Your Imperial Majesty," she grunted. "I assume full responsibility. Please accept my resignation from the Imperial Guard."

"Rejected," I told her. "We both know that was no ordinary assassin."

"You should get examined by a traditional healer," Sanjeet said in a rough voice when he was finished with my ear and ankle. When I shook my head, a vein in his brow ticked. "The arrow could have been tainted, Tar.

My Hallow is inefficient at checking for poison. For Am's sake. You don't need to be brave right now."

"We can't trust anyone," I said. "The person who tried to kill me is here, in the palace."

My council siblings collectively stiffened, and I looked at Bunmi for confirmation. The captain nodded, grimly. "How did you know, Lady Empress?"

"Call it a feeling." The moment I had seen the figure atop that building, my mind had seized at the puzzle, stacking facts and connecting images, like I had during the tests in the Children's Palace. Someone at An-Ileyoba wanted me dead . . . and they had almost succeeded.

The assassin had fooled Bunmi by knowing the correct all-clear signals, which suggested help from within the Imperial Guard. But the crown's forces were famously difficult to corrupt. Warriors who exposed traitors were awarded with cattle fields and a noble title, the latter of which no amount of money could buy.

Bribes, then, were unlikely to sway a Guard warrior . . . unless they had no need of a title. Unless, I concluded, the traitor was already a noble.

Dayo's brow furrowed. "The assassin was a courtier?"

"No," Bunmi replied. "But he was certainly hired by one." She produced a foul-smelling rag from her pocket. Inside it glistened a putrid yellow stone, stained with blood. At the sight of it, a memory ticked in my thoughts—the glittering green gem in Melu's cuff—the one my mother had used to enslave him.

Ai Ling recoiled at the sight of it, stroking her chin in the sign of the Pelican. "Is that—is that Pale Arts?"

Bunmi nodded grimly. "My warriors found this stone embedded in the assassin's neck. It's a practice called *ibaje*. Underworld artifacts bind the user to a task, give resistance to death, and bestow them with certain abilities. That explains, I imagine, why the assassin's arrows rarely missed. Ibaje objects are often worn—but when inserted directly into the body, they provide stronger, permanent power. They are poison, however, killing the user slowly and cursing them with deformity. Only one guild of assassins is depraved enough to carry them: the Jujoka."

I shook my head. "I've never heard of them."

"I have," Sanjeet said, gaze haunted and distant. As he knelt by my salon chair, his calloused fingers traced my jaw and hairline, over and over. Memorizing them. Convincing himself I was still here, safe—not skewered with arrows beneath the Watching Wall. When he spoke again, his voice was cold with rage. "The Jujoka are the most exclusive guild of mercenaries in the center realms. They can be contacted exclusively through ancient family liaisons. Even then, only the very, very wealthy can afford them."

"Someone within the guard—likely the child of a noble—must have provided the assassin tonight's passcodes and given him access to the rooftop," Bunmi agreed. "But we don't know who."

"It's likely more than one family," Ai Ling said grimly.

"These nobles like to do things in coalitions."

"But why would anyone want Tarisai dead?" Dayo asked. "She offered to sacrifice herself to the abiku, for Am's sake. She's a hero. Plus—"

In my head, I added what everyone was thinking, but not saying: Why bother having me killed, when the Underworld would likely kill me by my nineteenth birthday?

Bunmi made a scornful sound. "If those nobles are responsible, they are not only evil, but reckless. If the Empress Redemptor dies before fulfilling her promise to the Underworld, the abiku will wage war on us all. Even if we mobilize the Army of Twelve Realms, thousands will die. Millions."

Bumps prickled on my skin. I generally avoided thinking of my journey to the Underworld, letting the new alagbato crisis, as well as the task of anointing my own council, distract me. But after seeing those dirt-covered creatures skittering up the high-rise, stinking of decay . . . my death seemed more imminent than ever before. Why in Am's name had I thought I was strong enough to brave the Underworld? Had I gone mad?

I began to shudder violently, unable to stop. Immediately Sanjeet cradled my head to his chest, but I continued to shake. I felt his despair through the Ray as his Hallow searched me.

"I can't find anything," he whispered. "I don't know what's wrong, sunshine girl. Tell me—tell me where it hurts."

I barely heard him. The glyphs on my arms itched like fire ants as ojiji swarmed on the muraled salon ceiling, jeering through mocking, skeletal smiles.

Coward! Coward!

We were younger than you when your empire tossed us into the Oruku Breach.

You don't deserve to be afraid. Do more—do more.

Pay for our lives.

"Truth and lies," I breathed as my siblings watched me with growing concern. "Truth and lies. Which is which?"

"Tea," prescribed Ai Ling. She dug through Thérèse's herb basket in the corner, dumped leaves in a water mug, and pressed it under my nose. Fragrant leaves tickled my tongue as I sipped, and slowly, my limbs relaxed. The mocking voices disappeared, though I dared not look at the ceiling, in case those creatures still stared back.

One of Kameron's panther cubs mewled in the salon corner, and Dayo fetched it, hoping the furry bundle would soothe me. I stared at its limpid green eyes, and it squeaked, licking my face. Sighing, I held it to my chest, just as Sanjeet held me.

"The ojiji came back," I croaked. "Dayo and Bunmi saw them, down in the city. Children, just like the one who murdered Thaddace—Redemptors from Enoba's time. They saved me from the assassin." My council siblings shuddered as I fed the memory down the Ray bond: dead-eyed children hurling themselves from the high-rise, then rising from the dirt, limbs hanging grotesquely from their bodies as they turned to face me. Ai Ling and Sanjeet tensed in revulsion as I showed them the memory.

"What I don't understand," Dayo mused quietly, "is how those creatures are making it through from the Underworld. Maybe spirits can come and go as they please. But physical bodies? They could only enter our world through an opening."

Captain Bunmi stiffened, gripping her spear. "The Oruku Breach."

Sanjeet shook his head. "The Breach is guarded every hour of every day. I receive daily reports from Ebujo. Nothing has come through that hole since last month, when the abiku attended the Treaty Renewal. If dozens of undead children were pouring through the Breach, I would know."

"Unless they're coming from somewhere else," I whispered. "A new opening to the Underworld."

We all fell silent.

"Well," Ai Ling said after a pause, "wherever they're coming from, at least they're on our side. I mean . . . they saved Tar, right? So maybe they like her. Maybe those creatures are grateful that Tar's saving future children from their own fate."

Captain Bunmi sucked her teeth doubtfully. "I very much doubt that ojiji can be grateful," she said, brooding. "In my home village, wisewomen described ojiji as animate puppets—shell beings, with minds enslaved by the will of the abiku."

"Plus, an ojiji murdered Thaddace," I pointed out. "I don't want their help. If they don't care about the people I love, then how can they care about me?"

Ai Ling shrugged. "Who's to say? We don't know why the nobles tried to kill you either. But they did."

Sanjeet's arms around me stiffened. I turned to look at him, then followed his gaze to Umansa's tapestry of Malaki. He looked suddenly sick.

"It's Olojari," he said. "It has to be. The nobles lost wealth when Tar relinquished the mine. They're afraid she'll take more away from them."

Dayo frowned doubtfully. "Are the nobles really that greedy? After all, it's not like they'll be poor without Kunleo property. Their own estates are massive."

"But she's given the peasants power," Captain Bunmi observed, sharing an understanding look with Sanjeet. Out of everyone in the room, only Bunmi and Sanjeet had been raised as poor commoners. "With profits from the mine, the Olojari villagers could buy property of their own, instead of leasing land from the gentry. It might take years, decades even, but at the end of the day, peasants outnumber the gentry. Once enough commoners prosper . . . blood status will be all the nobility have left."

I nodded slowly. "And so they want me to disappear."

Sanjeet growled, and bumps prickled my skin. "I will disappear them first."

"Don't talk like that," I scolded him. "You're not a killer, Jeet."

"And you are not a sacrifice," he barked. Immediately he regretted it, and that expressionless wall rose around his features while he struggled for control of his anger. He left the divan and paced, linking his fingers behind his head. Words brewed behind his cold brown eyes.

The panther cub scrambled off my lap as I rose and went to him, wrapping my arms around his back. "Say it," I told him.

He did not move. "Say what?"

"The thing you can't sugarcoat." I spoke into his shirt.

He sighed—a cavernous, shuddering sound—and turned to stare at me. "I think . . ." He opened his mouth. Closed it. Opened it again. "You should take a step back from court life. Just for a while, until we can be sure the palace is secure. I think—if you relinquish your duties as empress—"

I stumbled back, blinking up at him. "What?"

"Just for a while, sunshine girl." His voice was tortured. Pleading. "You aren't safe here. You've been a target from day one, and—for Am's sake, Tar! You don't always have to be the hero."

In his eyes, I saw the same wistful longing from Kirah's face, and Mayazatyl's, and Kameron's and all the rest.

We just want you back.

"No," I rasped.

"Tar. Please."

"No!" I snarled. I marched to one of the salon windows and thrust aside the gauzy curtain, pointing down at the moonlit Watching Wall. "You're giving them what they want," I breathed. "What all of them want: every emperor and lord and priest who's ever ruled this palace. They wanted me to turn invisible. To run and hide. But I won't. Not like the others." Memories seeped into my body from the floor. The whispers of girls with dark skin and strident, fluting voices. Girls with mirror-black eyes and proud, broad noses; girls who laughed and teased and glowed with a Ray they could not suppress. I had dreamed about them once, as a candidate in the Children's Palace. Even then, I had loved them, before knowing who they were.

My ancestors. My Kunleo sisters, reviled and erased.

Exiled, for daring to shine like the sun.

"I bear the Ray," I said quietly. "Whether I live in a palace or a tent in the Bush. That's what makes me dangerous, Jeet. And until this world changes . . . I will always be a target. Whether you like it or not."

Then I walked to a kneeling desk in the corner, rummaged for paper and ink, and knelt to write.

"Tar," Dayo ventured, after a few cautious moments. "What are you doing?"

I finished writing, plunged my seal ring into wax, and stamped the paper. "Being empress," I snapped, then rose and headed for the exit. As I retreated, I heard them scramble to the desk, sensing their alarm through the Ray as they read my handwritten script:

BY EDICT OF TARISAI KUNLEO,
HIGH LADY JUDGE,
AND OBABIRIN REDEMPTOR OF ARITSAR:

All natural resources—quarries, hunting grounds, fisheries,
and lumber mills that have been heretofore claimed by House
Kunleo, throughout the twelve realms of Aritsar shall be
relinquished to the commoners of their native province
and released from the care of gentry.

Effective immediately.

"This is suicide," bellowed Sanjeet, coming to stand in my path. "Tar, you can't do this."

"I just did," I retorted, staring up at him coolly.

Ai Ling cleared her throat, awkwardly raising her finger. "Actually, Tari dear . . . you can't. Not right away, at least. It's imperial protocol. Any edict that primarily affects the gentry must be announced at a gathering where nobles can air their concerns. A Pinnacle—the highest of high courts."

The wind deflated from my sails. How could I have forgotten? Pinnacles were one of the oldest law rites in Arit history. I could try to pass the edict anyway, of course . . . but without respecting imperial protocol, I had precious little chance of the nobles obeying, even with the Imperial Guard at my back.

"Fine," I said, pinching the bridge of my nose. Arranging

a Pinnacle would take months—every noble clan in Aritsar would have to be invited, then given time to travel. "But it's still going to happen. Bunmi?"

The captain stood at wary attention. I snatched the edict from the desk and handed it to her.

"See that the criers deliver copies to every noble family in court and throughout the empire. Tell them a Pinnacle is imminent."

"Those resources are Dayo's property too," Sanjeet snapped, after Bunmi bowed and left the chamber. "Did you think of that?"

I paused guiltily, biting my lip. "I'm sorry I didn't ask," I told Dayo. "But this is what Malaki wanted. You were there. You saw my memories; you saw the broken stories of that mine. Well . . . this is how we fix it. I'm sure, Dayo."

Dayo fidgeted, glancing between me and Sanjeet. "I'm sorry, Jeet," he mumbled at last, rubbing the back of his neck. "But Tar's right. I don't like it any more than you do, but we've got to appease the alagbatos somehow. And the faster Tar passes this, the sooner our council siblings can come home."

Sanjeet shook his head, but turned to me one more time. "Please," he rasped. "Don't do this."

In that moment, I realized how fragile I must look to him. I was several heads shorter, and a minute ago I'd been trembling in his arms, bleeding in two places. It would have been so sweet to give in—to drown in those deep, molten eyes. Still, I inhaled slowly, floundering to stay afloat.

"You've seen the prophecies, Jeet," I told him. "If we don't appease the alagbatos, natural disasters could kill thousands. What am I supposed to do? Hide here in the suite and let all those people die for me?"

"People die every day," he said.

"Jeet." My voice was sharp. He had spoken with a clear-eyed calm that made me shiver. "How in Am's name can you say that?"

"Because it's true." His gaze was wet, unfocused. Faintly, I noticed Dayo and Ai Ling exchange an anxious look, then melt away from the room, sensing a need for privacy.

We were alone then, Sanjeet and I, suspended in a brewing storm that had loomed ever since I returned from Mount Sagimsan. We had tried to outrun it. Tried to shelter beneath sweet words, and desperate, hungry kisses. But now the clouds had finally caught up to us . . . so we opened the floodgates, and spoke in thunder.

"People are dying right now," Sanjeet said, in a voice so calm it felt cruel. "Good people. Innocent. Children you'll never even know existed, gasping their last breath in ditches all over Aritsar. And you'll never save them all, Tar. Whether you ride across lodestones, or make the nobles want to kill you, or hurl yourself into the Oruku Breach."

The speech hit me like a slap. In his twisted features, I saw the grief of a boy who had learned young that heroes do not win. That you can be the tallest boy on your street, strong like the Prince's Bear . . . and brothers will still get taken away. Mothers will still fail to escape. And the girl you love will still offer herself as a sacrifice to monsters.

I understood him. I did . . . but rage bubbled inside me as voices—Sanjeet's, Mayazatyl's, Kirah's, the ojijis'—jarred my ears from a hundred directions, brassy as kettle bells.

You seem determined to heighten security risks.

Now that you're back, all you care about is changing *things.*

We just want you back.

Some of us love Aritsar the way it is.

Your friends do not see what you see. They are blind, blind, and you are alone.

"Why doesn't anyone care?" I blurted. "Why is everyone so at peace with how things have always been? Children are *dead*, for Am's sake! Thousands of Redemptors who will never come back. And it isn't just Songland suffering. It's our people too; toiling, dying in mills and mines for generations of a greedy few. And we're just supposed to . . . what? Sit back and—"

"Let it happen?" Sanjeet finished bluntly. "Yes! Sometimes! Tar . . ." He ran a large square hand through his curls. "Have you ever considered that most people weren't born to save the world? Most of us are lucky just to find a home, a family to protect, and that's enough. More than enough, even. Sunshine girl . . . everyone can't care about everything."

"And you think I'm a fool for trying."

"I think," he said heavily, "that your life should not be a means to an end. No human being should be reduced to a function. The day we do that—it's the beginning of the end."

The words jolted me, ringing true like a song. But they

160

jumbled in my head with a dissonant tune, one no less true than the first.

The only thing more powerful than a wish is a purpose.

"You're right," I said slowly. I looked again at the vast twinkling city, watching my sprites mingle with the star-studded sky. "My life doesn't have to serve a purpose. But really, Jeet . . . would it be so bad if it did?"

Night wind whispered through the salon curtains, making them float like the ghosts above my head. He stood there beside me for what felt like an eternity. I shifted my feet. The bells of his mother's anklet chilled against my skin. I reached for his mind, and felt the grit of hands clenched tight, desperate to keep the ones he loved—*mother, brother, Dayo, sunshine girl*—from slipping through his fingers. When he spoke again, his voice was low, and resonant as the heart of a griot's drum.

"I once promised," he said, "that I would never ask you to be less than who you are. But if you set yourself on fire to warm a frozen world, I will not stand by and watch you burn."

"Then don't watch." I traced the stern ridges of his features, clearing a curl from his hooded brow. "Stand with me."

He rested his face against mine. I couldn't tell whose tears fell first. Salt stung our cheeks, prickling, gumming our features together like mortar. He whispered against my lips: "I can't, sunshine girl."

I nodded, smiled, and let my heart grow numb as an empress's sunstone. Then I stepped from his grasp.

"Then stand back, Jeet."

CHAPTER 13

HE WAS GONE BY MORNING.

Ai Ling bustled busily around me and Dayo, trying to lift the pallor that had fallen over the suite halls.

"Sanjeet would have had to leave for Dhyrma anyway," she said in a pleasant singsong, drawing away the mosquito curtains from where I lay side by side with Dayo. We were propped, uncomfortably, on a grand, fur-draped dais. "Just in case an alagbato makes trouble. And then there's the new opening to the Underworld to look for. But he'll come back, Tarisai." She patted my cheek consolingly. "I'm sure of it. Now remember to look sleepy, Imperial Majesties."

Morning light filtered into the high-ceilinged bedchamber, and we could hear the bustle of courtiers waiting outside the door.

"Maybe you should yawn," suggested Ai Ling. "Or look a little naked. It'd seem more realistic."

I snorted, lobbing a pillow at her. "This is awkward enough as it is," I said as she giggled, twirling away in her satin dressing gown. "Don't make it worse." Secretly though, I was relieved at Ai Ling's levity: It made the coming morning seem less ominous.

Once a month, the highest members of court attended the Emperor and Empress's Rising: a chance to wake, dress, and touch the reigning Raybearers, witnessing us living gods in our vulnerable state. It was a sham, of course. Dayo and I never slept in the formal Imperial Bedchamber. In fact, we had been awake for hours, rising before dawn to bathe in the palace bathhouses, and returning to the suite for breakfast and honeybush tea. Then—as the hour of our official Rising drew close—we had sighed, wriggled back into our night shifts, and climbed onto the dusty imperial bed to be awoken.

"The Rising should have a big turnout today," Dayo said, leaning nervously against the dais pillows. "News of your intention to hold a Pinnacle went out at dawn. I'm guessing the nobles will want a word."

"Of course," I muttered. "They'll want to kill me in the privacy of my bedroom. Why wait until I hold court?"

"Speaking of court," chirped Ai Ling, "you won't be there today. I've arranged your first meeting with Princess . . . I mean, Queen Min Ja of Songland."

"Chin up, Tar," said Dayo when I made a face. "It won't be *that* bad."

"My chin's fine where it is," I said sullenly. "Since you promised those strangers I'd share all my memories."

"You won't have to face them alone," said Ai Ling, patting my arm in sympathy. "I'll be there as Imperial Ambassador."

I gave her a grateful smile but winced internally. I didn't want my council siblings wading through the mire of my past any more than I wanted strangers there.

"I still don't get the appeal of Risings," Dayo said as he practiced a convincing yawn, rubbing his eyes theatrically. "Noble families scramble for the highest titles at court, and as a reward, we make them . . . rise at the crack of dawn and watch us get dressed?"

Ai Ling shrugged. "They'd be offended if you didn't."

Outside on the palace walls, the multitoned drums of the Imperial Guard announced the hour.

Battle stations, everyone, I Ray-spoke . . . and the bedchamber's double doors burst open.

Dayo and I sat up and stretched, doing our best to look regally awakened as courtiers trilled in grating, cheerful song.

Alive? Tell us!
Aheh, alive and well!
Thank Am, the oba has awoken!

Alive? Tell us!
Yes, we see her with our own eyes!
Thank Am, the obabirin has awoken!

The nobles circled the bed, crowing with exaggerated relief at finding Dayo and me alive. Then they dressed us, chanting songs at every interval—a blessing for each layer of wrapper, prayers for painting our faces, incantations for detangling and braiding our hair.

When at last we were handed our sandals, completing the Rising, a throng of courtiers turned their eyes on me, bowing and simpering with smiles that set my teeth on edge.

"We would like to give you a gift, Your Imperial Majesty," said a girl about my age. I recognized her from a flock of courtiers who smirked and tittered whenever I passed in the hallways. Her glowing, cobalt-black skin, set off by an *ashoke* wrapper, betrayed her to be a blueblood— one of the oldest and wealthiest families in Oluwan.

That's Lady Adebimpe, of House Oyega, Ai Ling told me through the Ray. *One of the most influential families at court.*

The lady curtsied, batting a palm-frond fan. "Our gift is long overdue, Lady Empress. You must forgive us for the delay."

I smiled at her tightly. "And does your gift include another arrow in the emperor's back? An arrow meant for me?"

Adebimpe's posse of courtiers froze, looking instantly uncomfortable, but the face of the lady herself betrayed nothing.

"Of course not, Lady Empress," she gasped, still bowed before me, lifting her eyes to mine with limpid innocence. "I was devastated to hear of what happened. We all were, weren't we?" Her followers oozed assent. "Your guards should have been more careful."

Whatever mischief she had planned, I wanted it now,

out in the open. She couldn't kill me with witnesses, and better a public humiliation than a dagger at night. "Then what," I asked, "is your gift?"

"Why, Lady Empress . . ." Adebimpe rose and gestured with a flourish. "An *akorin*, of course. You should have had one weeks ago."

I blinked in surprise, but it was true. By tradition, noble Arit families provided Raybearers with an akorin: a personal griot, tasked with immortalizing the Raybearer's deeds in song. Upon Olugbade's death, the court nobles had offered Dayo their most talented sons for griots, renowned scholars and skilled warriors, young lords, and even minor princes.

I, however, had received no one. I was the daughter of an exile, after all—a walking sacrifice at best. I had no connections or lands to offer them, and I would probably be dead within two years. I had assumed they wouldn't bother. But now—

"Your akorin, Lady Empress," Adebimpe sneered.

The courtiers stepped aside to reveal a squat, dazed-looking child. She looked no older than twelve. Beaded cornrows swung at her shoulders, and mottled stripes of skin, like bruises that had never healed, stretched from her ear to her hairline. She clutched a bundle to her chest.

The girl gulped and froze . . . but she squared herself, steadily meeting my gaze. "My n-name"—she grimaced, reddening—"is Ad-Adukeh, Your Imperial M-Majesty. I s-swear my drum t-to your s-service."

The nobles snickered behind their palm fans, and my

166

council siblings stiffened, recognizing Adebimpe's gift for what it was: an insult.

Imperial akorins were grown men in sweeping emerald kaftans, trained at the knee of the empire's most skilled griots, and seasoned with decades at the Imperial Academy.

They were seldom women, and *never* stuttering girls.

She blinked up at me, a sandy brown face with crescent-shaped eyes. Her wrapper was plain and fraying at the hem. I would later learn that she had blood from multiple realms—an *isoken*, perhaps with blood from both Oluwan and a realm of lighter complexions, like Moreyao.

I nodded at her, ignoring the nobles. "Where is your home province, Adukeh?"

She shifted her feet. "O-Olojari, Lady Empress."

My heart raced. I tried a smile, feeling as trapped as the child did. "No need to be nervous," I said brightly. "This isn't real court—it's just a silly Rising."

"She isn't *nervous*, Lady Empress." Adebimpe's smile brimmed with malicious glee. "She always stutters. Don't you, child?"

Adukeh inhaled, puffing up with anger. Then she shot me a furtive glance, touching the mark on her brow. "Th-There was an ac-accident. In the m-mine, when I was l-little. A sh-shaft collapsed, and . . . well. I c-couldn't talk for a while. Then, when I w-woke up, I sounded like th-this."

My cheeks heated. The nobles were rubbing it in my face—the power they still held over the people of Olojari.

The things they could do to hurt them, if I kept interfering.

"We found her busking outside the forge," crowed another noble. "Begging, really. She doesn't even have a *gele*."

He pointed at Adukeh's head. Most Oluwan ladies would never appear in public without their geles: towering headdresses made of starched fabric, folded elaborately to boast of marital status and rank.

"I do t-too," Adukeh retorted, and held out her bulky orange bundle. She unwrapped the stiff embroidered cloth, revealing the scuffed, hourglass-shaped gourd of a talking drum. Goatskin strings threaded the gourd from head to head, meant to be squeezed and released, changing the drum's pitch. "My grandmother was a griot," the girl explained to me. "My drum was hers, b-but I couldn't afford a c-case for it. So I use my g-gele instead. It's treated with st-starch, so it's very st-sturdy, and I c-can tie it to my back when I—"

The nobles howled with laughter, bangles jangling on their arms as their shoulders shook. Adebimpe watched me, hungry for my reaction. She wanted me to hop and shrill like a ruffled peacock—to stamp my foot, and dismiss Adukeh in fury.

"Stop laughing," I said quietly, and beneath my wrapper, the eyes of the lioness mask shone ever so dimly.

Every noble in the room fell quiet. Some gagged, as if something had knocked the air from their lungs. As their faces slackened in confusion, an eerie sensation made my skin itch. The last time nobles had obeyed me quickly had been at my Peace Banquet, when I ordered the continent rulers to sit down. To this day, I wasn't sure what had happened . . . and why the Songlanders had been immune to it. But I was too angry to wonder on it now.

I turned to Adukeh. "Play," I said.

The air thickened with whispers. The girl swallowed hard, but folded the gele over her shoulder and removed a curved beating stick from her wrapper folds. She clicked with her tongue and yelled the invocation of storytellers: *I have three b-bells in my mouth, I do not t-tell a lie!* Then she cradled the gourd in her arm, and struck.

The girl's music filled the bedchamber, reverberating from the lofty ceiling. Her stutter weakened as her song progressed, until it fell away all together. Hours could have passed, and I would not have felt them.

Adukeh sang first of my anointing: the day of the Children's Palace fire. She trilled to portray the screams of terrified candidates, and thrummed her fingers on the gourd, imitating the crackle of flames as I pulled Dayo to safety.

She pounded the drum on both sides, painting the din and chaos of the crowd as I revoked Thaddace's Unity Edict in every language.

She rocked, groaned, and chanted, reenacting my ride from Sagimsan, my body broken and stained with blood, the crack of the Imperial Hall doors bursting open as I ordered the Treaty to stop. Then at last, she finished— beating stick falling to her side, hips swaying to a stop.

No one was laughing now.

The courtiers stood agape, as though in a trance, and Adukeh knelt on the carpet, offering up her drum to me with both shaking hands. She said again, "I do not t–tell a lie."

My first impulse was to kneel with her. I wanted to clutch this girl to my chest, to steal every day of terror and abuse she'd ever had, hurling the memories into oblivion. The years in that mine had . . . *done* something to her— something unspeakable, and I would have known it even without the bruised marks on her forehead.

Adukeh sang with a skill too familiar with grief. For this child, evil was not the monster of a cookfire tale, but an intimate, constant friend.

But I did not hold her. Instead I kept my face solemn, and wordlessly unclasped a gleaming coral necklace from my throat. "Rise, Adukeh," I said, placing the necklace over her head, "akorin to the Empress Redemptor."

The girl froze, eyes wide as moons . . . and then she flashed a grin so radiant, it could have rivaled the power of my obabirin mask. A rush as heady as honeywine filled my head, nearly toppling me with relief.

I had helped someone as empress. I had *fixed* something— changed a life for the better. Self-doubt had itched on my shoulders, a mantle so constant, I hadn't noticed until it lifted. I savored the brief euphoria, immediately craving more. If I helped more people, fixed more problems, maybe the ojiji would be appeased. That's what they wanted, wasn't it? And what else was an empress for?

"Take the imperial griot to be fitted for her wardrobe," I said, smirking at Adebimpe. "She'll be staying here, in the Imperial Suite. Oh, and"—I glanced down at Adukeh and winked—"make sure she gets a proper case for that drum."

PART 3

CHAPTER 14

"TWELVE REALMS," I SWORE, HANGING BACK to hide behind Ai Ling. "It just looks so . . . intimate."

A low, sky-blue tent sat near a reflecting pool, perfume wafting lightly from the drapery. White gravel paths and fragrant orange trees dotted the side of Palace Hill. After the Rising, Ai Ling and I had hurried to the Imperial Orchard Garden, where I would hold my first meeting with Min Ja of Songland.

The outdoor gathering had been Ai Ling's idea. She insisted that gardens were more neutral than salons, encouraging friendliness and vulnerability.

Well. I felt vulnerable all right.

Cozy carpets and mudcloth pillows decorated the tent's insides, and brunch waited on carved teak trays, along with pitchers of water and spiked orange punch. The tent could easily have held five people, though we couldn't stand without the canvas grazing our hair. A brazier of kuso-kuso leaves lay unlit, and its presence confused me.

"Wasn't the kuso-kuso for *after* I anoint a council?"

I asked Ai Ling. "To communicate across distance?"

She shrugged. "I thought it could ease sharing your memories, as well."

Foreboding seeped into my stomach. Of course. Kuso-kuso caused a powerful trance state. One could dream several weeks' worth of memories in a single hour of sleep. If I passed on my memories as dreams, the vassal rulers could absorb my life in rapid time . . . and decide whether or not I had earned their love.

"You really do think of everything," I said, and Ai Ling held back the tent flap as I stooped inside.

We sat against the cushions, but before I could touch the food, Ai Ling dove to stop me.

"Wait," she barked. I watched with confusion, then dawning horror as she rushed to seize tiny portions of every dish, then stuff them daintily into her mouth. She chewed, swallowed, held up a hand to wait . . . then spread a close-lipped smile. "All clear, darling."

"Ai Ling," I gasped. "You didn't have to do that. What if—what if you had—"

"I wouldn't have died," she said calmly, sticking her finger in the wooden carafe of punch and licking it before I could stop her. Then, just managing to hide her relief, she poured me a glass. "At least . . . I don't think so. We've been building immunity to poisons since the Children's Palace. And we can't trust the palace servants—what if a noble bribed them? Anyway, better I get sick than you. You've got work to do."

"So do you," I sputtered. "Please, Ai Ling. Don't do that again."

To my surprise, she huffed with offense. "So you're allowed to risk your life for millions of people you barely know, but I can't get a stomachache for my own sister?"

I opened my mouth, then shut it. She was right. Still . . . "What would I have told Dayo if you died?"

"He'd have understood," she said after a pause, her brown gaze soft and serious.

She was right about that too. As I stared at her, I realized for the first time how similar her disposition was to Dayo's. It was hard to tell at first, with his bright-eyed optimism and her sharp political savvy, but whenever Dayo or Ai Ling determined a path to be *right*, however treacherous, they pursued it with unshakeable tenacity. How else could Dayo have kept me at his side all those years, knowing I was destined to kill him?

My appetite had vanished, but I nibbled a fig pastry so Ai Ling's risk wouldn't be in vain. The orange punch sparkled on my tongue, burning as it went down, roiling in my already-nervous stomach.

"Don't worry about Queen Min Ja seeing your memories," Ai Ling said after a moment, sensing my distress through the Ray. "What's it they say in Swana? 'For every field of cattle, a ditch of skeletons.' We all have stories we aren't proud of, Tarisai."

I scowled down at my plate of sweet fried *chin chin*. "But I tried to kill someone."

Ai Ling's jaded smile returned. "This is An-Ileyoba," she pointed out soothingly, reaching to squeeze my knee. "Who hasn't?"

I laughed shortly—and then, as I watched her, a memory slipped from my mind to hers. I jerked my knee away, eyes widening with horror. "Am's Story," I muttered. "I'm sorry. I didn't mean to pry. It's just, you reminded me of—"

"It's all right." She gazed into her chalice of punch. "I was thinking of it too."

I had seen Ai Ling's memory of Dayo's thirteenth birthday party, before he was immune to death.

Amidst mountains of presents and throngs of laughing children, a masked assassin had burst into the Children's Palace playroom.

The intruder flung darts into the necks of our guards. Sanjeet managed to grapple the assassin in a headlock, nearly subduing him, but the man grunted and reached up, fumbling for Sanjeet's neck. Only after three sleep darts did Sanjeet slump heavily to the floor. I rushed the intruder next, hoping to steal his memories, transforming him into a confused husk. But he tossed me aside like a sack of yams. The assassin unsheathed a knife and headed for Dayo, grim with purpose.

Then Ai Ling burst from the crowd of wailing children, balling her slender fists. "You don't want to hurt him," she squeaked, "do you?"

The assassin stopped, staggering back. Ai Ling's suggestion lodged in his body like an arrow. Still he grimaced, shook it off, and advanced.

"You don't want to hurt him," she repeated.

Again he shrugged off the invisible arrow, even more quickly this time. "Oh," he growled, "but I do."

Ai Ling's heart-shaped face blanched. "You don't, because you're a good person. It's beneath you."

The assassin hesitated, then laughed, hoisting her up by the scruff of her candidate tunic and jeering at her with rotting teeth. "You don't know me at all, little girl."

"Fine," she gasped. "You're a bad person, then. The worst. A piece of garbage, a rat who kills children, and . . . and no one will ever love you."

The man staggered back, dropping her. Ai Ling had struck at something the assassin believed already, tripling her Hallow's power. She stared up at him from the ground, tears of pity pooling in her wide-spaced eyes. But she wiped her cheeks and plowed on. "Admit it. No one cares about you. The people who say they do are lying, probably. So why go through all this trouble, when you're going to die alone? You don't want to be here." She glanced at Dayo, who stood frozen and vulnerable behind her. Then she turned back to the intruder and delivered the death blow. "I think . . . you don't want to be anywhere."

Then the whole room watched, dumbstruck, as the assassin nodded, sobbed . . . and plunged the knife into his own stomach.

The next day, Dayo anointed Ai Ling into his council. We had celebrated with a party, but from then on, the other candidates had shivered at the sight of her, covering their ears with whispers of *eviltongue* and *murmurwitch*.

"While we're confessing morbid secrets," Ai Ling told me airily, hair feathered out against the tasseled pillows as she reclined. "I had sex for the first time in a tent just like this one."

"Oh." A piece of braised goat froze on its way to my mouth. "Really? But—when? With whom?" I knew many council siblings had dalliances. But we were constantly together, and our schedules had always been so strict. When would Ai Ling have snuck away for an affair?

"Our last year in the Children's Palace." She stared up at the sky-blue canvas, rolling a tassel thread hard between her fingers until her skin turned white. "His name was Omar. He wasn't a candidate—just one of the temple boys who helped the griot priests during catechism. Goofy smile. Training to be a priest for the Wing, sworn to purity and all that. Anyway, I was impressed, and before we knew it . . . we were sneaking down to the gardens after dark. The sex was boring, really. Messy at first. And painful when he didn't do it right. Mostly, I did it to feel like the empire didn't own me. But I liked him a lot. He smelled too sweet, but in a good way, like incense. And I liked"— she ripped the thread from its tassel—"I liked that he called me *silvertongue* instead of murmurwitch. We got caught, of course. It's not hard to follow a boy who sneaks through the palace gates every night. But when the priests found us in the act, Omar . . . He shoved me away. Shook himself off, and shuddered like I was—was some dirty animal." She gave a hoarse little laugh. "Then he said I forced him to do it."

I gasped. "Ai Ling. The *bastard*."

She shrugged, though the corner of her mouth trembled. "Omar told the priests he couldn't control himself. That I'd put him under some kind of spell, and entrapped him with my *eviltongue wiles*. But I hadn't used my Hallow. Not since that assassin at Dayo's party, years ago. Anyway, I didn't get in trouble, obviously. The priests knew they'd be held responsible if word got out that their acolyte had lain with a sacred Anointed One. But I swore I'd never let a boy get close to me again. Not unless he trusted me completely, with no room for doubt, not even an inch. The kind of person with faith to fill an ocean. And if I found that person . . . nothing else about him would matter." Her eyes met mine. "Nothing."

I said, squeezing her hand and sending a pulse of understanding through the Ray, "I know a boy like that."

"I do too," she whispered. Then she smiled, swabbed a single tear from her eye, and sat up, crisp with composure once more.

The flap to our tent rustled.

Now, Tari darling, Ai Ling Ray-spoke. *Are you ready to show that queen your skeletons?*

CHAPTER 15

WHEN MIN JA'S SILK-SWATHED FORM APPEARED
in the entryway, she nodded stiffly in greeting, then glanced
at the array of treats and cozy hangings, stopping on the
brazier of kuso-kuso leaves.

"You've endeavored to make this painless, I see," the
queen of Songland remarked. Her voice was sharp as usual,
but humor shone in her hooded eyes. "A bit stuffy, though."

With a word and a sweep of her hand, Min Ja summoned
a cool breeze that rustled through the tent. I tried, and
probably failed, not to gape with wonder. I had only seen
Woo In perform wind *sowanhada,* the elemental language
of the Songland royal family.

Behind Min Ja, a second figure entered through the tent
flap: Da Seo, the shy consort I had met at my Peace Banquet.
Vivid moth-wing eyes shone over the mask concealing the
bottom half of her face.

Ai Ling shifted in surprise, glancing at three cups around
the breakfast trays. "Forgive us—we were only expecting
Queen Min Ja."

Min Ja raised an eyebrow. "I am about to do something more intimate with your empress than I'll ever get to do with my consort. And you expect me to send her away?"

"It's fine," Da Seo said, nudging the queen's side with her arm. "It's just for a few hours——"

"No," I said. "Stay, please—both of you." I offered Da Seo my own cup, pouring out a fresh helping of punch. "I know what it's like to face strangers without family."

She accepted, balancing it gracefully on the tips of her forearms. Min Ja helped her sip, gently dabbing the sides of Da Seo's mouth with her silken sleeve. As they sampled the brunch, Ai Ling and I prattled, praising what little we knew of Songlander art and culture until Min Ja put down her chalice, cocking her head with an arch smile. Her gaze was so penetrating, it was hard to believe she was barely ten years older than me. Raybearer or not . . . how could I ever be that confident?

"We both know," she said, "that you aren't here to discuss the finer points of green-glazed Songlander pottery. So . . . why haven't you asked anything about me? We're supposed to 'bond for life,' whatever that means. Aren't you curious?"

"Very," I admitted, sheepish. "Well—what was your family like?"

"Monsters," Min Ja replied. "Madmen, murderers, and cursed fanatics—all of them except for Mother, and even she had her moments. Next question."

I surprised us both by laughing. "Sorry. It's just . . . I'd say my family's about the same."

After an appraising moment, she shared my smile. "Most royal families are broken, though very few have the courage to admit it." Her gaze turned shrewd. "Is it true your uncle tried to kill your mother?"

"You're about to find out." I gestured stiffly at the kuso-kuso. "You said it was my turn to ask the questions."

"Testy," observed Min Ja, though her eyes twinkled. "I admire you, I think. I was determined not to. But you remind me of my favorite sister who was sent away—married off, when I was young. She never let anyone disrespect her."

"Thank you," I said, taken aback. "Well—I like you too. Woo In always spoke highly of his 'fierce big sister.' You can be yourself on my council. No diplomacy—nothing hidden."

Min Ja's merriment faded sharply. "Be careful what you wish for, Empress. Not everyone who gets to know me likes what they see."

"If they don't, they are fools," chirped Da Seo, jumping into the conversation with sudden gusto. "Lady Empress, don't listen to Min Ja. I know you've heard the rumors; she's only ever done what was necessary. Her brothers are a pack of beasts. She has nothing to apologize for—"

"Easy, Da Seo," Min Ja scolded gently, a blush rising to her cheeks. "You'll scare the Empress and High Ambassador."

Da Seo's nose crinkled above her mask. "I just think you should tell them, that's all," she mumbled. "Before they hear the story from someone else."

"Well?" the queen asked after a moment, staring coolly at me. "Have you heard?"

I gulped. "I'm not sure I understand—"

"You know," Min Ja coaxed. "The rumor that I killed six of my brothers in cold blood."

"Oh. Right." I exchanged a look with Ai Ling. Her face was expertly neutral, though she sent a pulse of warning through the Ray. "I don't listen to gossip, Queen Min Ja," I said at last. "So there's no need to worry."

"Well, it's true," Min Ja snapped. "All of it. So if you anoint me to your council, you'll have a murderer in your head for life." She sat back, crossing her arms defiantly, though just for a moment, her hands trembled. "So what's it going to be, Empress? Still want me on your council?"

You can get out of this, Ai Ling Ray-spoke, sipping her punch just a little too loudly. *Just say the word and I'll make an excuse. You don't need this. You don't need her to appease the abiku.*

My heart hammered as I watched the queen. Min Ja sat rigid-backed, tense as a cornered hare.

I remembered the last time I had felt that way: when Sanjeet had stumbled upon me at Enitawa's Quiver, with my hands drenched in Dayo's blood.

"Like I said," I told Min Ja, pouring her another glass of punch. "It's my turn to ask questions. What happened in Songland, Your Majesty?"

Min Ja paused, then tossed back her spiked punch in a single gulp. After glancing at Da Seo for courage, she said stiffly, "I was one of fourteen spoiled children," she said at last. "Born to eight royal wives and concubines. My sisters were all betrothed or married before I turned ten. The same would have happened to me, I suppose . . . if it weren't for my father's twisted sense of humor." She popped a piece of fried chin chin into her mouth, chewing with a tight-lipped smile. "He hated my oldest brother, and so decided to insult him in the cruelest way possible. On his deathbed, Father ordered Mother to pass over seven sons to name me her successor instead. Before then, Father had barely noticed I existed, except when I bothered him to protect Woo In." She played with the trailing silk ties of the pale jacket she wore over her skirt. "My succession was Father's idea of a joke."

"Funny," I quipped. "Mine was my uncle's nightmare." We exchanged a rueful smile. For a moment, the pain of understanding echoed between us.

"Anyway," she continued. "My brother Sungho was livid. He united my other brothers against me—all but Woo In. But you only get one family. I loved them, and I wanted to trust them—" Her voice caught. "So I begged Mother to keep them at court. Allowed them access to my rooms and parties. Then . . ." She trailed off, unable to continue.

Da Seo leaned forward, offering me her brow. "Lady Empress—you can take memories, yes? I will finish the story."

I nodded and touched Da Seo's smooth tan brow.

186

I am in the heart of Eunsan-do Palace, standing on paper one hundred feet long. My feet are bare. I inhale, letting the soft mulberry bark pulp of my canvas press into my heels. Dozens of courtiers fill the palace courtyard, but I have eyes for only one person: the princess, enthroned on her sheltered dais at the head of the tiled yard, resplendent in her pale blue birthday silks.

I grip my brush with tan, strong-fingered hands. The handle is as tall as I am, and the brush as thick as a horse's tail. But I wield it like a third limb, veins coursing with the sheer joy of my calling—my craft. I am handmaiden to Crown Princess Min Ja, and I am the youngest *dalpil-mu*— master calligraphy dancer—in Eunsan-do memory.

I dip my brush in a large vat of pine-soot ink. All the courtiers inhale, breathless in wait for my performance. But I don't move, taking time to perfect my blessing. One wrong stroke, one inauspicious word, and I could curse Min Ja with bad luck for the rest of the year. So I wait until I am ready . . . then I grip the brush with both hands and hurl ink onto the paper with a satisfying slap. Black droplets scatter across the creamy expanse, but only in the way I wish it to. My white clothes remain pristine, a symbol of my mastery.

I write with the passion of my whole body, standing on tiptoe for the delicate lines, and crouching low for bold, thick characters. My energy in each line is as important as the brushstrokes. I paint respect into the dots, lust into the slants, and pure, arduous devotion into the curling flourishes. The dance takes nearly twenty minutes, and when I am done, I step off of the paper and lift my brush, panting. The black characters glisten in the morning light, gleaming with holy energy. The court applauds, fluttering fans in approval, but I barely notice.

I have written my way across the courtyard to the feet of my princess.

I kneel before her, unable to watch as she reads the brushstrokes. She gasps, then sighs with both awe and confusion. I have written one of the riskiest blessings in a dalpil-mu's arsenal: *soul-sacrifice-life-eternity*, with characters written backward and forward. The words are a binding prophecy: a promise of protection. As long as my words lay unaltered, my princess will be safe . . . though at what cost, none could tell.

Little did I know how soon my blessing would be put to the test.

One courtier applauds louder than the rest: Prince Sungho, Min Ja's oldest brother.

"A toast," he proposes. "To my resplendent sister, our future queen."

He presents Min Ja with a bowl of rice wine, and my heart flips in my chest. Something isn't right. Sungho is charismatic as always, but I see through those long lashes, distrust that pearl-studded smile.

Min Ja lifts the small bowl to her lips.

"No," I shriek, leaping up the dais to yank the bowl from Min Ja's hands. The acrid liquid splashes from the cup onto my face and hands . . . and for the next minute, all I know is pain.

The world drops to white.

When at last I wake, Min Ja's beautiful, tear-streaked face hovers above me. I reach to touch her cheek . . . but nothing happens. I swallow hard in confusion at the bandaged numb weight below my elbows.

"The acid damage was too great," Min Ja whispers. "The healers say they'll need to remove them to avoid infection."

I stumble to her bedroom mirror, off balance because of my newly lifeless hands. Burns disfigure the bottom half of my face, and when I try to move it, my head explodes with pain.

"They will pay," Min Ja sobs, hugging me from behind. "Every last one of them. I will make them *pay*."

Her features are resolute. I believe what my princess says, and feel safe. Night will come soon for her brothers. But one thing too is grimly certain:

I will never dance with my brush again.

"It was all my fault," Min Ja whispered, once I returned from Da Seo's memory. "So I stopped being a docile sister, and transformed into a future queen. I threw another party. Discovered that all my brothers—except Woo In, of course—were in league with Sungho. So I gave them places of honor at my table." Her face took on a dreamy look, and she brushed a loose strand of hair from Da Seo's brow. "I brought concubines from Father's old court; his most talented dancers. They teased Sungho and the others, swaying with their fans, winding like butterflies. In finale, a dancer leaned over each of my brothers for a kiss . . ." Min Ja's voice shook, but her gaze was coldly peaceful. ". . . and slit his throat. They stole Da Seo's words, and so I took their voices as payment. They bled and died before my entire court—and no one ever threatened Da Seo or my throne again."

The queen reclined against the pillows, taking in my and Ai Ling's stunned expressions. "So what's it going to be, Empress? Still want me inside your head?"

I stared, the memory of Da Seo's dance still tingling through my arms, her love and primal devotion hot beneath my skin. Then I retrieved the sputtering oil lamp from its resting place on the breakfast tray, leaned toward the brazier, and lit the kuso-kuso leaves.

"If you'll have me in yours," I said.

Then the four of us joined hands, and for the second time—the cursed saga of Tarisai of Swana began.

CHAPTER 16

THE SMELL OF BURNING KUSO-KUSO LEAVES could stop a charging lion in its tracks, reducing it to a purring lapcat. But the moment that thick, heady scent touched my nostrils, every muscle in my body seized.

I had thought, just for a moment, that it was possible to tell the truth. That Min Ja might understand. But now, as my mind raced through its sordid collection of my weakest moments . . . I knew I was asking the impossible. The queen might be a killer, but at least her victims were monsters. When I had hurt Dayo, he had been innocent—more so than anyone. He had barely survived, and from there my body count only grew. Olugbade. Thaddace. Somehow, even the abiku massacre at Ebujo Temple felt like my fault.

And my motivations? My brave, noble reason for sticking a dagger in my oldest friend, and for betraying a secret that had killed both an emperor and a High Lord Judge?

A pat on the head from my mother. A chance to see her *smile*.

I couldn't show Min Ja my story. So instead, when the

kuso-kuso smoke filled the airy tent, curling around us in green tendrils . . . I held my breath. I measured each one, inhaling in slow, shallow gasps as the others took deep breaths, slumping in a blank-stared trance. Eventually, my shoulders relaxed too, but as my vision slipped into a dream, my will remained lucid.

The first rush of memories were my days at Bhekina House. My mind skimmed across the first seven years, which were hazy and imprecise—studying for Mother, waiting for Mother, performing for a lovely face that always tutted *no, not enough, what a shame.* Distantly, I sensed Ai Ling, Min Ja, and Da Seo possessing each memory. Under the influence of the kuso-kuso, they had turned into my shadow-selves, and beneath that pale blue tent, four Tarisais sat instead of one.

In the fog of my childhood, some memories glowed clear—crystalline stars against a vast, murky sky. In unfaded color and full volume sound, we relived the night I first met Melu of Swana.

After this memory, the story would curdle, growing sour and grim. My seven-year-old self would develop an irrational faith in The Lady's protection. That little girl would spiral into self-destruction, hurling herself into firepits and poisoning herself with spiders, marked every cheated death as proof that her mother loved her.

I winced, sick with repulsion. Had I really been that pathetic? What would Min Ja think of me? Someone as self-assured as the queen of Songland could never have been so desperate for a mother's attention.

Min Ja stirred, falling partially out of the trance as my focus wavered. "Tarisai?" she asked, words slurred by the kuso-kuso. "Are we still in your childhood?"

"Yes," I mumbled, and scrambled for control of my mind's helm. Like a master sailor, I nudged our ship slightly off course, veering around entire months of my childhood. When I relinquished control, the four Tarisais had arrived at the Children's Palace. There—jagged rocks avoided. No harm done.

But as soon as I relaxed, another impossible memory arose: the first time I had met Dayo.

My eleven-year-old self had transformed into a demon, red rage blinding her vision. I had wanted to hurt him. To *end* him. I had taken one look at his kind, dark face and breathed *Kill—kill—kill* . . .

No, I hadn't.

I hadn't done any of that.

I seized the helm again, only this time I was not veering around rocks. I was charting a fresh, new course, skimming over the water with a healer's scalpel, beating the waves into smooth, sparkling glass.

Now, when my eleven-year-old self met Dayo, her mind was undivided. She was pure and simple-hearted, brimming with innocent love. This girl had no loyalty to her murderess of a mother. She did not wonder, even once, if The Lady was right, and that boy might deserve to die. Instead, she vowed to free herself from The Lady's curse, and to protect Aritsar's prince for as long as it took.

Sweat beaded on my forehead with effort. When at last the brazier cooled, my shoulders sagged with exhaustion. The smoke in the tent had thinned as the kuso-kuso fumes wore off, and when the others roused and smiled at me dazedly, I smiled back, burying the guilt that weighed in my stomach.

I hadn't lied. Not really. I *had* fallen in love with Dayo at the Children's Palace, and eventually decided against The Lady's wishes. So what if it hadn't happened right away? I had still shown Min Ja my true self. My *truest self.*

The queen blinked and cocked her head. "Well?" she asked. "Do I love you yet?"

"You tell me," I said, smiling nervously.

Ai Ling suggested that we try the Ray, and when the queen shrugged her consent, I summoned on the heat in my chest, concentrating on Min Ja. She stiffened. Gasped . . .

And doubled over on the tent floor, retching, fists pressed to her temples.

"It hurts," she rasped. "Make it stop. Am's Story, make it *stop.*"

I severed the beam immediately, biting my fingernails in horror. "Sorry. I'm sorry. I should have warned you; it hurts when you're not ready. I didn't mean to . . ."

Da Seo was cradling the queen in her lap, whispering into her hair and staring at me with wary confusion. "I think we're done for today, Lady Empress."

"Of course." I bobbed my head. "We'll—um—try again tomorrow. Unless the queen isn't up for it."

"I'm fine," Min Ja said, wincing as she sat back up. "Am knows I've survived worse than a headache. But I won't be trying *that* again until we've seen more memories." She shook her head, as if clearing a fog. "How many years was that, anyway?"

"About twelve?" I guessed. "Give or take. We skipped around a bit."

"I'm trying to make sense of it," Da Seo murmured. "We lived through your entire childhood at Bhekina House. Even your babyhood. Still . . . I don't remember what it was like to be you as a baby."

I shrugged. "Neither do I."

"But you gave me those memories," she insisted. "I felt them, somehow, because my mind—your mind—was shaped by that period of time. Am's Story, I sound mad."

"No," Ai Ling said. "That makes sense. I've heard the mind never truly forgets anything. It only loses its ability to retrieve what it knows."

I frowned. "So I could pass on memories I don't even remember?"

"It's possible. Think of memories as books, and the brain as a library. You can only reach the books on the shelves closest to you. But that doesn't mean the other ones aren't there. And the knowledge from each book shapes how you think, even if you don't remember the books themselves." She paused, considering. "Maybe that's why you were able to pass on some parts of your childhood in a matter of minutes, while more recent years took hours. It's the difference between summarizing a scroll and reading every word."

I chewed my lip. How many unflattering entries had I unwittingly passed on to Min Ja? Perhaps that was why the Ray hadn't worked—my unconscious memories might have betrayed my monstrous nature, even if my conscious memories hadn't. And I couldn't let that happen. Min Ja's love depended on her thinking well of me. So next time . . .

I would simply have to take more control.

Nights later, I dreamed Sanjeet.

Not *of* him, but him directly, appearing in the nebulous ether of our sleeping minds, united across miles through the Ray.

I hadn't meant to. Dayo, Ai Ling, and I always slept with kuso-kuso under our tongues, hoping to connect with our distant siblings, and alleviate their council sickness from afar. I visited Kirah most often, nudging at the corners of her mind until she recognized my presence. Then we would dream together, suspended in her vivid thoughts for hours. Sometimes she reenacted her adventures for me, conjuring up the golden Blessid Valley dunes, where she currently hunted for riled-up alagbato—or the Great Moving City of Katsephut-Omar, which she had chased for days, hoping to catch her estranged family's caravan. Tonight, I had dropped eagerly asleep, hoping to see her again. But before

I lost consciousness, I must have spared a passing thought to someone else . . .

Because I woke in a crystalline garden hedged in cardamom and rosebushes. In the midst of trees covered in sparkling amber bark, Sanjeet's broad form sat hunched on a bench, faced away from me, while he plucked forlornly at a flower that appeared to be made of rubies.

Once I realized my mistake, I backed away, attempting to fall out of his mind, but he heard my footsteps on the silken grass. His tea-colored eyes met mine, froze . . . and then dimmed.

"You're not real," he said.

I blinked. "What?"

"For council members to unite in dreams," he said slowly, "they have to be thinking of each other at the same time. And she avoids thinking of me. So you're not really her." He laughed ruefully, turning back to the flower. "Just a figment of my imagination."

My heart twinged. I shifted my feet in the unnatural grass, considered telling him the truth. But instead I asked, "How do you know she isn't thinking of you?"

"Why would she?" he asked. "I left." His pain radiated through the air like weather, dewy teardrops sprouting on each plant. "I did the same thing her mother did. The moment she insisted on being herself, and nothing else—I disappeared."

"You could come back," I suggested, fighting the pain quickly stopping up my throat. "I know she can be . . .

difficult, sometimes, but she would rather have you there than gone—"

"I always wanted to bring her here." He stood, gazing wistfully around the shimmering clearing. "The enchanted Royal Garden of Vhraipur, in the heart of Dhyrma. Amah used to bring me here as a boy. Gems, silk, precious stones as far as the eye can see. You'd think thieves would help themselves. But if anyone tries to steal a bud out of its natural habitat"—he snapped the ruby rose from its stem, and the blossom crumbled instantly to dust—"it ceases to be."

"Jeet." I crossed the garden in two strides, seizing his arm with my insubstantial hand. "I'm really here—well. Not *here*—you know what I mean. But it's really me."

At my touch, he trembled, pupils dilating with grief and wonder. "Tar," he breathed, gathering me close. His dream self did not smell of anything, but I could feel his heartbeat, hammering fast against mine. "There's something you should know," he said, drawing back to cup my cheek. "I've searched for alagbatos. No signs. That's good; it means whatever you're doing is holding them off. But when I tried to find the new opening to the Underworld, stories kept cropping up. Leads about your ojiji. Something's going on, Tar. Something—"

Immediately a gush of wind swept me off the ground, and the treble cries of children filled my ears.

Sanjeet left you! Hurt you. He's trying to keep you from saving future Redemptors, keep you all to himself. Don't listen to him. Don'tlistenDon'tlistenDon'tlisten—

I fought and kicked, reeling with surprise. Until now, the ojiji had mostly left me alone when I slept and united with my siblings. They had never interfered with a dream before.

Sanjeet yelled after me, reaching desperately for the sky. His voice grew fainter with every word. "Ojiji . . . across Aritsar . . . noble families . . . danger. Please, Tar, be care—"

But then I was back in the Imperial Suite, jolting upright and covered with sweat. I snatched another kuso-kuso leaf from my nightstand, desperate to fall back asleep. But whenever I tried to connect with Sanjeet again, the ojiji were there, shrieking, crying, filling my head until I had no choice but to wake. At last, I gave up, collapsing on my back with exhaustion.

If he wanted to help you, breathed the child chorus, as this time I drifted into dreamless sleep—*then he shouldn't have left.*

Do more, Empress Redemptor. Do more.

You are alone.

CHAPTER 17

WEEKS PASSED BY IN A BLUR. I MET WITH MIN JA and Da Seo every morning in the sky-blue tent, chatting companionably over breakfast before inhaling kuso-kuso and succumbing to my coursing stream of memories. After my body adjusted to the daily trances, I began to have sessions in the evenings as well, with Chief Uriyah of Blessid Valley, and then with young King Ji Huan of Moreyao. I grew more adept at uprooting the barbs in my mind's garden, tearing out unflattering memories and replacing them with neat, manicured blooms.

In this version of my story, the one I showed the rulers, I had not *chosen* to erase my own memories, selfishly joining Dayo's council even though I had known it would put him in danger. No . . . my memories had vanished on their own. A traumatic side effect of the Children's Palace fire. A tragic injury—entirely out of my control. And I hadn't betrayed Thaddace's secret to The Lady. In fact, I hadn't known of Thaddace and Mbali's affair at all. His choice to save Mbali over the emperor had shocked me as much as anyone.

Most importantly: In this version of my story, I had no memory of stabbing Ekundayo Kunleo.

I had woken above his body, yes. And his blood had been on my hands. But I didn't remember it happening. I had been in a trance the whole time; a mindless pawn, waking from a horrible dream . . . not a monster who had lured him to Enitawa's Quiver, lucid, calculating, and coldly determined.

I told myself I was being fair. I didn't avoid *every* uncomfortable memory, after all. I let Min Ja see my failure to protect Ye Eun, my grief over the Unity Edict, and my struggle to accept my complicated Kunleo lineage. I even shared intimate moments between me and Sanjeet—my pain at his distrust after Enitawa's Quiver, and my lust for his touch, even as I feared hurting him.

Chief Uriyah's brow knit disapprovingly when he learned how I rebelled against the last emperor, and Ji Huan's cheeks flushed at my steamier memories with Sanjeet . . . but the rulers and I grew closer. Min Ja claimed to dream in my voice. Uriyah smiled, gravely but paternally, whenever we passed each other in the palace hallways. Ji Huan invited me for shy games of checkers in his private villa.

Still—whenever I tried the Ray, the rulers collapsed in pain. They had grown to respect me. Like me, even. But despite the hours we swayed in that tent, our minds suspended in the musk of kuso-kuso . . . the warm affection of the three rulers did not, even once, spark into love.

The ojiji scolded me as usual, flaying me with headaches,

ordering me to *do more*, and scolding me not to give up.

Earn the trust of the rulers, they chanted. *You will not be happy until you do. Be the empress Aritsar needs you to be.*

My stomach churned when I remembered what the first ojiji had said—the boy who had murdered Thaddace: *For our purposes, your image must remain unsullied. You must retain the trust of the Arit populace.*

What purpose, I wondered, was that?

As the days blended together, and my headaches intensified, I stopped wondering, and did instead what it always took to quiet the voices: I kept my head down, beat myself with righteous guilt, and worked harder.

My progress with one ruler crept along more slowly than all the rest combined. Zuri of Djbanti had missed four invitations to my sky-blue tent in the palace gardens. At first, I simply assumed he despised me as the other nobles did. Perhaps, I thought worriedly, he was as fickle as he was empty-headed, and had changed his mind about getting anointed.

Yet instead of returning to his home realm, the king remained at court: a phantom in the corridors, and a perfumed shadow at the edge of my thoughts. He appeared often at banquets, where he made a drunken show, but was mysteriously absent whenever I tried to visit his villa. I felt his eyes on me often when I held court in the Imperial Hall, a piercing gaze at odds with his pretty, vapid smile.

Only once did I dare approach Zuri in public. I came upon him one morning in the palace gardens, alone in a fragrant rosemary hedge maze. He saw me before I saw him.

I squirmed, wondering how long he'd been watching me.

The curving rosemary walls were short, barely coming up to Zuri's dark, tapered waist. Lush blossoms and small, gold-tipped onyx statues dotted the maze, making Zuri appear as a giant. His signature gold cuff glinted on his arm, and he smirked when I noticed him, raising his hands in mock surrender.

"That's quite a scowl, Tarisai. What in the Twelve Realms have I done to deserve it?"

"It's Lady Empress to you," I said. "And you've been ignoring my invitations. Why?"

He watched me for a moment with that inscrutable, thick-lashed gaze, making my cheeks grow warm in the interim. "I am not fond of kuso-kuso," he said at last. "And while I'd love to peek into that ravishing head of yours, I'm much less eager to have you see in mine."

I raised an eyebrow. "That's hypocritical."

"Very." He flashed that flawless smile. "Also, I was curious if you would force me to meet with you. Was looking forward to it, actually."

"Force you?" I echoed, horrified. "Why would I do that? The whole point of accepting the Ray is doing it willingly."

"Shame," he said, cocking his head. "I hate it when power goes to waste."

His twinkling eyes grated on my nerves. "Why do you always speak in riddles?" I demanded. "Why not just say what you mean? I'm getting sick of it. If you plan to let me anoint you, we'll be in each other's heads soon enough. So you might as well be honest now."

I regretted the words immediately. Suppose my anger repelled him? I still needed him on my council.

But to my surprise, at my outburst, his features shone with pleasure. He leaned over the short hedge, closing the distance between us. I tensed but did not move away.

Why in Am's name did he have to smell *so* good?

"Giving orders suits you, Lady Empress," he said. "You should do it more often."

"Another riddle," I droned.

"No. A compliment." He paused, considering me again. "You've asked me to speak plainly, and so I will. You have wasted your time at An-Ileyoba."

I recoiled. "Excuse me?"

"You've been empress for two months. Three, if we're counting since Olugbade's death. And you've yet to truly accomplish anything. You have more potential than all the monarchs put together. So why do you squander it?"

"Squander?" I sputtered. "Between drowning in court sessions and trying not to get *assassinated*, I've spent every waking minute trying to form my council. You know, so the continent doesn't get destroyed in a supernatural *war*? Is your head filled with mancala beans?"

He laughed appreciatively, then grew solemn. "Let's say you succeed in forming your council. When you travel to the Underworld—less than two years from now—you will almost certainly die. When that happens, your sole legacy will be that you temporarily united a dozen rulers. Are you content with that?"

Ice chilled my veins. He had said nothing I didn't know already. I knew how dangerous my Underworld mission was. But Zuri was the first to say it with such brutal plainness:

You will almost certainly die.

I had promised Dayo I would find a way to survive. Woo In had managed it, after all, and so had Ye Eun. But thousands upon thousands of Redemptors hadn't. And as stubbornly as I clung to hope, by any measure of probability . . . Zuri was right.

Still, I lifted my chin. "You've forgotten the terms of my treaty with the abiku," I told him. "My journey to the Underworld will end all Redemptor sacrifices, whether I survive or not. Millions of children growing to adulthood, instead of being slaughtered for peace—that will be my legacy. So yes, I'm *content* with that."

His eyes shaded with an emotion I couldn't name—something between frustration and admiration. Still he said nothing, only bending in an ironic bow of defeat.

His accusation still bothered me. "I've done more than form a council, you know," I added in an aloof tone. "I've been planning changes for the empire. A redistribution of resources—the largest in Arit history."

"Ah, yes," he said, features shining. "Your famous Pinnacle. Tell me . . . how do you intend to make the nobles give up those resources without a fight?"

He leaned over the hedge even closer—but this time the movement seemed unconscious, as if his attraction was earnest. I moved back, stiffly.

"I have a better question," I said, crossing my arms. "Why do the nobles in Djbanti hoard wealth? Your kingdom has some of the most abundant natural resources in the empire. Yet the majority of your people live in poverty."

For the first time, King Zuri looked uncomfortable. His earnest expression dissipated, replaced by the vapid mask he usually wore. "You'll have to ask my warlords," he drawled, waving a dismissive hand. "They're the ones who run my country. In fact," he said, giving me a sidelong glance. "Why don't you hold the Pinnacle in Djbanti? My family castle is located directly next to an imperial tannery. Game pelts are one of Djbanti's greatest exports. My warlords punish all peasants who poach on crown land—even those who hunt to feed their families. Seems fitting to hold your Pinnacle at the heart of injustice."

Suspicion narrowed my eyes . . . but I considered. Why *not* have the Pinnacle at Zuri's castle? Djbanti was a more central continent location than coastal Oluwan, so the nobles could travel there more easily.

"Fine," I said. "But don't expect me to go easy on your warlords. I know they hate my edict. All the nobles do, and the empire's too big for me to watch them all—I can't be sure they'll obey it. But I'm working on a strategy to make them cooperate. And if all goes well, I'll announce it at the Pinnacle." I smiled smugly. "Not bad for *squandered time*, I think."

"No," Zuri replied, his tone unnervingly soft. "Not bad at all."

I shifted my feet in the grass. "Enough for you to finally show up when I invite you?"

He smiled strangely, looking at me with familiar fondness—as though recalling a memory. "Believe me, Lady Empress," he said. "The moment you untap your full potential . . . your wish is my command."

CHAPTER 18

"ODODO THE HUNTER, UKPOPO, UKPOPO,
more handsome than princes; aheh, no lie!"

Adukeh, the former quarry girl who now served as my akorin, trilled in a melodramatic soprano as morning light streamed into the Imperial Bedchamber. She had christened Kameron's soot-black panther cub Ododo, and Dayo laughed as she danced with the animal, gyrating around the room.

"He'll charm you to pieces, a-bembem, a-bembem,
Unless you're a mouse; I tell you, no lie!"

Adukeh sashayed toward the sleeping dais, where Dayo and I sat cross-legged, awaiting this month's Rising. The twelve-year-old girl was officially the most cheerful person of the Imperial Suite. That wasn't saying much, of course, since only Dayo and I were left. Sanjeet, Kirah, and the rest of my council siblings had been gone for a month. Even Ai Ling had taken her leave to Moreyao, searching her home realm's rivers and lakes for an alagbato threatening to flood the villages. Between my pain at their absence, my ongoing failure to anoint a council, and the pressure of planning a

Pinnacle, few distractions cheered me up, even Adukeh's enthusiasm.

Some days, the only real exhilaration I felt was when those ghostly apparitions stared down at me, sending thrills along my spine of guilt and determination as they chanted:

Should have saved us. Should have saved us. Pay for our lives.

More and more, my soul seemed to hover with those grim-faced children, drifting through each day in hollow discontent. At night, I shared a pallet with Dayo, lulled to sleep by our synced breath—but I stopped trying to visit Sanjeet. Stopped visiting Kirah, and all the rest of my council siblings. I missed them terribly.

But I knew that during the day, I could focus more, work harder . . . if I just stopped dreaming altogether.

Do more. Do more.

Adukeh danced again by our dais. This time when she passed, the purple scar marring her face soured my stomach with rage.

Our empire had done this to her. Greed had caused that accident in the mines—and apathy, shown by bystanders like Sanjeet and my council siblings, too jaded to imagine a better tomorrow.

You are alone.

I inhaled. Exhaled, suspended in a bath of cold clarity. My council siblings couldn't help me. Neither could millions of others in this empire, blind to any problem beyond their social spheres. I couldn't blame them for not seeing what I saw. The ojiji, those guiding voices in my head, had made it clear.

And if only one person saw the systems—the brush-strokes, the tiny actions forming a mural of injustice—then *that* person was responsible. She had to do something. She had to fix it.

If the world didn't care about justice, then I would simply have to care enough for all of them.

"I could heal you," I said abruptly, interrupting Adukeh's song.

The girl stopped midverse, dropping Ododo. Her beaded cornrows clacked as she tilted her head in confusion. "Lady Empress?"

"I could heal you," I repeated. "So why won't you let me?"

Adukeh avoided my gaze, chewing her lip.

I touched the girl's blotchy forehead, my fingers itching to *do*, to *fix* something. "I could make the bad thoughts go away," I told her. The palace healers had determined that Adukeh's wounds were more than physical. "I think it would help, Adukeh. The trauma of your memories is hurting you. It's probably causing your stammer. You could feel so much better."

Adukeh stiffened beneath my touch, clearly struggling not to recoil. I sighed and released her, and she backed away, shaking her head.

"Ap-pologies, Lady Empress. I d-don't mean to b-be ungrateful. B-But—but—" She scowled at her feet. "D-Don't take my m-memories. P-Please. N-Not ever."

"It wouldn't be all of them, Adukeh. Just the bad ones."

"N–No!" She pressed her lips together. "B–Begging your pardon, Lady Empress."

I leaned back, frowning. "But you could have your voice back."

She clutched her grandmother's drum. "B–But . . . what good is a v–voice with no st–story to tell?"

Her words gave me pause. I blinked, considering, but before I could internalize what she'd said, the double doors of the bedchamber burst open.

Alive? Tell us!
Aheh, alive and well!

I'm sick of Risings, I Ray-spoke to Dayo as we were primped and serenaded. Colorful geles bobbed around the room as courtiers bickered over the right to tie a sash or polish a slipper. *I'm sick of everything. I'm still no closer to anointing my own council, and—* I bit my lip. *I never should have let those rulers into my head.*

Tar . . . are you all right? Dayo's large dark eyes locked on my face, narrowing with concern. *How could you think that? You've already accomplished more than anyone could have dreamed. Chief Uriyah has grown to like you, and that's saying something. Back in Blessid Valley, I hear he's called Uri the Droner. Not even his own grandchildren make him smile as often as you.*

"But it's not enough!" I said aloud, ignoring the confused glances of courtiers. My head was pounding— the light streaming through my bedroom windows sent daggers of pain behind my eyes. "Those rulers have to love me, or this is all pointless. I'm running out of things to show them, Dayo. I've inhaled so much kuso-kuso that my urine is turning green, and I'm fed up, and it doesn't help that I can't get a *moment* of peace and quiet in this place—"

The entire bedchamber fell silent, and only then did I realize I was yelling. The flock of courtiers, attendants, and children froze in place, exchanging looks.

I winced. "Apologies." I flashed a terse smile. "Too much pepper stew at breakfast."

Nervous laughter rippled through the room. Slowly, the courtiers resumed their chants and bickering. But Dayo chewed his lip with concern.

You aren't well, he Ray-spoke. *Tar . . . what's going on? Is it the ojiji again? We should take you to a priest. A shaman healer.*

A sea of small, dirt-smeared faces swam in the air above him.

Don't tell him. He doesn't understand. And he's busy; you're enough of a burden already. Don't tell him. Don'ttellDon'ttellDon'ttell . . .

I swallowed hard. If I told Dayo how often I now saw the ojiji, he would beg me to rest. To stop my sessions with the vassal rulers, my preparations for the Pinnacle. And if I slowed down, I wouldn't anoint a council in time for the abiku. More children would die.

To rest was to fail.

"I'm fine." I flashed a smile at Dayo, then turned to

212

accept my slippers from a courtier, thus ending the tiresome Rising ceremony. But when I saw who attended me, I recoiled in surprise.

Lady Adebimpe of House Oyega knelt before my dais, holding out my slippers, eyes fixed mutely on the floor. Her once lustrous dark skin had paled, as though she hadn't oiled it in days. The fat had vanished from her face and arms, leaving her sickly, and most alarmingly . . . her head was *bare*.

"Thank Am you are alive and well, Imperial Majesty," she mumbled, without a trace of her trademark irony.

Weeks after the attempt on my life, the number of courtiers attending my Rising had strangely doubled. Despite mocking me in the hallways less than a month ago, now ladies from the highest-ranking houses in Oluwan stumbled over one another to fetch my clothing, glaring at whoever reached me first. Until now, I had ignored this mysterious new attentiveness, chalking it up to some new noble game, a trend that would pass with the reason. But Adebimpe's presence gave me pause.

What, in Am's name, would possess the most fashionable blueblood in An-Ileyoba to attend my Rising without a gele?

"You're in mourning," I observed after a speechless few seconds. Red leather bands adorned Adebimpe's arms. She touched them, nodding woodenly.

"Yes, Lady Empress. You may—have heard. My betrothed died yesterday. An accident. Unexpected."

"Oh. I'm . . . so sorry. What a terrible loss."

She continued to hold out the slippers. I nodded awkwardly, and pity knotted my stomach as she bent over my feet, humbly securing each shoe.

"Um . . . you don't have to be here, you know," I said. "During mourning, it's customary to leave court. Why don't you take a break? Get some rest?"

Adebimpe's pupils dilated. For the first time, she fixed them on mine, and I saw that shadows pooled beneath her eyes. "Are you sending me away, Lady Empress?" she whispered.

"What? No. I just . . ." I noticed then that she was trembling from head to foot, a subtle, constant shiver.

Is she ill? Dayo Ray-spoke with alarm.

I'm not sure, I replied. *It's almost like she's seen a ghost.*

Adebimpe rose quickly to her feet and cleared her throat. "My father sent me here," she stammered. "Not just for the Rising. To serve you, Lady Empress. Lord Oyega would be honored for you to accept me as one of your personal attendants."

My eyebrows shot up to my hairline. The Oyegas had been one of the largest noble families to gain their wealth from the mine at Olojari. Why would they want to gift me anything, let alone a high-ranking lady?

"He makes this offer as an apology," Adebimpe explained, twisting the bangles on her tapered dark arms. "For all of the . . . inconveniences you've faced as empress."

I blinked, speechless.

214

"By inconvenience," I said presently, "do you mean the attempt on my life?"

Adebimpe's mouth opened, then closed, like a fish above water. "I only want to serve," she rasped. "Please, Lady Empress. Consider my request."

She could be trying to get closer to me. To snuff out my life in private, after the failed attempt at the Watching Wall.

But I wasn't so sure. Because when I looked into Adebimpe's eyes, all I saw was cold, primal fear.

"I don't really need more attendants," I told her, after a dazed pause. "And Adebimpe . . . you don't look well."

"I'm fine," she snapped, shrill with desperation. "Truly. I may be thin, but I'm strong enough to serve you, Lady Empress. My family has connections in the garment district. I can fetch you new wrappers. Fold your geles in the latest fashions . . . the other court ladies will despair of your beauty; look—" She seized a starched square of gele cloth from one of my wardrobe baskets. But before she could begin to fold, another blueblood girl snatched the cloth, cradling it to her chest and dancing out of Adebimpe's reach.

"I can do it better, Your Imperial Majesty," she gasped. "Adebimpe's too slow. If you pick me for your retinue, House Ibadan will supply you with jewels from all over the empire—"

"No, me," snarled a girl, wrestling the gele away. "My family's richer. House Olabisi will serve the empress better than Ibadan ever could—"

"Give it back!" Adebimpe screeched at them both, diving for the cloth . . . and too late, I heard the hiss of ripping fabric.

The girls froze, each clutching a piece of bright green gele.

I groaned internally. Whatever unusual game these courtiers were playing, I didn't have time to referee. Not with rulers to anoint, and alagbatos to appease, and a mob of ojiji to satisfy. A new headache began to blossom. Instinctively, my hand flew up to my temple.

And at that small gesture, Adebimpe collapsed to the floor, hyperventilating with sobs.

"Am's Story," I swore, alarmed. "I wasn't about to strike you."

But the lady didn't seem to hear me. She cowered at my feet, holding a woven grass fan in front of her face as if for protection. "Don't look at me," she whimpered. "Please, Lady Empress. Don't curse me with your evil eye. My family begs for forgiveness—"

"What in the Twelve Realms are you talking about?" Dayo asked with a nervous laugh. "Evil eye? Is that the newest silly rumor they're spreading about Tar?"

Adebimpe ignored him, continuing to wail. "We'll never plot against you again, Lady Empress. I swear. House Tunji was foolish to hire the Jujoka. My family severed my engagement to Banjoko Tunji as soon as we knew. We were barely involved, truly. I . . . I know we should have warned you, but it's over now. No more plots. We swear—"

My blood ran cold. *Jujoka*. Adebimpe had named that secret guild of assassins—the one Captain Bunmi had held responsible for the attempt on my life.

Adebimpe reached out a shaking, bony hand, attempting to touch the hem of my wrapper, but recoiled when one of my Guard warriors reached for his weapon.

"You don't have to keep hurting us, Lady Empress," she whispered. "We've learned our lesson. Banjoko's death was punishment enough . . . But when the others started disappearing—Lord Oyelana of House Ibadan, Lady Doyin of House Silva—*all three heirs* of House Ayodeji . . . we knew we had to make amends. That you h-hear everything. That whatever we say, even in secret . . . your s-servants are in the ground. Listening."

My servants. Instantly I was back at the Watching Wall, frozen as that pack of dirt-caked creatures scaled the high-rise walls. The ojiji appeared to me often, as ghosts, but had only assumed corporeal form twice—during the Emperor's Walk and at Thaddace's murder. Slowly, I remembered flashes of Sanjeet's warning in the dream.

Ojiji—noble families—danger.

I had thought the danger was for me. But I had not been the ojiji's target.

"The creatures ripped my fiancé limb from limb," Adebimpe said, staring in the distance at something only she could see. "My strong Banjoko. He—he was training in spearwork in the garden when those . . . things . . . came up from the ground. Children. Clawing through the dirt like beasts. They were gone as quickly as they came. And within days, any other courtier who had dared plot against you—even casually, or as a passing joke . . . they were gone too."

Slowly, every other blueblood in the chamber sank to their knees, babbling as they pressed their brows to the floor.

Forgive us, Lady Empress . . . my family had nothing to do with it . . . we'll make amends. More riches than you could ever . . . promise, just let us . . . don't take my brothers. They're all I have—

I pressed my fists to my pounding forehead, leaning against a wall for support. "You're dismissed," I rasped. "All of you."

If they heard me, they did not react, continuing to beg and wail.

"Please be quiet," I groaned, and when that didn't work, anger surged through me. "*I said be quiet!*"

My mask thrummed with heat, and the room fell deathly still. Breathing hard, I regained my balance, staring down at the crown of dumbstruck ladies.

"Adebimpe," I said, my voice still resonant with power, "if you are to attend me, you must change your reputation at court. No more tricks. No more coalitions with other bullies. Instead . . ." I sighed, gazing at the trembling girls behind her. "Find the weakest players at court. The ones that are poor, or plain, or unpopular. Lift them up, just because you can. For Am's sake—it shouldn't be so hard to be *kind* now and then. Can you handle that, Adebimpe?"

She nodded woodenly, as if in a trance. The mask on my chest cooled.

"Then you may attend me," I said. "But for now . . . you are all dismissed. I need to rest."

Reluctantly, the courtiers wobbled to their feet, backing out of the room in a hushed exodus. But Adebimpe paused at the door, meeting my eyes with a deep, terrible emotion I'd never seen on her before.

Reverence.

"Thank you for letting us cleanse our names, Lady Empress," she said. She sounded almost childlike. "For letting us please the gods. If we ever doubted that you had the Ray before . . ." She swallowed hard. "Well. We don't doubt it now."

CHAPTER 19

"TOO TIGHT, YOUR IMPERIAL MAJESTY?" Adebimpe asked a week later.

We sat side by side on my sleeping dais, as the moon cast silvery light into the bedchamber. For the past hour, her fingers had danced across my scalp, sectioning the hair in neat rows and saturating each tuft with soothing aloe water. Now she applied a fragrant pomade, twisting strands together with blurring speed.

"It's fine," I mumbled. "Thank you."

"Your curl pattern will be exquisite when we take these out," she sighed. Then, to my surprise, she picked up a wooden brush to tidy my edges . . . and snapped the brush, one-handed, in two. She tsked, tossing away the pieces. "Silly me. Sometimes I don't know my own strength."

I turned to stare at her. "Does that happen . . . often?"

She shrugged serenely. "All nobles are strong, Lady Empress. It's in our blood."

She held up an ivory hand mirror. Dozens of damp,

shoulder-length twists bounced around my shoulders, glistening with perfumed oil. "You can wear the twists down tomorrow. We'll hang the ends with ornaments. I found these at the old city market. Much better than those trashy imports I've been seeing around court, if you don't mind my saying, Lady Empress." She opened a wooden box. It was inlaid with ivory, and filled to the brim with colorful wooden beads and cowrie shells.

Didn't she used to hate you? Dayo's voice sounded in my mind. The whole time, he had been hovering nearby on a divan, pretending to read a scroll. There had been no more attempts on my life since the night of the Watching Wall. But Dayo still felt nervous about leaving me alone with bluebloods.

She did, I Ray-spoke back. *But not anymore.*

I examined Adebimpe curiously. Since her nervous collapse on my bedroom floor, she appeared to have transformed completely—no longer the haughty, sneering beauty from the palace corridors, snickering behind her woven grass fan. Instead, I'd caught her floating through the crowd at court gatherings, welcoming shyer noble girls into gossip and conversation. I'd even seen her defend a servant once.

Adebimpe wrapped my hair in a silk scarf and bid me good night. But before she left, I called out, "Adebimpe . . ." I chewed my lip, eyeing her eager face. "You don't have to work so hard to please me, you know. You just lost your fiancé." I thought briefly of how it felt when my mother died—how exhaustion had clouded every day. "I know how it feels to grieve."

She cocked her head. "Lady Empress . . . I didn't *love* my fiancé, you know."

I blinked, taken aback. "Oh. But you seemed so aggrieved. I mean, earlier—"

"Oh, I *used* to think I loved Banjoko," she said, waving a hand. "The blueblood power was strong in his veins. He used to slay hyenas with his bare hands. But the longer I've had to think about it . . . I don't actually think I wanted to marry him." Her eyes rose to mine. "I had wanted to *be* him. Powerful. Untouchable. Like a warrior, or a god. Like . . . *you*, Lady Empress."

I realized then, watching her shining gaze, that Adebimpe's new devotion was genuine. She respected me—thought I was some sort of goddess, not a seventeen-year-old girl who barely knew what she was doing. But I knew I wasn't worthy—the ojiji had made that clear. I had so much more to do. I wasn't enough.

Stop it, I wanted to tell Adebimpe. *Stop looking at me like that.*

But she didn't, continuing to smile at me beatifically as she took her leave, backing out of the room.

"It just feels wrong," I told Dayo. "I mean, obviously I'm glad the nobles aren't trying to kill me anymore. But now they're all terrified. This isn't how I wanted to win."

Dayo joined me on the bed, slinging an arm around me. "Maybe it's like Ai Ling said: Some people only love who they fear." He frowned at the floor. "I didn't agree with most of what my father told me when he was alive. But one thing he said made sense: You don't get to choose why people love you. But what you do with the love you receive . . . that's a choice you make every day."

My head against his, we lay together as the moon sank in the arched windows. In the citrus-scented night breeze, my oil lamps sputtered, sending dancing shadows up the walls.

"I wish Adebimpe *could* be like me," I said suddenly. "I wish I could share my Ray. Or at least a piece of it."

Dayo's brows shot into his hairline. "It's a nice thought," he said slowly. "But would that be wise? Adebimpe and her family tried to kill you."

"My mother tried to kill you," I pointed out, propping myself up on one arm. "So did your father. But the Ray chose them anyway. And the more I learn, the more I think the only decent way to use power is to share it with others. Maybe there shouldn't be rulers—at least, not in the way we think. Maybe emperors—and kings, and queens, and Raybearers—should just be people who make sure power flows to everyone."

"Sounds nice," Dayo said, yawning. "But Ai Ling always says that for an empire to run, someone has to be in charge."

I shot him a measured look. "You quote Ai Ling a lot these days."

He blinked sleepily. "Do I?"

"No matter what we talk about," I said, poking his ribs. "It's always, 'Ai Ling said this,' and 'Ai Ling thinks that . . .'" I cocked my head. "Something you want to tell me, Dayo?"

He chewed on his lip. "Ai Ling gives good advice."

"She's pretty too," I coaxed. "And smart. And more selfless than people give her credit for."

"So what? You're smart and pretty too."

"I saw you at the Peace Banquet," I said, rolling my eyes. "You've never danced with me the way you did with Ai Ling."

He grinned. "That's because you don't dance with anyone."

"Don't change the subject. For Am's sake—" I shoved him, and he snickered. "Just admit you like her! It's obvious, Dayo."

He sighed then and sat up, gazing out the chamber window. "Of course I like Ai Ling," he said. "I love her . . . just like I love you. And Kirah. And Umansa, and all our council. But . . ."

"But what you feel for her is special?"

He was quiet for a long moment. "It'll pass," he said at last, twisting the rings on his fingers. "Like all crushes do. I was in love with Sanjeet when I was little. And with you. But all those feelings changed when I got older. Wiser. And now—"

"Now you're in love with someone else," I said. "And she's just as crazy about you."

He ground the sole of his sandal. "You don't know that."

"She practically told me. And even if she hadn't . . ."

I raised an eyebrow. "Dayo, Ai Ling hides her emotions better than anyone. She has to; that's a High Ambassador's job. But at the Peace Banquet, she refused to hide anything. She wanted to be there, in *your* arms. Wanted the whole world to know how vulnerable you make her. It was beautiful, Dayo."

He brightened, then his dark brow creased, plunging into lines and shadow. I shivered at how much it aged him. "It doesn't matter," he said.

I scoffed. "Why in Am's name not?"

"You know why."

"I know you haven't asked her."

"I can't," Dayo blurted, with a sharpness that surprised me. "She already swore her life away. All of you did. You gave up your home realms. Gave me your *minds*, forever. How could I ask Ai Ling to give up even more? Especially—you know. The one thing everyone in the world wants?"

"Not everyone," I countered. "Not you, and others like you. The world is big, Dayo."

"Mine isn't," he said quietly. "The moment I was born a Raybearer, my world shrank to twelve people. And that was fine. I never thought I'd want more with any of you. Until . . ."

He trailed off, and I paused, considering. "If you don't ask," I said slowly, "you're making the choice for her."

"But what if she says no?" Dayo fidgeted. "Or worse—what if she says *yes*, and then hates me for it?"

"It's like you said," I murmured, reaching to tidy his messy tufts of hair. "We can't control why people love us, Dayo—or how much." I leaned over to kiss his cheek. "We only get to choose what we give in return."

His features remained stony, but before he could reply, a courier appeared at the door, panting, with a message.

"Apologies, your Imperial Majesties," he wheezed. "But the queen of Songland and her consort—well." He came to hand me a note. Min Ja's measured handwriting, ink barely dry, gleamed from the page. "They're leaving."

Wearing nothing but a purple cape over my night shift, I tumbled from a palanquin into the sleepy streets of Ileyoba: the residential district of the nobles and home to the temporary Songlander royal villa. Already the building seemed almost vacated. Servants poured out of the villa with the queen's possessions, loading carts with jeweled chests and silk-swathed baskets.

"In the name of the empress—let me see the queen," I hollered, barreling through lines of servants and flashing my imperial seal. "Please. Just for a minute."

When I burst into their private salon, Min Ja and Da Seo shot surprised, then guilt-stricken looks my way. Sheets covered the furniture. Both the queen and her consort were bundled in dark cloaks, dressed for a lengthy journey.

"We hoped to leave while you slept," Min Ja said, with

her usual bluntness. She gave an apologetic smile. "I do not excel at goodbyes."

"But why?" I panted. "What about getting anointed?"

Min Ja and Da Seo exchanged a meaningful look. "Little Empress," the queen said after a pause, "you don't need us to fulfill your promise to the abiku. And we've been in each other's heads for a month. I have a kingdom to run, and— Let's be honest. If we had enough in common for love, don't you think we would know by now?"

I opened my mouth, then closed it, heart sinking to my sandals. She was right.

At my forlorn expression, Da Seo tutted and came to plant a kiss on my forehead. "Cheer up, Lady Empress. I'm sure you'll woo the others. Any girl who survived riding through twenty-six lodestones can convince the Arit rulers to join a council. And now that we hear you've put your nobles in line, you can count on their support."

I sank despondently onto a sheet-covered divan. "You mean, now that my nobles are afraid I'll kill them."

Min Ja laughed. "In my court, we call that being popular. All hail Tarisai the Reaper: arbiter of death upon haughty nobles."

I smiled half-heartedly. "But I didn't want them to fear me. Not that way. I think I'd rather be hated as a weakling than loved as a monster."

To my surprise, Min Ja's face closed up immediately, and she expelled a short, bitter laugh. "You know," she said, "for all your speeches . . . your sacred Hallows, your magical sprite clouds . . . you really are still little more than a child."

I glared at her, taken aback. "What's that supposed to mean?"

"It means," she said, "that not all of us get to be noble. We don't all get to be the selfless heroine, flitting gracefully through life, adored by all. Some of us get our hands dirty. Some of us . . ." Her voice hitched. "Have scars."

"Min Ja," Da Seo intoned, a gentle reprimand.

Min Ja colored and sucked in a breath. When she released it, her voice was as calm and cool as ever. "Forgive me, Little Empress. That was unfair. I suppose you can't help being a saint, any more than I can help being a viper."

"I'm not a saint, Your Majesty."

"Could have fooled me." She shrugged and sighed. "Look . . . it doesn't matter anymore. We have enjoyed our days here—considerably more so than we expected to. If relations continue to improve between our realms, you may consider me an ally. It is a milestone no other Kunleo has achieved. You should be proud, Tarisai."

But I wasn't proud. I hadn't done enough. Even though I'd fought to give them my best story. Had shielded them from my rough points, my nightmares . . .

Then, with dawning realization, Adukeh's words echoed in my mind, punctuated by her proud, disfigured features.

What good is a voice with no story to tell?

I thought then of how vibrant Ai Ling had looked,

when she had shed her serene High Ambassador mask to dance in Dayo's arms. I thought of when my heart first warmed toward Adebimpe: when she had cowered in the suite, ashy-skinned and without the plainest gele.

In that moment, I had known Adebimpe better than in weeks of her flawless appearances at court.

"Don't go," I told Min Ja and Da Seo, rising to my feet with conviction. "I . . . I think I'm ready to prove I'm not a saint."

I had brought no kuso-kuso leaves, and so this time, Min Ja and Da Seo were wide awake when I fed them my memories. We sat on cushions in Min Ja's parlor, holding hands in a circle as the ugliest scenes from my life played out on an invisible stage.

First, I showed them the firepit.

We are a nine-year-old girl so desperate for her mother's touch, warmth draws her like a moth to a flame. She indulges mad fantasies, giggling at the kitchen fire in Bhekina House. She lets it caress her, imagining human fingers, and speaks to it—*Yes, Mother. I love you too, Mother*—until at last she topples in.

The servants scream prayers to the Storyteller, tossing

water on the fire and sustaining nasty burns as they haul the girl to safety . . .

And she's laughing.

The girl is laughing on the ground, chortling breathlessly as her clothes smolder. She clutches her waist, shuddering, wheezing: *See? I didn't burn. You're all so silly. I didn't burn, because my mother loves me. That means she'll come back. She has to come back.*

Doesn't she?

The girl rocks back and forth. By degrees, her laughter shrills into keening, wrenching sobs. The sound grates on our ears as we bleed into the next memory.

We are eleven now, meeting a doe-eyed prince for the first time. Dayo cowers behind a curtain in the Children's Palace, his dark face the picture of innocence. He smiles, gap-toothed, warming the girl from head to foot with curious affection.

And she wants to kill him.

The fantasy plays out in her head, over and over. First, her hands around his throat. Then his cries of protest, strangled and desperate. Then the light, fading at last from his guileless black eyes.

She recoils, knowing that the fantasy is evil. This boy is a good person, better than she'll ever be. He deserves to live, and so she should leave forever to keep him safe. It would be so easy to fail the Children's Palace tests on purpose. Then she would be sent far away, where she could never hurt him. It's the right thing to do, even though she likes the way he makes her feel. To stay is to actively put him in danger.

But she returns the boy's smile and says, "I'm not going anywhere."

The love-starved girl decides to stay by his side. She chooses to keep herself warm, even at the risk of setting the boy aflame.

At last, the girl is sixteen years old. The wind whips around Enitawa's Quiver, causing the tree's branches to shudder in high moans. The girl, or what is left of her, peels away Dayo's shirt and places her hands on his bare chest. He smiles at her trustingly. A silver dagger swings in a pouch at her side.

The girl wishes that she were an automaton, a mere *ehru* shell, doing its master's bidding. If she were a soulless monster, her betrayal of the prince would mean less. But her conscience is still present—a small vessel in a vast, raging storm, flailing to keep afloat. For the rest of her life, she will wonder if this is a battle her soul might have won. If only she had willed it a little harder, resisted a moment longer.

But instead, the ship slips beneath the waves . . . and the dagger slides into Dayo's stomach.

Min Ja, Da Seo, and I emerged from the memory in a chorus of gasps. Without the calming kuso-kuso, our transition back to the present is violent, and I could see the pain of each memory throbbing behind the queen's eyes.

I bit my lip, face heating with shame. "I'm sorry I wasn't honest before," I told the queen, gaze cast down to the elaborate lotus-patterned rug where we sat. I fidgeted with the tassel of my seat cushion. "I know it's probably too late. But I thought—after all the time you spent, getting to know me . . . I owed you this much, at least."

Min Ja nodded slowly and said nothing. She had wrapped her arms around herself, still shuddering from the grim montage. I winced and stood, backing toward the door.

"I interrupted your packing," I observed, bowing to Min Ja and Da Seo. "So I guess I'll go now. May Am grant you safe journey back to—"

"It gets better, you know," Min Ja interrupted. "The guilt."

We exchanged a long look, sweet in its painful understanding. "I find that a little hard to believe," I said.

"So did I." Min Ja winked ruefully at me. "You're not alone, Tarisai."

It was the first time she had used my name instead of Little Empress. At the word *alone*, I swallowed hard. The chorus of voices reminding me of my guilt, of my inadequacy to solve the empire's injustices, rang always in my ears, just out of hearing. I wished I could believe her. And more than that . . . I wished she would stay.

I looked at the queen's shining braided bun and finely chiseled features, lined with strength and hard-won good humor. I had come to love her, I realized: the fearless big sister with whom I might have shared a mind, even when miles of lodestone travel separated us.

I may not be a saint, Min Ja of Songland, I thought as I turned to exit the room. *But you aren't a viper either. Goodbye, almost-sister.*

I am not so easily gotten rid of, Little Empress.

I froze in the doorway. When I met Min Ja's gaze again, mouth agape, her sharp brown eyes were full of tears. She grinned as the Ray coursed between us, a beam of invisible sunlight, warming us from head to toe. Da Seo jumped at the suddenly crackling air. Realizing what had happened, she gasped with incredulous laughter.

I lost seven *sisters to marriage*, Min Ja Ray-spoke, and then she added aloud: "I will not lose one more to something as immaterial as distance."

CHAPTER 20

JI HUAN OF MOREYAO AND URIYAH OF BLESSID
Valley took longer to adjust to my new memories than Min
Ja and Da Seo, but to my relief and surprise, neither of
them left in disgust.

"So you really just *stabbed* Emperor Ekundayo?" Ji Huan
asked for the fifth time as I helped him fly a pelican-shaped
kite in the palace gardens. "Just stabbed him right there in the
open? Was it hard? Bet it was messy. With loads of blood."

"You saw what happened," I told him, squirming
uncomfortably. "I showed you the memory."

"Yes, but . . ." The young king nearly lost his grip on the
kite strings, eager brown eyes fixed on my face. After I had
shared my unaltered memories, Ji Huan's shyness around
me had evolved into morbid admiration. "It all happened
so fast. Could you show me again? Maybe that fight on
the palace roof too—when you made Anointed Honor
Thaddace kill Emperor Olugbade, and the High Priestess
fell but Woo In saved her. Then that part when you flew
through the sky, and arrows flew everywhere and—"

"No. Ji Huan, those memories weren't fun for me! You felt how much pain I was in. Why would you want to relive that?"

The boy looked sheepish. "I forgot about that part. I'm sorry, Lady Empress."

"It's all right." I sighed, melting at his dejected expression and ruffling his hair. "And we're friends now. Call me Tarisai."

"Sorry, Tarisai." He paused. "It's just— I've never gotten to do anything. At least, not go on adventures, like you. My uncles won't let me go anywhere." He shuffled his silk-slippered feet and cast a furtive look at two men with flowing robes and long, gray beards: the Lord Regents of Moreyao. They sat a short distance away, sipping tea on a blanket, and occasionally casting dour looks at me and Ji Huan.

"They won't even let me fly a kite without supervision," Ji Huan grumbled. "And I can't have friends they don't approve of. They're probably trying to read our lips right now."

I frowned in sympathy. "I used to live in a place like that."

"Bhekina House?"

"Yes." I still wasn't used to how much Ji Huan and the other rulers knew about me. My memories weren't my own anymore. My whole life, or copies of it, floated freely in other people's minds, free to be shaped to their prejudices.

"Even at the Children's Palace, eyes were always watching you," he said. "I know what that's like."

I took in his round innocent features, my former anxiety mirrored there. "Ji Huan, if you join my council, I'll never control whom you talk to, you know. There won't be any tests. No judging. All we have to do is be there for each other. Plus, thanks to Ray-speaking . . ." I tapped his head and winked at him. "We can talk anytime you like. And no one can read our lips."

He brightened. "Can I really tell you anything?"

My mind flashed back to another little boy, peeking out at me from behind a Children's Palace curtain.

You're going to be another one, aren't you? A person I like. A person they take away.

"Anything," I said, placing my hand over his on the kite string. Then, I let the Ray blaze around my ears and sent a message into the crackling beam: *Did I tell you about the time I threatened a Bush-spirit with a stick?*

"Yes," said Ji Huan, "but I want to hear it again, especially the part when you saved Anointed Honor Sanjeet from—" He broke off, realizing what had just happened. "I . . . I . . ."

"You heard me." I sighed. "And I'd much rather show you Bush-spirits than memories of me stabbing people."

Ji Huan dropped the string and pulled me into a hug, then stepped back just as quickly, flushing. The pelican kite escaped, dancing in circles on the wind, then drifting to a dot in the cloudless Oluwan sky.

Someday I'll be free like that, came Ji Huan's voice in my head. *But until then—tell me another story, my Tarisai.*

Uriyah's love for me was more complicated, and not in a way I liked. The old chief reminded me of Olugbade, in that he seemed especially fond of those more ignorant than himself—or at least, those he perceived to be. When I showed him my ugliest flaws, his features took on a paternal glow.

"'The wisest ruler must also be humble,'" he intoned, reaching to raise my downcast chin. "'Take heart, therefore, in your mistakes.'"

We sat together in Uriyah's study, at his villa in the Ileyoba district. Mountains of books and dusty scrolls surrounded us on the musty carpet, smelling vaguely of ink and camel hair.

"Thank you," I told him, swallowing my irritation at being patronized. "I'll certainly give that some th—"

"Cassius Mehedi the Surefooted," he interrupted, stroking his silver-streaked beard. "Ninth treatise, fifth verse. Mehedi's writings on humility are truly illuminating, and were my greatest comfort as a budding young ruler. I should have recommended them to you ages ago," he murmured, whirling around his study and selecting a pile of tomes. He dropped them in my lap, rheumy eyes winking with excitement. "Take these for tonight. I've included Ahwadi the Dune Dweller's verses on filial piety—due to the complex relationship you had with your mother—

and the poetry of Yakov the Wanderer, though I admit his work is elementary. You've read him, of course . . ." At my blank stare, he chuckled indulgently. "Ah. Well, don't be ashamed, child. In fact, I envy you. To be young again, at the very beginning of one's moral journey . . ." He trailed off, blinking at me wistfully. "There's nothing quite like it."

"Er—thank you," I repeated, shifting beneath the teetering pile of books. "But there's a lot I have to get done before my journey to the Underworld. I'm not sure I'll have much time for, um, leisure reading."

"Of course, of course," he said, patting my hand. "I understand completely." But before my shoulders could sag with relief, the chief added, "I'll summarize the texts for you. In particular, I think you'll truly connect with Elenya the Acolyte's musings on the nature of friendship and betrayal. I recall one passage in which she . . ."

My neck pricked with worry. Had I succeeded in giving my memories to Uriyah, only to be saddled with another arduous task? Would he need me to become an expert in philosophy before I could anoint him?

But over the next few days, as I fought to keep my eyelids open through lectures on royal virtue, I soon realized that the rate of my progress meant little to Chief Uriyah. It was my *potential* that enamored him—that chaotic canvas of my life's mistakes, waiting to be molded into a work of art. This would have annoyed me more, if it weren't for Uriyah's boyish joy in teaching. He seemed to crave a project: a willing vessel for his years of pedantic study.

As my headaches progressed, and the chorus of ojiji grew louder in my head, a strange relief enveloped me as I sat in Uriyah's dusty study. I nodded in the right places when he waxed philosophical, and watched his wrinkle-set eyes shine when I quoted a text correctly. Here was one person, at least, who I had not disappointed as an empress. Whose needs I could satisfy with nothing more than a listening ear—and a cup of honeybush tea, shared over the ramblings of dead philosophers.

I would never be as close to Uriyah as I was to Min Ja, or even to Ji Huan. But at the end of one lesson, when I Ray-spoke as an experiment, *Pride is a stumbling block to the young ruler . . .* and Uriyah absentmindedly Ray-spoke back, *Rinel the Goatminder, treatise five, verse twenty*—I was pleased to hear his voice in my head.

I woke hours before dawn, soothed by my Ray-synced breathing with Dayo. His familiar scent of shea butter and fresh linen made me sigh. Where he lay on my shoulder, a tiny pool of drool stained my night shift. I poked his nose fondly.

But as usual, peace lasted only a moment before the ojiji began their song in my head.

You're struggling. You're not enough of an empress. Not enough of a sister. It's why people always leave you. Why Sanjeet left you. Make up for it. Do more. Do more. Should have saved us. Should have cared.

Fever flared between my temples. In my exhaustion, I had long ceased to try to separate the ojiji's truth from their lies. Instead, I plunged into what shut their grating voices up, if only for a while: my work.

I wriggled from Dayo's embrace and padded into the salon, rifling through the chests for a pen and ink. Then I plopped down at my kneeling desk, scribbling furiously. I didn't realize I was talking to myself until a hand pressed my shoulder.

"Tar?" Dayo had roused, and was staring down at me, hair misshapen with sleep, brow creased.

I started. How long had I been sitting here? I glanced around the room. Minutes? Hours? The oil lamp wicks had burned to half their height. Dawn seeped through the salon skylight.

"Tar. Are you all right?"

"I'm fine," I said, my voice breathy and shrill. I beamed up at him. "Better than fine. You know I've been worried about how I'll enforce the new edict. Even if they seem to accept it at the Pinnacle, they know I can't watch them all." I dug through the piles of paper and waved a leaf at him. "Well. I've come up with ideas on how to keep them accountable. We could even enlist that vigilante, the Crocodile, to help us. It's risky, but I think it could work . . ."

"That . . . sounds useful." He squeezed my shoulder. "But why are you working now?"

"Couldn't sleep. Besides, there won't be time during the day."

In three more months, I had anointed seven more rulers: Uxmal of Quetzala, Sadhika of Dhyrma, Danai of Swana, Edwynn of Mewe, Helius of Sparti, Nadrej of Biraslov. After seeing my fraught memories of The Lady, even Beatrix of Nontes developed a perverse maternal affection for me, allowing for an anointing.

Two stripes remained pale on my lioness mask: one for Kwasi of Nyamba and one for Zuri of Djbanti. Apparently I only gained immunities when I anointed members of my empire—when Min Ja accepted my Ray, the stripes had remained as they had before. Redemptor marks covered my skin from toe to collarbone, leaving clear my neck, face, and the palms of my hands alone. Shadows pooled beneath my eyes, and every limb in my body ached with cold. I drifted through each day, a raft on a vast, numb ocean. Only those children's voices—a constant, bracing wind—egged me on.

Do more.

"These days," I said softly, "between Aritsar's mill and quarry workers, my old siblings, and my new ones, I never can decide who needs me more. No matter what I do . . . it feels like I'm betraying someone."

Dayo sat cross-legged beside me. "You aren't replacing our old council, Tar. That's not how love works. Besides," he added a little wryly, "if anyone could use a bigger family, it's us."

I didn't reply. Some topics—like our lack of heirs, with no clear way of getting them—were too heavy to discuss before breakfast.

My heart ached. The suite seemed barren with all our siblings gone. Especially without . . . I banished Sanjeet's face from my mind. That pain too could not be borne on an empty stomach.

He had left nearly four months ago. I heard news of him through reports from his guard captains, but in all that time, he'd sent me nothing, not even letters—until yesterday, when a package arrived at the palace: a long and bulky bundle.

It was an ivory-handled spear: perfectly balanced, with a head of razor-sharp adamant. Old Arit characters glittered on the shaft, in block script that I deciphered with a shiver.

WURAOLA

The name belonged to Enoba's sister—first of the Ray-bearers, though Enoba had stolen her birthright. No one had called me Wuraola since the memory of the Storyteller had possessed me on Mount Sagimsan, hurling my body to sacred ground. The name meant *girl of gold*, girl of sunshine. When I touched the spear's shaft, a wave of regret and longing passed into my skin. The memory of Sanjeet's emotions must have slipped into the spear as he engraved it. Perhaps he'd known they would be more eloquent than a letter.

"I still don't understand why you won't slow down," Dayo sighed, rubbing the back of his neck. "I'm worn out every day just holding court; approving plans that imperial experts assemble for me. But you're inventing new things from scratch. Tar—you've already done so much. More than anyone else could."

"But I'm not finished," I muttered. "I still haven't anointed Zuri, and only Am knows how long that'll take. There's also King Kwasi . . . though I think he'll come around. I just need to do him a favor."

"What's that?"

I smiled tiredly. "I have to take him shopping."

CHAPTER 21

"YOU THINK I'M FRIVOLOUS," THE OLD MAN accused. "A fop."

"Of course not," I said. "It's just, um, itchy. But really—it's beautiful, King Kwasi."

I stood with the portly king of Nyamba in a bustling tailor's stall, where I perched like a peacock on a rotating pedestal. Dressmakers clucked around me, sweat beading on their upper lips as they wrapped me in orange-striped fabric, pinning the excess in looping drapes across my hips.

"You hate it," insisted Kwasi, leaning on his walking stick. His jowls quivered in a pout.

"It's . . . not my usual style," I admitted, and the sulk vanished from Kwasi's features, exchanged for a wheezing giggle.

"Don't mind me, child," he chortled. "I'm just having fun. You should have seen the look on your face!"

I rolled my eyes but couldn't help smiling. The eighty-year-old king's delight in pranks could grow wearisome, but these days, I welcomed any diversion.

"Bring out more samples," Kwasi ordered the dress-makers, clapping his ring-adorned hands. "I believe we are coming close."

"Don't you think we've seen enough fabric today?" I suggested, watching with pity as the dressmakers scrambled. The head tailor, wholly unprepared for a king and an empress to visit in the same afternoon, shrieked orders at her staff and bowed to us so many times, I feared her bright pink gele would topple.

Still, Kwasi shook his head at me, tapping the side of his nose with a wink. "We are not going anywhere," he said, "until you've chosen something interesting. Should we look at the cobalt? The crimson? Or did we see that already? Maybe once more, just to be sure . . ."

I had spent the entire day in Ileyaso, the textile district of Oluwan City, puffing to keep up with the surprisingly nimble ruler. After weeks of absorbing my memories, he refused to try my Ray until I agreed to the outing.

"I cannot possibly love a person until I have seen them select a wardrobe," he had said, and then laughed as though he were joking, though I highly suspected he wasn't.

All the center realms—Oluwan, Swana, Djbanti, and Nyamba—were known for beautiful clothing, but Nyamba took the crown. I'd heard of Nyamban lords going bankrupt trying to follow their country's ever-revolving fashions, and of weavers with divine gifts, like Umansa and his prophetic tapestries.

I had grown fond of Kwasi. His boyish, good-natured

absentmindedness was how I imagined Dayo as an old man, though Dayo barely noticed the clothing on his own back, let alone anyone else's.

"Have I worn you out, child?" Kwasi asked, with real concern. All of a sudden, the shop had gone quiet. The head tailor and her attendants were staring at me on the pedestal, fidgeting with worry.

Then, as though having an out-of-body experience, I realized that I was doubled over, massaging both my temples and moaning.

"Someone fetch a healer," fretted the head tailor.

"No," I insisted. "It'll pass. I'll be fine."

The dressmakers gasped as the Redemptor marks on my skin began to pulse and shift, glowing with blue malevolent light.

A filthy child had appeared in the corner of the shop. I barely jumped—by now, I was used to the apparitions. But the ojiji's visions were growing more intense. They would not let me rest—would never let me be complacent.

Do more, the child repeated. *Justice for us all. Pay the price.* This one appeared to be from Songland, dirt streaking its transparent face.

Guilt weighed like lead in my stomach. I hissed under my breath, "Can't you see I'm trying?"

The child shrugged and disappeared. The marks on my body faded, dull and still again.

I'm crazy, I thought calmly. I am very, very ill. Part of me knew I should tell someone. Perhaps write to Kirah, or

246

confess my visions to Dayo, who grew increasingly worried. But what could they do? And really . . . what did it matter? Once I stepped into the Breach, I would soon cease to feel anything, let alone pain.

I revoked the thought immediately, shocked at myself. I planned to come back from the Underworld. Woo In had managed it, so had Ye Eun. And I had promised Dayo, promised everyone that I would try. Yet the thought remained.

You will almost certainly die.

Over the past few months, I had developed a sinister suspicion about what the ojiji truly wanted. Why they were never satisfied. Why there was always more to *do*, more to *pay for their lives*.

Deep down, I knew they wanted more than justice. They wanted revenge: recompense for the lives already lost—the blood already shed. And the worst part was . . . I didn't blame them.

I wasn't even sure if they were wrong.

Kwasi placed a soothing hand on my arm, rheumy eyes scanning my face. "It's that nasty council sickness, isn't it?"

"No. I don't get the sickness anymore."

This was true—I'd discovered it by accident after visiting Min Ja and Da Seo alone. The symptoms of council sickness had not surfaced—not since I anointed Dayo to my council months ago. Our Rays appeared to have struck a balance inside me, freeing me to travel without a sibling. Part of me felt guilty at how relieved this discovery made me. I loved my council siblings, after all. But in the last few weeks, any activity unrelated to *work*—courting vassal rulers, preparing for the Pinnacle, appeasing the ojiji—made me anxious with impatience.

They are blind, and you are alone. Justice. Justice.

You must care enough for everyone who does not care.

"It's only a headache," I told Kwasi, smiling wanly. "Happens a lot these days."

"I'm not surprised," he chided. "The bags beneath your eyes could carry half a day's shopping. Do you sleep at all, child?"

I avoided his searching gaze. "I'm fine," I said. "Just busy. You know how it is. Court sessions, judge rulings . . ." Trying to appease an army of ojiji ghosts.

"I may be a king," Kwasi replied, "but even I know that rulers can't do everything. Make some time for fun!" He made a sweeping gesture at the colorful fabrics festooned around the shop. At my glazed expression, he grunted. "You think I'm a shallow old fool."

I shook my head. "There's nothing shallow about appreciating beauty."

I liked Kwasi, and wanted to make him happy—so I perused the bolts of fabric, pretending to consider each one. Kwasi made a delighted sound when I stopped at a stack of cloth.

"These are Nyamban textiles," he said proudly. "Woven to reflect one's destiny."

As I touched them, he watched my face, keeping his own neutral. But I had been raised in the Children's Palace—I knew a test when I saw one.

At first, I picked up a colorful fabric with designs that mimicked the weave of a basket. The blocked pattern repeated in sky blue, crisp green, and bold streaks of black. Kwasi made a pleased sound.

"Nwentoma cloth," he sighed. "An excellent choice. And those colors have significance—blue for harmony, green for good health, and black for strength."

I nodded but had already put the cloth down, curiously drawn to a swatch peeking out from beneath the other bolts. I pulled it out, revealing a strange ream of black, white, and metallic gold, tiny hand-etched glyphs blocked together in stark patterns. The longer I watched, the more the symbols seemed to move, congregating in slow revolution around a symbol in the center—a prancing lioness.

"This one," I said immediately.

Kwasi's expression was hard to read. Something like awe . . . and profound, restless fear.

"Adinkra cloth," he said at last. "I am surprised it is sold here. Back home, it is only worn by high priests, or else those burdened with certain gifts—the ability to see other realms and commune with the spirits who live there."

I continued to stare, mouth agape, as the patterns moved for real—converging on the lioness, glyphs covering her body like tiny children until she disappeared. Then I blinked, and the pattern reverted, lioness intact. Kwasi swore softly.

"I have not seen something like that happen in a very long time," he whispered, and I gulped.

"Should I choose something else?"

"Of course not," he said, sucking in a breath. "My child, if there was ever a sign you were made for an outfit . . . that was it."

We paid the head tailor, who promised to visit the palace with my completed garment within the week. Then I turned hopefully to Kwasi. "Well?" I said. "Will you receive my Ray now?"

He gave a sly grin. "Not until we've found you some accessories. A silk sash, perhaps. Or some beaded tassels."

So our Ileyaso odyssey continued, Imperial Guard warriors following patiently behind with our purchases as we shopped our way through the district. When we came to an open-air luxury market of panther and donkey hides, Kwasi stopped to admire a dove-gray pelt, exclaiming at its quality.

Several hides hung on clotheslines between stalls and high-rise buildings. Out of the corner of my eye, I spotted a flash of dark green amidst the motley rows of animal skin. I squinted. Was someone standing on a window ledge?

"Marvelous. Just marvelous," Kwasi gushed, examining a pelt with dappled white spots. "Tarisai, wouldn't this be just the thing for your adinkra?"

I was barely listening. The hairs on the back of my neck stood on end. Heart racing, I swiveled to check on our guards. They stood nearby, armed and calmly scanning the area.

". . . as a trim," Kwasi was saying. "Or a mantle, draped over one shoulder . . ."

I was barely listening. When had I felt this cold foreboding before? A song from a harrowing, moonlit night stole into my memory:

Why, you ask? Why?
The Pelican has spoken!

"Get down," I roared at Kwasi, right before a mob of masked, mounted warriors clattered into the marketplace. Merchants shouted and scrambled for cover, and the Imperial Guards leapt to form a wall around me and Kwasi. But instead of whizzing arrows or slashing spears, I heard only the din of overturned carts and stalls, and the screams of confused shoppers, some of whom were pointing overhead.

High above, hazy through the smoke of street fires and rows of hanging pelts, a man stood on a window ledge, his green, tooth-encrusted mask glinting in the sunlight.

The Crocodile.

"Having fun shopping, Oluwanis?" he boomed at the crowd in a strident tenor that sent a thrill up my spine. Scaly leather bands glinted on his arms. "My, what a wealth of bargains! Aheh: The stalls are just brimming with good deals today! Some of you could buy this whole market, and your purses would not feel the difference." He laughed, a thundercrack that echoed through the stone square. "Well—how is this for a price? The lives of men, women, and innocent children worked to death in tanneries and textile mills throughout the empire!"

The crowd chattered objections, but the Crocodile talked over them.

"Try to forget it! Pretend that it isn't true. Pretend you don't know what it means when pelts run cheap, or when furs sell for a song. Go on—drape your grand mantles! Clothe your bodies with a child's suffering!" His last words were guttural, as if growled through his teeth. "But if you *will* wear the fruits of poverty and greed . . . at least show the world what it truly costs." Then he leapt from the ledge, disappearing from sight, and the sound of metal creaking echoed overhead.

Too late I saw them—several bins, perched in eaves above the marketplace. Before I could shout a warning, distant figures overturned the bins . . . and waterfalls of cold, stinking blood filled the square.

My Guard warriors wheeled in confusion, temporarily blinded. I gagged and spat, slipping on the slimy, wet ground. Horrified shoppers formed a clumsy stampede, leaping over ruined piles of pelts and separating me from Kwasi. All too soon I was alone, nearly crushed by a stall as a mob of vigilantes overturned it and set it aflame.

I scrambled backward, only to press myself against a wall as shrieking, blood-soaked people roared past. Bile rose to my throat as one man fell and was crushed immediately by the exodus. Breathing hard, I pushed my way to an upended stall and climbed on top of it, hoping to avoid the fray. People and pack animals crashed into the stall's sides. I swayed and cried for help, hanging on for dear life—and then a figure flew toward me from above. He dangled from a rope, riding the rows of pelts like a zipline: the Crocodile.

I turned around and tried to duck. But he reached my stall, seizing me across the waist. I yelped but held on to him reflexively, air knocked from my lungs as we whizzed over the crowd, through the market square, and into a quiet alley. When we stopped, I wrenched myself from the Crocodile's sinewy arms. He did not resist, setting me gently on my feet.

"Don't move," I panted, whipping out the knife I kept always in my wrapper. "Don't . . . don't you dare touch me."

"Thank Am." To my surprise, the Crocodile only chuckled, tutting with his hands on his hips. "My dear empress . . . I was beginning to think you'd never force me to do anything."

Then the man pulled off his mask, and I stood face to face with the grinning king of Djbanti.

PART 4

CHAPTER 22

"WE SHOULD GET MOVING," ZURI TOLD ME then, seizing my hand and towing me along. "The district guard will come trampling through soon enough, and they tend to slash first and ask questions later."

"What? Where are you taking me?" I sputtered, managing to snatch my hand from his grasp. "And why should I trust you? You just destroyed a marketplace!"

"I prefer to think I revealed its true nature," he said blandly. "And we're going to my villa. Unless you'd like to find your way back to the palace in a crowded city, with no guards, looking like that." He gestured at my gore-stained face and shoulders. When I glanced down at my wrapper, soaked in crimson, my stomach turned.

"It's only pig's blood," he said, then winced. "I'd try not to swallow it, though."

I needed, very badly, to be clean. I sighed, lowering my knife. He wore several weapon holsters, and we stood in an empty alley. If he was going to kill me, he would have done it already.

So I followed him, stealing through the district. He cut through streets like someone who had done it many times, and before long, we reached the wide, fountain-dotted streets of the Ileyoba District.

Imperial Guard warriors flanked the villa assigned to Djbanti delegates, and high, smooth plaster rendered the walls unscalable. But before the warriors could spot us, Zuri took my hand, muttered feverishly, and tensed in pain—just like he had done at Olojari, when he vanished into thin air. My limbs hummed, in sync with his vibrating form . . . and then the wide street disappeared.

We stood in an elegant, citrus-scented bedchamber. The brick pattern matched the building we had just seen on the street—we were *inside* the Djbanti delegate villa. I dropped Zuri's hand, stomach lurching with nausea and confusion. "I—how did you—"

"What?" Zuri strolled casually to an end table and offered me a towel. "Never traveled by lodestone before? I'd have brought you directly from the market, but the demonstration left me winded. I only had the energy for a short distance."

I took the towel gingerly, swabbing at my gore-covered face. "Of course I have," I wheezed. "That is *not* what that was."

"Stomachache feels about the same," Zuri countered, and then peeled off one of his leather bands. With a jolt, I realized it was the same arm on which he always wore his wide gold cuff. There in his skin, encased in festering, veiny flesh, were two hunks of stone.

Zuri was using ibaje—the same deadly Pale Arts as the deformed assassin from that night in the square.

The largest rock embedded in his skin was metallic gray, dotted with tiny ashen symbols. The second made my breath catch in horror—a multifaceted emerald stone, glinting with malevolent light.

"That gem," I bleated, brushing my chin in the sign of the Pelican. "It was in Melu's cuff. My mother used that to enslave an alagbato. Are you— Are you a djinn? An ehru?"

"In a way. To my own ambition." He smiled wryly. "That stone is known as *idekun*—a mineral that grows only in the Underworld, though it's available up here for a . . . generous price. It is said to amplify the wearer's natural power, but it also binds the wearer to a person—or a cause. Until that person is satisfied, or that cause is fulfilled—idekun torments you." He grimaced as the green stone flashed, seeming to lash him. But he shook off the pain and pointed to the larger stone. "I'm sure you recognize this one. It's a piece of lodestone. The lodestones scattered throughout the empire originally came from the Underworld—did you know that? Alone, this piece lets me travel to other stones. But the idekun magnifies its power, allowing me to transport anywhere."

"And that's why you haven't been caught," I murmured. "How you've been waking alagbatos all over the empire as the Crocodile, while still making appearances at court."

"You're quick. Though it's still hard to lead revolutions when I can't be everywhere at once."

"Aren't you afraid of being poisoned?" I sputtered. "That's Pale Arts. Ibaje never comes without a price."

"Of course I've paid a price." He chuckled, replacing the arm band, and his eyes looked bright and manic. "But at least, unlike the rest of my family, I got to pick my poison."

My vision spun. The empty-headed king of Djbanti—the gambling drunkard who couldn't tell one end of a scepter from the other—was the Crocodile. The name whispered in the streets and written at the top of my security reports. Leader of the most organized vigilante group in Aritsar, responsible for disrupting industries across the empire.

"Should be a bath ready," Zuri said, nodding at a corner of the chamber. Behind woven screens stood a carved wooden tub, perfumed steam curling into the air. "It's for me . . . but I think we can agree you need it more than I do."

Am's Story—even his *voice* sounded different, low and resonant, rather than the nasal drawl he had used at court.

"How?" I squeaked. "How can you be the Crocodile?"

He poured himself a drink from a tall, fluted carafe. "You mean, 'How can a man you can't stand turn out to have a brain after all?'" He smiled, a white flash against midnight skin. "Sorry. That's unfair." He swirled the drink in his hand—herb water, not wine as I expected. I wondered again if I had ever seen Zuri drink at all. At court functions, he slurred and stumbled around, but his cup was always full. "I'm good at playing an idiot," he said. "I have to be."

"Who knows?" I demanded. "Your servants, obviously. But the other rulers? Your government? All of Djbanti?

260

Did everyone know about this but me?"

"With a few exceptions, my servants believe I sneak out to brothels. As for the other monarchs and my warlords"—he took a long swill from his chalice—"they think I'm an even bigger halfwit than you do. Even the revolutionaries who follow the Crocodile are uncertain of his identity, though I'm sure some of them have guessed."

I crossed my arms. "Then the only people in the world who know you're the Crocodile—who know the *real* you—are a couple servants . . . and me?"

He smirked, slipping back into his court drawl. "Bold of you to assume I'm not really an idiot."

But something grim lurked in his expression. The longer I watched him, the more I realized I had stumbled upon the only person in Oluwan as lonely as I was.

I turned away, snuffing out the sudden kinship between us. "Why tell me?" I said. "I could expose you to the world. People might doubt the word of a servant, but they would listen to an empress."

He opened his mouth, then shut it. "You're staining my rug," he observed, and turned to pour himself another drink.

I glanced down. Red muck dripped from my legs, and my sandals had left gruesome smears on the carpet. My face and neck had grown stiff with filth.

"Enjoy the water while it's fresh," he said. "I'll send for some clothes you can wear back to the palace." Then he crossed the room to be as far as he could from the screened bath, busying himself with papers at a kneeling desk.

I sucked in a breath. The only thing I wanted more than to leave that room was to be clean.

So I ducked behind the screen, peeked over it three times to make sure Zuri was staying away, and peeled off my soiled clothes. I kept on my mask and sunstone pendant, unwilling to part with them in such strange territory. Then I climbed into the tub.

It was pleasant at first. A selection of oils and ash soaps rested within reach on a stool, and leaves floated on the water. Lemongrass steam rose around my ears. But the longer I soaked, the thicker and redder the water became. I blinked, entranced by my arms and knees, dark brown hills in a sea of blood. The scene from the marketplace repeated in my head, only now it mixed with the night when monsters tore an assassin apart. Then I was back in that palace hallway, Thaddace dead at my feet, and a child pointing, wailing, *Empress Redemptor.*

My heart slammed in my chest. I gripped the edges of the tub. I was naked in some stranger's villa, and there was blood everywhere, and it was on my skin and in my hair and undead children hovered in every corner and in less than two years I was going to die and—

"Tarisai?" Zuri's voice floated from beyond the screen. I realized then that my breaths were audible, coming in loud, hard sobs.

"L–Lady Empress to you," I gasped, trying not thrash in the water. "And don't you dare come in. I'm—"

I'm fine faltered on my lips. I had said those words to so many people. Even to myself, late at night, as my fingers trembled from writing notes and passing edicts. But the truth?

I hadn't been fine in a very long time.

Zuri's steps padded closer, and his shadow appeared near the screen. "You're having an anxiety fit," he said quietly. "It happens to some of my best men after missions go wrong. You feel like you can't breathe, but you can."

"Are you sure? I—"

"Work through it." His voice was stern, which made me angry. To my surprise . . . that helped.

I hiccupped. "There's so much blood."

"Close your eyes. Wash as well as you can. Then get out of the tub and don't look back."

I gulped but followed his advice, feeling blindly for a soft lump of soap and scrubbing until my skin felt raw. Then I fumbled out of the tub, taking care not to slip on the damp stone floor, and donned a furry pelt robe that lay draped over the screen. It smelled of him—agave and spear polish.

"There's probably still blood in my hair," I muttered. "My attendants will have a lot of questions."

"I—" Zuri's silhouette hesitated behind the screen. "I could help you wash it out. If you like."

For a horrifying, fascinating moment, I imagined being beneath him, awash with his scent as I sat against the tub, head tilted back as he ran his strong, dark fingers through my hair.

"Or not," he said at my stunned silence. "There's a turban on the stool. Should be clean."

I retrieved it and wrapped my coils, which had fallen out of their twists in the water. When I stepped from behind the screen, Zuri sat before an elegant luncheon. While I had bathed, servants had come and gone, leaving a tureen of peanut stew, a platter of doughy *fufu*, and a steaming pot of tea.

"Your clothes should arrive soon," he said, gesturing to the seat across from him. "Nothing too obviously Djbanti. It could be . . . complicated for the court rumor mill to know you were here. Bathing."

I cringed and nodded, hugging his robe closer around me.

"You should eat," he added, filling two polished wood cups with tea and offering one to me. "You've had a shock."

I accepted the cup after a pause, sinking down onto the cushion. "You didn't answer my question," I pointed out. "Why trust me with your secret? In fact—why have secrets in the first place?" I frowned down at my tea. "I understand concealing the Crocodile's identity. But you live a lie every moment of every day—even among your own people. What kind of king makes his own subjects think he's a fool?"

"A king who survives," he replied, handing me a bowl. "How much have you heard about the Wanguru—my family?"

I dipped a piece of fufu in the stew, chewing thoughtfully. "I know your older brothers died. Hunting accidents. It's why you came to the throne so young. Your parents died too . . ." I trailed off, a chill racing up my arms. "Am's Story. Was your family—"

"Murdered? Yes. Though my father might have killed himself. Too proud to live as a puppet, you see. I, on the other hand . . ." He flourished a hand, then smiled tightly. "Djbanti has long been controlled by merchant-warlords. Their riches outweigh my treasury, and if it were up to them, they would erase my family altogether. But the common people of Djbanti revere us, and so we remain. The warlords could snuff out a peasant uprising, of course, but civil wars are expensive, and would interrupt what they love most: their precious supply lines."

"So they made the Wanguru puppets, instead." I tried to hide the pity in my voice.

Zuri nodded once. "We look the other way as the warlords seize every mill, mine, and quarry that the Kunleos don't own already. And if any king dares show a hint of backbone, he's eliminated. When I was still a boy, I learned to keep my temper quiet, and my words pretty." He ran a calloused hand through his locs, which fell in sheets over his dark shoulder. "The warlord system was initially well-intended. Their merchants were supposed to compete with each other, keeping prices low for the people. Then they realized they were stronger together. They united and made pacts to drive up the price of basic goods, like rice and palm oil. My people were driven to desperation."

I put my bowl down, jaw tightening. "It's not just Djbanti," I said bleakly. "I've read every report I can. Nobles in Mewe and Biraslov practically enslave their poor, all to make a profit on wool and ice blocks."

"And so I invented the Crocodile," he said, leaning closer. "Hit the nobles in their profits. No point using cheap labor if your product's covered in blood. Or if your customers are afraid of getting doused when they buy it."

I made a face. "Is it always blood?"

He grinned. "Depends. We use ground itchwort for wool. Live beetles are fun for rice, though that sometimes can go awry."

I laughed, though my smile faltered. "You should be careful about tainting food. It may belong to greedy nobles, but those who buy it are probably poor—especially if it's the cheapest option."

His head tilted in thought then remorse. "You're right. I didn't even think of that. You were right about Olojari, too. If Malaki had truly destroyed that mountain, the damage would've been insurmountable." He pierced me with a look that made my pulse skip. "That foresight—that attention to detail, the way you solve puzzles no one else sees . . . it's why I want you, Tarisai."

I nearly spit out my stew. "Excuse me?"

He shrugged, the corner of his mouth twitching. "Is that a problem? Don't you want me too?"

"As a council brother," I said slowly. "To fulfill my treaty with the abiku."

"Yes, of course. What did you think I meant?"

My cheeks heated, and his grin spread like the crocodile he was. "I'd also like to be partners in crime," he said. "It's why I trusted you with my secret."

"Partners? Doing what?"

He sat back, appraising me. "I want to dissolve the government of Djbanti," he said at last. "The warlords, the Wanguru monarchy. All of it. I want to tear it down and replace it with something new."

My eyebrows shot up. "You want to depose . . . yourself? From being king?"

"We did not always have kings in the central realms," he said, suddenly restless with excitement. "At least, not in the way we see them now. Before the time of Enoba the Perfect, leaders were merely the hands of their people. Oluwan, Nyamba, Swana and Djbanti were ruled by *nkosi*—chiefs of small states, where even the poorest maize farmer had a say."

"The rulers shared power," I said, remembering the fantasy I had described to Dayo. "And made sure it flowed to everyone."

"Yes, exactly." He beamed at me. "And the foundation for change is already in place. The peasants of Djbanti are planning a revolt, selecting leaders among themselves. I've armed them when I can, though it's hard to sneak weapons into warlord territory."

I shook my head, impressed. "That's incredible. But what do you need me for? Won't it look suspicious for imperial forces to arm peasants?"

"I don't need your weapons. I need—" He paused, considering his words carefully. "Your influence. You'll be addressing my warlords when you hold the Pinnacle in

Djbanti. Somehow, I think you'll be very . . . persuasive."

I frowned. "Meaning?"

"That we want the same thing. For poverty to be a thing of the past."

A bit of his courtier smoothness returned to his voice. He was keeping something from me, and I didn't like it.

"I know you don't trust me," he said, after a moment. "But we'll be spending plenty of time together soon enough. I'm going to be your council brother, aren't I?

"I don't know," I retorted. "Are you? You still haven't joined me for kuso-kuso."

"I'd prefer to get to know you the old-fashioned way." He cocked his head in invitation. "Spar with me, Tarisai. How about a scrimmage on the palace training grounds?"

I bit my lip, fidgeting with the sleeve of his robe, unnerved by the masculine scent that lingered there. I had an involuntary flash of Zuri dancing around me at my Peace Banquet, making me spin until I was dizzy, a lithe shadow swirling just out of reach.

"Lady Empress," I muttered, feeling sullen. "You keep forgetting my title."

He bowed and extended a hand. "I'll meet you halfway. How about . . . Idajo?"

I shivered at the name. Tarisai Idajo—Tarisai the Just.

Still, my fingers closed around his. "You'd better make yourself useful, Crocodile."

He smiled, this time with no sarcasm or seduction. As he

looked at me, a deep, wistful memory seemed to pass over his face like a cloud. Curiosity got the best of me. His hand still in mine, I let my Hallow explore him . . .

Only to have my own power thrust back into my mind, like a wave breaking against a dam.

I blinked, dazed. "You're Hallowed too," I blurted, and he smiled tightly. Zuri had thrown up mental shields of jagged adamant, the strongest I had ever encountered.

"I am. An ability to resist the inherent gifts of others." I gasped, remembering that Ai Ling had found Zuri impossible to coerce. His smile wavered. "It is the main reason, I suspect, that I am alive, and my family is not."

"I'm sorry," I mumbled. I was still holding his hand. I squeezed it tighter, just for a moment, and he lifted my palm to his lips, kissing it briefly before turning to leave the room.

"My steward will escort you back to the palace," he said in a strange, subdued voice. "I'll see you later, my Empress Idajo."

CHAPTER 23

LATER TURNED OUT TO BE THE NEXT MORNING.

The monthly Rising had just finished, a gaggle of courtiers bustling out of the room after dressing me and Dayo. I did not hear Zuri enter the room until he began to applaud, leaning in the arched entryway.

"Well done, Emperor. Empress Idajo," purred Zuri of Djbanti, his nasal court voice back in full force. The gold cuff was back on his arm. "The fear you two inspire in that crowd of sycophants never ceases to impress."

I stiffened on the dais, my nails digging into the bedding. Despite seeing it with my own eyes, it was still hard to believe that this man and the blood-splattered warrior who had seized me on a zipline were the same person. Just like at the Peace Banquet, Zuri's long, neat locs twinkled with gold accents, and that metallic combination of iron and sweet agave wafted from his elegant frame.

Am's Story, Dayo Ray-spoke, grinning. *He's as pretty as you, Tar. Are you* sure *you don't want to make babies with anyone? Because—*

I nudged him, hard, in the ribs. He kept grinning, Ray vibrating with laughter as I glowered down at Zuri.

"I'm afraid my Rising is over," I told the king flatly. "If you wanted an audience, you should have come on time."

"I didn't want to crowd you," he said. He stood, looking me over with liquid, inscrutable eyes. "Not after what you went through yesterday. I figured you need as much rest as possible. I am happy to find you revived."

The concern in his tone sounded genuine. Still, my eyes narrowed. "If you're so eager for me to rest, why come at all?"

His features danced. "I have brought you a surprise, though I now know you are not fond of them. As your council nears completion, I realized you should begin training for the Underworld as soon as possible."

My frown deepened, but when Zuri cleared his throat, three people appeared in the doorway. My jaw dropped.

"Woo In," I squeaked. "You're all right."

The last time I'd seen the Redemptor prince of Songland, he'd been languishing with fever on the steppes of Mount Sagimsan. Aside from the arrow wound scar on his abdomen, he appeared to have made a full recovery. His jet, silky hair was longer than I remembered, and tousled, as if he'd flown to the palace. Purple birthmarks covered his sinewy arms and chest, partially concealed by his signature crisp blue cape.

His mouth lifted in a smile. "An honor to see you well, Lady's Daugh—Empress Tarisai."

A golden-cheeked infant squirmed in a sling on Woo In's

chest. Beside them both stood a young girl—a Redemptor, no older than Adukeh, with short bobbed hair and pert, jaded features. A massive, translucent blue bird sat on her shoulder, its eyes crystal white.

"Ye Eun," I breathed, sliding down from the dais to greet her. "I'm so glad to see you."

I hadn't known if I ever would. My last memory of Ye Eun was on Mount Sagimsan, her form growing smaller as I rode away on Hyung's steaming back, racing toward what I thought was certain death. My heart twinged—the way it always did around Ye Eun, the warrior of a girl whose innocence I had failed to protect. I took a step forward, unconsciously reaching to touch her.

The bird's feathers flashed with blue light. A cold blast seared the air between us, and I snatched my hand back. Glistening ice encased the tips of my fingers. The Imperial Guard warriors at the door gasped, reaching for their weapons.

"It's all right," I told them, shaking my smarting fingers. "That's not a monster. It's an *emi-ehran*, isn't it? A soul guardian." I smiled down at Ye Eun. "All Redemptors have them."

"Only if we survive the Underworld," Ye Eun corrected.

"Right." I frowned awkwardly. "Didn't you say your emi-ehran was a phoenix?"

"Hwanghu *is* a phoenix," Ye Eun retorted, stroking the bird's breast. "But their essence isn't fire. It's water. The language of my sowanhada."

I should have guessed that a Songlander girl as strong as Ye Eun was gifted in elemental speaking. Could she command water, like Woo In and Min Ja controlled the wind?

"Don't mind them," Ye Eun told the shimmering creature. "I'm not in danger—right now anyway. Go play."

Hwanghu nuzzled Ye Eun's cheek, threw us all a haughty look, then flapped its wings and dispersed into crystalline droplets, vanishing through the bedroom window.

I glanced around with sudden caution, searching for a flash of lurid orange and black, or the tip of a massive striped paw. "Uh—is . . . Hyung here too?" I asked Woo In. "I never got to thank him—them—for my ride. After bringing me to the palace, your emi-ehran just . . . disappeared."

"Sounds like Hyung," Woo In replied with a wry smile. "My pet cat, as Kirah liked to call them, always comes when summoned. But even after all these years, I've never quite figured out where they vanish to. I imagine Hyung in a void, playing with some cosmic ball of string."

"I suppose," Zuri said presently, bowing to me, "you'll want to know why your friends are here. Well . . . Woo In offered to bring Ye Eun to help you train for the Underworld. And I assumed the expense of their lodestone journey. It was no trouble, I assure you."

Dayo cocked his head in confusion. "That's very kind of you, King Zuri. But why does Tar need to train for the Underworld? After all—once she's anointed her council— she'll be immune to all thirteen deaths except old age. It may be . . . difficult for her to find her way back from the Breach.

But she'll be fine," he insisted, nervously. "I know she will."

"Except," Ye Eun said, crossing her arms, "there are more than thirteen deaths."

The air in the room chilled, plunging into silence.

"But how is that possible?" I asked. "I've never heard of more than thirteen. No one has." All of Aritsar knew the story. Warlord Fire, consort of Queen Earth, had grown jealous of her union with King Water, and had cursed Earth's children with thirteen deaths in revenge. But Woo In shook his head grimly.

"Ye Eun's right," he said. "Tarisai . . . there's something you need to know about the Underworld. Death is not a *concept* there. In the Underworld, the Deaths are living things—prowling monsters. And when I saw them as a boy, there were more than thirteen. *Way* more. Some of them were expected: Burning, Drowning, Heart-Death, the like. But others were strange . . . like Despair. Avarice. Yearning. I think, perhaps, there's a way humans can die while their hearts are still beating." His jaw tightened. "One of the Deaths didn't have a name at all."

My pulse raced, and I touched the mask beneath my clothes. I had thought that with a council of thirteen siblings, I would be inoculated against death—unless I stayed in the Underworld, dying eventually of old age. I now felt foolish for my hubris.

"Well," Zuri droned into the terse silence, "it seems you and your friends have a lot to talk about. So I take my leave. Don't thank me, please. Bringing your Songlander friends was the least I could do, after the impression I made at your Peace Banquet." He bowed once to Dayo, then lingeringly to me. "I look forward to sparring, Empress Redemptor."

He leaned to take my hand, kissing my palm again as he had in his private rooms. Then with a wave of sharply sweet cologne, Zuri was gone.

I faced Woo In, demanding without preamble, "How do you know him?"

An odd expression crossed Woo In's face. "It's . . . a long story," he said at last. His voice was quiet, gossamer—the same reverent tone he had once used around my mother.

My skin pricked with unease. "I'm assuming you know he's the Crocodile?" I had already broken my promise to Zuri by telling Dayo, though I didn't think that counted.

"Yes." Woo In sighed heavily, and a shimmering breeze stirred his silk cape. "Tarisai, there's something you should know."

"And?"

"And I can't say. I gave him my word."

I snorted. "Since when does the king of Djbanti control you?"

"He doesn't. But . . ." Woo In sighed, rubbing his temples. "I took something from him, not too long ago. Something I can't give back. Just like I took something from you." He winced, and we both shifted uncomfortably beneath the weight of my mother's death. "I'm sorry, Tarisai. I didn't know the knife was poisoned. The Lady anointed me, and I loved her. I never would have—"

"I know, Woo In," I murmured. "And I forgive you."

He nodded glumly. "I need Zuri to forgive me too. There is . . . honor between us."

"You and Zuri are friends?"

He clenched and unclenched his hands, choosing his words carefully. "I have associated with Zuri for *many* years."

The emphasis was meaningful, but the hidden message was lost on me. At my blank stare, Woo In shrugged and spread his hands. "Look. Insufferable as he may seem, I can tell you that Zuri means no harm. He is safe to anoint as a council member—even if your motives may not always align."

I pinched the bridge of my nose, shaking my head. "None of this makes sense. Why are you even here?"

"Like Zuri said: to bring Ye Eun. I'd train you for the Underworld myself, but my mother is uneasy with the idea of me staying at An-Ileyoba. Guess she's afraid I'll get sucked into another Arit conspiracy."

I raised an eyebrow. "I thought you hated Queen Hye Sun. For how she treated you when you returned from the Underworld."

"I did hate her." He paused, his gaze softening. "But I think . . . she hated herself more. She's different now than I remember. Wiser. In any case, her heart is fragile with age, and I won't tax it more than is necessary." For just a moment, he glanced searchingly around the room. "I . . . had hoped to introduce one of your council members to my mother. Is . . . is the High Priestess—"

"Kirah isn't here," I said bluntly. "If that's what you're

asking. She's gone to face an alagbato in Blessid Valley. Then she's off to Songland, to negotiate Arit reparations." When his face fell, I rolled my eyes, taking pity on him. "I'm sure she hopes to see you in Songland," I admitted. "And if you leave now, you could probably fly to Blessid Valley by nightfall."

"Ah." Woo In's eyes shone considerably brighter. "Well. Perhaps I will. If I can be of assistance, I mean."

In his sling, the baby roused, mewling softly.

"Ae Ri," I gasped, recognizing the black tuft of hair. "She's already so much bigger than when I saw her last. How are the other Redemptor children? Are they alone at the refuge?"

Ye Eun retrieved Ae Ri from Woo In's sling, expertly settling the infant on one hip.

"The Sagimsan Refuge doesn't exist anymore," Ye Eun snapped. "After you cancelled the Redemptor Treaty, Queen Hye Sun sent an order to Songland: all Redemptors were to be adopted into regular families. So the other children got taken."

"That's wonderful," I gushed, then knew immediately I had said the wrong thing. Ye Eun's face reddened.

"No one wanted me," she said quietly. "They said I'm cursed, since I've been to the Underworld already. And Ae Ri cried when the nobles tried to separate us. So . . ." Ye Eun chewed her lip, scowling at the floor. "I don't care where I live. But I'm not going anywhere without Ae Ri."

"You can stay here, in the suite," I said hurriedly. "Both of you. For as long as you like."

A small lump rose in my throat as Ae Ri fussed, and Ye Eun calmed her with a maternal coo. At twelve, Ye Eun was already a competent caregiver. But how long since anyone had mothered her?

My thoughts spiraled to The Lady. Already, the shadow she had cast over my life seemed eons away. Whenever I dwelled on it, my thoughts sputtered and fizzled, like oil drops on a brazier. I'd never been mothered either—not really. The Lady had seen me as a tool—an extension of herself. Then again, I had only seen *her* as a symbol. A totem for the familial closeness, the sense of belonging I craved. We had neither of us seen each other, not really. And we'd never have another chance again.

"May . . ." A sudden urge had overcame me. "May I hold Ae Ri?"

Ye Eun raised an eyebrow, then held out the fussing baby.

I cradled Ae Ri gingerly, and said the first thing that came to mind. "Sorry," I whispered. "Um. I know I'm bad at this. But you'll never go hungry here. And you'll still have Ye Eun to play with. Eventually, you'll come to like us. I think—"

Ae Ri lurched from my grasp, reaching for someone behind me with insistent grunts. I turned, and the baby catapulted herself straight into Dayo's arms.

Ae Ri and the emperor stared at each other, transfixed with delight. Solemnly, Ae Ri placed her pudgy hands on either side of Dayo's dark, scarred face, cooing as if she'd known him all her life.

"Hello," Dayo breathed, liquid with adoration. She beamed, and then claimed the oba mask on his chest, gnawing the rainbow lion mane.

"Well," I said, blinking once. "I guess . . . that decides that."

"We'll have toys brought up from the Children's Palace," Dayo said dreamily. "We'll hire a nurse, and a team of tutors, and make the salon a playroom. I think you'd like that, Ye Eun. And you too—wouldn't you, Ri-Ri?" He blew on Ae Ri's soft hair, glowing when she giggled. "You'll *love* the wooden giraffes. And the rocking zebra . . . unless you want a real one." He bounced her. "Should Uncle Dayo buy you a zebra? A rhino? You can play with Aunt Tarisai's elephant, if you like . . ."

My cheeks hurt from smiling. But sadness panged through me. I had wondered if I'd fall in love with Ae Ri, like Dayo had. If holding her would reverse that impulse inside me—that conviction against having babies of my own. But as precious as Ae Ri was . . . my mind remained unchanged.

One thing, however, I knew for certain: Nothing would ever happen to Ye Eun, or Ae Ri, or any other innocent born with maps on their skin. Not on my watch. And if I was to be the world's last Redemptor, I would have to learn what it took to survive the Underworld.

CHAPTER 24

"I HATE THIS," DAYO SAID QUIETLY AS AE RI fussed on his hip. "I hate everything about this."

"Again," I told Ye Eun.

"This is unwise," warned Captain Bunmi, pacing in the Hall of Dreams. I had asked her to stand watch, making sure no one interrupted us in the old Children's Palace, where I had been meeting with Ye Eun for a week, training for my journey to the Underworld. "Lady Empress, you aren't immune to organ-death yet."

"Do you want me to survive the Underworld or not?" I shivered in a thin embroidered shift. Ye Eun had advised against wearing anything else while I trained. The cold was the point. "Watch my sprites," I told Bunmi, pointing at the floor-length arched windows of the hall. Outside, my sprites twinkled worriedly against the zenith. The night of the Emperor's Walk, the sprites had dimmed when the assassin hurt me. I had experimented since, concluding that their lives were linked to mine.

"I'll stop training if they start dying," I said. "But not before."

280

Moonlight made ghosts of the sheet-covered toys and furniture. The mural of dancing children on the Hall of Dreams ceiling appeared more sinister than cheery, cherubic faces obscured in shadow. As far as Dayo and Bunmi knew, I had chosen to train in the Children's Palace for its seclusion. Ever since our council had moved to the Imperial Suite, not even servants visited this wing of the palace. In truth, I had chosen the Hall of Dreams to make sure I would not buckle to cowardice. Any time pain tempted me to stop training, these abandoned toys, these tiny bedrolls and empty miniature chairs would remind me of the children my ancestors sacrificed.

"Again," I repeated, and Ye Eun nodded, whispering to the crystalline emi-ehran on her shoulder. Hwanghu rose into the air, water running in rivulets from its translucent blue shoulders. Then it shrieked, a battle cry—and dove at me, shattering against my chest in a stinging wave of ice.

I gasped and fell to my knees, heart floundering at the living, malevolent cold, which coursed up my neck, across my collarbone, and down my legs and arms. Unlike normal water, this liquid was sentient, made of Hwanghu's soul and Ye Eun's will. Until she commanded otherwise, the water would remain on my skin: a frigid, lethal mantle.

"Get up," said Ye Eun. Her voice was surprisingly gentle. "Now, Empress Tarisai."

"I c-can't," I wheezed. "I c-can't b-breathe."

Ae Ri wailed, and Dayo shielded the baby's eyes, looking close to tears himself. "Don't worry, Ri-Ri," he said soothingly. "Aunty Tar will be just fine. You'll see."

"Make Hwanghu stop," Bunmi snapped, her hands balling into fists. "It's killing her."

"Her sprites are still shining," Ye Eun said calmly, glancing at the arched windows. "Get up, Lady Empress." She circled me slowly, bending so her steely, birthmarked features were close to mine. "When you enter the Underworld, the cold will be just as bad. Only you won't die. You'll just keep suffering and suffering, until you convince yourself to move." Her voice softened. "It gets better with every step. So get up."

"M–Make it stop," I whispered. "J–Just . . . make it stop."

"If you say that down there," Ye Eun warned, "the abiku will kill you. No creature of the Underworld can harm you without invitation. But they are listening, always, and those words will suffice."

"Think of something warm," Dayo suggested anxiously, sending beams of heat into my mind.

"Don't," I snapped at him. "Your Ray can't reach me in the Underworld." I had to do it myself. Teeth chattering, I summoned memories of fire, but that only reminded me of when Woo In had set the Children's Palace aflame, nearly murdering Dayo in the process. I shivered harder. Outside, the sprites began to wane.

"That's the sign," Bunmi growled. "Lady Empress—"

"No," I gasped. "Just a little longer."

"You need more than warmth," Ye Eun said. "Think of something that makes you feel safe."

Immediately, Sanjeet's face blossomed in my mind, followed by Dayo's, Kirah's, Mayazatyl's, Ai Ling's . . . I exhaled. I thought of my council siblings on the beach beneath Yorua Keep, doubled over with laughter as they splashed one another in the water. I let their loving voices hum through me, eleven harmonies filling the air in vibrant unison.

Tar is ours
Tar is ours
and Tar is enough.

Slowly, as though my joints were made of glass, I rose to my feet.

"One step," Ye Eun whispered. "Just one step, Empress. And in the Underworld, the rest will follow."

My lungs began to shut down, shriveling beneath the oppressive cold. Shadows crept at the edges of my vision. The ojiji apparitions had filled the room like fog, wheeling, keening.

Your siblings are gone. They left you. You didn't deserve them anyway. You can't do anything right. Give in. Pay the price. Pay for our lives.

Truth and lies. Lies or truth . . . who could tell? Maybe the ojiji were right. I was so tired, so fed up with fighting for a better world. I could give them what they wanted— pay the ultimate price. But even in my haze of exhaustion, my family's voices still rang in my ears, faint, but present all the same.

Tar is enough.

I stepped. Ye Eun made a swift gesture, and the ice water fell to the floor with a violent slap. My skin was miraculously dry, and beneath me, the water began to evaporate, rising into the air until Hwanghu regained their shimmering form. The emi-ehran looked smaller, now, and weaker. I wondered how many times the bird could disintegrate before dying altogether. But I chose to believe they would rise again, as all phoenixes were fated to do.

Though dry, my body still shook with cold. My hearing grew fuzzy . . . then without warning, my legs buckled.

Strong arms caught me before I hit the ground, and I peered up with bemusement at Bunmi's tersely wrinkled face. My fevered brain jumbled her features, morphing them until I stared up at Sanjeet's tea-colored eyes. He hadn't left me after all. He had been here, all along, and I'd just been too silly to notice. He frowned in concern, but I smiled up at him, dreamily.

"If you're not careful, Jeet of Dhyrma," I giggled, "your face will freeze that way."

"She's going into shock," said Sanjeet, though he sounded strangely like Bunmi. "Emperor Ekundayo—your Ray! Now!"

Heat surged through me as Dayo's Ray united with mine, sending doubled power into each of my limbs. Ye Eun brought over one of the billowing dust sheets from the Children's Palace furniture and tucked it around me.

I sneezed. My fingers and toes prickled with pain as blood seeped back into them. Outside, my sprites began to glow again.

"Thank you," I whispered to Bunmi, who looked like herself again. Then I lifted my head from her chest and found Ye Eun. "Again."

"No," barked Bunmi and Dayo in unison. Their voices hurt my ears, echoing from the hall ceiling. Sensing the tension in the room, Ae Ri began to wail.

"I need to train," I insisted. All around me, the wispy ojiji children floated, shrilling in a treble chorus. *Do more. Justice. Have to pay.* "I need to be the best Redemptor I can be."

"Why?" Dayo demanded, patting Ae Ri's back as her cries rose in pitch. "What's the point in learning how to survive if you kill yourself now?"

"Our ancestors sent thousands of children into that cold," I reminded him. "If they had to endure it, why shouldn't I?"

Dayo's full lips pressed together, and his large black eyes glistened with hurt. "I knew it. You aren't really training, are you?" he whispered. "You're punishing yourself. Something's wrong with you, Tar. You haven't been all right for a long time, and . . . I'm worried. All of us are."

He is blind, hissed the ojiji. *He is blind, they are all blind, andyouarealone—*

I wrenched out of Bunmi's arms and teetered to my feet. "I'm tired," I rasped, "of being treated like I'm crazy. Of being the only one who seems to care that our empire *killed* people for hundreds of years! We tortured children! We still do, if you count the quarries and mills. And I'm going to fix it." I swallowed hard, voice dropping to a whisper. "I'm going to be Tarisai Idajo.

"Again, Ye Eun."

"This must be doing wonders for your ego," I quipped several evenings later as Zuri deposited me in a heap on the courtyard training grounds. It was the fourth round of sparring I'd lost.

I squinted up at Zuri, irritable. The setting sun made a halo around his bare, glistening shoulders, winking on the metal cuffs in his locs. Far above, my sprites congregated in the sky, dipping and wheeling. The creatures had remained on edge ever since I started training with Ye Eun. I would have been training now, if Dayo hadn't fainted after my last session. Only then had I agreed to rest for a night—though by "rest," I meant studying for the Pinnacle and holding my first sparring session with the Crocodile.

"You aren't *that* bad," he said, smirking and helping me up. He gestured to a scrape on his chest. "You scored a hit."

"Once." A hiss escaped through my teeth as I retrieved my weapon. My leg throbbed. I wore a crimson training skirt, slashed on either side from hip to ankle for ease of movement. On my exposed thigh, a black bruise had begun to form. "Is that why you asked to spar?" I asked, scowling. "To show me how weak I am?"

"Quite the opposite."

"You have a fetish for vague answers," I muttered, brandishing Sanjeet's gift: the finely balanced spear, engraved with golden letters. Already the bruise on my thigh had begun to fade—thanks to my nearly complete council of Anointed Ones, I was immune to bleeding, even internally.

I had thought my growing resistance to earthly deaths would make me feel like a god. But instead, with every rapidly healing injury, I only felt more like a ghost—detached from this world, floating higher and higher until all that felt real was the ojiji's song.

Should have saved us. Should have cared. Do more. Do more.

Zuri and I dropped into a combat stance and circled each other again. My face heated, thinking of the time we had first met: whirling in each other's arms at the Peace Banquet. I fought in the Swana style, advancing with a spear and long leather shield. Zuri used Djbanti weapons: a pointed pole in one hand, used mostly to block and disarm, and a club in the other, for close-range offense.

"Come on, Empress Idajo," Zuri purred, "lure me in. Mesmerize me. The same way you've managed to lure in twelve rulers for your council."

"I didn't lure anyone," I objected, lunging for his side and grunting when he danced out of the way. "They chose me."

"Congrats on anointing Kwasi, by the way," he said, feinting and launching a blow I barely blocked. "I was worried my demonstration at the market might have ruined your outing."

"It helped, actually," I admitted, smiling in spite of myself. Kind old King Kwasi had already loved me, in his way. And when I disappeared at the blood-soaked market . . . Kwasi had been so relieved when I turned up later at the palace, clean and safe, he had accepted my anointing on the spot.

I lunged again, and Zuri skirted me. The force of my missed blow threw me off balance, and before I knew it, Zuri had thrust an arm around me from behind, pressing me against him, his club a bar across my throat.

"Do you know what your problem is?" Zuri said into my hair. "You fight like you're defending something behind you. Always pushing your targets back, instead of drawing them in."

I cursed the pleasant shiver that chased up my spine. "It's what they taught us in the Children's Palace," I whispered. "Protect Dayo. Preserve the Raybearer."

He murmured in my ear, "You were not born to be a bodyguard, Wuraola."

He slackened his grip then, expecting me to break away. But I remained in his embrace, heart hammering.

"I'm going to use my question now," I said.

I felt him shift, curious. "Question?"

"My prize from the Peace Banquet." I turned to meet his dark, calculating eyes. "You promised me I could ask you anything."

His expression turned carefully blank. "That I did."

"Who killed Thaddace of Mewe? And how do you know Prince Woo In?"

"The first question," he said, "is the one I asked you."

"I know. But it seemed like you were testing me."

He blinked, thoughtful. "I have no idea who killed your old mentor," he said, and from his steady gaze, I knew he told the truth. But when I sagged in disappointment, he added, "I rather hoped his killer was you."

I did break away then, whirling around, enraged. "Why in Am's name would you hope that?"

"Because a ruthless empress is a powerful one," he said. "And power can be harnessed." Then in a fluid movement, he slipped a hand behind my neck. I recoiled, but too late. He leapt away with his prize: my obabirin mask. It had hung from a cord, concealed beneath my blouse, before he slipped the cord over my head.

"Give that back," I growled. "Right now."

He twirled the cord on one finger. "Make me."

"Are you a child?" I gasped, incredulous with anger. "That's an imperial artifact. I could have you thrown in prison—"

"I wonder which ways our empress can die," he said in a singsong, counting the stripes on the mask, still sashaying out of reach. "One more ruler to anoint. One missing stripe left. That means, besides old age, my little Idajo can still die of"—he squinted, examining the mask—"organ-death. Ah. But I'd still have to be creative to kill you. You're immune to bleeding and battery, so a mere stab wouldn't work.

I suppose I'd have to carve out your heart altogether . . ."

My veins ran cold as he watched me, circling like a cat. But when humor crinkled his eyes, I realized he wasn't threatening me at all. He was trying to make me angrier . . . and it was working.

"I said," I rasped, vision tinting red, "give that back."

"No."

"*Do not*"—I roared, and as if with a will of their own, my arms rose, pointing the spear at him. Heat seared up the shaft, and the engraving, *WURAOLA*, smoldered against the wood—"*contradict me!*"

Zuri's smirk vanished. Then he trembled, and every limb in his body appeared to seize. Blue light emanated from his skin. His spear and club thudded to the dirt, and then, with rigid slowness, he came toward me, arm outreached. The mask dangled from his finger. When I snatched it, he fell to his knees, gasping, and the blue light faded.

"Zuri?" My vision cleared, anger draining away. "What's wrong with you?"

He clutched his chest, still breathing hard. But when he looked up, he smiled. "Well done."

Suspicion crept into my voice. "What are you playing at?" I demanded. "What did you just do?"

"My dear Empress Idajo," he laughed, gesturing at the spear I still brandished over him. "*I* didn't do anything."

Slowly, I lowered the weapon. "I . . . something happened," I stammered. "I wasn't myself. There was heat. I was so angry, and then . . ."

"And then I did what you said," Zuri finished, glowing with excitement. "I had no choice, because of the noble *okanoba* in my blood. Your anger awoke the full potential of the Ray inside you."

"I don't understand," I breathed.

"Have you truly never used it before?" His eyes narrowed. "Never once have you commanded a blueblood, and had them bend to your influence, without question?"

I began to say no . . . and then Adebimpe's eager, pliant face appeared in my mind.

That moment at my Rising—when I had ordered her to be kinder. To change her demeanor at court and protect the weak.

To this day, she had kept her word. I had seen her in the hallways, flocked by a cloud of shy, plainly dressed girls, fussing over them like a hawk defending her chicks. I had expected Adebimpe to improve for a day, perhaps two. But ever since, she'd been a different person.

There had been other times too—when I ordered the nobles at my Rising to be silent. When I had compelled the rulers to sit at my Peace Banquet. And now . . . when Zuri had fallen to his knees, offering up the mask when I willed it.

"It—it can't be," I stammered. "That isn't what the Ray is for."

"What makes you so sure?"

"Am the Storyteller," I snapped. "Or Am's memory, anyway. On a cave in Mount Sagimsan. I saw it all—where the Ray came from, what it's for, everything. Melu granted the Ray to Enoba the Perfect, so the emperor could unite a council and gain immunity to death. That's it."

"No," Zuri said quietly. "That is only one purpose of the Ray. Melu granted Enoba three wishes, remember? The first—to make one land out of many. The third—to unite souls. And the second?" He watched the memory dawn across my face, before saying it aloud: "*The power to rule an empire for eternity.* And what is power, but the ability to command the powerful?"

"How do you know all this?" I whispered. "And why haven't I heard it before?"

"The Kunleo family is fond of secrets," he replied vaguely. "I imagine Olugbade would have told Ekundayo, had he not died prematurely."

"You haven't answered all my question," I hissed. "How do *you* know Kunleo secrets? Does this have something to do with how you know Prince Woo In?"

His face went blank. "I only owed you the answer to one question. You wasted it asking about Thaddace." He flashed a rakish grin. "Dance with me at another banquet, and I'll answer more."

"Or," I said, "answer them now, and I won't lodge this spear in your backside."

He stepped closer, gaze cold and bright. "Why stoop to violence, when you can compel me with your mind?"

I stepped back, faltering. "I don't know what you're talking about."

"Don't deny what just happened," he snapped, suddenly severe. "You made me give you that mask. So . . ." He leaned in, breath tickling my cheek. "Make me say what you want to know."

My palms beaded with sweat. Whatever I had done to Zuri had scared me more than anything in months. I hadn't felt so angry, so powerless since . . .

Since I knelt over Dayo beneath Enitawa's Quiver, a knife sticking out of his gut.

At my horrified expression, Zuri sighed and held up his hands. "How about this?" he said. "I'll tell you everything I know, as long as you don't ask how I know it. Deal?"

I chewed my lip, wiping sweat from my brow. "Fine," I huffed at last.

Zuri retrieved his spear and club from the ground and resumed a sparring stance. I nearly refused to fight him, but my nerves were so wired from that strange, foreign energy, I couldn't keep still. I mirrored his stance, and our weapons clacked and swung. The more effort he put into the fight, the more his smooth black skin seemed to glow with power—a subtle, midnight blue. Should it ever strike an assassin to try, Zuri of Djbanti would be very, very hard to kill.

"Enoba the Perfect, first emperor of Aritsar, gave a gift to the empire's gentry," he panted. "Okanoba: a blessing on their bloodlines, giving them strength and longevity. This allowed them to subdue their native provinces, securing tributes for the emperor. Some nobles are aware of okanoba, though they do not speak of it often. For they know that just as Raybearers give okanoba . . . they can also take okanoba away."

I frowned with disbelief, but then I remembered Adebimpe, nonchalantly snapping a brush in two with one slender hand.

Okanoba also explained why my power had no sway over Songlanders. They had never sworn fealty to Enoba. My heart raced with the possibilities. Could I really turn anyone into a blueblood? Give them the gift of strength, health, longevity?

"The gift comes with a price," Zuri continued. "If anyone receives okanoba, their will is tied to the Raybearer's. The stronger the noble bloodline, the more the Raybearer could control them. So past Kunleo emperors struck an unspoken truce: They would allow bluebloods their freedom, so long as they stayed in line. The nobles at An-Ileyoba must have guessed that you and Dayo were unaware of your power," Zuri said, "or else they never would have tried to kill you."

At these last words, Zuri's face tightened, and his eyes glittered dangerously. After a dazed moment, I realized he wasn't angry at me. He despised the nobles—he *hated* them for trying to kill me. But why? Why should the king of Djbanti care whether I lived or died?

His rage rendered him sloppy. I managed to duck under his guard, slapping his knees with the pole of my spear. He toppled, dropping his club. I kicked it away and stood over him, spear pointed at his face.

"Yield," I said.

He stared up at me, inscrutable. "With all my heart, Idajo," he said. "The moment you admit what you are."

I sucked in a breath, knuckles clenching the spear shaft. "You won't turn me into a monster," I said. "I won't be made into someone's weapon. Not again. I lived that life already—for my mother." Then I flung my spear to the ground and turned on my heel, heading back to the palace.

"And what of the innocents toiling in mills and quarries?" he called after me. "Are you too pure to help them?"

I froze, stunned. He clambered to his feet, reaching me in a stride and wrenching me to face him.

"One word," he said, breathless. "One word from you, and every blueblood in this empire would relinquish Kunleo resources and abide by fair labor laws. You could be the heroine you were born to be. The one I know you are."

He reached out to stroke my cheek. For just a moment, I let him touch me—then I seized his wrist, digging my nails into his skin.

"I will help the poor of Aritsar, Zuri Wanguru," I said. "But I'll do it my way."

When I released him, he scoffed, "And what way is that? Scribbling more laws? Writing an edict on a calfskin and throwing a fancy high court where everyone agrees to obey it?"

"You'll find out at the Pinnacle," I snapped, giving him a taste of his own secret-keeping medicine.

"Why stifle your own power?"

"Because I want to be an empress, not a god!" My voice pinged against the courtyard walls.

His expression softened, and he regarded me gravely. "I understand you better than you know," he said. "But I learned, Idajo—the moment those warlords stepped over the corpses of my parents and brothers and placed a crown on my head. None of us are gods. We are merely tools, wielded by the strongest system. I am giving you the chance to choose what that system is." He retrieved my spear from the ground and held it out to me. "I can't force you to accept your power. But if you do, you owe it to Aritsar, and to yourself, to be ready."

After a moment, my fingers closed around it. The word *WURAOLA* glittered on the shaft, cold and bright, as the sun sank at last below the horizon.

CHAPTER 25

TWO DAYS BEFORE THE PINNACLE, FOG HUNG in clouds over the frothing brown Olorun River, which curved like a serpent around Oluwan City. Dinghies and private barges, manned by chanting teams of rowers, emerged and vanished like shades into the night. Even at this hour, the docks bustled. When Adukeh, my attendants, and I stepped down from our palanquins, several dozen leering faces turned to stare.

"L–Lady Empress?" Adukeh asked, clutching her drum as we hurried along.

"Not so loud," I shushed her.

The only people who sailed the Olorun at night were smugglers or nobility—and many who were both. Nobles liked to avoid the heat of day and could pay for the extra security that night travel required.

For anonymity I wore a linen cowl draped over my satin-wrapped hair. But my other clothing choices had been less prudent. My plain red wrapper, borrowed from a palace servant, was still much too fine, edged in gold thread that glistened in the dock torchlight. I had hoped to blend in with my attendants, but our escort of warriors betrayed one of us to be a noble, or at least, very well off.

Urchins and sailors grinned and licked their lips. I ignored them, hurrying Adukeh along. Better that men ogle our finery than look overhead, where one by one, hundreds of lavender sprites began to congregate, twinkling against the midnight sky.

"S-Sorry," Adukeh whispered. "B-But why d-do we need a b-boat? Wouldn't traveling by l-lodestone be f-faster?"

"Not where we're going," I muttered.

Somewhere in the dark, a vessel waited to carry us to the Wanguru Fortress of Djbanti, where I hoped to convince the empire's nobility to relinquish the crown's resources for good. I still wondered if accepting Zuri's offer of a ride had been a mistake.

Zuri's home court, the Wanguru Fortress, lay at the intersection of Oluwan, Swana, and Djbanti. Any stop on the continent's chaotic network of lodestones would place us too far away . . . and leave it to Zuri to own the largest smuggler's barge this side of the Olorun.

"Why can't you just whisk us to the fortress with those stones in your arm?" I'd asked him.

He had winced and smiled. "Because unlike the Crocodile, Zuri of Djbanti is not a dashing sorcerer, and must be seen traveling like a mortal."

I glanced at the scrap of calfskin in my hand, scrawled

with his clipped, elegant handwriting: *Seventh boardwalk. The Tsetse Fly shoves off at midnight.*

I counted the rickety docks, arriving quickly at the right one. A long, low vessel floated in the murky water, lamps and oars dangling off the sides. A shirtless man, dark and ripple-backed, waited in plain trousers near the gangplank. He turned, and his slow, broad smile flashed in the gloom.

"Glad you made it, Idajo."

I swore under my breath. Even in peasant clothes on a foggy, brine-covered dock, Zuri of Djbanti was maddeningly beautiful.

"Put a shirt on," I grumbled. "The mosquitos will eat you alive."

"I'm wearing salve," he countered, leaning his neck to my nose. "Eucalyptus. Can't you smell it?"

I could. It smelled delicious, which made my scowl deepen.

He laughed, and then raised his eyebrows. "You brought guests."

"Adukeh's the opening act of our Pinnacle," I said, patting her shoulder. "As for the guards and attendants . . . well. I'm not passing into your clutches without backup."

His smile widened. "Smart decision. Welcome aboard."

The *Tsetse Fly* appeared to be a sleepy cargo barge, deck filled to bursting with barrels of oranges, kola nuts, and palm oil. When I squinted, however, iron objects glinted from beneath the piles of fruit: weapons for Zuri's secret army of commoners. I quickly looked away, ordering my entourage belowdecks.

"Aren't you going below too?" Zuri asked as the ship shoved off, deck thrumming rhythmically beneath us. Drummer boys played at the ship's bow, syncing a team of muscled rowers. With a groan, the *Tsetse Fly* embarked into the night.

"I need to practice my Pinnacle speech," I said, then cringed as needles shot between my eyes. "Besides . . . I don't sleep much these days."

He nodded with approval. "Oppression doesn't rest. So why should we?"

I snorted, thinking he was joking . . . but his mouth remained serious. "I mean"—I smiled uncertainly—"you know we have to sleep sometime, right? We're not immortal."

"You will be," he reminded me, nodding at where the empress mask lay concealed beneath my clothes. "Almost, anyway. And when that day comes . . ." His expression grew starry. "You'll be able to accomplish more than ever. Always running, working, plotting. Fighting for the lowly and voiceless, from sunrise to sunrise. I envy you, Idajo."

My stomach sank at his words, but immediately I felt guilty. Zuri was right. Of course I needed to work more, work harder. How could I do otherwise, with a gift like immunity? Even now, I wouldn't die without sleep. Eventually I'd go mad—well, *madder*—but not for a while.

Zuri squeezed my shoulder, winked, then wandered away to speak with the bosun. I paced the deck, muttering my ruling for the Pinnacle until my tongue grew leaden. Both wired and exhausted, I leaned over the ship's braided rope railing and closed my eyes as the night wind blew back my cowl. Very faintly, the Ray hummed from the general direction of Oluwan City, which had shrunk to a smudge in the distance.

Miss you already.

It was Dayo. I didn't respond, feeling agitated from the last conversation we'd had before I left.

"Why now?" he had asked, looking forlorn in the Imperial Bedchamber as attendants bustled to pack my belongings.

I had blinked at him. "What do you mean?"

"All of this." He had waved at my desk, where a sea of notes, edicts, and Pinnacle invitation lists had gathered from the last few months. "Why try to solve these huge problems—*poverty, trafficking, corruption*—when you've got so little time to prepare for the Underworld? Why not just focus on that, and . . . well—enjoy life with me and the others? With what time you've got left?"

At his wide, guileless stare, I had suppressed a wave of anger, swallowing my loneliness. Of course Dayo wouldn't understand. No one would. Those who fought for justice were always alone—the ghosts who haunted me had made that clear.

"I'm doing it because—" The truth stuck like thorns in my tongue.

Because I'm the only one willing to feel guilty.

Because our ancestors killed children, and their ghosts are thirsty for blood.

*Because if I don't give the voices in my head what they want—
if I don't achieve justice for Aritsar—I might never come back from
the Underworld.*

But I'd given a half-truth instead. "Because I want a
legacy," I had told Dayo, kissing his scarred cheek. "I'm
not immune to death yet—not until I anoint Zuri. And if I
die, I want to have made a difference. I want . . ."

"To have meant something," I murmured now, words
lost in the Olorun fog.

A soft chuckle warmed my neck. "Done with speech
making?"

I hunched my shoulders. "What is it with you and
lurking? You're a king, not a drooling hyena."

"In due time, I hope to be neither."

I crossed my arms, appraising Zuri. "The abiku require
that I anoint twelve rulers, you know. So if you're going
to dismantle the Djbanti monarchy, I'll have to anoint you
while you're still king."

He raised a suggestive eyebrow. "Then we'll have to fall
in love rather quickly, Idajo."

My face heated, but I didn't break his gaze. "If you
succeed in dismantling the Djbanti monarchy . . . what
next? You won't have the resources of a king anymore.
Will you travel? Learn a trade?" I smiled ruefully. "Between
playing the fop for your warlords and razing markets as the
Crocodile, I can't imagine you've had time for fun since . . .
well. Ever, really."

To my surprise, Zuri's self-assured features grew

uncertain. "Haven't thought much about it," he said after a pause, face going carefully blank. "Don't need to. That's the price of ibaje magic. Once these stones have done their work . . . well. Let's just say I won't be in a state for touring the empire."

I looked with horror at the cuff on his bicep, noticing the raised, sickly veins that had begun to spider across his dark skin. "It's killing you," I whispered.

"Maybe," he muttered. "Maybe not. You never know with Pale Arts. It could be changing me into something else—perhaps one of those ghastly Underworld creatures you see scrawled in temple murals. I'd have to hide then, I suppose." He nudged my side. "Maybe I'll retire to where you grew up—if I can find it. Spend the rest of my days haunting the mango-scented orchards of Bhekina House."

I started. "How do you know about Bhekina House? Did Woo In tell you?"

He paused, gave a maddening shrug, and then smoothly changed the subject. "If you don't convince my warlords to stand down at this Pinnacle, I won't be retiring anywhere. Have you practiced wielding your Ray against any more bluebloods?"

I frowned. "I told you. I'm not touching the warlords' okanoba. I'm not an ehru-master, Zuri—we've had enough of those in my family."

His full lips pressed together. "You should be ready to use it. What if there's an emergency and you have to protect—Adukeh?"

"Don't use my akorin to manipulate me," I shot back, but the bait had worked. Adukeh was only a girl and we were headed for a coalition of nobles who might still want me dead. Was I putting her in danger?

"Practice on me," Zuri pressed. "Right now, while we're alone."

"We aren't alone." I shot a nervous glance at the drummer boys and bosun. "They'll see us. It'll look . . . well, unnatural. What if they start a rumor that I'm a witch?"

"You're a woman who rules equally with a man," he said dryly. "They'll always call you a witch. And if you beat me up, the sailors will be too frightened to gossip." He spread his chiseled arms, bearing his chest. "It'll be easy, Idajo. My father was king of Djbanti. My mother was a Nyamban princess. I'm *brimming* with okanoba. Command me, my great obabirin."

"A handstand," I bleated, hoping the indignity would make him resent me. But when the mask flashed beneath my wrapper, he grinned, immediately teetering upside down.

"Good," he panted. "Now make me do something hard. Something I don't want to do."

I gulped and shook my head. "Get up. And I'm not going to hurt you."

"Come on," he goaded, upright again. "You hate me. So why not show it?"

"Stop being stupid. I don't hate you."

"No?" He cocked his head, locs falling in thick strands. "Could have fooled me."

304

"I can't stand you," I said, flushing. "There's a difference."

He smiled, leaning close. Eucalyptus and peppermint washed over me in a cloud. "Still," he said, "haven't you wanted to see me squirm? What about when my agents covered you in blood at that market? Or the time I tricked you into dancing at your Peace Banquet? Or—" He paused, as if considering whether to cross a line. "Shall I tell you a secret? I know what High General Sanjeet has been up to." I started, but before I could interrupt, Zuri continued, "And no, it isn't searching for alagbatos, or even finding the new entrance to the Underworld. My spies keep me informed— he finished with all of that over a month ago. Now he's doing something new . . . almost as if he's *trying* to stay away from Oluwan. Funny—I used to be jealous, watching the two of you. I could have sworn you two were in love. But he's been away so long, I must have been mistaken—"

"You *shut up*," I snapped, heat surging through the mask. Before I knew it, Zuri was clutching his neck, eyes wide as he doubled over onto the deck, seeming to gag on his own tongue.

The bosun hurried over in alarm, and for half a second, I watched, fascinated and horrified. Then I snapped back into sanity, kneeling by Zuri's side.

"Breathe," I yelped. "For Am's sake, Zuri. Breathe, I command it." Only then did his rasping ease, and his hands dropped from his throat . . . but it didn't end there. When I commanded him, a fleeting thought had overcome me: *Okanoba is more trouble than it's worth.*

And though I had not directly commanded that thought—my will took shape in Zuri. I could sense the power fading from his body, leaving him alive, but weakened. Smaller. Even his muscles seemed diminished. Panicking, I willed the reverse . . . and Zuri grew vibrant again, his breaths strong and even.

The bosun stared daggers at me, but Zuri only laughed, waving the man away.

"Admit it," he croaked, "that was fun for you."

I collapsed against a barrel of oranges, feeling sick. "It wasn't."

"Not even a little?" He rolled onto his stomach, propping his chin in his hands.

"I took it," I breathed. "Just now. I took your okanoba away."

He nodded slowly. "Yes. Then you gave it back. I told you that was within your power. You could try it again."

"When Blessid Valley freezes over."

"Make me tell you things." He used his wheedling courtier voice. "How I know Prince Woo In. Where I found out about the power of okanoba. Why I won't let you see my memories."

"You'll let your guard down eventually," I countered. "I have to anoint you, and for that, we'll need to share memories with kuso-kuso."

"No," he sighed, scooting over and plopping his head onto my lap. His locs splayed across my thighs. "I'll only need to love you."

I cursed my stomach for fluttering. "Does your neck hurt from carrying an ego that big?"

"Sometimes. It's exhausting." He reached to chuck me under the chin. "I'm comforted that no matter how much I irritate you, you still need me alive."

"Not forever," I replied dryly. "I promised the abiku I'd anoint a council, not retain a living one. I could anoint you, then kill you after. I'd still have met the Underworld's requirement."

"Mm. Guess I'd better stay charming, then." He waggled his eyebrows at me, then frowned up at the sky. "Those sprites are a hazard, you know. Won't be long until people figure out that purple 'stars' follow wherever the empress goes. Your days of anonymous travel are numbered."

As if with a life of its own—my hand rose to trace Zuri's hairline. He relaxed beneath my touch, smiling as though familiar with it. As though embracing me beneath the moon was a long-cherished memory.

"To be fair," I said, glancing up at the lavender whirls of light, "they *have* tried to be more discreet."

We laughed quietly as the sprites arranged themselves like constellations, twinkling in a desperate imitation of stars. The bosun squinted at them doubtfully, rubbing his eyes.

"Brats," I sighed. "But I think I'd miss them if they left."

"I envy them. They get to hover at your side without getting slapped."

I glowered down at him, chewing the inside of my cheek.

His gaze was distant. Again, I felt the strange sensation that he was lost in a memory.

"I wish you'd just let me use the kuso-kuso," I said at last. "What if I can't anoint you in time?"

When he spoke again, the courtier's drawl had vanished from his voice. "I think, Idajo," he said, "you severely underestimate how easy you are to love."

When he cupped my face and kissed me, his lips were soft, like the sun through palm leaves. Then he stood and disappeared below deck, leaving me alone with my sky of sentient stars.

CHAPTER 26

ZURI INSISTED WE HOLD THE CEREMONY AT the crack of dawn, in the central compound of the sprawling Wanguru Fortress.

His home castle was made up of long, low mudbrick buildings, etched elegantly with geometric patterns and dotted with fortified towers. Upon our arrival, I immediately wished I could spend more time in Djbanti. A cerulean sky stretched over neat, bustling towns and villages surrounded by lush brush forests—purposely untamed to preserve the Djbantis' expert pastime: the hunting of beasts, providing the exquisite pelts that Djbanti exported throughout the empire.

Beggars lined the well-ordered streets, their gaunt faces a stark contrast to the old, elegant mudbrick high-rises. Clearly, the commoners of Djbanti had not always been poor. Hollow eyes watched our procession to the fortress, and children fought dogs for scraps in the alleys. The damage wrought by Zuri's warlords grew clearer by the hour. More than ever, I was desperate for my Pinnacle to succeed.

"D-Don't worry, L-Lady Empress," Adukeh whispered,

squeezing my hand. Her throat glittered with strings of coral akorin beads. She and the other attendants preceded in a grave procession through the fortress hallways. "After my p-performance, those nobles will *have* to listen."

I smiled and winked at her, moved as usual by my akorin's unshakeable confidence. "If you can't put the fear of Am into those nobles," I told her, "no one can. The audience won't know what hit them."

By tradition, all Pinnacles involved some form of entertainment, usually something flattering and benign, like *oriki* praise poems in the guests' honor, or dancing parades of animals from each realm.

But for my Pinnacle, I had asked Adukeh to sing the scariest tale she knew. The idea had delighted her, and even now she muttered the lines to herself, caressing her grandmother's drum.

The main gathering area of Wanguru Fortress lay in a vast limestone courtyard, overlooked by towering statues of lions— patron beasts of Djbanti royalty. I could hear the audience's rumble long before we entered—noble clans teemed in every inch of the standing space. In the courtyard's center, Zuri sat enthroned on an echo-stone dais. He wore a richly patterned wrapper and sash in black and crimson—the royal cloth of Djbanti. More ornaments glittered in his locs than I had ever seen on him before. When I appeared, he leapt up, sweeping a bow and gesturing toward his throne.

"The court is yours, Imperial Majesty," he slurred, with a lurch so convincingly clumsy, I thought he was drunk for real. Then he settled onto a lesser gilded stool, and emitted a hiccup so violent, I bit my lip to keep from laughing. I couldn't giggle now—thanks to the nervous energy roiling in my stomach, I wouldn't be able to stop.

As I ascended the dais, Adukeh hollered the traditional entry song with barely a stutter. "*Of what use—Of what use is an empty throne?*"

A sea of noble faces, bodies swathed in fabrics from all over the empire, glowered at me from behind lace fans and woven palm fronds. Zuri's warlords stood out among them—seven burly, smug-faced men in war paint and lion pelt mantles. They shot sneering looks at Zuri, and glared at me, but in a bleating chorus, they echoed the call-and-response with everyone else.

We have found someone worthy—(Have you found someone?)
Aheh, Kunleo is worthy to fill it—(Yes, Kunleo is worthy to fill it!)

How many of these nobles had been terrorized by my "servants"—the ojiji who had murdered my enemies in droves? Sweat sprung from my palms, but I clenched them, head high, and sat on Zuri's throne.

The adinkra cloth from my outing with King Kwasi— black, white, and metallic gold fabric—hugged my hips in an arresting gown, leaving my shoulders bare. My jewelry I kept simple: a gold cuff choker and my rising sun crown, a complement to the stark glyphs on my adinkra and the blue patterns covering my skin.

"You look," Zuri said, "like someone to be feared."

"In the words of my council sister Queen Min Ja," I whispered back, "that's what makes me so popular."

Adukeh's voice pinged from the echo-stone, words sliding in the tonal scale of ancient Arit orators. "N-Noble clans of the t-twelve Arit realms. Your obabirin b-bids you welcome to the first P-Pinnacle of her est-esteemed reign."

On cue, my attendants passed bowls of kola nuts around the courtyard. Every clan leader took one, politely biting the pieces of small, hard fruits and spitting onto the floor: an acceptance of my peace offering. I wondered how long peace would last once I started talking.

"In honor of this m-momentous g-gathering," Adukeh went on, clearly rallying her courage, "I, a f-former quarry girl, will t-tell you a story."

Members of the crowd jeered at Adukeh's impediment. She stole a glance at me, and I smiled, mouthing what I'd told her this morning:

Make history.

Adukeh's eyes glittered. Brandishing her drum like a weapon, she tore on, her stutter growing weaker with every word.

"Hear a song of life and d-death," she bellowed. "Hear the t-tale of Egungun's Parade. I have three bells in my mouth. I do not tell a lie."

Then she trilled, throwing her shoulder into beating the drum. When she started the song, my attendants and I joined in, crowing out the well-known refrain:

Egungun, I hear him! He was the first man.
Egungun, my ancestors' ancestor.
Egungun wins souls with the beat of his drum—
Egungun, he leads the parade.

All around us, the court of nobles murmured, alarmed and discomfited. The tale of Egungun was said to have sinister power—that when sung, it awoke beasts who lurked in the Underworld, eager to pull souls into the depths below. As a result, the story was only told in whispers, or jeered at criminals on their way to execution, hoping to heap bad luck on already-doomed souls.

But Adukeh grinned and pressed on, declaiming in a strident sing-chant:

"There was no death in Human-town. Watch my eyes, I am not a liar! There was no death in Human-town; we walked the earth as gods. Our children lived forever until Warlord Fire cursed us. Hear the sounds of beasts baying: *gorrun-go, gorrun-go*! The Warlord has sent his thirteen monsters; they prey on Human-town!"

Adukeh hunched over as she drummed, baring her teeth in her best imitation of snarling beasts.

"Each monster is a death that you or I may die," Adukeh continued, "and the strongest, Old Age, shall catch us all. Hear a wail lift up from Human-town. The children of Earth and the Pelican have known pain, but death? This is a journey no human has taken. Who will be the first?

"'Me,' intones the Gray-Beard Man, and so we call him,

for we have lost his name to time. 'I was the first that Earth shaped from blood and clay. My limbs are weak, and when the Warlord's beast growls for me, I shall not outrun her.'"

Adukeh stroked her smooth chin in imitation of Gray-Beard, and then shifted, rolling her shoulders like a wolf on the prowl.

"This very night, she comes: Old Age, with her mane as white as coconut, scratching her claws—*krit, krit*—on the walls of Gray-Beard's house. He does not run, our Gray-Beard. No, he kneels at her paws and bows his ancient head. He says, 'I am ready.'

"This pleases the Warlord's beast. So she allows him to take one item with him: his favorite drum. Then Old Age smites Gray-Beard with her chilling breath—*saa, saa*—and takes him to a forest deep in the Underworld, where animals unlike you or I have ever seen live.

"'Select a companion,' Old Age tells him. 'For beyond this forest lies the path to Core: the paradise that gives rest to all souls. But for every step of your journey, you will feel any pain that you caused on earth.' Then Old Age vanishes. A black dog, tall and fat as a harvest cow, comes to Gray-Beard: Aja, the first emi-ehran. Faithful Aja! Hear it pound its massive tail—*khoum, khoum*—to embolden Gray-Beard's soul. Together, they descend into Core."

Adukeh played an interlude on her drum and danced, swaying her hips and stepping rhythmically on the balls of her feet.

"This is the part you will not like. You will want to run

me, an honest griot, out of town. You will throw rocks and say, 'Ah-ah, you are trying to scare us! It isn't true!' But I swear on the hide of this drum: I will someday walk that painful path to Core, and so will you.

"*Aieeee!* Hear Gray-Beard shout! His body aches. His cheeks sting from the blows he rained down on his siblings as a quarrelsome young boy. He doubles over. He jerks, as if he has sprouted invisible wings, now bruised and broken: the death of birds he once struck down for sport.

"'If these are the crimes of my childhood,' sobs Gray-Beard, 'how will I endure the wrongs I committed as a man?'

"He falls to his knees. The pain is bad, bad now. He feels the shame of the peasant who swept his front step, teased and spat upon by Gray-Beard's children. He feels the thirst, the hunger of the poor who toiled in his mills, and mined his quarries."

The crowd's foreboding hum grows louder—these lines of Egungun's story were new, clearly added by Adukeh.

"Gray-Beard flees from the path," says Adukeh, "away from Core! He beckons to Aja—'Come with me, my faithful friend!' But the emi-ehran stays put, staring with sad eyes at the path. Aja's message is clear: *I am your companion for this journey only.* So Gray-Beard wanders the Underworld for seventy days," Adukeh intoned. "But the loneliness is too much for him to bear. So he returns to that harrowing path! Aja nuzzles his face—*gurunun, gurunun*—and they walk on.

"The journey to Core can take years, or no time at all.

It depends, you see, on all the pain that you have caused out of malice or neglect. But Gray-Beard is very old, and so the path stretches on for miles. He would go mad, I think, if not for the love of Aja, and the boon of his drum.

"*Egungun, Egungun, Egungun!* The sound shores up Gray-Beard's limbs. He plays the drum until his hands are calloused. His heartbeat tunes to the rhythm. The drum is part of him now, and swallows his name. Egungun—and so we must now call him, for Gray-Beard is no more— laughs with every painful step. Gray-Beard knew nothing but shame, but Egungun is wise. See his feet swell with love for those he has hurt! See him pity his enemies, who will someday die and walk the path before him!

"Hear a song rise in Egungun's heart. There are many verses, but time has lost them. This part, however, I know:

> *Walk on, beloved, walk on!*
> *There is life at the end of the world.*

"Will you sing now, to strengthen him? I will, for what else is a griot's purpose?

> *Egungun, I hear him! He was the first man.*
> *Egungun, my ancestors' ancestor.*
> *Egungun wins souls with the beat of his drum—*
> *Egungun, he leads the parade.*

Then Adukeh, every muscle in her body shaking with

fear and triumph, swept a solemn bow. From behind me I heard fervent applause—Zuri, standing and clapping. I did the same, and the nobles reluctantly joined in, scowling at Adukeh as she scrambled off the stage and my attendants ushered her away. Only then did I address the court, smiling tightly at the crowd.

"Here is the part that you will like," I said, voice reverberating through the courtyard. "My akorin did not finish her story. Egungun reaches the gates of Core. The Ira, guardians of all souls, invite him in, but Egungun refuses to enter. He knows that every other human soul will suffer on their journey, as he did. So he returns up the path, and to this day, we hear Egungun's drum pound through the Underworld, guiding tormented souls to their final rest at Core. Giving hope to all who join Egungun's Parade." I paused. "Today, I give all of you a chance to turn back. To redeem yourselves for the abuses, the poverty that flourished under your watch. You may get away with it now . . . but will you escape the consequences on your journey to Core?"

To my endless relief, some of the nobles actually appeared chastened. But most of them scoffed, and loudest of all were Zuri's warlords, jowls shaking with laughter.

"Is this why you have come all this way, Imperial Majesty?" called the boldest one—a warrior with elaborate bone piercings—grinning at me with gold-capped teeth. Zuri had warned me about him: Lord Gakuru, overseer of Djbanti's largest limestone quarries and tanning houses.

"Do you mean to scare us with cookfire tales? Either your throne has power to enforce the laws it passes . . . or it does not. This very Pinnacle is a show of weakness. We are not children to be chastened with wagged fingers."

The warlords chuckled. I heard Zuri shift behind me, and though I knew he could not show it, rage was rippling through him.

I smiled coldly. "You are not children," I agreed. "Some of you are greedy, ready to grasp at land and resources no matter who it hurts—and that is exactly what I'm counting on."

Confused chatter from the crowd. I glanced back at Zuri, who watched me with deepened curiosity.

"As your Empress Redemptor and High Lady Judge of Aritsar," I declared, "I hereby pass the Watchman Edict. As of the next moon, the crown will strip lands from any noble clan who refuses to cede the Kunleo-owned resources in their jurisdiction. The crown will then award the confiscated land to another clan . . . whichever one reports the crime."

I watched wheels turn behind the warlords' pompous faces, from which the smugness gradually faded.

"You will police each other," I said simply. "Many of your clans have been rivals for decades, and each would leap at the chance to gain your neighbor's property at the first whiff of illegal operations. The burden of proof will be on the reporter. But with lands to win," I added, "I'm sure you'll be resourceful. So . . ." I crossed my arms. "What have you to say, nobles of Aritsar? Any objections?"

I braced myself for an onslaught, but to my fascination, the courtyard had gone quiet. Greed hung in the air like a sensual veil of smoke. Already I could sense them plotting, panicking, wondering how soon they could unveil the illegal operations of their neighbors.

Behind me, Zuri gave a low whistle of admiration. "Diabolical, Idajo," he slurred. "Wish I'd thought of it myself."

Again, the kola nut bowls were passed around the courtyard. I held my breath as, one by one, the clan leaders of Oluwan, Swana, Quetzala, Mewe, Moreyao, and every other Arit realm bit and spat, accepting my edict and hurrying from the courtyard . . . all except the warlords of Djbanti.

"Unlike our fellow Arit lords," Gakuru hissed, "we Djbanti are not easily led by imperial tricks. The clans of other realms may squabble in rivalry, but we warlords learned to stand together ages ago. We know from experience that when nobility unites—in trade or in war—no one may stand against them. Not even a king." He sneered at Zuri, then turned to me. "Not even an empress."

"You will accept my edict," I snapped. "No matter how powerful your forces are, they cannot stand against the entire Imperial Guard."

"But of course we accept, Imperial Majesty." Still grinning, Gakuru bowed, bit a kola nut, and spat loudly on the ground. "Just don't expect to receive any *reports* from Djbanti anytime soon."

My face flushed. Slowly, my heart sank to my sandals. This had been my plan's weakness—at the end of the day, I still depended on nobles to be my eyes and ears. If Zuri's warlords were unwilling to report disobedience, then how could I eradicate dissent?

I turned to Zuri for help, but he only raised an eyebrow, nodding at my chest, where my mask lay hidden beneath my wrapper. "You know what to do."

I froze on the dais, temptation stirring in my veins. With a word, I could wipe the grin off Gakuru's face. I could make every one of those slimy warlords bow. With a flash of my mask, I could save every child like Adukeh.

"There's nothing wrong with using power, Idajo," Zuri said. His courtier drawl was gone. He spoke quietly, though the echo-stone undoubtedly allowed the court to hear him. "You aren't an ehru-master. You are a gear in an imperial machine—just like everyone else. You are a tool—so be a useful one."

Slowly, my hand rose to my mask. I met Gakuru's mocking eyes, and fury roiled inside me, ready to spew in a word: *Bow. Bow and obey.*

But then my spear shifted in its holster, reminding me of its presence. I reached up and touched the shaft, feeling a spark of Sanjeet's essence in my fingertips. Just then I remembered a night so many months ago, when Sanjeet embraced me in the palace salon, whispering in my ear.

No human being should be reduced to a function. The day we do that—it's the beginning of the end.

"I'm not a tool," I rasped, after a deafening silence. "And I refuse to make one of anyone else. We'll find another way to help your people, Zuri. I promise. We'll build the Djbanti you want, together." I reached to take his hand. "But this . . ." I gestured toward the mask beneath my clothes. "This isn't it."

To my surprise, Zuri did not look disappointed—only resigned. He stood and touched my cheek, gaze reaching past me to the fortress walls. "I hoped you wouldn't say that, Idajo. It would have made this day so much easier."

Only then did I notice a roar in my ears—and this time, it wasn't due to sleep deprivation. Faintly, beyond the fortress walls, shouts and the pounding of feet and the clanging of iron against iron sounded.

A runner boy in Wanguru colors stumbled into the courtyard, eyes glinting with fear. I noticed that he bowed to the warlords instead of to Zuri. "The peasants," he wailed. "Workers, everywhere, in every region—they're setting fire to your villas. Laying siege to mines, claiming ownership of the tanneries. They're armed. I'm not sure how. But now they're coming for the fortress, and . . . it's a revolution, Lord Gakuru."

CHAPTER 27

GAKURU'S SHOULDERS TURNED TO STONE. His gaze fell like thunder on Zuri. "This," he rasped, "is your doing."

"However do you mean?" Zuri's voice was soft. He smiled down at the warlords from his dais, dark features cold and resplendent, like a marble-faced god. For a breathless moment, I lost myself in that charismatic rage. I knew then that I could drown in a man like Zuri, sinking like a pebble in his well of righteous blood.

Gakuru unsheathed a knife from his weapon holster. "Your days as king have always been numbered. We knew you were up to something, we were only unclear on the details. But now the game is up, my *king* . . ." He bared his gold-capped teeth, knuckles tightening around the knife. The other warlords drew their weapons as well. "And we have armies a thousand strong. They will cut your peasants to pieces, and by the time we are done with you—"

"By the time you leave this courtyard," Zuri interrupted, "you will not have a single gold coin to your names. Your

322

warriors may fight, but they will lose. Your lands will be razed, redistributed among the people, and your mills and quarries, stripped of your names." His eyes gleamed. "Consider this day a gift from my parents and brothers."

Gakuru snarled. "You will soon join them." He raised the knife to throw it . . . and then froze, blade clattering to the ground. Around him, the other warlords dropped their weapons as well, arms frozen in the air. Their mouths gaped like fish, blinded by light that had flashed from my mask, shining through the cloth of my adinkra gown.

"Stop," I hissed. But I hadn't even needed to speak aloud. Like an instinct, my Ray had seized their okanoba as a viper took its prey, squeezing their wills into submission.

"Witch," Gakuru gasped. "*Witch!*"

"Run," I told Zuri and my entourage, who still hovered nervously by the dais. "It's not safe here. Get out, all of you. Barricade yourself somewhere in the fortress."

My attendants fled from the courtyard, and though my guards hesitated, they jogged after my handmaidens when I commanded them a second time.

"I'm not leaving you," Zuri said, taking my hand. He beamed at me, glowing with the lurid power of his ibaje . . . and we vanished together.

Stomach sloshing, I reappeared next to Zuri on the fortress's highest turret, which offered a grim view of the battle unfolding below.

"You planned this from the beginning," I panted. "You didn't expect me to convince the nobles at all. You were using my Pinnacle to distract the warlords." I stared at him, puzzled by the revelation. "Except for just now, when I used it by accident. You didn't need me to control their okanoba."

"But I do. Now more than ever." He spoke fervently, wind whipping his locs as he gestured at the carnage below. "You're the only chance those peasants have to survive."

I followed his gaze, stiffening with horror as I realized how unequal the battle was. Armored warriors, faces painted with the colors of their liege warlords, swarmed the peasants like ants. The commoners outnumbered them, but even armed with the few weapons Zuri had managed to smuggle them, they were vastly unskilled and slowly but surely dropping beneath the merciless clubs of the warriors.

"How in Am's name do you expect me to stop this?" I snapped at Zuri. "You sent innocent, untrained people into battle! All of them could die!"

"Or none of them." Against all reason, Zuri was smiling, gently gripping my shoulders. "We're almost there, Idajo. The warriors will only fight for as long as their warlords are alive."

He pointed to the center of the fray, where Gakuru and his peers cut down peasants left and right. The warlords were easy to make out: their skin gleamed with the power of okanoba—a merciless, malevolent blue.

"Kill them," said Zuri. "Order their hearts to stop and the battle will end immediately. Thousands of lives saved . . . and a new Djbanti born."

"Zuri, what are you talking about?" I wrenched from his grasp, my head reeling. "I can't just murder seven people in cold blood."

He blinked. "If you don't," he said calmly, "thousands of peasants will die."

"Peasants you incited to rebel!"

"Yes. Incited to stop bowing to people like those warlords. To people like *me,* for Am's sake. To royal families, who have profited off the backs of the poor for decades."

"You're using me," I whispered.

"Of course I'm using you." He blinked at me without an ounce of shame. "To save thousands of people. Just like you're using me to complete your council and save thousands of Redemptors."

"That is not the same," I snapped. "I never manipulated or lied to you. If I kill those warlords, you might not abdicate the throne of Djbanti. You could just seize all their land for yourself. Rule with absolute power."

He exhaled slowly. "There's no reason for you to trust me," he admitted. "I wish I could prove myself, but I can't. Still, Idajo . . . if you don't deliver justice to Gakuru and his fellow cretins, the blood of innocents will be on your hands."

"Don't," I shrilled. "Don't you dare blame me for a massacre you orchestrated."

"You could kill me," he said, with sudden inspiration. "If I don't abdicate. You could use my okanoba to stop my heart. That's it—there's your insurance. If I break my promise, you stop my heart where I stand."

He was right. And even if I didn't have that power . . . deep down, I knew Zuri wasn't lying to me. I may not have known him as well as I thought I had, but anyone could see that Zuri was extraordinary. He would never connive for a life of mere wealth and comfort. It was too unimaginative. Every muscle in his body strained for purpose. If I did what he wanted, Zuri would toss away his crown without a second thought. And those people below . . .

My eyes slid to the peasants. The longer I waited, the more people fell. How many times would my cowardice cost human lives?

"You already used your okanoba to save me," he said fiercely, drawing me close. His hands found my waist, and my breath shortened. "Deep down, we think the same, Idajo. You stepped into your power like a second skin. It was beautiful. You used it then, for one life. So why not now, for many?"

The logic entrapped me, clouding my thoughts. Already I could feel the heat rising in my chest. I wouldn't even have to speak—if I thought of Gakuru's cruel features and let the reins on my anger slacken, he and the other warlords would drop dead. Still—

I balled my hands into fists. "When I saved you, I didn't have to kill anyone. I didn't play god."

By degrees, he read the stubbornness on my face, and his hardened with disappointment. Then his features grew strangely peaceful—distant. Resigned. "Well then, Idajo," he said, still holding me, "you had better anoint me right now."

My heart pounded. "Why?"

"Because I'm going down there," he said. "It's as you said—that battle is my doing. I won't let those peasants fight alone. So in case I don't see you again—"

"Stop it," I rasped, scanning him with fearful eyes as his words sank in. "Stop talking nonsense. And I can't anoint you. You don't love me."

He smiled, as calm as a madman. "Yes, I do."

Reeling with anger and grief, I flung the Ray at him out of contempt, knowing he couldn't hold it—knowing it would hurt him. *You don't love me,* I Ray-spoke.

But he didn't fall or cry out and press his temples. Instead, his voice sounded in my mind, setting all my nerves on edge.

Wrong again, Idajo.

I watched, speechless, as he drew a knife from his pocket, making a shallow slit in his palm. Then he sheathed the knife and took my hand. "Isn't this how we seal it?" he asked. "The blood oath."

I nodded woodenly, wondering how he knew that—anointings were usually done in private. Still, I allowed him to make a cut, pressing our palms together. I inhaled sharply as my Ray flowed into him: a permanent, thrumming tether.

That's better, he Ray-spoke, then looped his fingers beneath the collar line of my dress, pulling out my obabirin mask by its cord, and setting it to rest on my chest.

327

Twelve bold colors glittered on the face of the lioness: every immunity but old age.

A thrill ran up my spine: I was a full Raybearer. I had fulfilled the command of the abiku. My mask was complete.

"How?" I asked, as he tore his tunic to wrap our hands. "How is this possible? Zuri, you barely know me."

He shook his head, features glowing with that expression I'd seen twice before: hazy, as though recalling an old, fond memory. Then he drew me into a kiss—deeper than the one on the boat, stealing the air from my lungs as, dazed, I kissed him back.

I loved you once before, he Ray-spoke. *A version of you. It's how I knew you'd be perfect.*

A cold, stinging suspicion crept into my veins.

He was vulnerable now—I could tell, from the way he trembled against me—and so when I sent my Hallow into his mind, the usual barriers were gone. He stiffened as I rummaged through his memories, my lips still pressed to his—but he did not stop me. Then I froze and pushed him away, eyes wet with disbelief. In his mind, I had found the face I was looking for. He had kissed her once too. He had *bonded* with her—lived as one of her Anointed Ones.

"Mother," I gasped. "You . . . you were one of hers."

He continued to smile. "I was, my Idajo. And in a way . . . now I'm hers again."

My head pounded with horror. It all made sense now. His infatuation. His knowledge about the Ray. His insistence on mental barriers—he knew that if I'd discovered his

328

ties to my mother, I would never have let him get close.

"She understood, my Lady," Zuri said dreamily. "The need to knock old regimes down before you can build them up again. I was going to build a world with her. Like I'm building a new world with you."

"Woo In," I whispered, backing away. "You were council brothers. He kept your secret because he felt guilty about killing The Lady."

Zuri didn't seem to register my repulsion, smiling as though we shared an inside joke. "I gave you hints, you know. When I told you I was Hallowed. And when I told you of my parentage—you know how partial The Lady was to isokens."

"You don't love me," I croaked, my shock giving way to rage. "All this time—all you saw was an extension of my mother. You love an *idea* of me."

He reached with his bandaged hand to stroke my hairline. "But that's what the Raybearer is, Idajo," he said fervently. "The Raybearer has never been about a person—not really. It's about an idea. Min Ja and the rest may love the real you. But they also love what you represent: rebirth. Redemption. The tale of a monster turned heroine." He pressed a final, lingering kiss to my forehead, and gestured to the chaos below. "I hope, Idajo, that you'll be the story they need too."

Then, unsheathing his club and battle pole, my newest council brother glowed with the sickly tendrils of ibaje . . . and disappeared, leaving me alone atop the tower.

Clanging weapons and the sick cacophony of blows roared in my ears. The battle below raged on, and before long I spotted Zuri, using the Ray to locate him in the fray. He had donned his Crocodile mask and fought alongside the commoners, skin burning cobalt, dealing death like a fluid, lethal dancer. His okanoba allowed him to fight with the strength of two men . . . but it wasn't enough.

Even now, I could see the battle turning in favor of the noble warriors. In less than an hour, I would be staring over a mass graveyard. Even though I hadn't started this—even though I knew it wasn't my fault, my stomach went leaden as the ojiji chorus sounded in my head.

See how death follows everywhere you go? For shame, Empress. You will never make up for this. You will have to pay—have to pay.

I shuddered. They were right. In my cowardice, I could not bring myself to kill, even to protect the innocent. The lost lives of every Djbanti commoner rested on my shoulders, and for that I deserved to pay. Unless . . .

My eyes slid to Gakuru and his six companions. Even as they murdered dozens, they were nauseatingly resplendent, the subtle glow of okanoba lending glory to their cruelty. My jaw set with rage. How dare they abuse so rare and powerful a gift? They didn't deserve to be called nobles.

They didn't deserve their okanoba.

And with that thought, I took my hands off the reins of my will.

My mask flashed, a burst of light over the battle. None

of the fighters noticed, too caught up in combat . . . but in an instant, the seven warlords of Djbanti fumbled their weapons, clutching their chests and wheezing. Their smug stature disappeared, and they stared at one another in disoriented confusion. I had not killed them. But the glow of their okanoba was gone—leaving seven old, winded men in a field of peasants out for blood.

"Now," I growled, though I knew they could not hear me. "Let's see how you do in a fair fight."

In seconds they were set upon, commoners covering their bodies in a wave of flesh and iron. I could not determine the exact moment the warlords died—but judging from how quickly the peasants dispersed, whooping in victory, I guessed it had been quick. I squinted. No—one of the warlords still lived, albeit barely: Gakuru dragged himself up from the bodies of his fallen peers, clutching his side. A nearby peasant warrior cried out, preparing to finish the job, but Zuri got there first, plunging his pole in Gakuru's side. I exhaled with relief . . . until, with a dying lurch, Gakuru ripped the crocodile mask from Zuri's face.

The whoops of nearby peasants grew dull with shock— and then, as they recognized the king of Djbanti, they advanced with roars of rage.

"No," I breathed, and then hollered at the top of my lungs, though I knew the enraged commoners could not hear me. "No, don't hurt him! You don't understand; he's on your side!"

But my cries fell on deaf ears. Of course they did—as

far as these starved, abused commoners knew, Zuri was just like the warlords. Just another noble, feeding off the sweat on their backs. Of course they thought that. It was exactly what Zuri had taught them.

"Stop," I rasped. But my Ray had no power over those without okanoba. So I did nothing—only stood on that tower and watched as combat pole after combat pole lodged in Zuri's torso. Before he fell, he looked up . . . and tears filled my throat in wonder and horror.

Zuri was smiling.

Smiling, because at last, he had been a successful tool.

This was what he'd wanted all along, I realized. He hadn't planned to live past today. Hadn't wanted to. I remembered now how he had evaded my questions on the *Tsetse Fly*, when I asked his plans for the future. His whole life had revolved around bringing about his revolution. To birth his new Djbanti. It was beautiful, Zuri's cause—of that I had no doubt. It was selfless, unambiguously *right*. But he had given himself nothing else to live for. His world had gone adrift, and so . . . he had chosen to fall out of orbit.

In that moment, I saw my own future. Zuri had called us the same, and he had been right. As every care, every other focus in my life winked out, tunneling to a single focus until I could only find joy in one goal—*do more*—I was fast approaching Zuri's ending. And it had taken this— the dreadful glory of Zuri's death, the rapture of his dying face—for me to realize I didn't want it.

This was not my ending.

I did not want a hero's death. I did not want to die in the Underworld, my story reduced to a function, a meal to sate the appetite of ghosts.

Craven, hissed the ojiji. *Deserter. Justice—justice! Pay the price. Don't you care?*

"I do care," I told them, out loud. "I want justice—for you. For everyone. But I have to find a balance. It isn't enough to pay for past abuses. I have to find a future to live for too."

The voices paused, considering. *Well then,* they asked, voices dripping with contempt, *what will you live for, Empress Redemptor? What could be more important than us?*

I had no answer. My mind yawned blank as wind howled around the tower, raising goose bumps on my skin. Faintly, I realized that the battle had not ended with Zuri's death. His prediction had been wrong—once the warlords were dead, some of the warriors did not immediately retreat, continuing to cut down commoners.

I gripped the tower balustrade, swearing in helpless rage. *"No!"* Had all of it been for nothing—the Pinnacle, Zuri's sacrifice? Would today still end in a massacre?

Then drums sounded in the air—first far away, then nearer, and in a sequence I recognized. Before my eyes, cohorts of plainclothes warriors seemed to pour in from nowhere, flooding into the front lines and overwhelming both warlord and commoner forces.

"Lay down your weapons," barked a familiar voice.

"Down! Let the peasants go free. There will be no more slaughter today." My vision blurred with incredulous tears. For there on the battlefield, leading the charge against the warlords' forces, was High General Sanjeet of Dhyrma.

CHAPTER 28

WHEN I DESCENDED FROM THE TOWER, a different battle seemed to be raging in the fortress—one of panicked greed instead of blood and justice. Djbanti courtiers fought with one another in the mudstone fortress corridors, barking at servants, stuffing sacks with tapestries, earthenware, sconce figurines of gold and ivory—any riches they could carry from the now-fallen royal house of Wanguru.

I glided through the looting mobs, numb and directionless until a voice Ray-spoke in my thoughts, low and anxious.

Where are you, sunshine girl? Answer me. Please. Tar, are you all right?

I was too dazed to respond, but could sense the speaker moving toward me, searching the fortress, rounding corners until he appeared before me in a corridor, his armored chest rising and falling.

I said nothing, not quite believing he was there. I'd certainly had more implausible visions. Though in those, I saw floating, undead children—not a man with tea-colored eyes, blood-spattered clothes, and a musical, cavernous voice I had not heard in months.

"Tar," he breathed, dropping his scimitar to the ground. Absently, I wondered why he wasn't wearing his Imperial Guard uniform. "I was so worried. When we saw the peasants had killed King Zuri, we couldn't find you, and I thought . . . but you're alive. Am's Story"—his gaze dropped to my mask, which glittered with all twelve colors— "you're more than alive. You're . . . done. Then you managed to anoint Zuri before he—"

I nodded.

"Oh, Tar." Sanjeet reached me in a stride, holding me to his chest. I shook in his arms, tears pouring from my unblinking eyes as I inhaled his familiar scent. Earth and leather polish. Solid. Grounding—the opposite of the heady rush I'd felt around Zuri.

"Adukeh," I asked.

"She's safe. Evacuated with the rest of your attendants— only you were missing. You can't stay, Tar. The battle may be over, but this territory will be volatile for a long time. Djbanti's government is changing hands, and that transition won't be pretty."

"It's what they wanted," I whispered. "The commoners—they deserved a change. Justice. A chance to rule themselves."

"I know."

"You do? How?"

He didn't answer, brow furrowing as his Hallow crackled

over me. "I know you can't exactly *die* anymore, but . . . Tar, you're not well. When's the last time you got any sleep?"

I smiled up at him as fever overcame me, phantom tutsu sprites spinning in my vision. "Gods don't sleep, Jeet," I mumbled. "They only rise and fall."

His brow wrinkled with concern. "Tar."

"I need help," I said.

The words echoed in my ears. I blinked, stunned at how natural they sounded. Why hadn't I said them before?

The answer appeared in an instant: the entire corridor filled with ojiji. Crying children, tears running tracks down their filthy cheeks, their voices shrill and ravenous. Angry.

Sanjeet is blind, they chanted. *You cannot ask him for help. He will never understand, he will think you are mad; he will get in your way. Only you can help us, Empress Redemptor. Only you understand. You are special. You are alone—*

"That's what Zuri thought," I whispered. "Zuri thought he was alone. That he was the only one who could save those people, and now . . . he's dead. That's what you want for me too, isn't it?"

"Tar, who are you talking to?" Sanjeet's tone was calm, but his eyes shone with terror.

You are unworthy. You have to pay—

"How can I be both special and unworthy?" I demanded, yelling over the screeching ojiji. Sanjeet gripped my shoulders, making sounds as if to soothe a panicked animal, and I laughed, smiling at him. "It doesn't make any sense.

But those voices—they've never tried to make sense. They wanted me to feel guilty. Worthless, exhausted, so I'd go to the Underworld and choose to never come back."

"What voices?" His gaze was serious. "Tar, are you talking about the ojiji?"

"Yes. I think the abiku are using them. Controlling them, somehow. They made me think I was alone. But I was wrong. Jeet . . . I'm not fine. And I haven't been for a long—"

The children screamed.

Something warm trickled down my neck. I touched my ears—they were running with blood.

"Help," I said again, before collapsing against Sanjeet's chest, my world fading to white.

When I awoke, a hot, fragrant mist enveloped me, prickling my underarms and forehead. Then a bracingly cold wave slapped my face. I jerked upright, opening my eyes just in time to see a bird with crystalline blue wings flap away.

"Sorry," said Ye Eun, "I *told* Hwanghu to be gentle."

"What in Am's name . . ." I croaked.

I was outdoors, and it appeared to be twilight, my sprites barely visible in the sky. I was lying on a translucent jade altar, which rested on the banks of several steaming pools. The spring lay in a mossy clearing, surrounded on all sides by vine-covered rock face. Ye Eun was kneeling by my side, wearing nothing but an unbleached shift. A short distance away, Ae Ri sat among the moss in only a nappy, splashing her pudgy hands in the water.

"Ye Eun, where are we? And how did you—"

"Drink," she ordered, holding a drinking gourd to my lips. The mist had saturated her short black hair and strands clung to her stony face. "You're thirsty."

She was right, and so I obeyed, gulping down several ounces of metallic-tasting water. "You slept for a week," she explained. "The Well priests had to force drinks down your throat until I used sowanhada. I learned how to command the water to stay in your mouth. Eventually, you'd swallow it." She cocked her head, raising her eyebrows at my lioness mask. "You wouldn't have died either way, I suppose. But you wouldn't have gotten better either."

I drew my knees to my chest. Besides the mask, I wore only a strip of linen, tied gently across my breasts, and a matching loincloth that hung to my ankles. Every inch of my map-covered skin beaded with sweat. Someone had sectioned my hair into neat twists and massaged my scalp with tingling peppermint oil.

I sat in a temple, of course. If Ye Eun's mention of priests hadn't been enough, the stone goddess towering nearby would have confirmed it. The natural rock face had been carved into the shape of a winged, plush-lipped young woman emptying a jug. An enormous waterfall gushed from her vessel, landing with billowing clouds of steam into the springs below. Turquoise pricks of light danced on the water's surface, diving, chirruping, leaving trails of rainbow bubbles: *ombitsu* sprites, much rarer than tutsu, and said only to appear where water was exceptionally pure.

"That's supposed to be Iyaja," said Ye Eun, nodding at the mountain sculpture. "The spring's alagbato—King Water's favorite daughter. She blesses mortals with good health. If you believe in all that."

I sucked in a breath. "Then I'm not in Djbanti anymore."

The sects of Arit religion made for wildly different places of worship. In Oluwan, Ember-sect halls devoted to Warlord Fire were most common, built near volcanoes and holy forges, and bustling with merchants of coal and gemstones. The Temple of Iyaja, a collection of springs and tunnels carved into a mountain, was the only Well-sect shrine to King Water and his pantheon near Oluwan City. The ancient hot springs—which mysteriously spouted salt water instead of fresh—were said to cure troubled souls of evil spirits. I glanced around. My altar stood a stone's throw from several cave openings. Drumbeats and string music floated out from the gloom, interspersed with distant chanting.

Ye Eun leaned against the altar, eyeing me keenly. "Do you feel different now, Lady Empress?"

"Different how?"

"I don't know. Different. From before."

"I'm certainly weaker," I mumbled. "And hungry. And . . ." I trailed off, finally identifying the strange weight-lessness I'd felt since waking.

No headaches. For the first time in months, not even the slightest twinge.

The chorus of ojiji, which I'd grown to regard almost as my conscience, waiting always at the edge of my thoughts, had vanished completely.

Relief and unease washed over me. What did it mean? Had the spirits given up on me—did they no longer think I could bring the justice they craved? It was nice not to be in pain, but . . . without them, how would I know what to do?

Ye Eun handed me another gourd, this time filled with broth. I gulped it down too quickly, feeling instantly queasy. "They brought you back to An-Ileyoba first," Ye Eun said. "When you didn't wake up for days, the whole palace was worried—especially the emperor and the High Lord General. None of the healers could figure out what was wrong. Then the sprites said to bring you here."

I shook my head—knowing I couldn't have heard right. "The *sprites*?" I stared up at the hazy twilight sky where the tutsu twinkled faintly.

"It's hard to explain. I'll let the High Lord General do it. Are you still thirsty?"

I nodded, and she gestured at the spring, squinting hard in concentration. A bubble of water lifted into the air, hovering toward us. When Ye Eun muttered something, the bubble seemed to shake itself free of crumbling white powder, leaving the water clear—she had ordered the liquid to remove its own salt. I held out the drinking gourd, and the bubble burst over it, allowing me to drink.

"You get lots of visitors, you know," she said, gesturing toward the cave openings. "The emperor comes every day, and all of the realm rulers. Sometimes they watch you when I'm not here. Of course, the visitor who comes most often is—"

"You're awake," said a deep voice. I turned just in time to see Sanjeet, frozen in front of the caves. He stared at me, lips parted like I'd risen from the dead.

"Jeet," I murmured. Like me, he was mostly naked, wearing only a long white loincloth. Mist beaded on his wide copper shoulders and glistened in his curling hair.

He reached the altar in three strides and knelt to clutch my shoulders. "How do you feel?"

"Tired. But . . . rested, if that makes sense."

"And the ojiji?" he asked, careful to keep his tone neutral. "Are you still . . . seeing them? Hearing things?"

I shook my head. "I don't know what was happening to me, before. But something about this place . . . It clears my head." My face heated. After months of absent silence, Sanjeet's presence still felt unreal—especially here, in this clearing of mist and rainbowed light. "Jeet, what's going on? And, um—why aren't we wearing anything?"

Ye Eun stifled a giggling snort, scooping up Ae Ri and disappearing into the tunnels.

Sanjeet blinked, glancing down at his hairy muscled chest. "Oh. The priests don't allow normal clothes into the spring. It's said to defile the water." He bit his lip, scanning me anxiously. "I'm so glad you're all right.

I'll explain everything, I promise, but . . ." He glanced at the sky, which was fading fast, streaked with shadowy indigo. "You're supposed to dip in the spring before sunset. It's part of your treatment. I can carry you." He shrugged, looking sheepish. "I've been doing it every night for days."

I nodded shyly and placed my arms around his neck for balance as he scooped me up from the altar. The spring deepened quickly as he waded in, hot water lapping at our bare skin. When he set me down, my feet barely touched the bottom. Beneath the water, his hands closed around my waist, steadying me.

"There," he sighed as steam rose around us. Then he swallowed hard, drawing me close so his chin rested atop my head. "I was beginning to think the treatments weren't working. If you'd slept another day, Dayo was going to rush Kirah home from Songland. She's probably coming anyway. News of your illness spread fast. As we speak, the entire empire is burning incense for your recovery."

This close, I could feel his heartbeat, erratic as his chest pressed against mine. "Jeet . . . What happened at the fortress?"

He sucked in a breath. "Well. The good news is, while the transition wasn't pretty, Djbanti's revolt was incredibly well organized. The commoners have seized control of the realm and elected their own chieftains to divide property and carry out the people's demands. If you and Dayo choose to recognize their new government, I'd guess Djbanti will resume trade with other realms in a matter of months."

"And the bad news?"

"Djbanti's nobility—cronies of the former warlords—have taken sanctuary in Oluwan, and they're demanding support from the crown."

My eyes widened. "Why would they expect help from us, after our Imperial Guard warriors defended the commoners? I'd have thought the nobles would be furious."

"Ah . . . the nobles don't exactly know about that part." Sanjeet sighed and released me, running wet fingers through his hair. "At least, not yet. My warriors and I were wearing plainclothes. I had to make sure we weren't recognized, since we were technically breaking imperial law."

He was right. Anointed Ones weren't supposed to interfere in a realm's internal conflict; that job belonged to the vassal rulers. The imperial councils only ruled on a larger scale, mediating peace and trade between realms, and hearing escalated court cases.

My eyebrows rose. Since when did Sanjeet start conducting subterfuge missions on behalf of commoners?

"There's a lot to explain," he mumbled.

"I'd say." I smiled at him, intrigued.

"It's a long story. And I'm not a hero for most of it. Maybe when you're stronger—"

"My ears are strong enough."

He hesitated, then nodded, looking thoughtful and grim. "After I left An-Ileyoba—that night after our fight—I wandered Dhyrma for a while. As you are aware, tracking alagbatos is no easy task. Paying charlatan shamans, camping in wait for spirits . . . It was numbing, and I liked it that way. Scout all day, drink all night. Dream of you, if I was lucky. My plan was to live that way until you returned from the Underworld. And if you never returned, well . . . the alagbatos weren't going anywhere. And neither was the wine." He gave a tight, self-deprecating smile. "I told myself to be content. After all—that's what I told you to do. I had a home, if I wanted it, and a family—Dayo, our council. Everyone I loved was safe and cared for. Except for you, of course. And . . ." He stiffened then, running fingers through his wet hair. "I started wondering about my brother Sendhil. I hadn't contacted him in years—was afraid to, really. But I tracked him down. I expected to find him snug in some luxury Vhraipur apartment, bullying his way through the Dhyrma social scene. He was Hallowed to sense people's vulnerabilities, after all, and so he'd certainly have plenty of money: The Imperial Treasury cares for the relations of Anointed Ones. But when I found him . . ."

His jaw hardened. I lifted my wet hand to his face, and let the memory unfold inside me.

CHAPTER 29

A LANKY BOY WALLOWS IN THE DIRT, PROPPED
against the side of what looks like a brothel. He sings to
himself, tossing back a leather flask, and I can smell the
stink of liquor from yards away. The boy shares my russet
complexion, my chin and prominent ears. Despite his
dissolute appearance, he's clean-shaven. I'd smile if I weren't
so horrified—my brother never could grow a beard.

"Twelve Realms, big brother," Sendhil slurs without
rising. He looks me up and down with a sneer. "Looking
at you now, I'd never recognize the champion pit fighter
of Vhraipur. Much nicer clothes, for one thing. No
bloodstains. Or do the servants take care of those for
you?"

"It's good to see you, Sendhil." I ignore the barb—I had
known this wouldn't be easy. "I . . . know I wasn't there
for you when we were boys. That I haven't been there for
you. And I'm sorry. But now, I hope at least we can . . ."

I trail off, taking in his clothes—a disheveled soldier's
tunic, cobra sigils emblazoned on each breast.

346

The guilt drains out of me, replaced by disbelief that chokes my throat, and I barely manage words at all.

"You're still with the mercenaries," I say.

And he shrugs. My poor, brilliant, *idiot* of a baby brother—shrugs. "What else would I do?"

"Anything!" I rasp. "Am's Story, Sendhil! The crown has been paying your expenses for over two years. And you're Hallowed. You see weaknesses in character; you can make people feel things—feel anything. You could have been an orator. Or . . . a priest, a mummer, I don't know. The point is, all this time, you could have lived for something greater. Could have helped people—"

"Like you."

"Yes," I retort. "And instead, you sit around and kill people for a living."

"Like you."

I open my mouth, then shut it, air deflating from my lungs. "Imperial Guards don't kill during peacetime," I stammer at last.

"But you're trained to." Sendhil smirks, then winces, rubbing his temples and nursing the flask again. "Listen, Jeeti, I don't know why you're here. If you hoped to rescue me, well . . . I don't need rescuing. I made friends in my cohort. Just like you did back in Oluwan, with your magical friends in your ivory tower. So don't worry about me. As long as that pretty money keeps coming from the capital . . ." He raised his flask. "We're square."

"Sendhil, those mercenaries are not your friends. They

made you do monstrous things. They—they broke you—"

"So what?" Sendhil shoots back, clumsily rising to his feet. "The world is broken! We of all people should know that, Jeeti. Do you know who tried to help people? Do you know who tried to make a difference? Amah."

It takes everything inside me not to hit him.

But I don't. Instead we stare at each other, a distorted mirror. It is unclear, at least to me, which of us is the righteous gazer, and which, the tarnished reflection.

Sendhil tosses back the last drops from his flask, his weapon-scarred hands shaking. Then he stumbles toward the brothel door.

Without turning around, he pauses, just for a moment, and says, "Don't live for something greater, brother. Just protect what you've got. And this time"—his jaded brown eyes fall on me for a final time—"don't let go."

"I wanted to be angry," said Sanjeet, once our minds separated and I was myself again.

The sun had vanished, plunging the spring into shadow but for the pulsing light of ombitsu sprites, and the glow of my tustu overhead, forming their purple lattice in the evening sky.

"To hate him," he continued. "To prove him wrong. But I couldn't. Sendhil was right: We were the same; both aimless, both lacking in conviction. Equally content with our status quo. The only difference was that my clothes were more expensive, and people genuflected when I passed." He frowned, watching absently as ombitsu sprites trailed rainbows around the waterfall. "I distracted myself for a while, tracking down the new entrance to the Underworld. I found it. It's not far from the Oruku Breach, but there wasn't much I could do—only set guards to watch and warn you that the ojiji were targeting nobles. I could have come home after that. But it felt wrong—returning to wring my hands over you, while you fought for justice. So I decided to fight a noble cause of my own: I tried to catch the Crocodile."

I sucked in a breath, and Sanjeet noticed, eyes shading with an emotion I couldn't name.

"I assume you know Zuri's secret. I didn't know he was the Crocodile until that day in Djbanti. But I'd been obsessed with the vigilante for a while, sending spies to track his movements. I visited the sites of his demonstrations, talked to the commoners there. And after a while . . . I can't explain it, Tar. But the more I saw—the children pulled from mills and quarries, the hope in peasants' eyes . . . It was like something woke inside me. Passion—something I've been afraid of my whole life. I knew how dangerous it was to long for change, especially change of a system, something beyond any one person's control. But I couldn't help it. For the first time I felt . . . restless. I chafed at the apathy of others, chafed at all the time I had wasted. That's when I sent you that spear. I finally felt like I understood

you, just a little bit. And I wanted to say I was sorry."
He bit his lip. "But I couldn't come back. Not yet. My
spies brought word of a revolution planned in Djbanti, the
day of your Pinnacle. I thought of sending word to you,
but didn't want to risk such a message being intercepted. I
knew I had to go. Not to protect you—you haven't needed
that in a long time. But to help those peasants, however I
could. So I doffed my uniform and hid my seal ring. Some
of my warriors, also in plainclothes, volunteered to go with
me. And it looked like we came just in time."

He paused, watching my face. I swallowed, unable to
hide the grief there, and he nodded.

"We weren't able to recover his body," he said quietly.
"Apparently the peasants took it, and no one's seen it since.
I can't imagine what it must have been like to lose a council
brother. Well, I can, after Dayo almost died, but—" He
shook his head, his voice going carefully toneless. "I heard
rumors that what you had with Zuri was special. From
what I've heard of the Crocodile, I'd guess you two had a
lot in common."

"He was like my braver twin," I said after a long, heavy
pause. I smiled weakly. "He used me, and I hated that. But
even more, I hated that I understood him. His anger. His
pain, loneliness. Zuri was more of a hero than I'll ever be."
I bit my lip. "I've never met anyone like him. And I don't
think I ever will."

Sanjeet avoided my gaze then, fighting to keep his face
emotionless. "I'm glad he was there for you." A beat passed.

"I'm glad you had someone who stood with you, instead of standing by."

I moved through the water, closing the space between us and resting my head against his. "Jeet."

"I was insufferable," he said softly. "And—" He frowned, swallowed, then said the words in a rush. "I can't beat a dead man's memory. Zuri understood you. He didn't leave you, for Am's sake, or try to cage who you are—"

"Jeet."

"Let me finish." He smiled, clear brown eyes sharp and resigned. He shifted in the water and then cupped my face: a warm, wet hand against my cheek. "I know I'm not him," he whispered. "I know it's unfair for me to hope. But if there's a chance. If—if, after you've had time to grieve— someday, we might—"

I pressed a finger to his lips. He blinked, dazed, as I placed his arms around me. Then I braced myself on his shoulders, wrapping my legs around his waist so he held me, weightless, in the water. "Jeet . . . I wasn't in love with Zuri."

His breaths came short. "You weren't?"

I shook my head.

"Oh." He looked so dumbstruck, I laughed. I kissed his nose, then each of his bushy eyebrows, smiling when they knit together.

"I assumed," he mumbled. "I mean—you spent so much time with him. And you called him a hero."

"That's because he was." I smiled sadly. "But you can't

hold a legend's hand, Jeet." I screwed up my face. Zuri had been right—the Ray didn't require someone to truly love you. Only the idea of you. I had always been an idea to him, and enamored as he had been with The Lady, I suspected even she had only been a tool in his revolutionary imagination—like a keen knife, or a gleaming sword. And when she lost her usefulness, he had simply exchanged her for a younger, sharper copy.

"Zuri didn't want the girl," I said. "He only wanted the empress." I sighed, wrapping my legs tighter around him. "Only you ever tried to love both."

The doubt left his eyes, replaced by warmth as my thighs pressed his hips. We kissed—gently at first, shy pecks containing apologies for fights before. Then my tongue grew bold. His skin tasted strongly of salt, seasoned by the spring. I clutched him closer, sharply aware that the cloth binding my breasts had soaked sheer. A sound escaped him, and his mouth dipped beneath my collarbone, moving my obabirin mask aside. I moaned, seeing stars. In the dark, I could not see below the water. But I felt—and wanted—every inch of him.

My head swam. Inhaling so much steam had made me giddy, and I'd had nothing but broth and water for days. Part of me also knew that if we kept this up much longer, my qualms about *risks* and *heirs* would fade quickly to white noise, no matter how imminent those risks were. Still, my hands gripped his back, and I let his mouth explore a few blissful moments longer before I broke the embrace.

"We should—" I gasped. "We should go inside."

He nodded reluctantly, eyes glazed with hunger.

A pile of linens lay stacked neatly beside the jade altar. We climbed from the pool and wrapped our shoulders in the perfumed towels. But before we could leave the clearing, my tutsu swarmed.

"What in Am's name," I said, moving to shield Sanjeet. But to my surprise, he didn't seem afraid.

"Oh. I forgot to tell you," he said. "After you fainted, we—ah—received a message from . . . an old friend. It was on her advice we brought you to the temple."

I watched, speechless, as the tutsu hummed and spun, growing denser as they descended. At last, the glowing swarm took the shape of a hunched, scowling old woman. Hands on its hips, the being made of tiny sparks stood before us in the clearing.

"Well, Wuraola?" it demanded. "How did you like your bath?"

"Old Mongwe," I squeaked, gaping at the priestess's shifting form. "But . . . how? You're— How are you—"

"I cannot see or hear you. Talking through these sprites is exhausting enough as it is, let alone trying to cast a message *back*," the hermit priestess huffed, speaking over me. "So this better be you, child, and not some other yam-brained royal. I told the sprites to find the wuraola, but they can be thick-thick in the head, especially during mating season—"

I tried again. "How—"

"—or if they sense that the land is in mortal danger,

which, if I'm being honest, is more often than not these last hundred years. Anyhow. I assume you want to know how I've appeared before you. Well, I haven't! I'm home in Swana, inhaling a fresh brew of kuso–kuso leaves. The fumes let my soul leave its sorry sack of bones every once in a while, which is nice for errands, when the weather is bad."

Mongwe paused, observing the air where she assumed I stood.

"The sprites whispered of you," she said quietly. "*'Mongwe,'* they whined, *'the Wuraola is in a bad-bad way.'* It took me an age to make sense of their stories. Shades that return more than once? Children like reanimated corpses? But once I figured out it was ojiji . . ." She inhaled sharply. "I know their tricks of old. You have been in grave danger, child, and you are not cured yet. Though you're feeling better now, I expect. Baths can treat a staggering number of ills, and you won't find a more luxurious tub than the pools of Iyaja." She chuckled to herself, then sobered. "The temple has bought you time, but once you leave it, the hauntings will return. The ojiji will do their best to confuse you, but remember this: Do not confuse guilt with conviction. Guilt is self-centered, and leads only to destructive obsession. But conviction brings balance—a sense of purpose beyond oneself. The abiku want to keep you when you descend to the Underworld. I don't know why. But let me be absolutely clear." The old woman hovered close, her stern, sparkling eyes inches from my face. "Wuraola: Under no circumstances should you enter the Underworld, unless you are certain that you will return alive."

I opened my mouth to object. She seemed to sense this.

"No buts," she snapped. "Yes, breaking your vow to the abiku would mean disaster. A supernatural war, and a terrible one. But those futures pale in comparison, I fear, to what the abiku could accomplish with you in their clutches."

I frowned with confusion. How could a supernatural war be *better* than my death in the Underworld?

Her wrinkled features grew distorted. The sprites began to wane and disperse, and so Mongwe spoke quickly. "The kuso-kuso is fading. Malevolent spirits work against me, and I may not soon visit you again. More advice: In the Underworld, the abiku may not touch, harm, or kill you without your consent. These are the laws of the Storyteller— laws to separate life and death—by which even the abiku must abide. Spirits of dead humans are different, but they seldom leave Egungun's Parade. Oh—and no matter how you much you want to, don't you dare trust the—"

But then Mongwe vanished, and the sprites dispersed, ascending from the clearing in a buzzing cloud.

"Don't what?" I yelled after them. "Don't trust the *what*?"

But Mongwe was silent, now nothing but a purple scatter of lights across the sky.

CHAPTER 30

"YOU *KISSED* HIM?" KIRAH SPUTTERED, WISPS of hair escaping from her prayer shawl. "You *kissed* the king of Djbanti?"

I laughed, tossing a fig at her as our legs dangled over the edge of the Children's Palace roof. The fruit missed her, bouncing on a balustrade and tumbling to the courtyard far below.

"Out of everything I just told you, *that*'s what you remember? Kirah, there was a whole battle! A Djbanti revolution."

"I know! But . . . *Zuri?*" she squealed, and wrinkled her nose, an expression I had sorely missed these past several months. Then she looked apologetic. "Sorry, I shouldn't make fun. Now that he's . . . you know—"

"No, it's all right." I smiled at her. "You're allowed to tease, after the hard time I gave you about Woo In. By the way, have you finally forgiven him and admitted you're crazy about each other?"

Kirah's moonlike face flushed. The setting sun dyed

An-Ileyoba in rose gold, and orange blossoms floated on the Oluwan City breeze. I could almost pretend we were small girls again, braiding each other's hair and trading secrets before scampering back down to the Hall of Dreams. I'd asked Kirah to come here for old times' sake—and to avoid Woo In, who followed Kirah around the palace like a sullen, lovesick lapdog.

Woo In and Kirah had only just returned to Oluwan, their peace campaign in Songland a tentative success. With Min Ja's blessing, they had brought an entire barge of Songlander merchants and dignitaries to Oluwan, all of them eager to establish their presence in the Arit capital.

"My relationship with the prince of Songland is political," Kirah said primly. "We work well together, yes, but the priorities of our realms come first—"

"You sing his name in your sleep," I deadpanned. "You dream about him flying you around the moon, and going on mountaintop picnics, where for *some* reason, neither of you have any clothes on—"

"Am's Story, stay out of my head at night!" Kirah snorted, and I only smirked.

"It's hard when you dream so loudly."

She was quiet for a moment. "We have talked about it," she admitted. "Once, in Songland, we all but confessed everything. That he likes me, and I like him. I didn't even mind that he wasn't a council member. But . . ." She swallowed. "He's eight years older than me, Tar. I thought I didn't care before. But he's been so many places.

357

Done things I haven't. And no matter how much I dream of him . . ." She hugged her knees to her chest, wrinkling her priestess kaftan. "I don't want to look up to the man I'm in love with. I'd rather see eye to eye."

I shrugged. "Chuck him, then. Never thought he deserved you, anyway. What kind of a prince takes a cat wherever he goes?"

Kirah dimpled, then grew serious. "A year from now, or two, or three—after I've traveled the continent and seen everything I've ever wanted . . . maybe I'll let Woo In fly me to the moon. But for now?" She stared serenely at the city skyline, twilight shading her wistful features. "I might grow some wings of my own. High Priestesses are supposed to resolve disputes between the Arit religious sects. They usually work from one temple here in the capital, but what if I traveled to other temples instead? There are so many places in Aritsar I haven't seen. So many people who need a healer."

I pouted. "You've only just got back, and now you want to leave me again."

"You're one to talk," she shot back, though she looked immediately regretful. "Sorry," she mumbled. "I just . . . Sometimes, I get a little tired of pretending it's not happening."

"I know. It's all right." I stared at the marks on my arms and legs, which glistened as whispers filled my ears. After leaving the Temple of Iyaja a month ago, I had followed Old Mongwe's advice, ignoring the ojiji who haunted me.

My headaches had remained at bay, though translucent children still mobbed me in the palace, their words nipping at my ears.

Unworthy. Unworthy. Pay the price. Paythepricepaytheprice—

My eighteenth birthday was tomorrow. I had anointed a council in less than half the time I'd asked of the abiku, and still had a year before I had to enter the Underworld. But—much to the chagrin of both my councils—I had decided to go early. The longer I waited, the more it seemed like I was preparing for death—and Mongwe's warning weighed like a stone in my stomach.

Under no circumstances should you enter the Underworld, unless you are certain that you will return.

"Have you rehearsed your answer for the Bridge of the Warlord's Deaths?" Kirah asked, and I nodded. Ye Eun had drilled me in every Underworld riddle and obstacle I would encounter, forcing me to memorize the map on my skin. "Say it," Kirah insisted. "Say your answer until you believe it. Why should you live?"

I sighed, wetting my lips. "I should live because I'm saving lives. I'm doing the right thing. I'm a good empress. A good person."

Not enough, hissed the children. *Not enough.*

I told myself it didn't matter what the dead Redemptors thought. Ye Eun had said that the Deaths would have to let me pass, so long as I believed my answer. And I believed it. Of course I did.

Didn't I?

"I wish the ojiji would leave you alone," Kirah said softly. "I can't believe you didn't tell us how bad it had gotten."

I chewed my lip. "It's complicated," I said at last. "The thing is, even though the ojiji are cruel, they tell the truth as often as they don't."

"Tar, how can you say that?" Kirah shook her head wildly, shaking the tassels on her prayer scarf. "Those voices called you worthless. They isolated you on purpose. Stopped you from asking for help, made you do everything yourself."

"They're trying to wear me down," I admitted. "So I'll feel hopeless enough to stay in the Underworld. Still . . . they drove me to *do* things. Good things. The Pinnacle, the battle in Djbanti—none of that would have happened if I hadn't felt so guilty. I want the voices to go away, Kirah, but . . . I'm afraid of what happens when they do. What if being free—feeling happy—makes me blind again? Ignorant of all the injustice around me, like I was before?"

Deep in thought, Kirah scowled at the priestess pendant around her neck—a golden pelican, inlaid in mother-of-pearl. She clutched it with pale knuckles, as if trying to squeeze out an answer.

"What was it you told me Old Mongwe said?" she asked suddenly. "About guilt?"

"That it's useless." I sighed, remembering the hermit's opaque words: *Guilt is self-centered, and leads only to destructive obsession. But conviction brings balance—a sense of purpose beyond oneself.*

"And what you said," Kirah pressed. "When you convinced Thaddace to leave that prison?"

I blinked in confusion. She gripped my shoulders, hazel eyes alight. "It was important, Tarisai. You said you heard it from someone—someone powerful."

I remembered then—the voice from the shrine at Sagimsan, turning my limbs to water as the breath of the Storyteller swelled on the mountain air.

"Do not ask how many people you will save," I murmured. *"Ask, to what world will you save them? What makes a world worth surviving in?"*

"That's right." Kirah nodded fervently. "And what made Thaddace keep going—what made him *try*—it wasn't guilt. It was love." She reached out and squeezed my hand. "It was love, Tarisai."

I'm scared, Empress Tar, Ji Huan Ray-spoke, his voice cutting through the din of my birthday banquet.

Instead of a stately festival in the Imperial Hall, I had opted for an intimate party in the palace orchards. Encircled by gold-dappled trees and a breeze perfumed with orange blossoms, all twenty-one of my living council siblings knelt in the grass, feasting in flower crowns around a long, low table.

I sat between Sanjeet and a shy Ji Huan. The boy king laid his palm in his silk-robed lap, examining the now-faded scar where he had combined his blood with mine. He seemed surprised when I placed an arm around him. *Why are you scared, Ji Huan? It's just a party.*

He blinked. *Sorry. I didn't mean to tell you that.* He flushed pink. *Even before I was anointed, I talked to you in my head all the time. I guess now I Ray-speak by accident.*

Well, your secret's out. I nudged him in the ribs. *What are you afraid of?*

The boy picked glumly at the colorful wax-dyed tablecloth, piled high with sweet plantains and *suya* meat skewers. *We're all together now,* he said at last. *But soon, we're all going back to our home realms. Our council—it isn't like your other one.* Jealousy seeped into his voice as he eyed my original council siblings, who crowded together, laughing at one end of the table. *We don't all get to live together in one big palace. Soon I'll be back in Moreyao, alone again. I'll get sick.* He shivered, and suddenly I felt cold too, thinking of my years in an icy bubble at Bhekina House.

I touched Ji Huan's cheek, willing him courage through the Ray bond. *That's council sickness for you. But we can speak across the distance with kuso-kuso, remember? And Moreyao borders the Blessid Valley. You'll see Chief Uriyah all the time.*

And you'll visit me too, he added firmly. *When you come back from the Underworld.*

My throat closed up.

The certainty of his tone sent thrills of panic up my spine. Immediately, the table went quiet, twenty-one sets of eyes turned on me. I winced—my anxiety had been so strong, they'd felt it through our Ray bond, even with my mental shields up. It must have shown on my face as well—Adukeh, Da Seo, Ye Eun, and Woo In also looked concerned, even though we weren't bonded through the Ray.

Sanjeet's hand closed over mine. "Is it the ojiji?"

I shook my head, forcing a grin to calm my party guests. "No. Just—ah—running through my training from Ye Eun. Strange that in a matter of weeks, I'll meet literal Deaths. Kind of exciting, when you think about it."

Nervous laughter all around. "If you get scared in the Underworld," suggested Ai Ling after a pause, "just look at your mask. You've beat so many deaths already."

I lifted the obsidian lioness, smiling wryly at the glittering rainbow stripes. "Funny—in all my rush to pass edicts and prepare for the Underworld, I've barely tried out my immunities. Maybe I should jump off a battlement. Or provoke a blueblood into stabbing me. Or spend a night in the Bush and see if I get hexed."

"Don't say those things," Sanjeet grumbled. "Not even as a joke."

"Sorry." I replaced the mask beneath my wrapper. "It's just weird to think I'm immune to more than burning. Like, if I went swimming in the ocean, could I breathe underwater?"

"Nope," said Dayo, looking up from cutting grapes in half to feed Ae Ri, who babbled on his lap. "I tried that once when I was little. You won't die, but you *will* vomit salt water for an hour."

More laughter around the table, genuine this time.

"I've always wondered what it was like for you," Ai Ling said, drawing thoughtful circles on Dayo's shoulder. "Growing up, knowing that someday you'd be—well, almost a god."

Absently, he leaned his cheek against her hand. "It still hasn't sunk in for me, really. And I don't think it ever will. Still . . . it's no wonder people worshipped our ancestors."

Ae Ri made an insistent grunt toward the orchard pen, where my birthday present from last year—the pale pink baby elephant—placidly rolled a log in the grass.

Ai Ling pulled the little girl from Dayo's arms, and together, they took Ae Ri to pet the elephant's trunk. I smiled as I watched them, thinking just how much they looked like a family.

"You know," Dayo told me over his shoulder. "You never did name your birthday present."

But before I could respond, Ae Ri wrapped her arms around the animal's muddy trunk, and lovingly cooed her first word.

"Dog," she said, with finality. "Dog."

I nodded solemnly. "Dog it is."

My gaze traveled to the massive black tapestries on An-Ileyoba's walls, which blazed with Dayo's and my new seal: dual Kunleo suns. I wondered, as I often did, what Zuri had made of the empire. He had spoken so glowingly of the way things were before in Aritsar—the days of elected nkosi chiefs, giving both poor and rich a say. Often, when

I slept in my pile of council siblings, lulled by their soft, synced breaths, his words about the Raybearer echoed.

The Raybearer has never been about a person—not really. It's about an idea.

But that idea, whatever it was, had always been bound to the Kunleo bloodline. What happened when that ended? After all, Dayo and I still didn't have a plan to make new Raybearers. And even if we did . . . what would stop our heirs from being selfish, like Olugbade, or manipulative, like The Lady? Why did the health of the empire, the lives of millions, have to depend on a tiny subset of wealthy people being *kind*?

Unworthy, hissed the chorus of treble voices. *Unworthy, pay the price—*

My heart hammered. But before my distress could seep into the Ray bonds of my siblings, I stood suddenly. "Theo, Adukeh—did you bring instruments?"

"Always," said Theo, untying the harp strapped to his back. Adukeh patted her drum primly, as if insulted I'd even ask.

"Good," I said. "Because I have a birthday wish." I gulped, holding out my hands to Sanjeet. "A dance."

Again, the table went quiet.

"Tar," said Sanjeet slowly. He rose from his seat, looking like he wanted to scan me for a fever. "You . . . don't dance."

"Exactly." I placed his hands on my hips, smiling up at him wryly. "So after this, the Underworld should be easy."

I pulled him toward the clearing, and the rest of my party guests followed as Theo and Adukeh struck the opening bars of a joyful, infectious rhythm.

I was still terrible at the ijo agbaye. Seconds in, I had lost the beat, colliding with Sanjeet and bruising my right toe. But we were laughing so hard, I didn't care. Theo's musical illusion Hallow filled the air with amber gems and honey-colored butterflies that beat their wings in time to the music. Mayazatyl gyrated with Umansa and Kameron, and Min Ja forced a wobbling Uriyah into the fray. Kirah spun with Woo In, giggling as he swept her up in a glittering wind. Even Ye Eun joined the fun, bouncing a giggling Ae Ri on her hip. A short distance from everyone else, I noticed Dayo and Ai Ling, swaying as if to a melody all their own. Her jet hair had fallen out of its ornamented bun, making soft wisps around her face. When the song began to bleed into another, Ai Ling stood on her tiptoes and pressed a kiss to Dayo's mouth. I gasped and stifled a grin, wondering if anyone else had noticed.

Startled joy washed over Dayo's features . . . followed by regret.

"Ai Ling," I heard him say as Sanjeet and I danced close by. "I know how you feel for me. And I feel the same for you. But—"

"I've had sex before," Ai Ling said matter-of-factly. "And do you know what he said when we were done? *Murmurwitch*." She sucked in a slow, shaky breath. "But . . . you've never said that. You've never even wondered.

366

All you do, Dayo, is love the person in front of you so stubbornly, they love you back. So don't you dare say you can't make me happy." She wrapped her arms around his neck. Dayo swallowed hard as he stared down at her, tears pooling in his pure black eyes. Then he kissed her, laughing against her mouth, full lips parted in an incredulous smile. "I will always want you, Ekundayo of Oluwan," Ai Ling said when they parted, tracing his burn scar. "And I will never ask for more than you want to give."

Another song ended. Min Ja clapped her hands, gesturing for a retinue of Songlander attendants who waited on the sidelines.

"In celebration of my little sister's eighteenth birthday," she said, smirking at me, "my retinue has prepared something special. May I present the famed dancers of Eunsan-do Court."

And don't worry, she Ray-spoke, eyes twinkling. *They're not going to kill anybody . . . this time.*

I laughed, and then joined the court in clapping to the beat as veiled dancers took to the clearing, fluttering fans as musicians played a mélange of strings. But at a break in the music, Min Ja stepped forward again. She laid a blanket on the grass, then a small brush, a bowl of ink, and a long, wide roll of paper.

"Da Seo has a present too," she told me, then stepped back. "A blessing for the empress."

Da Seo stepped forward, squaring her shoulders for courage, and slipped out of her elegant silk shoes. Then she sat before the paper and removed her veil, revealing the scarred mouth and neck I had once seen in her memories. The party grew hushed.

Then we watched, entranced, as Da Seo reached for the brush with her toes and painted on the scroll with a strong, steady foot. She switched the brush to her mouth for the finer details, curling the characters with flourishing charisma. The ink glistened, waves of power rising from the script, and when I made out the words, which she had written in Arit instead of Songlander, tears stung my eyes.

BEHOLD WHAT IS COMING.

The ojiji could have screamed at the top of their lungs, and I would not have heard them. The strokes of Da Seo's script glowed in the dappled sunlight, shining like my twenty-one council siblings' faces as I took them in, branding their features on my heart's eye. In that moment, a warm, rebellious certainty thrummed through my limbs, pinning my feet to the soft, fragrant ground.

I will come back, I thought, speaking not to my siblings but to the world fathoms below, where spirits vied to keep me forever.

You will try to hold me, to knock me down. But I will always get up. And I will come back.

Behold what is coming.

PART 5

CHAPTER 31

THE LAST TIME I WAS PARADED THROUGH THE city of Ebujo—home of the last known entrance to the Underworld—townspeople had sung to celebrate my future. They still sang now, lining the streets and shaking *shekere* gourds. But this song was eerie and transcendent.

A tribute to a fallen god.

> *Where has our Lady Sun gone?*
> *Down-down, to the bottom of the world.*
> *Not dead, ah-ah! Just sleeping.*
> *Night is short*
> *When your servants sing forever.*

They were trying to comfort me with caterwauling voices and fragrant petals tossed onto my litter. They showed gratitude, promising me immortality—swearing to tell my story.

Yet as I rode beside Dayo on that flower-covered litter, I wanted to cover my ears. To make the crowds disappear, to fade into merciful silence. Because in every single one of those mournful, worshipful faces, one thought was clear:

The Empress Redemptor will not survive the Underworld.

Don't listen to them, Dayo Ray-spoke, sensing my revulsion through the bond. *They don't know your strength like I do.*

I smiled at him worriedly. *I'm surprised there are any crowds at all.*

In anticipation of my trip to the Underworld, most of Ebujo had evacuated days ago. For miles around the city, in thousands of tents and makeshift camp towns, the Imperial Army of Twelve Realms waited—some million warriors strong—headed by Sanjeet and my living royal council siblings. Some of the warrior cohorts had begun traveling to Ebujo over a year ago, when I had first announced my agreement with the abiku.

No one wanted a supernatural war, and if the abiku held up their end of the new treaty, there wouldn't be one. The moment I entered the Underworld, the empire's debt to the abiku would be satisfied, whether I came back or not. But despite the crippling expense of mobilizing the army, we couldn't leave the fate of Aritsar to chance.

"You're sure I can't come in? Just to see you off?" Dayo asked me for the hundredth time, when our procession stopped at the temple.

I squeezed his hand. "I told you—I need to do this alone. If everyone else is there, it'll feel like saying goodbye."

"You're letting *her* come in with you," Dayo mumbled

sullenly, pointing at the palanquin behind us, from which Ye Eun was disembarking.

"I was so surprised she asked, I couldn't say no." I glanced warily at the looming temple doors. "If I were her, I'd never want to see this place again."

He eyed me up and down. "Shouldn't you at least wear a cloak? It's supposed to be freezing down—where you're going. At least take a shield. Or armor."

I shook my head. "Ye Eun and Woo In warned against it. Living souls are weak in the Underworld—every ounce you carry feels like ten pounds." I wore nothing but a simple woven wrapper: cerulean, to remind me of the open Oluwan sky. I had no weapon. No supplies—not even a map. Instead, Ye Eun had made me stand naked in front of full-length mirrors, memorizing the glowing twists and turns inked onto my skin. If all went as planned, I could find my way through the Underworld with my eyes closed.

Dayo held my hand so tightly, when he finally released, it felt like I had shed a second skin. Then I took off the lioness mask, pressing it to him. "Hold on to this."

"Tar, *no*—"

"Just for a while." I kissed his cheek. "Do you love me now, Ekundayo of Oluwan?" I asked, echoing the question he had once asked me.

"Always have," he whispered. "Always will."

I pressed my brow to his, flooding both our minds with the dual-Ray, inhaling Dayo's scent—the warm, sweet essence of my other half. "Then wait for me," I murmured.

And I rose from the litter, entering the temple without looking back. The Ray sweltered over my skin—a hot beam at my back, as though Dayo's vision were a coal, growing cooler and cooler until the vast stone doors shut, separating us for what could be eternity.

Ye Eun and I entered the temple's central chamber—a vast, ceilingless room of pale limestone, shot through with veins of purple—memories seeped into me from the floor, and bile soured my tongue. Only two years ago, I had seen dozens massacred here, murdered by monsters that rose from the Oruku Breach: the yawning chasm at the far end of the chamber, guarded by warriors, and glowing with malevolent blue light.

"You shouldn't be here," I told Ye Eun as we neared the chasm's edge. I choked out the words, trying not to breathe—the pit stank of sulfur. Standing near it made me want to scrub off my own skin, as though the stench alone could infect every pore.

Ye Eun sighed softly, foul wind from the Breach tousling her short hair. "I know," she said. "But it was the only way I could make sure you'd enter the Breach."

"Make . . . sure?"

"I can't let Ae Ri be sacrificed." Her gaze was frank. "Not like I was. She's all I have."

I breathed a laugh. "If I hesitated, were you planning to push me?"

"Yes."

"Ah." I gulped. "Well, no need for that." And despite

Ye Eun's motivations, I was grateful for the company.

The faint voices of the singing townsfolk, combined with the fainter roar of the largest army in five oceans, rung in my ears as I stared into the wide, smirking Breach. It reminded me of an eye: a perimeter dazzling with color, with a void at its center that seemed to go on forever.

"Ye Eun?" I said, pulling my gaze back to her face.

"Mm?" Her arms were crossed tightly across her chest. Though she avoided looking at me, water glinted on her cheeks and her chin quivered.

"Can you promise me one thing?" I asked. "Once this is all over . . . Live for something besides Ae Ri."

She blinked with surprise. "But she needs me."

"I know. But she'll grow up. Her family will expand." The image of Dayo and Ai Ling cooing over Ae Ri flashed in my mind. "So will yours. And protecting someone else isn't a purpose, Ye Eun. I learned that the hard way." I smiled at her sadly. "What did you enjoy before all this? Back when you thought heroes could save the day?"

She bit her lip, tracing the purple patterns on her thin arms. "I liked flowers," she said at last. "They were hard to grow on Mount Sagimsan. Too rocky. But I always managed. I think . . . maybe somewhere sunny, like Oluwan, I could grow lilies again."

"That's a start."

She inhaled thoughtfully, then reached in her pocket and pressed something into my palm: a tiny white blossom, pressed and dried. "It's from your flower crown," she mumbled. "The one I made you when we first met. I don't know why I kept it. But . . . I liked having it in the Underworld."

My fingers closed around it. "Thank you."

Another beat passed in silence. The chilling blue light danced across our faces.

"It's probably easier if you go backward," Ye Eun blurted. "That's the one thing I regretted when I did it. Going face-first. Backward, you can keep your eyes on the light until it's gone."

I swallowed hard. "Backward it is then." I turned around, placing my heels on the edge of the Breach. My heart pounded against my chest. "Ye Eun?"

"Empress?"

"I—I think I want that push, after all."

She chuckled quietly and nodded, tears running over her pursed mouth. "For Ae Ri."

I took in her brave, slight features, hardened by invisible scars. "And for lilies," I said.

Then I placed her small hands on my shoulders. When at last she pushed, a small wail escaped her lips—and my heart leapt into my throat as I fell down, down, to the bottom of the world.

The vertigo of freefalling lasted only a moment, replaced by a sickeningly slow descent, as though the air had thickened, and I fell through cold, brackish water. Around me was darkness—not black, but dense with clouds of murky green and cobalt. The mouth of the Breach faded quickly to a bright pinprick, but Ye Eun had been right—having something to look at comforted me, if only a mite. I learned immediately that screaming was a bad idea—the fog had a taste, and it was foul.

Down, down, down.

My hair billowed in a cloud around my ears. I could hear music—but not the songs of Ebujo City. A chaos of drumbeats and voices filled my mind, overlapping snatches of stories in whispered languages, as though the fog were full of memories. When at last my descent ended, I lay in a cavern lit by ghoulish floating lanterns. I had landed roughly on a pile of something uneven . . . but before I could investigate, I gagged, choking.

No air.

There was no air down here—inhaling, exhaling made no difference. My heart raced, sending sharp pains through my chest. *Make it stop*, I wanted to say as I flailed and gasped, a fish on a riverbank. *This was a mistake. A bad dream. Make it all stop.* But I didn't—because that was what *they* wanted. The abiku couldn't touch me without an invitation, but if my words gave them the smallest opening, they would take it.

Ye Eun's calm voice echoed in my mind from months of training. Six steps to remember—six tasks to escape the Underworld.

First, remember that you need not die.

Clenching my fists, I forced my strange, airless breaths to slow.

"Still alive," I croaked. My voice made clouds in the dim chamber. Already the cold was setting in, turning the ends of my fingers to stone. I closed my eyes, focusing on my decelerating pulse. An hour could have passed—or ten. Ye Eun had warned me that time passed differently in the Underworld. Depending on where I was, and what delusions the spirits made me suffer, what felt like a week could be a day in the world above . . . and vice versa.

You are all alone again, sighed the chorus of ojiji spirits, who had a tangible presence, like feathers brushing over my skin. *Alone, alone, in a room with no windows. Just like in Bhekina House. Did you ever have friends, Wuraola?*

"Still alive," I yelled over them. "Still alive. Alive, and there's nothing you can do about it." I tried to laugh then, but it hurt my chest, and I stopped. Instead, I chanted the names of my siblings—all twenty-two of them, as I struggled to a sitting position.

Second, came Ye Eun's voice, *fight the cold*.

Invisible stones weighed on my limbs. Even my head was a burden. The cold seeped into my joints, as though I were slowly turning to marble, but after months of enduring Hwanghu's icy essence, ambushing me from head to toe . . . slow, I could handle.

When I moved, the pile beneath me shifted, and I slid to a packed dirt floor. Objects clattered around me as I fell: tiny weapons, like slings and daggers. Defensive charms.

Child-size cloaks, bundles of food. Small stuffed toys. The belongings of past Redemptors—objects for comfort and survival. Every single one abandoned once their unfortunate owners had learned what things weigh in the Underworld.

If it weren't for the cold, I might have added my wrapper and sandals to the pile. But though their weight hindered me, whatever lay beyond this cavern, I did not want to encounter naked. I checked my hand: Ye Eun's dried lily blossom was still there, stuck to my palm. I peeled it off and carefully fastened it behind my ear. Before me were two long tunnels jutting in sharply different directions. Most paths in the Underworld, I knew, led more or less to the same place, though some routes were more convoluted and treacherous than others.

Third: Follow the map.

The patterns on my arms and forearms had begun to glow. A new glyph appeared—a bursting sun, symbolizing myself, pulsed in a small round chamber on the tip of my longest right finger. I scarcely needed the map, since Ye Eun had told me what to expect—but I was grateful for a real-time guide. Farther down my arm, some of the glyphs coalesced around a crosshatched square, shifting into words I could understand: *BRIDGE OF THE WARLORD'S DEATHS.*

Fourth, cross the bridge.

After squinting at my arm, I entered the tunnel to the right. The tiny sun glided along my skin, a gentle pulse as it mirrored my trek through the Underworld.

"Dayo, Kirah, Sanjeet."

I wielded their names like a mantle against the cold, gritting my teeth to keep them from chattering.

"Theo. Mayazatyl. Thérèse."

I turned a corner—and nearly pitched headfirst into a pit teeming with scorpions. I stumbled backward, then stopped, glancing at my map. The sun pulsed in the middle of a tunnel . . . and did not show a pit. I forced myself to laugh—a weak, rasping sound, but a laugh all the same.

"Zathulu!" I cried out, charging into the writhing bowl of scorpions. "Umansa!"

No creatures scattered up my limbs or stung me with pincers. And after I leapt, my feet hit bare, solid ground. The illusion had vanished the moment I challenged it. I laughed again, though it dissolved into a cough—the air still stank of death.

"Emeronya," I sang, letting my voice echo off the sickly green stalactite. "Kameron. Ai Ling . . ."

I cycled through all my original siblings, and the vassal rulers too, until my tongue ran dry, blending the consonants together. How long had I been walking now? A day? Two?

My muscles ached, as though I had crossed a continent, but that meant little. My body seemed suspended—I was frozen and exhausted, but not thirsty or hungry. Even without my Raybearer immunities, as a living soul, I could not die in the Underworld unless I wished to—so I could not starve or faint of dehydration. Without such markers, however, measuring time was impossible. Ye Eun had warned me not to sleep—staying still would make me even colder, and every time I closed my eyes, it would grow harder to open them.

Phantom voices whispered from alternate tunnels, long, winding routes that my map warned would lead me in circles.

I quoted one of Chief Uriyah's dusty proverbs, mimicking the old man's chiding baritone. "'The wise young ruler is not led by passing fancy,'" I told the tunnels, and continued on my way.

Then came Kirah's voice. "Tar?" It was so real, I could almost see her in the distance, her tasseled prayer scarf rippling in the frigid cavern wind. "Help me. I don't know how I got down here, but I don't have a map, like you. Don't leave me. Stay, we'll escape together . . ."

I bit my lip and ignored the false spirit, charging on. "Min Ja wouldn't fall for that," I said aloud. "She would stab her own brother, if he meant her harm. So I'm not listening to you."

Days or hours later, I came to a crossroads and stopped to consult my map again. Then someone else spoke, in a strident, resonant tenor that made my knees weak.

"Well done, my Idajo," said Zuri of Djbanti. "I knew you'd keep your promise to the Redemptors."

CHAPTER 32

THE SHADE HOVERED RIGHT IN FRONT OF ME, swathed in grand, robe-like shadows. As when he lived, his skin was brilliant and black, his smile square and flawless. Gold cuffs winked in his locs, as though he were back in court again, but his voice was low and genuine—the one he had only ever used with me.

Tears sprung to my eyes. "You're not real," I said.

"I'm not *alive*," he corrected. "I died, Idajo. And this is where the dead go."

"The dead go to Egungun's Parade. You're not real."

His features crumpled with pain. "Not all of us can bear the parade, you know," he said quietly. "With every step, you feel the pain that you caused others in life. Some of us prefer to wander the Underworld. And there was one sin I just couldn't relive." He stepped closer, and I could *smell* him—the heady scent of agave and iron, mixed with the Underworld's sulfur. "The pain I caused you, Idajo."

I should have walked right by him. I knew where to go—the pulsing sun was on my thigh now, indicating the correct tunnel to reach the Bridge of the Warlord's Deaths.

But instead I asked, "What do you want, Zuri?"

"To apologize." He gave that sad half smile I had so loved when he was alive. "For keeping secrets. I said we were a team, and you deserved my trust. In the end . . . you always tried to do the right thing."

He emphasized the last phrase, which for some reason made me squirm. "Well," I said. "You've apologized. So let me pass."

"Of course. But I want to make amends." His brow wrinkled, as if torn with indecision. "Tar . . . there's something you should know about the abiku. They're up to something. I caught a glimpse of it when I left the parade, something to do with the old Redemptors. The ones whose souls they stole."

My pulse raced. "The ojiji?" I breathed, reaching out to take the memory from him.

He drew back, frowning. "It was . . . obscene. At least ten thousand children, lined up and drilling, like they were part of an army. Something rotten's going on. Those children should have passed into Egungun's Parade the moment they died in the Underworld. If they're still down here, it means their souls have been enslaved for five hundred years."

"I know." Disgust and pity churned my stomach. That boy who had murdered Thaddace—he had seemed so confused. All his memories appeared to have vanished—or at least have weakened, as though his soul was trapped in the preserved corpse of his body.

"Whatever the abiku are planning, it's happening soon," said Zuri. He turned on his heel, gesturing for me to follow him down a tunnel—the opposite route of where my map told me to go. "If we want to stop them, we'll have to hurry."

Heart pounding, I began to follow him down the murky, narrowing tunnel . . . and then I stopped.

He glanced back at me, raising a concerned eyebrow. "Idajo?"

"This is the wrong way," I said.

"I know." He sighed. "But we can come back here once we've saved those children. You have your map, don't you?"

He was right—I could always turn back. But for every moment I spent in the Underworld, I grew weaker. And the weaker I became, the more likely I would give in to the abiku, begging for the sweet release of death.

Zuri shifted on his feet—so impatient. So full of life, anxious to be useful. Nothing he'd said so far rang false in my ears. Still, my eyes narrowed.

I had always been good at puzzles.

"All right," I said softly, smiling at him. "I'll go with you."

"Good. There's no time to lose—"

"I'll go with you," I said, "if you kiss me."

He blinked, then grinned. "I'll kiss you all you want Idajo. After we stop the abiku, we can—"

"I'll go," I said, choosing my words carefully, "if you kiss me right now."

Zuri nodded, coming toward me with confidence. Again his cologne overcame me. "Have it your way." When he leaned in, I trembled.

"Ask me," he whispered. "Ask me to kiss you."

"I'm ready."

"I know." His beautiful dark eyes searched mine, warm and pleading. "But I want you to ask, Idajo. Because—"

"Because you aren't Zuri," I said calmly. "You are one of the abiku. And for as long as we're in the Underworld, you can't touch me unless I tell you to."

He froze, looking puzzled, and then he—it—smiled, mouth stretching wider and wider, teeth sharpening to points as the spirit shrank to a child's height, Zuri's form and features melting away.

"Such a pity, Wuraola," sighed the abiku, in a voice like rust on iron. It stared up at me, a creature with ashy gray skin and red-pupil eyes. "If you had only come now, your journey would have been so much shorter. But never worry." A narrow white tongue flicked out of the creature's mouth, licking its thin, cracked lips. "You and your friend will join us soon."

"All my friends are safe—far away from you," I snapped. "Be gone!"

And with a cackle, the abiku obliged, bursting into a cloud of flies and vanishing in a swarm down the opposite corridor.

Once the creature was gone, I collapsed against the

damp cavern wall, trembling with relief and anger. Had this been what Old Mongwe's warning was about? Before vanishing into the sky, she had said not to trust something—or someone. Perhaps the false Zuri had been the obstacle she feared.

I charged on down the correct path, steps buoyed by my victory over the Underworld spirit. This time, I stopped for nothing, not even a distant voice that sounded strangely like Ye Eun, or a shriek of a water phoenix, echoing through the caverns behind me.

After another round of day-long hours, I emerged from the tunnels and found myself standing on the ledge of a vast canyon. To my surprise, there seemed to be a sky here—or something like it. A deep emerald zenith twinkled overhead in either direction, as far as the eye could see. The smell of sulfur remained, but it combined with something organic—pungent and sweet, like decaying leaves on a forest floor. The canyon was so deep, I could not see the bottom. A stone bridge stretched across the chasm. It was wide—hundreds of yards across—but purposely unfinished: a formidable gap yawning in its center.

I clenched my fists. Ye Eun had prepared me for this. All I had to do was walk across—and to fill the gap, I need only answer a question.

My sandal touched the smooth, bone-white stone of the bridge—and I gulped. Every single step echoed through the canyon. Hurriedly, I made my way to the gap, muttering the names of my Anointed Ones like an incantation. *"Ji Huan. Beatrix. Min Ja, Kwasi, Danai . . ."*

I peered over the edge of the gap . . . and voices roared up from the deep. Husky, *ancient* voices shook the stone beneath me, rattling the drums in my ears.

"WELCOME, WURAOLA."

I wet myself.

Dozens of beasts, each the size of a small house, emerged from the darkness in a cloud of wings, fur, and claws. They landed with a *whoomp* on the bridge, surrounding me in a semicircle. Woo In had been right.

There were far more Deaths than thirteen.

"Well, girl," they rumbled as one. "What have you to ask the beasts of Warlord Fire?"

The sight of them awoke something primal in me: the pure, manic revulsion that every living thing held for death before its time. My nerves demanded that I run, and I heartily agreed with them. But still I stood firm, summoning my training from Ye Eun.

Remember that you need not die.

"Th-Thank you," I bleated after regaining control of my voice. "I . . . I need to pass. P-Please, kind beasts."

The beasts roared again, shaking, and I realized after a stunned moment that they were laughing.

"She calls us kind," rasped a beast with hair like bristles. Its scaly tongue smoldered, a dying coal, and flicked the creature's eyes as it spoke. "Death is often kind, to those exhausted by the boon of living. Are *you* exhausted, Wuraola?"

"N–No," I stammered, lifting a stubborn chin. "I want to live."

"Oh?" Another creature crept closer, eel–like, with veiny, translucent skin and unblinking, fishlike eyes. In a low, gurgling voice, the beast who could only be Drowning asked the question I had been waiting for. "And out of all the souls of the Overworld—the mortals who have died, and are dying, as we speak—why should *you* be allowed to live?"

I inhaled, then blurted the answer I'd rehearsed with Kirah: "Because I'm saving lives," I said. "I'm a good empress. And a good person."

Again, laughter shook the bridge, causing bile to roil in my stomach.

"Such hubris," hissed Poison, a boil–covered beast with foul green breath. "Only a year ago, your hands ran with the blood of an innocent prince."

"And from birth," grunted Organ–Death, a tusked boar with twitching arteries bulging like vines beneath its skin, "your days were gilded in wealth and privilege. Everything you own—your crown, your palace, even the friends you call your Anointed Ones—was bought with the lives of children."

The words lashed like whips. Organ–Death spoke the truth. Without Redemptors, Enoba Kunleo the Perfect could never have brought peace to Aritsar. And without peace, he could not have reigned as emperor.

All this time, one beast watched me without saying a

word: a sharp-clawed lion with blank, milky eyes, and a floating translucent mane. A sickening metallic smell filled my nose as I watched it, and I knew instinctively that this was one of the Unnamed Deaths—a terror beyond words.

"I'm trying to make things right," I croaked at last. "But how can I change Aritsar if I'm dead? I deserve to live because I care. I can fix it!"

"All you could achieve," wheezed the hairy, snub-nosed beast of Suffocation, "was fulfilled when you entered the Underworld. The new Treaty is complete. You are the last of history's Redemptors. In death, you have accomplished far more than your life ever did."

"To the thousands of souls already lost," added a frost-white wolf, crouching to its massive haunches, "to the Redemptors sacrificed before you . . . you are no savior. The only thing you have left to offer them is justice: an eye for an eye." From the hunger in its cloudy yellow eyes, I knew without a doubt that this was Old Age—one of the beasts, along with the Unnamed Deaths, who could still kill me. "Your life," it said, "for the ones your ancestors took."

I had heard these words before, of course: in the pounding melody of my headaches, the song at the edge of my nightmares.

Pay the price.

I slumped, my courage draining away. Perhaps this was why Zuri had let those commoners murder him. Had he been right? After defeating the warlords, had his death been the only thing left to give?

My chin hardened. Yes, Zuri of Djbanti had died for justice. But he had also died to escape—to kill the guilt that had plagued him all his life. He had looked at comfort with disdain and regarded rest as weakness. Zuri had died because it was easier to be legendary than human.

"My death won't solve anything," I said. "And maybe my life won't either. But . . ." My hand rose to my ear, and Ye Eun's lily blossom fell into my palm. A complicated memory passed into my skin: snippets of her marred innocence, her jaded hope, at battle inside her. I thought of Thaddace, growing ashen as the life left his body, and of Adukeh, glowing with pride in her coral akorin beads. I thought of panicking in Zuri's bathtub, covered in blood, and of the rainbow spring, washing me clean as Sanjeet bathed me in kisses. I thought of Da Seo's memory, in which violence stole her words, and of my golden-hued birthday party in the orchard, where courage brought her words back.

Then I smiled up at the Warlord's Deaths, who shifted their great heads in confused surprise.

"I want to live," I said, replacing Ye Eun's lily behind my ear, "because life is . . . is *worth* it. Because as long as we can imagine a better world, we should stick around to see it. Even if it doesn't exist yet. Even if we have to build it from scratch, brick by muddy brick."

Their ancient, glittering eyes bored into me, searching for a shadow of doubt—a thread of uncertainty. I closed my eyes awaiting my fate.

But when I opened them, the Deaths had vanished. No—they had moved into the gap, mending the bridge with their vast, heaving bodies. They had accepted my answer. I . . . I had won.

I willed my legs to move, but they remained frozen. I was supposed to step on the Deaths—Ye Eun had told me this—but the idea of touching death itself turned my very mortal stomach.

Again, they laughed. "You may fear touching us now, Wuraola," came the phlegmy chuckle of Contagion. "But all Redemptors forget fear once they meet their emi-ehran."

I blinked. What did they mean, "once I met . . ." But then my gaze locked on the end of the bridge, where a being slowly materialized. Water pooled in my eyes as my limbs relaxed, overwhelmed by a sudden, profound peace—and a feeling that I'd known this being a long, long time. Every human soul, the priests taught, was assigned a guardian spirit after meeting death: a companion for comfort as we marched in Egungun's Parade. But since Redemptors met death while still living, their emi-ehrans followed them out of the Underworld—a companion for the rest of eternity.

"She's beautiful," I breathed. Emi-ehrans possessed no sex according to legend. But without speaking aloud, the creature told me its gender—and in the same deep, silent voice, she asked me for a name.

I walked as if in a trance across the lumpy, textured backs of the Warlord's Deaths, my former fear vanished like smoke. The beasts dispersed as soon as I crossed, but I barely looked back, reaching out instead to touch my very own emi-ehran.

In the world above, I would have called her a rhinoceros. She was just as massive, towering yards above me, with the same ridged body and sharp, clever horn. But her horn was translucent crystal, and her skin the color of midnight, sparkling with sapphire stars.

No. Not sparkling. *Blinking.*

Each sapphire was an eye, fringed in silver lashes. They covered her like a mantle, each one wiser and farther-seeing than I could possibly imagine.

"Iranti," I murmured, a word in old Arit. "Memory." The name had tumbled from my lips, as though I'd been carrying it all my life—and perhaps I had. The creature nodded her assent. Then she named me back, in a language without words: a sequence of grunts and musical notes that I loved at once. After I voiced my acceptance, she jutted her horn, gently resting its tip between my eyes.

I gasped. My Hallow dove into the Underworld floor, submerging me in an ocean of color and voices. My whole life, I had always struggled to retrieve memories older than a few decades. But somehow, Iranti had amplified my Hallow, allowing me to see . . . centuries. Millennia. Billions upon billions of stories spinning around me until my chest tightened and my temples began to throb, and I—

Iranti drew back, tickling my cheek with a puff of warm air from her nostrils. An apology, I realized. She hadn't meant to hurt me. Only to show me what she, what *we*, could do. Together.

"You can find anything," I whispered. "Any story, from anywhere. And you'll help me carry them, won't you?"

Her many eyes glinted, as if with humor, and again she spoke in that voice that was not quite a voice: *Iranti never forgets.*

I touched my brow to her cheek, nuzzling her wrinkled face as her eyes blinked against me. "Let's get out of here," I said.

Name your emi-ehran had been the fifth task on Ye Eun's training. Now only one, the sixth, remained:

Ascend the Stair of Mirrors, not heeding your own reflection. Stop for nothing. Trust no one.

Escape the Underworld.

CHAPTER 33

THE STAIR OF MIRRORS, YE EUN HAD WARNED me, would be the most treacherous part of my journey. But I found that hard to believe. After all, I wasn't alone anymore—Iranti's body radiated heat like a heavenly brazier, thawing my extremities from head to toe. When we arrived at the stairs' bottom landing, hope flickered inside me.

Compared to the rest of the Underworld, the stairs were pleasantly bright—a steep, spiraling staircase several yards wide, lit ethereally by floating green lamps. The lamps were amplified, however, by the mirrors; the floor, ceiling, and walls enclosing the staircase were all hewn from dizzyingly spotless glass and when we entered, every movement we made seemed to echo on forever. When Iranti mounted the staircase, I half expected the steps to shatter—but the glass remained firm beneath her massive plodding feet and did not smear beneath my filthy ones. One last trek—one steep climb—and I would arrive at the Oruku Breach again. A free empress at last, and a live one.

At first, it was easy to ignore my reflection. I looked terrible, of course. A girl with puffy, bloodshot eyes, a stained blue wrapper, and skin made ashy from dust stared back at me from every direction. But after days or hours of that joint-grinding climb, the girl in the mirrors began to change. On one wall, a girl with my face and body appeared to address a crowd. This Tarisai, however, was several inches taller, black hair billowing around her in a coiling halo. She radiated grave wisdom, and the adinkra gown I had worn at my Pinnacle suited her muscled, commanding frame much better than my average one. I couldn't hear what she was saying, but I knew, instinctually, that masses would die to serve this girl. She stopped speaking then, glancing over her gold-powdered shoulder to meet my eye.

I froze in surprise . . . then she smiled, holding out a hand *through* the mirror. She mouthed, eyes bright with ambition, *Ask me to guide you.*

I was supposed to ignore her. Ye Eun's instructions had been clear. And yet . . . griots described the Underworld as a portal to many dimensions, not just a liaison between Earth and Core. Perhaps this other Tarisai was the empress of a mirror world. One where peasant and Redemptor blood had never been shed. One where I had been so prepared, so capable that I had never made mistakes.

What if this better, improved Tarisai could help me? Impart knowledge that could change the trajectory of Aritsar, and make me the ruler I so ached to be? Surely I wouldn't have to stay in her world forever. Just a little while, and she could tell me what I'd done wrong. Prevent me from causing future catastrophes.

She nodded encouragingly, seeming to sense my thoughts. *Ask*, she mouthed again, and I opened my mouth . . .

Only for Iranti to stamp in the stairwell, shaking her great head and grunting so loud, I was jarred out of my trance. All of her eyes seemed to scold me, wide with warning.

I stared at her, dazed, and then I realized the mistake I had almost made. If the mirror Tarisai was, in fact, another abiku, trying to lead me off the path . . . it would need my permission to touch me. *Ask me to guide you* may not have been explicit, but the words were enough to seal my doom.

I shuddered, stumbling back, and the Majestic Tarisai scowled and vanished, leaving behind my dreary reflection beside Iranti's.

Onward we climbed. The mirrors showed spear-toting, Vigilante Tarisai, her clothes modeled shamelessly after Zuri's, leading the oppressed in an armored charge toward liberation. Then came Cherished Tarisai, a grinning, round-cheeked little girl surrounded by imaginary family members, all of whom were delighted by her childish antics, and who caressed her without an ounce of fear. There was even Dancer Tarisai, resplendent in body paint and the envy of every festival, navigating her many partners with grace and rolling her perfect hips in sultry time to the music.

The hardest of my mirror selves to ignore was Mother Tarisai—a serene, doe-eyed woman decades older than I was, cooing as she held up a plump, gurgling infant.

A proud, bearded Sanjeet circled both mother and child in his arms. She looked so peaceful. So confident that she would never hurt the treasure in her arms—would never betray or leave it. For a brief, achingly sweet moment, I let myself pretend that this Tarisai truly existed. That it wasn't an abiku trying to murder me, but an alternate universe in which Raybearers didn't exist, and healing was certain, and curses never lasted longer than a single generation.

I moved on, smiling sadly to myself, but to my shock, the child Tarisai appeared again.

Only . . . it wasn't the giggling, doted-upon girl from earlier. This reflection was slightly older, perhaps nine or ten, mousy and fidgeting, and we were not quite twins, though her features strongly resembled mine. What's more . . . she wasn't standing in some idyllic scene, pantomiming a reality for me to envy. Instead, she stood still in the stairwell mirror, staring directly at me. Waiting. My mouth went dry.

I was staring at The Lady.

"No." I clenched my fists and walked quickly past her. The Stair of Mirrors was supposed to show *my* reflection. "I'm not The Lady," I snapped to the Lady-abiku in the mirror, who followed after me as I mounted the stairs with renewed rigor. "So if you're trying to entice me, you'd better try something else. We are *not* the same."

"I know that," the child wailed. "I know that, Made-of-Me."

I nearly toppled onto the hard glass stairs, grasping Iranti's horn for balance. "You can talk," I rasped. "The other ones. They . . . they didn't talk." I shuddered. Did these illusions get more powerful as I went along? Perhaps this meant I was almost to the Oruku Breach. I shook myself to regain my bearings and charged on.

"Wait," ordered the reflection. Still, the abiku followed me, the spitting image of my mother as a young girl. "Wait. Please Made-of— I mean—" She cringed. "Please, Tarisai." I paused, just for a moment . . .

And the illusion reached through the mirror, placing a firm, cold hand on my arm.

I jerked back, heart pounding. "You're not allowed to do that," I shrieked. "Abiku may not touch a living thing in the Underworld without permission. It's—it's—" It was the Storyteller's law. Which meant, in theory . . . it was unbreakable.

The reflection sighed, holding out her hand again. "I am not an abiku, Tarisai. I am your mother. Your real one." She fidgeted. "I know I look . . . different. They say the longer a soul stays down here, the more themselves they become." Her musical voice, higher and thinner than the one I'd grown up with, yet altogether familiar, sent shivers up my spine.

"You're lying," I whispered.

But she had touched me. Ye Eun and Mongwe would have warned me if there were exceptions to the Storyteller's rule.

"I don't understand," I said at last. "Why are you here? Why didn't you go to Egungun's Parade?"

The child stared at me for a long moment, her brilliant black eyes wet and tortured. "I tried," she said at last. "I tried to do the parade. I knew it would be hard, but I didn't think . . ." Her strong chin quivered—then tears rolled down her dark, soft cheeks. "I have hurt so many people. And in such different, terrible ways. How could I have been so bad?"

I watched with morbid fascination, struck by a need to comfort her. Then the impulse cooled, congealing into rage.

No. *I* was the child, not her. *I* was the one she had chosen to bring into the world, then starved for love and forced to attempt murder. *I* was the one half-delirious in the Underworld. *She* should be comforting *me*. And yet— And yet—

It was so hard to be angry at someone so small and insubstantial. I had never seen The Lady cry before. I hadn't known she could. There was so much about my mother I hadn't known.

"So you're stuck down here," I monotoned at last, shuffling my feet. "In the Underworld, instead of going to Core."

She nodded woodenly. "But I can rejoin the parade anytime I like. My emi-ehran's waiting for me there." She smiled weakly. "I'll go back to them. Soon, I expect. But I had to see you. I . . . I shouldn't have locked you in that house. Always so cold, so lonely, with no one to talk to . . ." She shuddered and rubbed her arms, as if reliving my childhood misery. "And your suffering got so much worse after meeting the prince. It's no wonder you tried to forget. But I was mistaken, Tarisai. And I'm sorry for the mother I wasn't, even though I *was* only trying to secure your future."

I smiled grimly. That last phrase—that thread of my mother's indignant pride, which she could not relinquish even here, in the heart of hell—removed any doubt that this shade was my mother.

The Lady—the great and powerful Unnamed Raybearer, commander of an alagbato, feared by kings and emperors— was here in front of me. And she was sorry. *Actually* sorry.

"I forgive you," I said, and to my surprise, I decided that I meant it. For now, anyway. Some days I would change my mind. My mother's toxic legacy was permanent, like the scars on Dayo's face, and whenever I dwelled on it, I'd be livid all over again. But for now, standing before that fidgeting shade of a little girl, surrounded by my reflections, I felt only a sad, resigned peace.

"I can do you a favor," The Lady said then, holding out her dainty hand through the mirror. "The abiku have dug another route out of the Underworld. It's closer than the Oruku Breach. I could take you," she said eagerly, gesturing to her translucent hovering feet. "I can fly, after all. You've got several days' travel left using the stairs to the Oruku Breach. But there's a new exit to the Overworld now, much closer. I could take you."

"Really?" I breathed.

"I think the abiku have been working on that exit for

years," replied The Lady. "I've been curious: Have you heard any news of creatures appearing in the Overworld? Escapees through a new breach?"

My eyes widened. She was telling the truth. There *was* a new exit from the Underworld—Sanjeet had found it.

"I'll take you," The Lady said again, extending her hand through the mirror. "Please, Tarisai." If she had smiled then—that warm, radiant beam that had always molded my will to clay—I would have turned away, leaving her in the Underworld without a second glance. But instead, she only stared. Agitated. Desperate. I had seen that look before, on the face of a little Kunleo girl staring up at her brother, begging him to see her and let them be a family.

That earnest, heart-shattering look hadn't worked on Olugbade. And by rejecting his sister—betraying her pure trust—he had created the wounded monster who would grow into The Lady.

"Please," the girl whispered. "Let me make amends."

I inhaled slowly. I did not *trust* The Lady. Not exactly . . . but I knew, deep down, that I could not reject her in the same way her brother had. No one deserved that heartbreak twice. Not even my mother.

I glanced tiredly at Iranti, whose muscles were tense. The emi-ehran's short tail flicked with hostility, then she moaned in her wordless, tonal language. Of her complicated song I could make out only one theme:

Danger.

"I know." I sighed, stroking her face. "But what could

hurt me, now?" I had survived the deaths. I had outwitted every attempt of the abiku to trick me. And what was more, I had not slept in what felt like days or weeks. Every limb in my body screamed for rest. The thought of my journey being over . . . of seeing my council siblings again, in hours instead of days—it made hope surge through my veins, like the heady rush of honeywine.

I leaned to whisper in Iranti's ear. "If The Lady's lying, we can always find our way back. I have a map, so there's no risk. I know the rules, Iranti: I need not die."

I turned to enter the mirror, but my emi-ehran stayed put, staring pleadingly with her sky of eyes.

"I'm going," I repeated, and she huffed a great sigh . . . then disappeared. I frowned, but knew at once that she hadn't truly gone. Not completely. I could feel her, somewhere in a near ether, waiting to reappear when I called.

"I'll see you on the surface, then," I told the air, and took my mother's small, cold hand. The moment I did, both my feet left the floor, and I passed into the mirror, glass rippling around me like rings of troubled water.

CHAPTER 34

THE LADY AND I WERE FLOATING IN ANOTHER cavern, filled with sulfurous green fog. My stomach flipped at the height, but the girl tightened her grip on my hand, smiling reassuringly.

"Won't be far now, my daughter," she said, still with that desperate, nervous gleam in her eyes.

We flew up, up, toward the emerald underworld sky, and parallel to what seemed like an ash-covered mountain. The fog cleared, allowing me my first aerial view of the Underworld.

The expanse of it numbed my senses. Shadowy cliffs and valleys teeming with shades; threadbare forests that spread for miles; gray ash dunes and winding, bone-white rivers.

The only lively feature was a colorful ribbon, long and quivering, seeming to stretch into eternity. I didn't realize what it was until I heard the drumbeats, faint but reverberating, possessing my limbs like a manic spirit. Immediately, my soul felt lighter. Why had I felt so weary about my journey through the Underworld? Why had

I worried that it would never end? All stories came to completion, and no hill was too steep—no step too painful. I laughed, eyes filling with tears. I had been touched by the music of Egungun—and I was witnessing his parade.

"My emi-ehran is down there, somewhere," The Lady sighed. "They refused to come with me when I left the parade."

"I bet they miss you," I replied after a moment. "What do they look like?"

The corners of her eyes creased with fondness. "A fox," she said. "As stubborn and cunning as I am—though its eyes are soft, as mine once were. We understand each other, my Ifaya and I. They were the first to name me—and I, them. I'll go back to them. As soon as I've made amends for my sins."

"You mean, after you help me?"

She blinked slowly. "Yes," The Lady said, squeezing my hand just a little too tight. "After I help everyone."

We flew higher, leveling out over the plateau of a charcoal mountain. A glittering amethyst lake covered most of the plateau, and in its center lay a tiny island mound with a shrine of polished black marble.

"We're here," The Lady announced, flying over the water and landing on the island.

Immediately my nose wrinkled. A faintly familiar, metallic smell wafted from the shrine, which featured a tall, narrow statue. Fog, so cold it stung the back of my throat, curled over the glittering amethyst water.

"What is this?" I asked, rubbing goose pimples on my arms.

The Lady didn't answer at first, pulling me into a tight embrace. Her child's form barely reached my chest, and her skin was chilly, as were the tendrils of her robe as they wrapped around me.

"It's your way home," she whispered.

"Oh." My brow wrinkled with confusion. The statue depicted Warlord Fire, flames bursting from the god's handsome face in a malevolent halo. One hand was clenched above his head in a fist, as though ready to smite, and the other held an outstretched spear, its tip capped in pearly ivory and pulsing with pale light. It didn't look like the Oruku Breach, but then again, I didn't have much experience with supernatural portals.

"You're supposed to touch it," The Lady explained, nodding at the spear. She swallowed hard. "You won't feel any pain. Or loneliness either. That should make up for Bhekina House, shouldn't it?"

I stepped out of her embrace, unsure of what she meant. "Well," I said, glancing warily at the spear. "It's better than climbing the stairs, at least."

The Lady nodded, her eyes wet and wistful. "Best do it quickly."

"All right." I leaned in to plant a kiss on her stony cold cheek. "Goodbye again, Mother. Until we meet again in Core."

Then I turned toward the statue. The strange scent

intensified, making my eyes water. Where had I smelled it? I had been in the Underworld so long, memories jumbled together. Ah well—it wouldn't matter, once I was back home. With a last look over the sprawling shadowed landscape, I lifted my hand to touch the spear.

And then The Lady's arms locked around me from behind, yanking me to the ground.

"Get back," she shrieked. "Don't go anywhere near it!"

She flew us away from the island mound, dropping me in a heap on the banks of the amethyst lake. Scrambling to my feet, I stared at her in confused alarm. "Mother?"

She was covering her face, mouth open in a static sob. Slowly she sank down by my side, looking younger than ever. Her shade robes flickered around her as she drew her knees to her chest.

"I'm sorry, Tarisai," she rasped. "I-I don't know what came over me. I just thought—if I gave the abiku what they wanted—if I could free all those children . . ."

As she babbled incomprehensibly, I remembered where I had smelled the statue before.

The milky-eyed beast at the bridge: one of the Unnamed Deaths.

"That shrine isn't a portal at all, is it?" I said, in a low, strangled voice. "It would have killed me."

The Lady nodded slowly, bright eyes peering out at me from behind her hands. "I'm so sorry," she whispered again.

"Why?" Hot tears rolled down my cheeks, but my voice remained calm. "Why did you try to kill me, Mother?"

She began to rock back and forth, keening into her fists. "To free the others," she said. "All of them." She pointed over the edge of the plateau. Woodenly, I rose to my feet and glanced below. Immediately, my veins turned to ice.

For miles beneath the plateau, lines of ojiji children stretched in every direction, drilling in perfect synchronization. Their eyes were dull and empty. Most were from Songland, though a minority looked to hail from all twelve kingdoms of Aritsar. Purple Redemptor birthmarks glistened on every single child.

"No," I croaked. "But—but this doesn't make sense. There must be at least ten thousand Redemptors here. A hundred, even. And that would mean . . ."

"It would mean," The Lady finished, "that except for the few who escaped the Underworld, in all five hundred years of sacrifices, not a single child has made it to Core. They never got to enter Egungun's Parade. They never got to travel to paradise, or receive their final rest. Once they succumbed to the Underworld's torture and gave the abiku permission to kill them, they were brought here." She indicated at the amethyst lake. "To be cursed by the shrine. It killed them, of course—but unlike every other kind of death, it also stole their memories. And a soul without memories is like a ghost—never leaving its body, even if that body is dead. What's left is the perfect weapon: a soul that can be commanded and a body that cannot die. One of those ojiji could kill one hundred Arit warriors in a matter of hours. A hundred thousand . . ."

"Could defeat the Army of Twelve Realms," I whispered.

The Lady nodded. "I think the abiku must have been planning it from the very beginning. It's why they agreed to Enoba's treaty in the first place. The abiku, while strong, could not defeat the massive Army of Twelve realms . . . but if they could get their hands on live humans, eventually, they'd have immortal forces strong enough to rule the world."

"But the abiku are bound by the Treaty," I protested. "It was sealed by blood oath, which binds even demons. They can't attack us anymore—that was the term of my sacrifice."

"The abiku may not attack the Overworld themselves," said The Lady, "But their undead puppets can. And for centuries, slowly amassing an army of non-abiku was their only hope of ruling the Overworld . . . until you offered yourself as a sacrifice.

"They were going to use you," she murmured. "To kill you, steal your memories, and send your puppet body to rule Aritsar while they controlled you from the Underworld. As empress, you could revoke the old treaty, allowing abiku once more to roam the Earth. But to turn you into a puppet, they needed you to enter the Underworld alive. This pool is the only way to kill someone using the Warlord Fire's special Death."

Of course. The last year whipped before my eyes, every puzzle piece falling into place. Why the ojiji had protected me. Why they had guarded my reputation and won me the loyalty of the nobles. Why they had insisted I make a council of rulers—so I would have unchecked power when they stole my soul and unleashed me, their puppet monster, back into Aritsar.

I knew then the rest of Old Mongwe's warning.

Don't trust The Lady.

"You were going to let me die," I whispered. "To let them trap my soul in my dead body forever."

"Not forever," The Lady protested. "They said they'd let you go eventually. When their work was done. And you wouldn't have suffered—well, maybe when you first touched the stone." She bit her lip. "But after that, you wouldn't have felt anything. Wouldn't even remember. And in exchange . . ." She stared out over dotted lines of Redemptors. "They promised to free all of these children. To let their souls travel to Core, instead of staying trapped in those corpses. Don't you see, Made-of-Me? I finally had a chance to do something good. To make up for how I betrayed Woo In. To save thousands of Redemptors, instead of hurting people, like I did when I was alive. I . . . I thought then, when I went back to Egungun's Parade . . ."

"It would hurt less," I finished, feeling my blood begin to boil. "You were going to lessen your own pain by killing me. By making me betray all my friends—again!"

"Just for a little while," The Lady insisted, features wild with desperation. "For a greater cause."

"I forgave you." Hot tears coursed down my cheeks. "I trusted you, and you tricked me. You didn't even give me a choice!"

"But I did, in the end!" The Lady clenched her small fists. "I stopped you from touching it, didn't I? I knew it was wrong. But I'm still learning, Made-of-Me. I'm trying to be a good person."

"My name," I reminded her, "is Tarisai. And I never want to see you again."

The little girl's face crumpled as though I'd punched her. And in spite of everything—in spite of the unspeakable betrayal she had almost wrought . . . I still felt pity.

"You will see me again," she said, after a long pause. "In Core. That's where everyone goes, after Egungun's Parade. And when you do—" Chin wobbling, she touched my shoulder. "I'll be better. A good person. I'll show all of you. You'll see."

I turned away, letting the cold Underworld air dry my cheeks. "I hope so, Mother."

Another pause. "I still can help you leave the Underworld."

"Stop lying."

"I'm not," she wailed. "The new breach is real. But it's not the stone. It's there." She gestured down into the valley. For the first time, I noticed what looked like a rift in the air on the other side of the valley: a floating, iridescent streak, cycling through a spectrum of colors, into which a stream of undead children were marching.

My stomach dropped. The undead army had already begun its assault on the surface.

"I could fly you down," The Lady suggested. "It wouldn't

take long. You could go back home. Please, Tarisai. It's the least I can do."

Then she smiled her famous smile as her eyes searched my face, hungry for absolution. I watched her in silence, savoring my favorite features—the first I'd ever loved.

Then I said: "Goodbye, Mother. For real this time."

"But—"

"I'll see you in Core." I closed my eyes and sensed her hesitate for a moment, hovering in front of me. But when I opened my eyes . . . she was gone.

CHAPTER 35

I MADE A SILENT PLEA TO THE AIR, AND A SHORT distance away Iranti materialized, plodding toward me with long-suffering dignity. I sighed, laying my head against hers. "Thank you," I told her. "For not saying 'I told you so.'"

She huffed a sigh, then spoke in her song of sounds and symbols, extending two words into my mind: *Friend. Coming.*

"Yes," I told her. "We'll always be friends."

She wagged her head—I'd misunderstood her. She concentrated harder. *Friend. Coming.*

And just then, the shriek of a phoenix echoed across the mountainside.

I stared in shock as Ye Eun appeared over the mountain ridge, stumbling onto the plateau. Overhead, Hwanghu flew loops in the emerald sky, leaving icy streaks across the zenith.

I recoiled. Were they both abiku illusions?

But that theory vanished the moment Ye Eun reached me, seizing my hand. "You're all right," she panted, eyes wide with relief. "Hwanghu's been scanning the Underworld, looking for you everywhere."

I pulled her into a hug, heart racing with disbelief. She was the first live human I'd seen in . . .

"Ye Eun," I breathed, "how are you here? And how long have I been gone?"

"I'd guess about two weeks," she said. "I'm not sure, though. After the battle started, I knew something must be wrong. So I left Ae Ri with her nurses and came in to find you."

"Battle? What battle?"

Her gaze was empty. "They started coming a day after you entered. Undead children—Redemptors. Hundreds of them . . . and they haven't stopped coming. The attack came from that new portal to the Underworld north of Ebujo City, instead of the Oruku Breach in the temple. The Army of Twelve Realms lay mobilized in wait for them, but . . ." She shook her head, looking haunted, and placed my hand against her forehead.

I am standing on the walls of Ebujo City, watching chaos unfold below. Though I inhabit the memory as Ye Eun, my heart is moved as Tarisai, and tears of pride spring to my eyes: Warriors from all twelve realms of Aritsar fight side by side. They advance, united to defend the city from the armed, deathless killers pouring from the ochre breach.

Sanjeet, Dayo, and Captain Bunmi lead the fray atop armored war buffalo, beating back the undead creatures with a cohort of Imperial Guard warriors.

In truth, it is not an Army of Twelve Realms, but thirteen, for Songland has arrived. From atop a turret, Min Ja directs a unit of fire-speaking sowanhada warriors, her long jet hair streaming like a pennant. The warriors punch the air in unison, sending up a spray of flame, which Min Ja directs in a lethal wind toward the invaders.

The battleground is a patchwork of realms. Quetzalan war machines ignite cannons, sending frozen balls of holy water into the Breach, while Moreyaoese archers shower the enemy with arrows. Biraslovians in horned helmets ride packs of snow-white battle wolves, providing cover for Swanian and Nyamban warriors, who hurl spears with deadly accuracy. Warriors of the new Djbanti commonwealth fight shoulder to shoulder with Spartian soldiers, and Mewish berserkers, fierce in bright blue war paint and capes of tartan, share mounts with Dhyrmish charioteers. Blessid and Nontish healers retrieve the fallen, tending to wounds with grim efficiency.

Yet for all its colorful glory, dispatching hordes back into the breach like a well-oiled machine, the Army of Twelve Realms was flagging. How could it do otherwise? Their enemy could not die. For every cursed Redemptor set aflame or corralled into cages or hurled back into the Underworld . . . there were ten more behind it. And they'd only continue coming.

I pulled out of Ye Eun's mind, heart racing. Sanjeet. The vassal rulers. Hundreds of thousands of Arit warriors all doomed. Am's Story, even the cursed Redemptors were victims in all this, souls trapped, forced to desecrate their bodies with blood and murder.

"Well?" Ye Eun breathed. "What did you do? Why are those Redemptors doing this?"

I swallowed hard. "It didn't start when I came here. The abiku have been planning this for a long time."

"And you, Wuraola," hissed a triad of rasping voices, "have the power to stop it."

Ye Eun and I whirled. Amidst a noxious cloud, a gaggle of ashen abiku had appeared in the clearing, baring their sharp smiles.

I shivered. "What's that supposed to mean?"

Their all-pupil eyes flashed, beady and crimson. "We extend the same offer that we gave to your mother." They pointed to the statue of Warlord Fire. "Die so that more may live. Give your memories to the shrine, and once you have, go above world, and be our empress. Revoke the Treaty. Weaken the continental realms . . . and in return, we will use our powers to destroy the shrine, freeing your memories, and those of the ojiji army."

I eyed them suspiciously. "Why would you give up an undead army? You're already defeating the Army of Twelve Realms. With enough time, your enslaved child soldiers could decimate the entire continent. You've won, so why offer me a deal?"

"You misunderstand our goal, Wuraola. We never wanted to obliterate humanity—not even in the time of Enoba. No, Little Empress, we wanted to rule it. To expand our territory from this realm of death and smoke to the young, unmolested Overworld. There we may grow strong, as we once were, at the dawn of time." Their eyes glittered, gray faces taut with longing. "But we may only do so if you revoke that accursed Treaty."

"Why would I do that? Why would I allow you to take over the continent?"

"Because the alternative," sneered the abiku, gesturing at the mobilizing army below, "is death for everyone, and eternal damnation for those poor, poor Redemptors. The choice is simple, Wuraola." The demons were morphing, growing before my eyes, shedding their usual skins of monstrous children to stand before me as winged beings, smoldering in dark green flame. "A new age for humanity, in which they finally serve the abiku—their natural superiors . . . Or the end of all life on your continent. Decide quickly, Wuraola." They glanced again at the lines of child soldiers and smirked with wide, scaly mouths. "Your friends in the Aboveworld don't have much time."

The memory of Dayo and Sanjeet—of Min Ja, Ji Huan, Uxmal, and the others leading cohorts against the undead masses, faces streaked with sweat, voices hoarse as their strength begins to quail flashed in my mind. I ran puzzle after puzzle, desperate to craft a solution. But every single answer to this problem involved a deadly sacrifice.

I reached for Iranti, asking her permission. Her fate was tied with mine, and so where I fell, she would follow. Grief filled her many eyes as her horn grazed my fingers. But with a nod of her dark, galaxy-wide head, she gave her consent.

"Well?" demanded the abiku. "Do we have a deal, Empress Redemptor?"

I closed my eyes, feeling the sulfurous wind of the Underworld beat about my hair. I touched Ye Eun's lily and said goodbye to everything I'd once known: the color of being alive, the weight of a living soul.

Then I commanded Iranti, aloud so the abiku could hear: "Take me to the Warlord's shrine."

"No," whispered Ye Eun, her stony face wet with tears. "There has to be another way."

I only smiled at her, leaning down to kiss her forehead— then pulled her lily from my hair and tucked it behind her ear. "Don't worry," I told her. "No matter how bleak the world gets, I'll make sure there's always a corner to plant flowers."

Then Iranti knelt, allowing me to climb onto her vast leathery back, and carried me into the amethyst lake. When she set me down on the shrine's small island, the abiku cackled with anticipation, sending bursts of pale green lightning across the sky.

The handsome, merciless face of Warlord Fire stared down at me. The metallic smell of the Unnamed Deaths filled my nostrils, turning my stomach. My gaze fell to the statue's outstretched spear, its tip capped in chilling white ivory.

"For a world worth surviving in," I whispered. Then I nodded at Iranti . . . and in one deft movement, she lowered her horn to press between my eyes, and I touched a finger to the spear of Warlord Fire.

I screamed, immediately seeing red.

Blinding, searing pain—shooting up my arm, enveloping my skin like a wave of crackling acid. I was dying. It was killing me—grasping at everything I was. Hungry to extract every memory, every day and hour, the marks on my soul that made me Tarisai. In only an instant more, it could have me. It would all be over. I would fall into a deep, dreamless sleep, my soul a slate wiped clean. My body a willing puppet for the abiku: their instrument for a new age of terror. Perhaps it wouldn't be so bad. Perhaps humanity would fight back. All I had to do was let them have me, just for an instant more and the pain would disappear.

I clenched my fists. Not all pain was worthless.

Sometimes, pain could write a story.

"Now," I shrieked at Iranti. With a burst of heat, she magnified my Hallow as I thrust it into the statue, inverting the shrine's power, taking its memories before it could steal mine.

Every nerve in my body begged for me to stop, alight with torture. But I pressed on, on, absorbing the complete and unabridged memory of one Redemptor's life—then ten—then a hundred. My skin sweltered where it touched the spear, and I watched my finger pale as the life leached out of it—from dark brown to tan, and from tan to clammy white. I couldn't feel it anymore. A small part of me knew that I would never feel it again. But I stood firm, sobbing with agony and triumph as my body blazed with stories.

I was a young Redemptor girl from Dhyrma, the daughter

of beggars, thrust into the Breach before I even turned five years old. I was the son of Djbanti hunters who tried to hide my Redemptor marks with mud and clay, living in denial of my fate until monsters attacked my village, and guilt drove me into the Underworld. I was thousands and thousands of Songlander children, raised in the shadow of an empire that only valued their bodies once they were dead. I am generations. Three thousand lives. Four. Six. Seven.

A hundred thousand lives and more, teeming throughout my body, expanding in my soul like rice absorbs water, rising until the pot threatened to overflow.

Too late, the abiku realized what I was doing. They screeched, filling the sky with their wrath, but all in vain. I was still a living, breathing human, and they could not touch me.

Once I had stolen every last story from the Warlord's shrine, I broke contact with the spear, gasping with pain. I collapsed, too weak even to thrust my arms out and break my fall.

"Ye Eun," I croaked, barely loud enough for her to hear me on the opposite bank. "It . . . it's your turn now."

Faintly, I sensed Ye Eun splashing through the lake, swimming to my aid on the island mound. She knelt at my side in her dripping clothes, Hwanghu flapping anxiously on her shoulder.

"You can save them," I told her. "The Redemptors. All of them."

"How?" she asked, voice breaking with sobs. "How am I supposed to do that?"

"It's like you always said." I smiled. "You've never needed me. Just like Songland never needed Aritsar. I had to undo what my ancestors did, but the song of the Redemptors was never mine to finish." I gestured toward the plateau's edge, where far below, droves of hollow-eyed children marched into battle. "You're the hero of their story, Ye Eun," I whispered. "This has always been your fight."

Then I dropped my head, spent, and thrust my hand over the edge of the island. My fingers dangled in the water, and with my last ounce of strength . . . I released them. All hundred thousand lives' worth of memories, surging into the lake with a gurgling roar.

Ye Eun stiffened with understanding, then rose to her feet, crying out Hwanghu's name. The bird let out a jubilant shriek before plunging into the lake, disappearing into the amethyst depths. Then Ye Eun lifted her hands high above her head. The island shook as the entire lake rose into the air, water floating and twisting in a dripping mass until at last, beneath Ye Eun's masterful control, it took the shape of a giant, broad-winged bird. Moving her arms with fluid grace, Ye Eun directed the bird down into the ravine of Redemptors.

"No!" screamed the abiku, but they could do nothing as the bird broke shape, dissolving into a flood of memory.

As I lay on the island, I could not see the Redemptors. But later, through Ye Eun's memory, I would witness thousands of children gasping with joy and pain as their souls were restored. Released at last, their cloud of laughing shades flew to Egungun's Parade, letting the prison-like cages of their bodies crumble to dust. Outside Ebujo City, the Army of Twelve Realms would watch in confusion as their undying adversaries dropped one by one, bodies washed away by a cleansing river of amethyst.

When Hwanghu returned and Ye Eun knelt by my side again, she was grinning and laughing, eyes as bright and childlike as the day I'd first met her. "It's over," she said. "I did it, Lady Empress. They're free . . . we all are."

I tried to smile back, but shadows were closing in on the edges of my vision.

"Lady Empress?"

My hand still dangled over the edge of the island. Faintly, I felt her lift it and gasp.

"Your finger," she whispered. "It's . . . it's not good, Lady Empress. If I leave it, the death will spread through your whole body." She murmured something, drawing water from Hwanghu's wings and shaping it into a glinting ice knife. "I'm sorry, Lady Empress. But . . ."

I nodded and looked away. I barely felt it as the knife sliced through ruined bone, severing the snow-white index finger of my left hand. Ye Eun sealed the wound with ice and ripped her blouse to wrap it. Then she heaved my limp body onto Iranti's starry back, climbing up behind me.

"Let's go home, Lady Empress," I heard Ye Eun say, moments before I slipped from consciousness. "Let's go plant some flowers."

CHAPTER 36

"I NEED A FAVOR, ADUKEH."

My akorin snapped to attention, her crescent-shaped eyes fixed on me as Ododo, the almost-grown panther cub, tumbled from her lap. She'd been teasing him with a piece of fish, which he pounced at triumphantly, spiriting the morsel away before Adukeh could change her mind. "Anything, Lady Empress."

Morning light streamed into the Imperial Bedchamber. Adukeh sat in a corner, and I could barely see her through the army of clothiers and beauticians fussing over me, Dayo, and my council siblings.

From the windows, the cheerful clamor of several thousand Arits wafted up to the bedroom—the guests to our coronation, feasting in the courtyards before the official ceremony in the Imperial Hall.

I asked, half yelling through the fray, "Adukeh, how quickly can you make up a song?"

She dimpled, breaking at once into a comic soprano: "Come and see my empress, nse, nse. Tell me, is she mighty?

Bem-bem-bem. Ah, but see her akorin! Nse, nse—isn't she a genius? Bem-bem-bem."

My council siblings and I laughed, though they fell silent when I cried out, cradling my left hand.

"Forgive me, Lady Empress," gasped Adebimpe, covering her mouth in horror. While slipping bangles onto my wrists, she had squeezed my hand by accident, grazing the tender tissue that had once been my index finger.

I smiled at it ruefully. "It's all right. It's my fault for being vain enough to remove the bandage."

It had been two weeks since I returned from the Underworld. The amputated finger was barely scarred over, though it was healing nicely.

In an instant, Sanjeet was at my side, pressing my palm to his lips, eyes scanning me anxiously as his Hallow checked for infection.

"No fever," he observed, broad shoulders sagging with relief. Sanjeet stood resplendent in a heavily embroidered tunic of black and gold. Kohl lined his tea-colored eyes, and his beard and bushy eyebrows had been trimmed and manicured, framing his face in sleek, dark lines. "Though your pulse is elevated. You're still recovering, sunshine girl. Until we're sure Warlord Fire's Death has left you, go easy on your heart. No exercise or sudden shocks."

I grinned at him wickedly, filling his mind with the Ray. *No shocks at all? You didn't feel that way last night when we—*

He smirked, cutting off the thought with a kiss on my lips. But I could feel his trepidation. Once I had returned from the

Underworld, little more than a barely warmed corpse draped over Iranti's back, Sanjeet had gathered me to his chest, sobbing tears of relief into my neck. Of course, Dayo and the others also celebrated my return, but for two whole weeks, Sanjeet had not let me from his sight, changing my bandages on the hour, spooning stew down my throat. Carrying me to the bathhouses each morning, and cradling me close at night. Even now, I could see, he couldn't quite believe I'd come back. That unlike Sendhil, or his amah, or many others he'd held dear, I was his forever. I hadn't disappeared, vanished into memory smoke. And I never would.

My attendants herded Sanjeet away, fretting he'd ruin my makeup. I didn't blame them—the beauticians were artisans, and today, I was their masterpiece. After a few more finishing touches, they presented me to the floor-length mirror.

Dayo's reflection appeared beside mine, and his heavily draped arm slipped around me, squeezing me tight.

"It's how I'd always thought you'd look," he whispered, tears sparkling in his pure dark eyes. "When you came back."

For banquets, my attendants made me look warm and alluring, like a pretty flame. But today, for my coronation, I looked as untouchable as a star. Lovely and terrible: the glittering empress from the Watching Wall.

My arms, cheekbones, and clavicle glowed with gold powder, as though I were cut from polished stone. Crimson paint dotted the bridge of my nose and spiraled above each eye. A necklace of stacked metal rings glinted around my neck. Swirling cornrows decorated the front of my scalp, while the rest of my hair floated in a dark, ethereal cloud. The halo-crown of Aiyetoro shone against the coily mass—an upright disc of mirror gold, like the sun bursting from my scalp, restored from its two-hundred-year hiding place in the Oluwan crypts.

My garments matched the cloth of Dayo's agbada: finely woven ashoke so purple it was almost black, shot through with thread of gold. The crisp cloth furled around my body in a wrapper, sash, and jewel-studded train. But as Dayo watched me in the mirror, I knew which part of my outfit he liked best: the rainbow-striped mask on my chest, which he had fastened around my neck the moment I returned from the Underworld.

"You look beautiful, Lady Empress." Adukeh's reflection fidgeted behind us, though her stutter had grown almost imperceptible. "Did you still need a favor?"

I turned to face her, bangles clinking on my wrist as I bent to touch her arm. "Do you remember the memories I once showed you of my childhood? Of Bhekina House and the Children's Palace?"

Adukeh looked offended. "Of course." She tapped her temple. "A griot never forgets."

"Good." I pressed my lips together. "Then when the emperor and I enter the Imperial Hall, I want you right at my side."

Her jaw dropped to the floor. "Lady Empress!"

"On one condition," I said, closing my eyes as the revelries began in the Imperial Hall below, vibrating the floor of my bedchamber with a raucous chant. *Eleven moons around the throne, eleven moons in glory shone; they shone around the sun . . .*

"Sing to me, Addie." I reached for Adukeh's hand and squeezed. "Keep my story in your head. The waiting, the questions. The normal, boring parts. The parts that make me human. Can you do that? I . . ." I stared down at my missing finger. "I don't want to forget."

Within an hour, Dayo and I stood hand in hand before the towering Imperial Hall doors, sun-and-moon patterns and glyphs in old Arit carved into the alagbato-hewn mahogany. Our council siblings—as well as Iranti, whose vast neck Ye Eun had draped with blooming flower wreaths—stood close behind us. Adukeh trembled at my shoulder.

Are you ready for this? Dayo said into the Ray-bond, linking all twelve of our anointed minds. He could not have spoken aloud. Even behind thick doors, the rhythmic din from the Imperial Hall drowned out all sound.

I guess we'd better be—Oh gods oh gods oh gods—why does it have to be so loud?—is my collar on straight?—please, I've been ready for this since the Children's Palace . . .

Voices poured into my mind, along with a din of emotions. Then Dayo sent a wave of calm, flooding our thoughts like a low, bubbling tide. Our breaths synced, as they had when we slept together in Yorua Keep. We smiled at each other like milk-sated babes—nothing calmed anointed blood like the Ray.

Imperial Guard warriors prepared to haul the doors open, reaching for the thick cords of rope. But before they could heave at the tons of solid wood, I raised both my hands, calling out to the memory of the iron, drawn from the heart of Malaki the alagbato.

I did it, I told her. *I kept my promise . . . and I always will. I will protect this land's stories.*

The doors burst open, and the sound of my own name reverberated through each of my limbs and invaded my eardrums.

Tarisai for the morning!
Ekundayo for the evening!
And peace for moons to come.

Drumbeats echoed through the lofty dome, along with shaker gourds, a brassy child's choir, and thousands of voices. Guests teemed on tiered benches from floor to ceiling—citizens from each region of every realm in Aritsar.

Why, you ask? Why?
The Pelican has spoken!

Olugbade's council waited for us on the great dais of echo-stones. Today was the last time they were allowed in the palace, and they occupied the ancient carved thrones.

Previously, their seats had surrounded only one chair, its high back inlaid with ivory and chiseled with an Old Arit word: *oba*. But now, a second polished throne stood beside it, and though I could not read it from far away, I knew the word sculpted into its frame: *obabirin*.

My legs threatened to buckle. I had held court as empress already, but I had done so from one of the minor thrones. Until now, a very small part of me had still felt like I was pretending. That I would wake up and find myself in Yorua Keep, poring over court cases with half my memory gone, the Ray safely dormant in my chest, the last two years vanished like a feverish dream.

But there it was: a throne built for me. And a sea of voices, propelling me forward, filling every corner of my brain until every thought was *obabirin, obabirin.*

Me, me, me.

My heart pounded, drunk on the sound. The Ray crackled against my ribs like coals on a brazier. After a moment I realized I was laughing—or hyperventilating, it was hard to tell. Was this what it felt like to be a god? With thousands calling out in worship, as though my name were the only barrier between them and death? It was too strange for words, and yet . . .

I liked it.

I liked it a lot. And a manic thought passed through my mind: *Why not believe them?*

It had happened to Olugbade. Only a man who felt equal with gods would feel so comfortable ordering the

430

death of his own sister. But I wasn't like him, surely.
I could bask in this heady, inebriating praise, and be better.
Stronger . . .

Then a voice rose at my side, small and high and clear,
audible only to me amidst the chaos.

Do you see her?
A girl in a mango tree, aheh—
Waiting for her mother.

I stared down at Adukeh, my manic self-obsession
draining as she sang. Suddenly, I was small again. Not a
glittering statue. Not a towering god. Dancers paraded
before me, throwing fistfuls of petals in my path. A
moment ago, they would have been faceless to me, mere
ornaments in my parade. But now each person burned
on my mind's eye. Each was another life for which I was
responsible. Another story entrusted to my protection.

Do you see her?
The girl on a castle floor,
Asleep in a dozen arms.

The loneliness of my childhood washed over me,
a splash of cold water. I had been human once. Less
so now, with every death I had conquered—but I was
determined to remember. The feeling of being weak and
voiceless. Of screaming, clawing at windows boarded shut.

Not everyone was lucky enough to be a Kunleo, with privilege hidden away in their bloodline, waiting to whisk them away to palaces and Anointed Ones. My Ray may have empowered me, but I would not let it erase the past. The heat in my chest spread across my shoulders, a mantle as well as a burden.

Thank you, I mouthed to Adukeh, and she beamed, continuing to compose verses. I lifted my chin—not with pride, this time, but to gaze at the ocean of worshipping strangers, and to strike a silent pact.

I would not forget.

Adukeh stopped singing when we reached the lofty dais. The old Council of Eleven rose from their thrones, and Mbali, resplendent in gold-hemmed priestess robes, raised her hands, quieting the massive hall to a rolling hiss.

A lump formed in my throat. I hadn't seen Mbali since the day of our failed heist, when an ojiji had murdered Thaddace. Mbali knew that I was not his killer. But I couldn't be sure she'd forgiven me for his death until she stared down from the imperial dais, features lined with their signature blend of grief and compassion.

Dayo and I ascended to the thrones. First, we knelt before the old council, and one by one they asked if we would defend Aritsar and uphold the legacy of Enoba the Perfect. We replied *I will* eleven times, though in my head I replaced *Enoba* with *Aiyetoro*. Dayo also swore to defend Oluwan, since he would be king as well as emperor.

The former High Priestess produced the horn of an

antelope, into which she poured a carafe of sharp-smelling pelican oil. Her fluting voice amplified by the echo-stone, Mbali announced, "As the antelope cuts through the savannah, and the grass may not hinder it, so the commands of Ekundayo and Tarisai Kunleo must come to pass." The hall held its breath as she touched the tip of the horn to Dayo's lips, then mine, invoking them with the ritual power of *ase*—divine authority. Then we rose as one, presented by Mbali to the masses.

"Behold," she said amidst wall-to-wall joyful roars that rattled my bones. "Your Emperor and Empress Redemptor."

The next part was my favorite: watching all my council siblings get crowned. I had not anointed them, so only Dayo placed the circlets of moonstone on their heads, but my heart swelled as Kirah, Sanjeet, Ai Ling, Umansa, and all the rest were presented to the hall, taking their places beside us on the eleven gleaming thrones. I crowned my council of vassal rulers next, though they did not take places on the dais—their thrones belonged in their home realms. On a stool beside my throne lay Zuri's crocodile mask, on loan to me from the citizens of Djbanti. They had long since learned of their former king's heroism, and sang his name with honor in the streets of their commonwealth.

Strangely, his body was still to be found. I knew better than to hope. If he was alive, after all, I'd be able to feel him through my Ray, and when I reached out into the ether, searching for a thread of his vibrant soul . . . I found nothing. So he was dead. He had to be dead.

Didn't he?

I smiled ruefully. Perhaps some puzzles could not be solved for a lifetime. When I came to the crown that would have been Zuri's, I blinked back tears and placed the gold circlet on the spiked green mask.

"May we dance together in Egungun's Parade," I murmured.

The choir returned with more anthems and dancing. Then, as was custom, the vassal rulers of each realm showered us with gifts. Last to approach the dais was Queen Danai, her dark, elegant features shining with secrecy. "I am afraid," she announced, "that Swana's gift for your Imperial Majesties could not be wrapped."

Then amidst shouts and gasps, the scent of violets and freshly cut savannah grass filled the hall. Like a falling star, a tall, pole-like figure descended through one of the lofty arched windows, sprites dancing at his dark temples. Hair burst from his scalp in dense, shimmering coils, and long wings blurred around him in an azure haze.

Courtiers scattered in different directions as the alagbato floated over them. He was at least three times larger than when I'd last seen him. Perhaps even this size was a courtesy—in his truest form, I had no doubt he was as giant as Malaki, hovering over Swana in enormous, terrifying glory. The alagbato's long, narrow feet came to rest at last on the marble hall tiles. Wings folded neatly on his back, he waited, amused, as Imperial Guard warriors rushed to block the dais.

"No." I waved them away, rising from my throne. Tears pricked at my eyes. "It's all right." In an instant I launched down the dais steps, nearly tripping on my rustling purple train. The towering immortal knelt just in time to catch me as I launched myself at his shimmering torso.

He laughed, wings stirring to lift us both before he set me, firmly, on my feet. "Well met, *Behold-What-Is-Coming.*"

I regained the formality of an empress, though I shattered it with a childish smile. "You are welcome in our court . . . Great Melu, Guardian of Swana."

The packed hall erupted with gossip. Only my council siblings knew for certain that Melu was my father, though rumors of my unnatural blood had floated ever since the sprites appeared outside An-Ileyoba.

I didn't know why I was so happy to see him. He had never been much of a parent. Then again, neither had The Lady, and I had ached for her every moment she was gone. Perhaps no matter how many councils I joined, part of me would always crave a face like my own—would always search Melu's wrinkled lines and shadows, hoping to find a sliver of myself there.

"I thought you never left your homeland," I babbled. "I mean, I know you *can*; you're not an ehru anymore, but . . ."

"I rarely do," Melu confirmed, smiling mysteriously. "But I thought today's events merited the journey. Alagbatos do not grant favors often. It goes against our nature—yet I am here to grant one. It is not every day that both Rays of Enoba are restored to their full power."

Melu reached into a woven pouch at his waist and produced a gold hinged bracelet.

My breath caught in my throat. "No," I said. "No. Melu, I'm not going anywhere near that thing."

"Do not worry, Behold-What-Is-Coming." He laughed again, this time a little sadly, and gripped the jeweled bracelet with both hands. "I see you recognize ibaje—the Pale Arts your mother used to enslave me, as did Enoba before her. Thankfully, the idekun stone was embedded in this cuff and not in my skin. It amplified my powers, allowing me to grant wishes beyond human imagination."

White light pulsed between his palms and at once the cuff smoldered to ash. The powder slipped through his fingers, caught at once on a supernatural wind that scattered the dust through the windows. But when only a pinch of ash remained, Melu closed his hand, and said, "Even the palest of arts might be repurposed—for the right cause."

He held out his fist. Hesitantly, I cupped both my hands, and he dropped the remaining ash into my palms. "One wish," he said. "And if it is within my abilities, I will grant it. But the ash will not retain its power long. You must decide now."

At once, the floor vibrated with voices, masses frenzied with excitement. I blocked them out, my mind racing.

What do you want, Wuraola?

I dismissed the obvious wishes. Love, power, riches . . . I had all those things, and more than I knew what to do with.

So what *did* I want?

Could I eradicate suffering? Disease? No—even pestilence was a living thing, and I remembered that killing was beyond an ehru's power.

My eyes fell on Zuri's mask, glittering beneath his gold council crown.

So often, I remembered the distant world he had described—that state of Aritsar before Enoba established his empire.

We did not always have kings in the central kingdoms. Once, leaders were merely the hand of their people.

I thought of Olugbade and The Lady, loving siblings doomed to bitter rivalry, playing a game with rules that had been decided long before they were born. I thought of the Unity Edict—inflicted on the empire by rulers so disconnected from the general populace, they thought they could *force* harmony. I thought of me and Dayo, wringing our hands at the thought of heirs—of passing on legacies to children unfit or unwilling to bear them.

Again, Zuri's words echoed in my head: *Accepting the Raybearer has never been about loving a person—not really. It's about loving an idea.*

I opened my eyes, taking in the sea of spectators. From jewel-encrusted queens to paupers in their festival finest, cheeks gaunt. I had only one burden left: the future of my people. Then I glanced back at Dayo, asking him a question through the Ray. His eyes widened with shock.

Please, I told him. *It's the only way forward.*

Slowly, he nodded, solemnly gripping the arms of his throne.

I pressed my lips together . . . and in that moment, I decided.

"I wish," I whispered, though my voice ricocheted from the echo-stones, "that the Rays of Enoba would no longer be bound to a man and woman from the house of Kunleo. That instead—from this day forward—the Rays and their power would belong to the people of Aritsar. That the next Raybearers could be anyone—from a queen to a pig farmer. So long as those two Raybearers are worthy—those best suited to bring peace to the empire."

Then I blew the ash up at Melu.

He inclined his head, slanted eyes gleaming with fire. "It is done," he intoned, and the hall erupted with shocked cries.

Did she really say anyone? But what does that mean? She couldn't have meant it.

Melu cocked his head at me. "You do realize, daughter," he said, "that in a world where the Ray chooses those most worthy, heirs do not exist. No bloodlines. No royal families."

"I know," I murmured. And since Melu knew a great deal that no one ever told him, I wondered if he knew my stance on future motherhood. I picked at my nails. After my wish to Melu, a quiet, hazy corner of possibility twinkled in my mind. Without the Ray, a child wouldn't be my *legacy*: the small, frightened receptacle of all my life's ambitions. A child—should I ever choose to have one— would be just that.

A child.

For just a moment, I let the thought waft around me like a riddle, twisting this way and that, before I plucked it from the air, locking it away in the box of my heart. It would keep there just fine—if I ever wished to open it again.

Melu raised a sparkling eyebrow, then shrugged and went on. "The masks of oba and obabirin, of course, will retain their power. But due to the wording of your wish, even those will not necessarily choose a man and a woman. The next Raybearers truly could be . . . anyone."

I nodded, exchanging a smile with Dayo. "I know."

"But how will you find them?"

I grinned up at Melu. "I seem to recall knowing an alagbato who is very good at finding things. And even if you weren't . . ." I touched the rainbow lioness on my chest. "These masks tend to make their way to the people meant to have them."

Melu's features shaded with gravity. "There is one more aspect of your wish you have not considered," he said. "If the Ray is bound only to those best suited to lead the empire in peace, that could change at any moment. Suppose a ruler becomes unworthy? The Ray would leave them, entering into another host. The former Raybearer would lose all their power—including their immunities to death."

I inhaled sharply. "Then let the Ray leave."

More excited whispers.

Melu asked: "And what if the old council cannot love the new Raybearer?"

After a long pause, I replied, "They don't need to love the Raybearer. They just need to love the story that the Raybearer represents." My heart twinged, thinking of Zuri. "The story of peace. Of justice at any price."

The hall plunged into echoing rumbles, voices raised in eager discussion. I chewed my lip, feeling vaguely as though I'd tossed a honeycomb onto a mound of ravenous ants. How long, I wondered, would it take me to sort this one out?

But before the hall could descend into disorder, one voice rose over the others, chanting in her sharp strident voice: Min Ja of Songland. Danai joined her, followed by Uriyah, Kwasi, and all the rest of my vassal rulers, voices lifted in song.

A sun for the morning, a sun for the evening,
And moons for years to come.

Then a hundred-voiced chant grew from the farthest standing tiers, doubling, then tripling into thousands. Before long, the hall was on its feet, rocking, dancing, crying out with passionate conviction.

Tarisai for the morning!
Ekundayo for the evening!
And peace for moons to come.

My legs trembled at the sound. It was different from when I first entered the hall, different even from the cheers after my First Ruling, which were heightened by gossip and scandal.

This sound had kindness to it, like the third chord in a harmony, wrapping around the hall.

Love. This sound, this new, chaotic ocean roaring my name—it was filled with love.

"Prove it, little sister," Min Ja yelled, pointing at the mask on my chest. "If the Ray could leave you anytime, we'd better check if you're still worthy."

A nervous thrill chased up my spine. Still, I cried: "*Obabirin!*" The word ricocheted from the echo-stone, and the hall held its breath.

I glanced up at the domed skylight, just in time to see a pelican soar across the clouds. Then the eyes of the lioness flashed, filling the hall with golden light.

I have three bells in my mouth, I do not tell a lie.
Once, a girl tasted death and spat it out—pah, pah—
for she did not like its story.
Should I say her name? Aheh, but you know it already!
Many moons ago, the Idajo walked the earth.
Some say she never left. (Do not suck your teeth, I am not a liar.)
Yes: Some say she visits in dreams, riding Iranti, her beast of
many eyes. And if your soul is made of gold, and your mind filled
with peace . . . she may visit you, child, and peek into your story.
Who knows? Maybe she will find you worthy.
Maybe you too will wear the mask of Wuraola.

—From the songs of Adukeh: Master Griot, and akorin to the
Empress Redemptor

CAST OF CHARACTERS AND THEIR HOME REALMS

Adebimpe (Ah-deh-BIHM-peh), Oluwan
Adukeh (Ah-DOO-kay), Oluwan
Ai Ling (Eye-leeng), Moreyao
Aiyetoro (EYE-yeh-TOH-roh), Oluwan
Beatrix (BEE-ah-treex), Nontes
Da Seo (DAH-SOH), Songland
Danai (DUN-AYE), Swana
Edwynn (EHD-win), Mewe
Ekundayo (EH-kuhn-DYE-oh), Oluwan
Emeronya (EHM-er-OH-nyuh), Biraslov
Fergus (FEHR-gus), Mewe
Helius (HEE-lee-yus), Sparti
Hye Sun (HEH-sun), Songland
Ji Huan (Jee-HWAHN), Moreyao
Kameron (KAM-ruhn), Mewe
Kirah (KEE-rah), Blessid Valley
Kwasi (KWAH-SEE), Nyamba
Mayazatyl (MYE-ah-ZAH-tuhl), Quetzala
Mbali (Mm-BAH-lee), Swana
Melu (MEH-loo), Swana
Min Ja (MEEN-jah), Songland
Nadrej (Nah-DREJ), Biraslov

Olugbade (Oh-loo-BAWD-day), Oluwan
Sadhika (SAHD-ee-kah), Dhyrma
Sanjeet (Sahn-JEET), Dhyrma
Tarisai (TAR-ree-sigh), Swana
Thaddace (THAD-us), Mewe
The Lady, Unknown
Theo (THEE-oh), Sparti
Thérèse (Tay-RES), Nontes
Umansa (Oo-MAHN-sah), Nyamba
Uriyah (Yoo-RYE-ah), Blessid Valley
Uxmal (OOX-mahl), Quetzala
Woo In (OO-een), Songland
Zathulu (Zah-THOO-loo), Djbanti
Zuri (ZOO-REE), Djbanti

AUTHOR'S NOTE AND ACKNOWLEDGMENTS

Redemptor is the hardest thing I've ever done.

Raybearer took me twelve years. But I had to write *Redemptor*, the first sequel I've ever attempted, in nine months, during a period of brutal depression, a global pandemic that killed millions, the hastily rescheduled release of my first novel, and the largest Black civil rights movement to date in world history, abutted with violent state retaliation.

There are pages and pages of this book I don't remember writing. Some days I would write, collapse in exhaustion, and wake to lines in my own handwriting that hadn't been there before. A year-long whiplash between grief, anger, and white-knuckled fear does strange things to memory. Tarisai's Hallow, in a way, mirrors the way our bodies have an instinct to carry difficult stories, but also to fade the ones we can't quite handle—and least not yet.

Tarisai has been my companion since I was thirteen years old. But I've never felt closer to her than I did while writing this book. Her confusion, headaches, and sense of isolation were my own. But so was her stubborn determination to complete what she had started, buoyed by the potent love that surrounded her.

To cross the Underworld, she repeated the names of her loved ones, summoning each individual's unique traits to power her journey. In no particular order, I'm honored to do the same here.

Mom, my first griot.

Dad, my tireless champion.

Rachael Bug, my constant joy and sister-grown-dearest-friend.

Auntie Lisa, my beacon of love and lifelong fairy godmother.

Mama Marva, who adopted me.

Tia Thee Therapist, who is to this day helping my brain function.

Lisa-Marie, who helped me love my ailing writer's body through dance and art.

Miss Viv, my model for a stability and love that could only exist in a lifelong teacher.

Melissa, one of my original "council members," who never gave up on our friendship.

Otana, the first non–blood relation I ever remember truly loving, which perhaps laid the foundation for what this book is all about.

Jibiana, who will someday—benevolently and with cheerful enthusiasm—rule the entire free world.

Clare, Latosha, Reed, Monica, Ian, Kristina, Rob, Robyn, #BobYourFriend, Wendy, Matt, Lauren, Michael, Ali, Will, Kim, and all the rest of my church family, for their endless, nurturing care.

Grandma, for teaching me the meaning of unconditional love.

Uncle Femi, for his enormous fatherly heart.

Auntie Monica, for being the glue of every community she chooses.

Auntie Ifueko, who adopted me as passionately as I adopted her.

Auntie Tonia, who helped me connect to my roots in a way no one else has.

Shaiah the Bee, for letting me be her honorary big sister.

Kenzie, Naomi, and Imelda, for being their extraordinary selves, and Faith, for sharing them with me.

Gail Carson Levine, for her kindness, and for inspiring me to make worlds of my own.

Shannon Hale, for modeling a level of empathy in writing I hope to reach someday.

Joniece Abbot-Pratt and Weruche Opia, for lending their voices to bring Tarisai to vivid life.

Rosiee Thor, for going above and beyond as a sensitivity reader.

Maggie Lehrman, my editor, for accepting my specific brand of weird and making it shine.

Pastor Colleen, for being the mother's heart of God I so desperately needed.

Charles Chaisson and Hana Anouk Nakamura, for giving Tarisai a face and designing yet another a heart-stopping cover.

Namina Forna, for being my fast friend and champion, but also simply for being her warrior-hearted, brilliant self.

Ronni Davis, Dhonielle Clayton, Bethany C. Morrow,

Rosie Brown, and Nic Stone, for being my guardian angels. I will never forget.

Michael Prevett, my film agent, for being my tutor and champion in the world of television rights.

Becca Seidler, for her love and constancy in the roller-coaster ride that was my life these past two years.

Karisa Keasey Marsland, for being my kindred spirit and lionhearted friend, and for accepting my tear-soaked calls at all hours of the night.

Maureen, Jessica, Isabel, Nikki, Maddi, and Pippi at Once Upon a Time Bookstore in Glendale, California, for adopting me as their author even before *Raybearer* came out.

Kim-Mei, for being the kind of agent most writers can only dream of. Editor, advocate, accountability-prodder, at-times-emergency-therapist—I have no idea how I got lucky enough to go on this journey with you, but I sure am glad I did.

Tara, the kind of friend who only comes once in a lifetime. I will never understand how so extraordinary and empathetic a person can keep reinventing herself, while her soul burns so faithfully the same.

Reggie the schnauzer, my living emi-ehran. *(Tell us—what good is an empty lap? Aheh, Reggie is worthy to fill it, yes, Reggie is worthy to fill it.)*

David, my Life Person, both Sanjeet and Zuri in one: rock and revolutionary. I love you. Thank you for choosing me.

Thank you for choosing a Hot Key book.

If you want to know more about our authors and what we publish, you can find us online.

You can start at our website

www.hotkeybooks.com

And you can also find us on:

We hope to see you soon!